Darleen Innis gardens by day and pieces quilts at night or when the weather keeps her indoors. She writes from her home outside Athens, Ohio.

Women of the Guild

Darleen Innis

Women *of the* Guild

A CIP catalogue record for this title is
available from the British Library.

ISBN 978 1 83794 036 3

*Vanguard Press is an imprint of
Pegasus Elliot Mackenzie Publishers Ltd.*
www.pegasuspublishers.com

First Published in 2023

**Vanguard Press
Sheraton House Castle Park
Cambridge England**

Printed & Bound in Great Britain

This book is dedicated to Barbara Cramer and Jaska Kaneff

I wish to acknowledge the help of many people, including my husband, Chris, for his patience. A thank you also to my writers' group for honest and constructive feedback: Barbara Donahue, Nan Mykle, Svenn Lindskold, Ruth Reilly, Jesse Stowe, Shei Shine, Marilynn St. Lawrence and Febry Amanatillah. Cynthia King needs to be mentioned because she listened to the hours of ramblings, as the idea for this book began. And finally, to LiLi Cole, Ruth Day and Eric LeMay.

1

$\mathcal{N}$ora Radnor shifted uneasily in her seat. As an Appalachian, she found any discord unnerving. When arguments occurred so openly within her guild, The Tea Basket Quilters, Nora felt a deep angst. As the eldest member and one of the founders, she held more than mere affection in her heart for the organization. Any dissent within its ranks was like an attack on her child. The guild, in essence, was her child, as she had no children of her own. She considered all of the members as close friends — as sisters. Any time an argument arose among them, Nora's heart rate increased, and her temperature rose. The ninety-year-old would have to wipe her damp hands against her slacks and consciously will her breathing to slow. This was one of those moments.

At the far side of their meeting room, Evelyn North yelled her objections, her wrath directed at the four officers seated at the table in front of the group. "You're making a huge mistake! This is no way to raise money. I could do better myself."

Evelyn always wore jogging outfits over her thin frame. Today's ensemble was bright green. Her loose running pants were paired with a coordinating sleeveless top, which exposed her bony arms. Evelyn's hair was the color of a naval orange. Even her attire screamed loudly.

Guild treasurer, Rosie Dyer, stood unmoved at the dais. The vote had been in favor of the motion — her motion. Rosie's eyes narrowed. She folded her arms. She found Evelyn's objections more than a nuisance. Such a display violated Robert's Rules of Order. The woman's tirade bordered on verbal aggression, a tactic for which Evelyn was well-known. This outburst was typical of the many preceding it over the years. But Rosie, as a professional real estate agent, had faced down even more inconsiderate troublemakers on the job. She had dealt with shoddy contractors and demanding buyers. These people might not have been happy about a situation, but manners are manners. Neither those people nor Evelyn had any right to be rude. That kind of behavior was absolutely unacceptable in Rosie's opinion. On this day, Evelyn North was behaving as rudely as all of them combined.

"You may not like it, Evelyn, but the motion carried, and this guild is going to hold a small quilt auction," Rosie said firmly, then glanced to the guild president, Carolyn Ashcroft, seated beside her, for confirmation.

Poor Carolyn seemed helpless to intervene. She continued to clutch her hands as if in prayer, muttering under her breath, "Oh, my. Oh, my," as she sat, paralyzed with fear, in the chair next to Rosie. Tiny beads of sweat appeared on her upper lip. She fanned air across her body using her loose-fitting jumper, then switched to a pocket-sized battery-powered plastic fan hanging from a lanyard around her neck. Instead of responding, Carolyn inhaled the cool flow of air from the tiny fan clutched tightly in her hand.

"Well!" huffed Evelyn North, her normally pale complexion pink with agitation. "We'll just see about that!" She tossed back a tangled mass of orange curls once held in place by strategically placed bobby pins. She snatched her purse up off the floor, and shaking a boney finger at the board of officers, leveled directly toward Rosie, like a pistol, she said, "I'm resigning. This board is full of fools! I'll prove to you that a raffle will raise far more money for that Gammill. You can collect hundreds of little quilts for your foolhardy auction. Nobody in Athens will pay anything for them! You'll see. You'll have few dollars for all your time, and I'll own the Gammill! I quit!"

Evelyn spun like a whirlwind on the heels of her running shoes and stormed briskly past the membership. Two bobby pins fell to the floor in her wake. An unruly curl suddenly set free, dropping over one eye as she glanced back with malice at the entire body. Women seated around the room gawked slack-jawed in her direction. She bolted through the front door of the meeting room. A rush of hot humid air blew back into the hall, wafting past every member.

The room she vacated was populated in stunned silence by members of the Tea Basket Quilters. The building, in particular this first floor, had once served as a store, back at the turn of the century. Now the wood-frame structure served as the guild's permanent home. The first floor was used primarily for their meetings. Fortunately, glass in the upper half of the old door did not break when Evelyn slammed the door shut behind her.

A collective sigh of relief escaped Nora and several other members of the Tea Basket Quilters. Members glanced around, some looking concerned, others in disbelief.

Nora leaned over to whisper to the black woman seated by her side, her friend and confidante, Phoebe Prescott. "I think she means it this time."

Phoebe brushed a piece of lint from her slacks and shrugged. "Don't care. Never liked the witch, anyway."

Phoebe found most of the members to be friendly and helpful, but not Evelyn North, whose name she often purposefully mispronounced as 'Evil Lynn.' The woman had a nasty habit of being critical of others. She body-shamed anybody who was overweight. Phoebe got the feeling that Evelyn also disliked people of color.

The town of Athens was a diverse island of liberalism and tolerance in the center of an otherwise rural county, populated mostly by conservative whites. It was anchored by a university that brought students of color to its undergraduate programs and people of all nationalities to various advanced degree programs. The town itself, as a result, was very diverse. Phoebe discovered that her quilt guild reflected the town's sense of inclusion. She felt quite at home among the Tea Basket Quilters and had been a member for many years. Evil Lynn was the exception. That woman never attempted to make one overture toward establishing any kind of friendship with her, or anyone.

Phoebe was retired from a nearby technical school. She quickly replaced student term papers with quilt patterns and seed catalogs. She loved making intricate machine-pieced quilt tops in her spare time, which was every day. She also enjoyed losing herself in the hard work of gardening. Her good friend, Nora, who had never held a job outside the home, preferred hand applique to machine piecing. Old Nora hired a yardman to do all her flower gardening. Phoebe was most comfortable in T-shirts and jeans and loved toiling in dirt. Nora wore fashionable, bright silk tops with contrasting linen slacks, more suitable for sipping tea on her very comfortable patio furniture. Phoebe was twenty-odd years younger than Nora. However, not divergent tastes in clothes, not preferred favorite forms of quilt construction, and certainly not birth years, could hinder their enduring friendship and love of the Tea Basket Quilters. Only their approach to dissidents within the ranks gave them reason to disagree.

"Oh, Phoebe!" scolded Nora. "Don't say that. She *can* be a pain, but the guild *needs* all its members. I wish she weren't so quick to anger."

To Nora's other side, Lois Caldwell, another friend, spoke up, "She scares the bajeebers outta me, I'll tell ya."

Lois was as unlike both Nora and Phoebe as anyone could be: a large woman who never came to town unless she was attired in a voluminous cotton dress. Lois was neither highly educated like Phoebe nor wealthy like Nora. But her love of quilting also found kindred spirits and friendship among these women.

"I, for one," said Phoebe, "am glad she's gone. We can surely find somebody to replace her, who likes making quilts instead of trouble... like you, Nora. *You* don't cause trouble or try to divide people. You're the kind of person we need. She's not."

Phoebe looked directly into the older woman's eyes. "I do wish you'd run for president next year. You know everybody and everything about the Tea Basket guild. You're such a good quilt-maker and have so many friends here. I'm sure we'd have a great three years under your leadership."

Nora blushed. "No, no, dear. I'm no leader. Younger girls need to do that job."

By then, the current guild president, Carolyn Ashcroft, had recovered sufficiently from her stress-induced hot flash to turn off her little fan and wrap her gavel on the table, calling for silence and order in the hall. The women quickly stopped talking to each other. The hubbub subsided. Carolyn finally stood to address the membership.

"Yes, er, well, before Evelyn, er, spoke," she stammered, "we were talking about our decision to enter the contest for the Gammill longarm quilting machine offered by Molly at the Thimble and Chatelaine Quilt Shop. As you all know, from your empty wallets, if we can win and install that machine upstairs, here at our guild home, we can each save hundreds of dollars. So I would like to see a show of hands, please, for those of you who are willing to serve on an ad hoc committee to put our auction together."

Members looked around cautiously, no one wanting to go first, just in case that might make her chair of the committee.

Finally, Rosie Dyer, now seated next to Carolyn, spoke up. "It was my idea, so I'm very willing to work on it," she said.

After that announcement, several hands immediately shot up. Phoebe Prescott raised her hand. Simone LeBlanc raised hers, and her friend, Ximi Ling, the only Asian member of the Tea Basket Quilters, raised her hand. Finally, Nora Radnor's hand went up.

"Thank you, ladies, for volunteering. I'll leave you all to decide when to meet, select a chair and get started. The 5K will be held this October, so we have several months to find, or make, little quilts for our auction. Everyone should be thinking of what they can donate. All the proceeds will go to Molly's Thimble and Chatelaine team. Molly will give all the money she collects from guilds to the organizers on the day of the race. I'll be sure she knows we'll support her effort, and try to win that Gammill. The committee can brief us on our auction plans, in what?" She looked toward her treasurer. "Say a week?"

Rosie nodded affirmative.

Carolyn then called for a motion to adjourn. That was followed by a second from the floor, and that was followed by a united chorus of female voices saying, "Aye," all in favor.

"Well," said Phoebe. "Looks like we're going to have an auction."

Nora smiled with pleasure and adjusted her oversized, red-rimmed glasses. The two friends rose from their seats and attempted to make their way toward Rosie at the head table. They snaked through other ladies dashing off for another cup of coffee from the little kitchenette in the back of the meeting room. Lois rose from her seat, going directly toward the kitchenette.

The Tea Baskets had a permanent home, thanks to the generous bequest from one of their departed founding members. As a result, the Tea Basket guild owned the old building located at the corner of Morris and Shannon. The first floor offered a wide, open space with a small kitchenette, and a restroom off to the side. The open space was furnished with folding tables and chairs, suitable for either meetings or classes.

Members used four individual rooms upstairs as work areas. One group worked in the room reserved for applique enthusiasts. They had arranged several tables and comfortable chairs about for those doing handwork. They also scattered chairs and tables near electric outlets for machine applique. Another group met in a room claimed by paper-piecing addicts. There, ladies arranged several stations for a sewing machine with an adjacent small table for cutting every seam allowance after being stitched. They equipped a third room for machine piecers. The walls had been rewired with numerous outlets for sewing machines and extra lights. To the delight of some Tea Basket Quilters, this arrangement proved very convenient for those who owned multiple sewing machines. Those members left one of their machines in the room plugged in and ready to sew.

The members maintained yet a final room on the second floor, which was very large and nearly empty. This room was where members hoped one day to install a professional longarm quilting machine, like the Gammill being offered as the incentive prize from the Thimble and Chatelaine. Until they owned such a big machine, only one side wall was used as their design wall.

A short line of ladies were queuing up for the restroom. Other members, with fresh cups of coffee in hand, were heading toward the stairs that led up to the second floor. At the top of the steps, they split off into groups to sew in the various rooms of their choice. At the officers' table, Ximi Ling and Simone LeBlanc were already engaged in conversation with Rosie about their new, small quilt auction committee.

Phoebe sensed Nora to be under a bit of stress. Normally cheerful and animated, her friend seemed somewhat withdrawn, the walk up to join the group a little slower than usual. Nora's silk blouse this day, printed with bright pink and blue flowers, with a hint of metallic thread, didn't glow with her smile as intended. The bow under her chin drooped. The smile which normally adorned her painted lips — pink today, to match one of the flowers in her blouse — was absent. *Evil Lynn's drama, no doubt, set old Nora on edge,* Phoebe thought. Phoebe cared little for drama queens.

"Evelyn was really steamed!" said Ximi to Simone.

"I know!"

"Oh, girls," Nora said, as she joined the circle of women standing around the table, "I called one of my friends the other day, who told me Evelyn's been planning to form a new guild for some time. And I hear she wants to take our members with her. But I never suspected she'd *resign*. Maybe she really is going to form another guild."

Nora was the central clearinghouse for any gossip and all vital information about her guild. She maintained a circle of friends on speed dial with whom she chatted on a daily basis, sometimes more than once every day. There was nothing going on in the Tea Basket guild that went unnoticed by its eldest member.

"I guess we can always use another guild in the area," Nora sighed.

"Too bad Evil Lynn has to create one out of spite," Phoebe said.

"You know, I'd heard she planned to cause a *big stir* at the meeting. Now I know what that meant," said Nora.

"Some people are never happy about *anything*. I swear. What on earth can she hope to gain? Friends? Does she even have any friends?" asked Simone.

"Seems she's out to prevent us from winning that longarm quilting machine," answered Ximi.

"It's pure spite, that's what I think. And I wouldn't be a bit surprised if she isn't out to destroy our guild in the process," said Nora. "I'm furious."

Rosie remained silent until most of the women in the meeting room had vacated. Then to no one in particular, she spoke. "She can be *very* vindictive and difficult. Remember when she was our president a few years ago? She ran the guild like her own private club. Nobody got to do anything *they* wanted to do. The program was Evelyn's way or no way. Those were three boring years. That's probably why she's not been asked to preside again. Since Carolyn's tenure comes up at the end of this year, I'll bet a thousand dollars Evelyn knew she wouldn't be approached again by the nominating committee. So she's leaving, and in a snit to boot." Turning to the four standing beside her, she asked, "How much do you think Evelyn's scheme will hurt our auction? Or our guild?"

Phoebe was first to suggest an answer. "If she takes a lot of members with her, I'm sure the number of quilts for an auction will be down. But I can't imagine our guild will suffer much with the loss of a few members. We have a vital group. It seems to me that she's not that well-liked. I doubt there are many Tea Basket friends eager to join her. I don't know if she even has any friends."

"Well, let's hope she doesn't siphon off too many gals. Or too many of the *good ones*!" added Nora.

The circle of Tea Basket Quilters forming the new auction committee looked from one to the other. There was little they could do about Evelyn, whatever Evelyn's intent. Members were free to do as they pleased. If they left, they left. If they chose to stay, well, maybe their auction would do better than Evelyn or even they could imagine.

Maybe.

With that hopeful thought on the mind of each, the committee members agreed to convene the following day with ideas for their auction.

"Are you staying to sew?" asked Nora of Phoebe.

"Yes. You?"

"I have to. I have applique enthusiasts waiting upstairs," Nora explained. "Some of the ladies wanted a demo on reverse applique, today. So I need to go up."

The two friends made a brief stop in the kitchenette for hot coffee, where they found Lois polishing off the last of the cookies put out for refreshment. Nora and Phoebe said their goodbyes to Lois, then climbed the steps together to the second floor where they parted; old Nora off to the applique room, Phoebe in the opposite direction to the big empty room, her favorite spot to work alone, laying out blocks on the design wall.

The Tea Basket Quilters were extremely fortunate to own this permanent space. Most quilt guilds had to rely on the hospitality of churches, where they could convene in basements, halls or in classroom space. That arrangement usually required they make regular donations to their hosts. But rented space was only temporary space. They would have to gather up all their work, haul away sewing machines, put away tables and chairs and vacate immediately after every meeting.

Nora lived nearby to the Tea Basket hall. She would drive over every morning, unlock the front door and put on a pot of coffee. Those members with tiny houses found the arrangement ideal. They could spread out fabric and supplies in their room of choice and know everything would be exactly where they had set work down, when they could return. Those with naughty cats who laid on their mistress's work, leaving behind fine cat fuzz, also loved the arrangement. Members compelled to decorate for all occasions were delighted to do so with abandon and thus promote the guild with a constantly changing, twin-window display, flanking the front door. They hung quilts and lights and arranged tasteful knickknacks to the enjoyment of themselves and to passersby. They constantly updated the pair of floor-to-ceiling windows with each new season, holiday or special community event. Soon they would do something to announce their little quilt auction.

A wooden sign hung under the awning. The words, 'Tea Basket Quilters', painted in blue, could be read below a blue, red and white rendition of the traditional block bearing the same name.

The Tea Basket Quilters had acquired their permanent home after one of their elder members passed away. The wood-frame structure had once been used by her family, as a small neighborhood store on the east side of Athens. The old building sat idle for decades after the family closed down the business. Now the building was a hive of guild activity every day. It became a second home for some, particularly to Nora Radnor. With guidance from an attorney, the deceased had set aside sufficient funds to cover annual real estate taxes, insurance, and upkeep for decades yet to come. Once the Tea Basket Quilters took possession, every inch of space was put to use. They even found use for the small garage at the back of the lot. There they stored quilt show supplies, needed only on occasion, and extra folding tables and chairs for classes.

Members recruited help, from talented husbands and strong sons, to renovate a small space in the back of the first floor to serve as a small kitchenette. They updated a tiny bathroom along an adjacent wall the following year. Then they created ample workspaces in the second-floor rooms to meet their collective quilt-making needs. The largest room could easily house any longarm quilting machine which required at least fourteen feet in length and eight feet in width. This room measured twenty feet by forty feet. The only thing inside the room was their design wall. Two Tea Basket husbands had laid white carpet over one end wall to serve the purpose. A bench was positioned in the center of the room, facing the carpeted wall. A small table was placed near the wall to hold waiting squares, before being pinned up onto the carpet for arranging and viewing. A member could sit on the bench to inspect her layout from a distance. She could work alone or with friends and then, if necessary, get up to make necessary adjustments to perfect her layout. That was where Phoebe went this day to work alone.

Nora found four eager guild members in the applique room, chatting, and admiring small pieces of fabric each had brought for her class.

2

*E*velyn North walked briskly down the steps and away from the Tea
Basket's front door. She flung her purse over her shoulder, like a rifle on a
strap. She fumbled inside for an extra bobby pin to capture the wayward
lock that dangled over her eye. When she reached her black Prius, she
touched the handle. The car's security system unlocked. She jumped in. She
jabbed the start button on the car's console, then checked her image in the
rearview mirror. In exasperation, she tried to secure the drooping orange
curl. She stabbed the bobby pin into the rebellious lock. A few strands
managed to escape capture and fell again. With obvious irritation, she
stuffed the curl behind her ear and pitched the bobby pin back into her
purse. Without looking, she jammed her running shoe down on the
accelerator and executed a smart U-turn on Shannon, heading for the public
library.

A red pickup truck stopped abruptly to avoid broadsiding the little
Prius. Unseen by Evelyn, branches, leaves and debris tumbled off the
truck's bed onto the street. The driver swore aloud and flipped a one-finger
salute at the lunatic woman driver who never once looked his way.

The public library was just a few blocks from the Tea Basket hall, so
the journey took only a couple of minutes and two turns before Evelyn
arrived. She didn't stop at any of the stop signs. She barely slowed down
for them. She jammed the car into the first open parking place she saw,
slammed the gear shift into park, punched off the engine and jumped out.
Seventy years, and arthritic knee joints from multiple marathons, did not
slow her down. Her spindly legs carried her faster at a walk than others her
age could run. Only cataracts bothered her these days. She wore a two-
weeks-old pair of glasses which still gave her fits. This was the third pair
she had to buy in just as many months. And still she could not get the correct
prescription lenses. Her optometrist wanted her to undergo cataract surgery.
She vehemently refused.

Doctor's stupid. Maybe I can't see so well, but I can certainly set up a meeting. They're going to be really sorry they planned an idiotic auction. I'll put a guild together, and we'll win that Gammill. No question about it. First, I need a meeting space. The library will have exactly what I want, and it'll be free, to boot.

Crashing through the doors, she shoved aside a small child proudly carrying a library book, trotting alongside her mother, who herself toted a canvas bag filled with books on loan. They were trying to leave through the same set of doors where Evelyn arrived. Evelyn bolted past them in her haste and sped up to the front desk, without acknowledging their presence. The little child, a girl, started whining from her new position, having fallen in Evelyn's wake. The mother had to drop her book bag to comfort the fallen child and was too busy and too polite to address the rude woman who had flattened her daughter. The librarian stood at a computer, checking out books for an elderly man at the counter. Evelyn didn't wait for the librarian to look up to acknowledge her.

"I need a meeting room for about ten ladies," she demanded, as she approached the counter.

The librarian, a patient man wearing his black hair in a long braid down his back, looked briefly up, then went back to his task. "Sure. Just be a minute." He calmly completed his checkout procedure for the elderly patron. Once finished scanning the book barcodes, he stamped the books with their due date then handed them over. Finally he turned to Evelyn, who stood impatiently tapping a toe.

"What's your group's name? And when do you need a room?"

Evelyn was quick to respond. "We're the Shining Star Quilt Guild. I don't care when we meet. What do you have open?"

"Shining Star Quilt Guild? That's a new one. Didn't know there was such a guild in the area," he said, as he fished around to no avail for the scheduling book hiding somewhere under the counter. Perhaps the booklet was inside some drawer. He began a systematic examination of all the drawers behind the counter. A minute later, the notebook located and slowly opened up, he flipped through several pages, one at a time, very carefully scanning each page, before at last finding the one he needed to schedule Evelyn's meeting.

"We're new. Getting started. We don't have a set meeting time yet. Whatcha got open?" she said, drumming her bony fingers on the countertop.

"This week or next?" he inquired with a smile, his pencil now poised to make an entry.

Evelyn hated this hippie. *The Judge would have tossed your butt in jail,* she thought to herself. The Judge had been her father. Strict. No nonsense. Demanding. Rules are rules. No hippie would dared have stood before him wearing a long damn braid of hair. What was that kind of guy doing, working in a library? Really! Everything was going to pot. Pot. *Yes, he probably smokes lots of pot,* she thought.

"This week," she demanded curtly.

"We have only one opening. Friday. Four o'clock to closing. We close at five."

"Friday at four will work. I'll take it," she announced.

"You'll need to fill out this reservation form," the hippie-librarian with the long black braid said, handing a single sheet of paper across the counter to Evelyn. "Just a formality. When you're finished on Friday, we'll need you to report how many people attended. Do you need anything special, like power point equipment? Lectern? Will you offer refreshments?"

Evelyn snatched the form out of his hand and fumbled in her purse once again, this time hunting for a pen which wasn't there. She squinted, adjusted her useless glasses, pursed her lips even tighter and huffed.

The hippie-librarian silently offered Evelyn his pencil.

She grabbed the #2 and began scribbling her name, the name of the group and 'guild formation meeting' as the reason for the meeting room use. "No. We don't need anything. Just the room." She finished scribbling and held the completed form up in front of the librarian's nose.

He calmly accepted the sheet of paper.

Evelyn spun on her heels, about to leave, when the librarian gave a big throat-clearing, "Eh hem!"

She turned back around to stare.

"Pencil?" he said, nodding toward Evelyn's hand.

Evelyn realized that she still gripped the yellow pencil in her hand. She tossed it and turned to storm out through the library doors. This time she nearly ran over a couple who had been riding on the bike path and were just then returning loaner bikes to the library. Evelyn did not excuse herself.

The couple looked at each other. The man shrugged. The woman glared after her. Evelyn adjusted her glasses then returned the glare with pursed lips.

From the library, Evelyn jogged rapidly across the parking lot back to her Prius, touched the door handle to unlock the car once again, then leaped inside. Though her arthritic knees ached and sweat had begun to trickle down her back from the day's heat, she felt elated. She was now on a mission. No one and no act of God would stand in her way. She felt positive that the Gammill would soon be hers. With the library secured as a meeting place, the next item on her agenda was to acquire members. Her first recruit would be the simple, enormous, old Lois Caldwell, easy to sway and most compliant.

Evelyn drove, not to Lois' place in the country where the old woman lived alone on the family farm, but to the fairgrounds on the other side of town where Lois often spent time each summer working in the office. Evelyn knew that Lois rarely stayed at the Tea Basket hall to sew. Lois was all things rural. In spite of her age — late seventies, Evelyn guessed, by the looks of her — the biddy kept a few cattle, a henhouse filled with chickens, and even drove a tractor and a truck. She also helped hired men bale and put up hay. Lois always said she didn't have a lot of time for such pleasures as staying to sew with the others. But if Evelyn told her to stay, the woman would. Evelyn guessed she was probably still in town but had surely made her way, by then, over to the fairgrounds on the west end of Athens.

Lois' hard life was certainly not the sort Evelyn could abide. Evelyn would never shed her jogging suits for dungarees and ratty shirts. In spite of the heat, Evelyn's lime-green running attire failed to keep her cool this day. Evelyn hated the way the top trapped perspiration against her torso, but wearing only a colorful exercise bra to guild would have been unthinkable. She was proud of her thin body free of fat.

Well, maybe I should have worn just a jog bra. Give the old crones something to gossip about, as if I haven't already given them something! Some of those old girls, like Lois, for instance, would greatly benefit from weight management. They eat anything and everything in front of them, without a second thought. They even gobble up second helpings. God, they're pigs.

Evelyn floored the black Prius down Home Street, past the hotel and the restaurant. She slowed only a moment at the stop sign at State Street, a main artery of town and always busy. She then took a sharp right in order to get onto the bypass. Several cars already formed a queue, waiting for the light to change from red to green. Evelyn would have rolled right through the light and up onto the ramp if not for them blocking her way. She found herself momentarily stuck. The pause of one minute lasted far longer than she liked, idling silently, fuming, inside her hatchback, drumming bony fingers on the steering wheel, while forced to wait… wait… wait.

Finally onto the ramp, she accelerated the little car into the fast lane, no one in front of her. She pushed the speedometer over sixty, avoided the Stimpson Exit and barreled on down the highway. She accelerated past cars in the slow lane along a stretch of highway that overlooked the shallow and meandering Hocking River bordering the University Golf Course. She noticed several hackers standing by, while one of their foursome sliced into a sand trap.

"In this heat? Idiots!" she said aloud to herself. The mention of the day's heat made her ramp up the fan on the car air-conditioner.

At the roundabout on Richland Avenue, Evelyn did pause, however briefly, to make sure no one was driving at her from the left. Quickly wiggling through the congestion, she continued to follow the highway flanking the Hocking riverbed, past the old lunatic asylum on the hilltop to her left. Wild Canada geese grazed peacefully along the mowed bank. Soon she passed White's Mill, long a landmark of Athens. The mill had changed hands several times over the past decades, becoming most recently a combination garden center with an artsy section added to the store. Evelyn wasn't sure if changes in ownership had improved the store or not. She never had reason to stop in. She noticed, as she drove by, that they still seemed to sell the same flowers and shrubs in the outdoor lot. *No doubt they still sold bales of straw. Probably sold the same bags of fertilizers all summer, and the same collection of bulbs every autumn.*

"Gardeners are nuts," she said to herself.

At the Union Street traffic light, which remained green just for her, Evelyn turned right and crossed the bridge, letting her double back along the Hocking. She could see the fairgrounds on her left, after a short distance. She veered onto the main roadway on the grounds across from the grocery store at the fair's main entrance. The grounds were idle this time of year, since the fair was still many weeks away. She felt certain she'd find Lois up in the fair office. She wondered if Lois was a member of the fair board.

Old woman's probably working diligently, no doubt, on some mundane matter. Maybe not. Maybe she only works for the fair board. Probably needs the extra cash. Or maybe she just likes milling 'round with her fellow farm folks a lot. Whatever.

Once atop the hill, above the racetrack, Evelyn turned off the quiet Prius and ran up the steps to the fair office. She did indeed realize she was on the right trail. Within a foot of the closed door, Evelyn caught a whiff of her quarry's heavily scented perfume. Evelyn pulled open the door to spot Lois seated inside at a desk.

Lois Caldwell was not a woman to which time had been kind. She likely tipped the scale at two hundred and fifty. She sat alone, munching chips from an open bag on the desk, as she stared at a computer screen. She was dressed in a simple, inexpensive, pale, printed housedress which fell loosely to the floor around her. To Evelyn, she resembled a giant, speckled hen perched on a nest. In this case, the nest was a swivel office chair, lacking arms hidden somewhere under the enormous tent of the dress whose skirt edge fell all the way to the floor.

When Lois heard someone enter the office, she quickly cocked her head to see who it was. The movement made the sagging skin under her chin waggle. Her beak of a nose pointed up toward Evelyn. She blinked in surprise at the green stick of a figure standing now in front of her. The resemblance to a scared hen was complete.

Lois quickly recognized the red-headed rebel from today's guild meeting. She felt her heart skip a beat. "What?" she asked. "What on earth brings you here, Evelyn?" Such bluntness was not how she might have welcomed another visitor or a familiar friend into the office.

Evelyn didn't ask for permission to come round behind the counter. She just did. Looking directly into Lois' questioning eyes, she leaned in close and replied, "I've come for you."

"Me?"

"Yes, my dear. I need a secretary for my new guild. I'm calling it, 'The Shining Star Quilt Guild'. I've given this a lot of thought, Lois. Perhaps more than you realize. Perhaps more than anyone realizes. My guild will be great!" she exclaimed. "Furthermore, I'm certain that my guild — my efforts — will win us that Gammill! So what do you say? Join me?"

Lois blinked, frozen in place at her desk.

"C'mon! You're a great quilter. You know lots of people to sell raffle tickets to. And you've always wanted to be an officer, haven't you?"

This was one secret that Evelyn had learned about Lois. They hadn't talked much, but once, during a class when they had set up sewing stations next to each other, Lois rambled on and on during the entire day. One of the desires she confessed to Evelyn was that she longed to be an officer of the Tea Basket guild. But of course, as an excuse, she said that she just didn't really have the time. Not that anybody had ever approached her, but that she was so very, very busy with the livestock and her vegetable stand every summer at the farmer's market.

Lois cackled nervously. Evelyn had an ability to get others to do what she wanted. Lois knew from experience that Evelyn was skilled at manipulating her to do her bidding. Of course, she longed to hold an office in a guild, but in reality, she really had little free time to spare. Lois preferred working behind the scenes whenever possible. Lois didn't have education beyond high school, which had been so very, very long ago. That lack of schooling, in a community and a guild of others who held advanced college degrees, often made her doubt her own abilities and made her feel inadequate.

How can I refuse? How can I accept? How can I do what Evelyn needs in a secretary? Lois slipped her hand into the open bag of chips, avoiding further eye contact, wishing for a way to escape. But there was no escape from Evelyn.

As if reading the woman's mind, Evelyn leaned in closer, in spite of the fumes of perfume and potato chips. She put a cold hand over Lois' ample bare arm. The move prevented Lois from withdrawing another handful of chips. "I'll do the work. All I need you to do is make raffle tickets and get them out to everybody. That's all. Once we have a quilt, you can get started. For now, just make one sample ticket and bring the sample to our first meeting. The library in Athens. Four o'clock Friday. You can make it, right? You can make one sample ticket and attend the meeting?"

With some difficulty, Lois withdrew her arm from Evelyn's grasp. Her hand free, she delivered chips to her mouth. She munched. Her wattles waggled. She rolled the hidden office chair slightly back, putting a little distance between herself and Evelyn. She needed time to ponder the offer. Or was it an order? If she did as Evelyn told her to do, she wondered if she could still remain a member of the Tea Basket Quilters.

Maybe Evelyn won't like it, but maybe I can be a member of both guilds. Evelyn has just resigned, right? How would she ever know?

Lois sighed. People always find out stuff about you. "Well, OK. I'll be your... your...?

"Shining Star Quilt Guild secretary!" Evelyn announced, glancing proudly around the office. "A very important job requiring a very responsible person. Looks like you're adept in an office setting and know how to get around a computer. You'll be perfect!"

Lois found the prospect of becoming a guild secretary quite flattering. But she remembered her limited free time. She also remembered Evelyn's temper. "But I can't stay at your Friday meeting very long. I have evening chores to do, you know."

Evelyn smiled, her thin lips not parting. "Excellent. Meeting will only last an hour. I'll see you Friday. Have a draft raffle ticket ready to share. We only need one sample."

With that, Evelyn spun around. Another bobby pin fell to the floor. An errant red curl drooped again over her cheek. Once again, Evelyn tucked it behind an ear and bolted for the door. Without so much as a thank you or a goodbye to Lois Caldwell, the new secretary of the Shining Star Quilt Guild, Evelyn departed.

Lois blinked, sighed and stared at the fair board office door closing behind Evelyn. Without thought, Lois dove her hand once again into the half-empty bag of chips.

In the short span of time Evelyn had been inside the fair board office, the interior of the Prius, sitting in full sun, had heated up considerably. She pushed a button to roll down all the windows and paused inside only for the briefest period of time to contemplate who next to call upon. She quickly decided that Isabelle Hart would be her next recruit.

The complete opposite of Lois in appearance, Isabelle 'Belle' Hart was stunningly beautiful for being mature. Though her hair was silver, Belle always meticulously styled hers, unlike Lois, who often looked like she'd just taken off a bandana after bailing hay. Belle had the most dazzling blue eyes, with a figure right out of Vogue. Belle lived very near both Rosie Dyer, treasurer of the Tea Basket Quilters, 'the one who brought up the cockamamie idea to hold a small quilt auction', and Carolyn Ashcroft, 'that wimp of a guild president'.

Not knowing if any of the three might already have gone home to their well-to-do subdivision in The Plains, Evelyn decided to head home for a break. She'd relax, make some plans, toss back a Bloody Mary and give Belle a phone call later in the evening. Off she drove, down the hill from where the fair office was perched. She double backed the way she had arrived, turned right at the county health department and sped back down Union, on her way out of Athens toward 682. She, too, lived in The Plains, but in a different, less expensive, more modest subdivision than Carolyn, Rosie and Belle.

Her own home was smaller and contained fewer amenities than theirs. Evelyn's house had been constructed to her specifications from the ground up. Every detail was just to her desires. The house sat in a section of The Plains which was slightly more elevated than the entire town, so named "The Plains" because the town itself sat atop a plateau of sorts above the Hocking River valley. Evelyn had been able to build her house thanks entirely to the profitable sale of The Judge's estate several years earlier. After he died and left her — his daughter and only heir—'that stinking monstrosity of a house of his', she sold his property off. She acquired a tidy sum and used some of that to build her dream house on a little lot at the edge of town.

By taking 682 off Union Street to The Plains, Evelyn avoided all but the one traffic light at that intersection. Fortunately, someone in government passed a law that drivers could turn right on red. Evelyn preferred to skip the conditional part about 'after stop' and so arrived home in record time. There were no unanticipated obstructions along the way, and she encountered no idiots driving slowly. By pressing the remote button to her automatic garage door opener three houses from her driveway, Evelyn was able to pull right into her garage without stopping. The garage door was still traveling upward as she drove the car in. She pressed the fob again before she even came to a full stop within the garage, sending the door back down before she turned off the engine.

Evelyn liked her house. The garage had space for two vehicles, though Evelyn found it prudent to only own one car — her Prius. She was unlike some of the other Tea Basket Quilters who owned multiple cars, or one car and one truck, like Lois Caldwell. These women acted as if they needed a vehicle for every season: four-wheeled drives for winter, convertibles for summer, sedans for Ohio's autumn and spring monsoon seasons.

Ridiculous, thought Evelyn. *Why waste good money on tags, insurance and upkeep? One car ought to be good enough for anybody. It'd be smarter to spend money on, say, a trip of a lifetime, like a cruise around the world, than to blow it on cars. Yeah, I'd take a world cruise. Maybe someday I will.*

With vague thoughts of Spanish coasts and Alpine mountains scrolling through her mind, Evelyn snatched her purse off the passenger seat and walked briskly through the side door into her kitchen. Her kitchen was small but spotlessly clean and tidy. She rarely cooked food. Evelyn rarely ate. Dropping her purse on the only chair at the small breakfast table by the window, she passed immediately to her liquor cabinet for a bottle of Vodka, then opened a cupboard, taking down a cocktail glass. From the refrigerator she retrieved a large jar of chilled tomato juice and a small, yellow container shaped like a lemon. In practiced movements, she proceeded to make her favorite beverage of choice — a Bloody Mary. She gathered crushed ice from her freezer to strain the concoction through, then finally, one ice cube from the refrigerator's ice cube dispenser.

From the kitchen, cocktail glass in hand, Evelyn headed for her sunroom perched off the carpeted living area which, like the kitchen, was spotless. Mounted on one wall, which caught and reflected back her own image, was a black, large-screen television. The big screen seemed out of place amid her otherwise color-coordinated furnishings in shades of pastel greens, green being her favorite color. The sunroom was pleasant. Her destination was a single, white, wicker porch swing suspended from the exposed white rafters. She pried off her running shoes and curled up on the floral cushions on the swing. There she sipped her cocktail as she mentally reviewed with pleasure the progress of her day so far.

Evelyn let her thoughts wander.

My resignation from the Tea Baskets might have caused the old biddies to rethink that foolish plan for a small quilt auction. Wait until they find out

I'm creating the new Shining Star guild. They'll be sorry they didn't listen to me.

She let out a contemptuous snort of superiority and took another sip of her cocktail.

I was a great president of theirs. I'll be a great president again; this time, of my own guild. Soon. Quite soon.

She imagined leading her new guild to soaring heights. She'd bring in members with experience, not neophytes with little ability, not owners of ancient sewing machines that hadn't seen service in years.

My members will be experienced piecers and quilters. I'll have Lois design a questionnaire. They'll have to complete this questionnaire before being admitted for membership. Screen out the weak ones. Make sure my members know what they're doing. Mine will be an exclusive association of all the best piecers and quilters in the region.

Evelyn smiled with satisfaction as she imagined her members accepting first-place ribbons at local quilt shows, of having their photographs hit the front page of the local rag, then their stories appearing in various quilt association magazines.

Winning that Gammill will benefit all of us who prefer our quilts be machine quilted. The Tea Baskets will have to continue to pay professionals to quilt theirs. Ah, another thought; I'll have to get the Tea Baskets who own their own longarm quilting machines into my guild, too. Have to make sure Lois adds a line in the questionnaire about that. Siphon them off. Make things just a bit tougher for the old biddies back on Morris St. Make them come crawling to my guild for the service. Maybe I'll ask some of the quilt shop owners to join my guild. Now that'd be a coup!

Evelyn took another sip. Then another. As the cocktail began to work soothing magic, she settled back deeper into the cushions. Her eyes closed briefly, then opened. Her gaze fell on her collection of succulents and cacti, scattered artfully around the sunroom. Some had long, threatening barbs. Others had prickly stems that seemed to invite an unsuspecting fingertip to touch what appeared to be soft, but was not. A couple cacti bloomed. Evelyn resembled her cacti. Her appearance, and her speech were sharp and prickly.

In spite of air-conditioning and being partially shaded by large maple trees at the edge of her lot, Evelyn's sunroom provided just the right climate for her Cactaceae to thrive. The room with plants pleased her. Her sense of satisfaction confirmed that her decision to sell off her father's cold mansion and build this ranch house had been the right one.

Her father, Judge, Zachary North, owned a three-story brick and mortar Victorian atop one of the tallest hills overlooking Athens. The mansion was his opulent pride and joy. Evelyn found only discomfort within its walls. Every room was cold, figuratively and literally, filled with her father's austere, demanding and demeaning attitude. She started running in her teens, to escape his control for at least part of most days. At first, young Evelyn found running painful, but not nearly as painful as what The Judge could exact on her with his sharp tongue. Going out for the high school track team required hours of practice: first around the football track, then later running up and down hills around Athens for conditioning. Training hard was physically exhausting. Evelyn learned to tolerate the physical pain more than she could the emotional pain that waited for her at home. She'd arrive back at the mansion, following practice, totally exhausted. She would often fall asleep in her bedroom, missing dinner.

"This family dines at six. If you can't be here by then, we're not waiting!" she remembered him shouting at her when she came home late after one long practice run.

Who needs to eat with you anyway?

After that, Evelyn began to pack both her lunch for school and a small snack to follow practice. The Judge was none the wiser.

As weeks turned into months, her young body developed the stamina and strength needed to excel at her sport. Her long legs often brought her across finish lines first. She added cross-country to her regimen. She ran fast enough to make it to regionals, then on to state finals. She brought home ribbons, medals and trophies, seemingly non-stop. But there was no room in *his house* for her awards, at least not where visitors could admire them. So Evelyn made a space for her running awards inside her own bedroom. They adorned one wall. Then two walls.

The Judge scoffed when she asked for a trophy case. He thought running was something girls shouldn't do.

"Boys are better at sports. Just a great waste of time for girls," he said.

He wanted Evelyn to study more and ready herself for college.

At first, Evelyn only entered local 5K's. Eventually she added 10K's. Once she was old enough to get a driver's license, she signed up for half marathons anywhere a tank of gas would take her. Without an income of her own, The Judge would only allow her to top up her car's tank once a week. So she would often run to and from high school, just to save enough fuel in the car to get her to and from an away race on weekends. Eventually, Evelyn was winning marathons in her age division.

With grades good enough for admittance into Ohio University, The Judge seemed relieved, though not quite pleased. He still wanted academically more than she could achieve. A general studies non-major in college was useless in his opinion. He decided she should be in pre-law, English or political science. He wanted her to move on to law school. Pass the bar. Become a practicing attorney like he had. Maybe to sit someday on the bench just like him.

Evelyn didn't have the mental stamina nor the desire for a career in law. She enrolled in college, but she enrolled in classes held at the branch in Ironton, trying once again to put herself as far away from her father as possible. He was, of course, furious when he found out where her classes were held. When her first quarter proved to be a disaster, in his eyes, he berated her endlessly. She had passed every subject that term, but just barely. She failed to get the four point GPA he'd expected.

In disgust, or perhaps her own disappointment, she dropped out of the university completely, much again over The Judge's objections. That's when her father refused to support her any longer. So she found part-time work to pay her own tuition, cover room and board, and enrolled down the road at the local technical school with dorms on campus. That winter she landed a part-time student job with the college, and from there, she proceeded to work her way through their two-year program.

At the technical school, she became a star. Having selected office management, Evelyn achieved her associate degree on time in two years. She immediately landed a full-time entry-level staff position within the college. From that moment on she never returned home. From a clerk in the college Financial Aid office, she managed to climb the ladder of her own success until she became a secretary for one of the deans. She remained at the college until she retired thirty years later. The Judge never forgave her for failing to become an attorney.

When The Judge died, she felt nothing except a sense of relief. She wasn't at all sad. She shed not one tear at his passing. He was someone she had chosen to avoid, a person she had not spoken to since her college days. Everyone who was anyone in the local legal profession attended his funeral and signed his remembrance book. Evelyn wore black, attended the visitation hours at the funeral home, shook hands, accepted their condolences and was the first to toss a handful of dirt on his grave. Having no other heirs, everything Judge Zachary North had owned passed to Evelyn. Not long after the burial, she promptly disposed of anything that could remind her of the man. That included his house on the hill and every stick of furniture inside.

She stashed the money from the sale of his estate into her own once meager bank account. She engaged a CPA to prepare her inheritance taxes, then paid the state its pound of flesh. With what remained, she was able to afford the construction of a new ranch house with a sunroom and a garage. She erected the structure on a small lot, free and clear of all debt. She still retained a lovely nest egg for a time she was sure she would need *something*. She had been quite able to live comfortably in a rental for all those years on her salary from the college. Then later, in her new house, thanks to The Judge, her retirement income was more than adequate to meet her needs. Her investments continued to grow in size, thanks to the CPA and some careful long-term investments he had recommended. Evelyn's life was good at last.

The daily drive to work on campus had been brief. Sometimes she'd jog the bike path to the college then run home in the evening, just to stay in shape for marathons, which she continued to enter on occasional weekends throughout most of her working life. Eventually, her knees began to give out. Her doctor advised she give up running. That's when she turned to the sedentary diversion of quilt making. She found the quiet repetitive action of sewing surprisingly pleasurable. This new creative skill led her eventually to the doorstep of the Tea Basket Quilters. She became one of their members. She advanced her sewing skills, added new forms of quilt making to her repertoire, learned to do hand quilting, then learned how to maneuver the handlebars of a professional longarm quilting machine. She rose through their ranks to become their president for one three-year term.

Now she found herself creating a new guild, one that would put the Tea Baskets to shame.

By the time Evelyn had sipped the last of her cocktail, sleepiness was overtaking her. She set the empty glass on the floor and stretched out on the wicker swing where she promptly fell asleep, dreaming pleasant thoughts of success.

Nora Radnor amazed the three Tea Basket Quilters surrounding her as she demonstrated, with ease, two methods to execute reverse applique. Her students were new members and also new to piecing. With assistance from the guild secretary, Nora provided written instructions with drawings for those who learned best from the printed word. For the ones needing a visual demonstration, she sat in a chair with them hovering over her shoulders as she slowly and carefully took them through the process.

The tallest student was Avery Underwood, recently unemployed by choice, who was built more like a tall boy than a woman. Her blue eyes never left Nora's hands as the old woman carefully took the tip of a needle and turned under a small one-fourth inch edge of fabric, pushing the tiny fold back under itself. The hole around which she worked exposed beneath it a different colored fabric. Avery watched as Nora's hidden hand, holding the needle under the piece being appliqued, pushed the tip out through the fold, completing the stitch.

"Point the tip of the needle toward your heart," Nora explained. "Make the thread disappear into the fabric fold of a seam allowance that you just created by having turned under this top fabric."

"I see," Avery said, while adjusting her glasses and bending closer to the work in Nora's lap. "But I can still see your stitch there on the edge of the fold," she said.

"Very observant, Avery. That's because I've used a dark-blue contrasting thread on the white fabric for demonstration only. Blue on white is easier for you to see than white on white. When you do your own reverse applique, you should choose thread in a shade that's the same or only slightly darker than the top fabric you're turning. And if you plan to enter your work in competitions, I recommend you use matching silk thread, not cotton. The silk will virtually disappear!"

Avery smiled appreciatively. She liked Nora, the oldest of the guild members. Everyone was generous to share their knowledge and skill whenever asked. Belonging to the Tea Baskets made Avery glad she had decided to return to the town that had been home during college. Now that she was no longer a student, just somebody looking for a place to call home, the Tea Basket hall proved to be a most enjoyable and resourceful home in its own right. Avery found every hour spent there to be a delight.

Armed with new knowledge, Avery and the other women retreated down to the first floor when Nora concluded her mini class. They returned their empty coffee cups, washed them out and put them away. Avery planned to visit the County Highway Department the next day to drop off her resume. She needed a few hours to update her information before printing out an updated copy. She planned to drive to her small apartment to finish the document. After that, she would practice the applique method she had just learned. She decided to try making a sample block using scraps... with highly contrasting thread to better see what she could do.

Nora gathered up her samples and arranged them neatly in a small fabric tote. She carried the tote down the hallway, to check on Phoebe's progress. In the empty design room, Phoebe sat alone, pondering a display of blocks now neatly pinned to the wall of white carpet. She had made a scrappy log cabin quilt which could have been arranged in several different combinations. The pattern that Phoebe pinned up to the wall was called 'Barn Raising'.

Nora took a seat on the lone bench beside her friend. "Looks nice," she said, as she admired the play of dark and light stripes arranged on point.

Phoebe smiled.

The two old friends lapsed into silence. Nora pondered the worst possible outcomes for the Tea Basket Quilters, while she fidgeted with her tote. How many members might Evelyn North steal away? Phoebe imagined the potential loss of a Gammill longarm quilting machine valued in five digits. She wondered who she might find to perform machine quilting for this top now pinned to the wall, after all the squares were finally sewn together. Could Molly at the Thimble and Chatelaine do it? How much would it cost? This was going to be a quilt worth keeping. She'd have to have custom work. Whoever did the work, their fee would certainly be expensive.

3

*M*embers of the new committee charged with the task of putting on the auction, met the following day as agreed. Nora Radnor arrived early to unlock the front door and make coffee. Always fashionably attired, her outfit consisted of a shimmering, white silk shell under a Kelly-green linen jacket. Her ensemble was complete with tan linen slacks and a pair of matching tan Taos flats. Nora always tried to match lipstick to the outfit she wore. However, green lipstick was not something she could ever imagine herself wearing, nor, she imagined, that any cosmetics company would make. So this day, Nora matched her lipstick shade to her red-rimmed oversized glasses. A small emerald dangled from a fine, gold chain around her neck. Her ears were adorned with matching emerald studs.

Nora knew the women on this committee preferred coffee with punch this early. No need to make a pot of decaf. Instead, she busied herself making a pot of regular and setting out creamer, sugar — both real and artificial — and five mugs.

Rosie Dyer was the next to arrive. She joined Nora in the kitchenette. She walked straight back to the coffee cups. Rosie, a plump woman in her sixties, had pink cheeks, a grandmotherly smile and silver hair cut into a carefree, boyish bob. As a successful real estate agent, she was skilled at making customers feel relaxed and at ease when escorting them about town or the countryside in her blue five-passenger Ford Edge Crossover. Everything 'Rosie' was blue. Not only was Rosie's vehicle blue, she wore blue shades of business attire every day of the week. This day was no exception. Her blue iPhone rang at all hours. Sometimes calls came from staff in the real estate office. Other times calls came directly from buyers who got her number off signs in front of the properties she'd listed. Always dressed in a business suit meant that she was always ready to work. In her spare time, Rosie enjoyed losing herself in quilt making. Even Rosie's quilt tops were done in various shades of blue. She constructed her quilts using primarily blue cottons, and at other times, she pieced with blue batiks. She was occasionally known to wear stray blue threads on her otherwise tidy business suits.

Rosie had a knack of convincing homebuyers to purchase and 'sign on the dotted line' when they teetered on indecision. That skill came in handy for guild, too, as she easily convinced several members with limited piecing skills to tackle an imagined-to-be-difficult method of block creation called paper piecing. She adored paper piecing above all other forms.

Simone LeBlanc and Ximi Ling arrived together, soon after Rosie. They were friends who often paired up for classes, road trips and committee work. Neither liked being a leader. Ximi was the only Asian member of the Tea Basket Quilters. Like Phoebe, she discovered a group of women who openly accepted her into their company and friendship. Simone, also a single woman, was her best friend.

Last to arrive was Phoebe Prescott, attired in dungarees and a T-shirt, which was her preferred style of dress every day, especially when gardening. Of this group, Phoebe lived farthest from Athens. She kept a few hens for eggs, and two female pugs for companionship, at her cabin on several acres in the country. Today, the pugs, named Stitch and Medallion, accompanied her into the hall, trotting obediently beside her feet. In one hand she carried an oversized tote bag. Rolled up inside were two pads, to ensure comfortable resting spots for her fawn-colored pugs. In the bottom of the bag she carried a small, three-ring spiral binder and a pen intended for taking notes at today's committee meeting. Phoebe walked to one of the tables where the women were assembling. She selected a chair, dropping pads on the floor, flanking both sides. She pointed to the pads and commanded the pugs to sit and stay.

They obeyed willingly, proceeding to circle multiple times around on their beds in order to find a comfortable spot, while Phoebe made her way to the last empty cup waiting on the kitchenette counter.

Rosie switched the blue iPhone over to silent, laid the device beside her own notepad and took a sip of her coffee. Phoebe joined her, the pugs and the others already seated around a table.

"I'm happy to chair this committee, girls, unless one of you wants the job," announced Rosie.

They all smiled at her. Nora raised her coffee cup, by way of a salute. Phoebe clicked on her pen to take notes. No one objected.

"OK. That's done. Next. Ideas? Anyone?"

Everyone began talking at once.

"Holy moly! One at a time!"

Everyone giggled.

"How about 'age before beauty?' Nora?"

Nora adjusted her giant, red-rimmed glasses in feigned anger at the remark about 'age'. "Well, girls, as I see it, we need a suitable place to hold this auction. The venue must have plenty of room to display our little quilts. I imagine we need to allow buyers access, let them roam around at their leisure, to view them before the actual auction begins. We need a good auctioneer, too. One who doesn't charge much. Oh, and we have to get the word out. Publicity will be very important."

Everyone nodded in agreement.

"What about the quilts?" Rosie asked.

Phoebe spoke up. "I think we should ask every member to make one quilt for the auction, or to donate one already made, no matter how old that quilt may be."

"That might not be enough," thought Simone out loud. "If we only auction off one per member we'll have, what? Maybe sixty. There are always members who don't or can't participate. Let's say the average sale price is $30. Not much, I know. But let's assume that's the average, for now. What would that give us?"

Rosie, who was good with dollar amounts, had the answer immediately. "$1800."

"OK, two quilts then," corrected Phoebe. "Maybe an old one and a new one."

Ximi spoke up next. "Didn't we gross around $4000 on our last quilt raffle? Maybe asking for two isn't even enough, considering."

Everyone suspected that the 'considering' comment was in reference to Evelyn's threat from the previous day. Phoebe doodled on her notepad, drawing a stick figure witch flying on a broomstick. Simone took another sip of coffee. Nora sighed heavily.

Rosie decided to act so that the committee didn't drown in gloom and worry. "Who among us can find us a venue? Who can contact an auctioneer? What about putting the question of number of donated quilts to the entire membership when we report to them next week?"

"I'll be happy to get our auctioneer," announced Nora.

"I agree. Let's let the members decide the actual number of quilts to donate," said Phoebe. "Maybe they'll even form small groups and make an extra one or two!"

Simone nudged Ximi's arm. "I guess we can scour the town for the venue."

"Agreed," Ximi said.

"Good," declared Rosie. "I think I'll ask our guild secretary to survey all members, just to find out how many quilts they might *already have* that they're willing to donate to the cause. Do you all agree to that?"

Everyone nodded.

"That was easy," Rosie said. "Aren't we a *great* committee? I think we're done for now. Let's not beat a dead horse, just yet. We'll reconvene in two days, after you have some time to actually locate a venue," she pointed to Ximi and Simone, "An auctioneer," pointing to Nora, "and I'll see what I can come up with for possible publicity. I simply love it when there are no problems! Same time in two days? Same place?"

The ladies nodded while they scoffed and snickered good-naturedly about 'no problems'. Everyone sensed that a problem would certainly surface. Would it be named Evelyn?

"What about me?" asked Phoebe. "What do you want me to do?"

"Moral support for now," said Rosie. "I have a feeling this task will not stay easy. I'll need your real help when things fall apart."

Nora asked, "Anybody staying to sew? We still have half a pot of coffee to consume."

"I want to stay for a bit. I need to label rows and columns on the design wall upstairs, then take my blocks down," said Phoebe.

The others indicated they were leaving, but the immediate plan was to consume the coffee and chat a little while.

Nora drained the remaining coffee into their cups. The Tea Basket small quilt auction committee diverted their conversation to the topic of utmost interest — Evelyn North's recent tirade and threat. Everyone agreed that her behavior was reprehensible, but none of them cared to confront her about it. Most were not unhappy that she was gone. No doubt, if any ever came face to face with her again, which in the small town of Athens would surely happen, they planned to avoid her. Ximi, the shyest among those seated around the table, announced what they all were thinking. If Ximi saw Evelyn first, Ximi planned to do a one-eighty before Evelyn spotted her.

Phoebe rolled her eyes and snorted in agreement.

Nora looked worried. "What if she intends to take our members away? Maybe she's really bent on destroying the Tea Baskets, not merely winning a Gammill."

"I think we'll be OK, in spite of her efforts, dear," Rosie reassured her. "We can surely survive any storm she may send our way."

With that, Simone and Ximi drained their cups, rinsed them out and were the first to leave so they could begin work immediately on their assignment. They decided they would hunt for a place to hold the auction by making the rounds of Athens from the comfort of Simone's condo. From there, they rationalized, calling places by phone would be cheaper, faster and easier than driving cars all over town. Besides, Simone had recently baked her favorite dessert, a peach cobbler, which was 'going to waste', as she put it, 'just sitting on the kitchen counter.'

Once they arrived at Simone's, both friends kicked off their shoes in the hallway. With a serving each of cobbler in hand, a phone book open between them and cell phones out, the two friends began their quest for an empty venue and empty plates. Simone had used two highlighters, one in yellow and another in pink, alternately marking various phone numbers in the yellow pages. Simone reserved the pink numbers for herself to call and instructed Ximi to call the yellow highlighted numbers.

Ximi quickly scanned over her list to contact. Her eyes stopped at the unfamiliar name of a martial arts studio. It had to have been a new business, because Ximi didn't know the place. Familiar with the insides of many martial arts academies, she suspected this facility would not serve the guild's purpose. But still, she was intrigued at the discovery. She would have to check out the business for herself. Ximi was well trained in several forms of martial arts, particularly Hapkido, 'the way of coordination and internal power.' She was the only girl in her family, with three older brothers. Her brothers obsessed over the sport. Once in a while, as youngsters, when neither parent was watching, the boys would occasionally practice their kicks and takedowns on her. In order to defend herself against them, she started to take lessons too. In a few short years, Ximi exceeded all her brothers' skills, quickness and finesse. She then practiced her kicks and takedowns on them when their parents were away.

Ximi rejected the martial arts studio and suggested they call only those places that might have both room for an auction and ample parking for their needs. That list was fairly short because Athens had few such places. Their first concern was if anything was actually available. Parking was always an issue, thanks to twenty thousand students in a town of fourteen thousand residents, with only one parking garage available to the general public. The university had a parking garage, of course. But the structure was located on campus, at the bottom of a steep hill below the new student center. The location, design and construction obviously served to be of convenience to those attending university-related events held inside the student center, not for the convenience of townies.

The only public parking garage was a four-story antique structure half a block from the courthouse downtown. On-street parking downtown was risky anytime semesters were in session, with students around. Their search would have to extend beyond the city limits. Another two plates of cobbler disappeared.

Two hours passed as they called all the highlighted phone numbers. They marked off each dead end. An entire cobbler was gone, but the two friends were still at the beginning of their quest. All the yellow numbers had been called, all the pink numbers, too. No place they had contacted by phone had what they needed. The businesses that might have had space wanted money — lots of money — up front, for rent. Parking was then nonexistent. The community center with excellent parking, which they had hoped would be available, was booked solid. Rent there was also steep, even if the facility had been available. The task of finding a venue was proving much, much more challenging than either of them had anticipated.

Their search had also brought to mind a new concern. Just how, exactly, would they display quilts prior to the actual auction? For instance, they realized the big multipurpose room at the community center, or anywhere in town, for that matter, almost always had cement block walls. They had no idea, between them, how to temporarily attach small quilts to concrete walls. How would buyers inspect the little quilts before the auction took place? They decided to try calling area churches next. But maybe, first, they should take a walk around the neighborhood. Multiple slices of cobbler weren't sitting well with failure.

After Phoebe removed her labeled blocks from the design wall, Nora said goodbye to her and the pugs, then locked up the Tea Basket hall and drove the short distance home to begin her search for an auctioneer. She carefully edged the old Buick into the garage and lowered the door with her remote. As soon as she had entered her living room, she sat down with cell phone in hand. She held the device in one hand and scrolled through its digital address book with a manicured finger until she came to the name, 'Hart'. She pressed the number and waited.

"Hello?" came the familiar sound of a Southern accent.

"Hello, yourself, Belle. It's Nora."

"Ooh, baby doll, how are you? Haven't seen you in a day!"

'Baby doll' was Belle's favorite greeting. She used the term for women as well as men, for friends as well as strangers, as if Belle Hart had ever met a stranger. Everyone was Belle's friend. The 'baby doll' greeting she repeated so often was genuine.

Belle admired all things genuine and expensive. She wore the best clothes money could buy. She never shopped the limited choice of stores in Athens, but rather went to big cities. She was known to travel to Columbus or Cincinnati if she went shopping for a couple of days, and as far away as New York City for longer buying trips. Her closet at home was brimming with exquisite garments.

Belle sewed on the most expensive sewing machine made. Off its feed dogs, she produced the guild's brightest, most colorful and dazzling quilt tops among all the members. She excelled with color. However, when it came to her vehicle, although she drove an expensive Cadillac Escalade, the car was plain white, an exact copy of her husband's black Escalade. Their vanity plates read, 'His Caddy' and 'Her Caddy'. Her husband, Vernon, or Vern, as everyone called him, was the only gem she owned that required constant polishing. Vern seemed to need constant affirmation of her love. He was always asking if she loved him, which of course, she always assured him that she did.

It was Vern who Nora really wished to speak to, but Belle would do. Nora liked Belle. She thought Belle had a sincere sweetness about her. She seemed open and honest. Her marriage to Vern Hart seemed picture-perfect. Only occasionally did Nora get the feeling that Belle was guarding something from her past. She never spoke about her life long ago. Nora was puzzled when she could never get Belle to talk about her days as a youth, whereas Nora's early days were an open book. She enjoyed sharing stories about growing up in Athens nearly a century earlier. As far as Nora could tell, Belle didn't exist before Vern. So Nora chose not to pry. After all, everyone had something about them that wasn't perfect.

"Belle, dear," began Nora. "As you know, we're going to need an auctioneer for our little soiree." Nora gave a long pause, waiting for that Southern voice of surprise, or even curiosity. Obviously, her not-so-subtle hint wasn't working. "I was really hoping you could help us out." Another long pause.

"Me-e-e? Why, Nora, baby doll, *I'm* no auctioneer," feigned Belle, knowing full well what was about to come next.

She could barely restrain her delight. The idea that Vern would be asked to auctioneer the sale of small quilts had occurred to Belle at the meeting the previous day. That thought popped into her mind the moment Rosie spoke the word 'auction'. She had wondered how soon this call would arrive.

"Might you be wantin' my dear husband, Vern, to be our auctioneer?" she asked.

"You know it, Belle. Do you think he'd have time or be interested? I'm assigned to locate an auctioneer. Of course, I thought I'd try to 'keep it in the family', so to speak. So I'm here to ask you first. To ask Vern. Do tell me what you think."

Belle wasn't about to tell Nora what she was thinking, not at that moment. Her mind was racing, as her thoughts usually did. Thoughts which were all a little too embarrassing to speak out loud. What she thought was maybe... maybe if Vern auctioneered at the guild sale, that would gather points for Belle, so that she might someday be considered for an officer's position. Not that Belle thought without him she might *not* be considered. She longed to sit at the dais, to serve the guild as, oh, maybe treasurer, like her neighbor, Rosie, whose house was only a few blocks away. Maybe she would someday be asked to serve as president, like her other neighbor, Carolyn, the wife of a doctor. *Wouldn't that be something? President!*

"Oh, Miss Nora, I just *love* the way you all think of us. Vern's at his auction house right now. I think he has a big estate sale coming up this weekend. I'll give my sweetie a call right away. Do you have a date set that I can share with him?"

"No. No date. The girls, Ximi and Simone, are looking for a venue. I'm hunting for an auctioneer. It's like a big jigsaw puzzle at this stage. First we find the pieces. Then we have to see if we can fit them all together. Maybe if Vern can be our auctioneer one day, or one evening, he can let us know when he's available. How does that sound? Then the girls finding a venue can nail down a site that fits his schedule. Of course, things could work out the other way 'round. The venue might dictate when we hold our auction. So you see, it's complicated. But you will ask him? Won't you?"

"Bless your heart, Nora, dear, of course I will. I'll talk to Vern real soon. I'll get back to you as soon as I can. That sound OK, baby doll?" Belle crooned.

"Oh, yes, indeed, Belle. I think Vern would be perfect for our little sale." Then, as a sudden afterthought, she added, "Be sure to ask him what his fee will be, please?"

"You got it, baby doll."

As soon as Nora disconnected, Belle was punching up her husband's number on the cell phone in her hand.

Vern was intent on ticking off items listed on a clipboard. These were the pieces from the Morgan Estate that he'd be auctioning off that weekend. Two young men, hired as laborers, were positioning furniture in the order Vern planned to present them for sale. Vern would direct their movement of furniture by pointing a yardstick to various locations corresponding to plans drawn on his clipboard. Their T-shirts were wet with sweat from their efforts.

The Hart Auction House was a vast pole barn set on a polished cement slab atop a hill on the outskirts of Athens. A small stage occupied one wall. A sound system allowed Vern to walk anywhere to sing his auctioneer's refrain. A tiny office at the opposite end, near the public entrance, housed his teller on auction days. She checked IDs and financial credentials, assigned buyers their numbers, and cheerfully accepted their cash, debit cards or checks after their successful bids. Inside the little room was a desk and chair for her and the usual trappings of any small office. It also contained an oversized antique safe. Vern had come by the six-foot steel box many years previous, which failed to sell at an auction, but not because it wasn't a beautiful object. It was. It was just that no buyer seemed to have the means to transport such a heavy thing. So Vern bought it instead, and he hired a forklift to set it in place, where the steel safe protected his documents and auction day cash.

Vern's auction house was climate controlled. It had radiant heat embedded in the cement floor for the comfort of his winter bidders. The walls and ceiling were well insulated. Three air-conditioning units out back chased away heat and humidity for summertime bidders. Today, all three air-conditioners were working overtime to keep up with the recent heat wave. Reports on the radio announced there would be no relief any time soon. The radio was on in the little office, tuned to a local station. The weather report was just being announced.

'Today's heat wave is expected to reach the upper 90s by one o'clock, with no chance of rain. The evening's low is only expected to drop down into the upper 80s.'

Vern figured his electric bill would go out of sight this billing cycle. *I really should consider installing solar panels someday.*

It had taken Vernon Hart years to amass sufficient funds to have the auction barn constructed without the need of a bank loan. Vern was good with money. He earned it. Then he saved it. Then he very carefully spent a little of it. His services were always in demand, so he had kept busy earning and saving. He liked his work. He met interesting people. He had even met his wife on a trip south to Ironton, one of many little towns along the Ohio River, where he would sometimes conduct an on-site farm sale.

Vern had done well for himself over the past three decades. His successful endeavor allowed him to own the auction house, free and clear, a fine home and two new Cadillacs, one for himself and one for the beauty that was his bride. He also owned, outright, a little riverboat to enjoy now and then, that he christened *Mistress*, which he moored down on the Ohio. Sometimes he wished he could live full time with Belle on *Mistress* and forget all about responsibilities of running the auction house. But of course, that was never going to happen. His auction house was like a magnet. It drew him to his work every day. He loved it. He loved his work. As he checked off a bureau listed on the clipboard, he noted its position amid the other items. That piece of furniture was followed by a cherry dining table with eight chairs. His mind wandered. He thought about how very lucky he was to have all of this, and Belle, too. Yes, life was good to Vern.

He also loved Belle more than he could express to her. He loved her more than he loved his work, more than he loved anything or anyone else. Vern Hart was not the kind of guy able to talk easily about his feelings. Instead, he happily showered her with whatever she wanted. He enjoyed spoiling her. He would never, ever abandon her like his own father had abandoned him and his mother when he was young. But he worried, constantly, that this blue-eyed beauty might up and leave him someday. After all, Vern wasn't what one would call an Adonis.

He pushed back the bill of his trademark black ball cap. The words, 'Hart Auctions' were embroidered beneath a red heart centered over the bill. Vern dabbed a bit of perspiration from his brow with a sleeve and adjusted his bifocals which had managed to slip down his nose. His round face glanced down at his clipboard, then up to each sale item in turn, until at last he was confident that the big items were all properly in place. He excused the two laborers for a well-deserved break. That's when his cell phone, tucked inside a rear pocket of his jeans, rang out with the tune of 'Bad to the Bone', a signal that his Belle was calling.

"Why, Mrs Hart, what a pleasure to her from you, my dear. What's up?"

4

*E*velyn awoke with a start. She had drifted off and slept far longer than intended. Hours had passed. The whole day almost! She had fallen asleep sitting up. Her neck ached, and her knees creaked with stiffness as she unwound herself from the cushion on the swing.

Evelyn rushed to her desk as best she could. She limped toward the spare bedroom that served as her home office. Having worked in an office her entire adult life, she found it unnatural not to have a desk with a phone and the trappings of an office. The running trophies from high school through her final marathon adorned three walls. *The Judge would not appreciate this*, she thought. On her desk she searched for a red three-ring binder labeled 'Tea Basket Quilters'. Then she remembered that she'd filed the binder up on the bookshelf amid other binders, each labeled and shelved neatly above the desk.

She pulled the appropriate binder down and flipped through pages, past carefully filed minutes and copies of program handouts, until she came to the roster. The list included phone numbers of all Tea Basket members, their addresses, offices they held and committees they chaired or belonged to. Evelyn searched for Belle Hart's name. She squinted, frequently readjusting her glasses, until finally able to bring the phone number into focus. She picked up her house phone and dialed.

The line was busy.

"Oh, crap!" she muttered, slamming the receiver back down on the cradle.

She had a new idea. "I'll call that new woman — Avery something-or-other," she announced to no one.

Evelyn took longer to locate Avery's number than it had Belle Hart's. Whenever a new person joined the guild, the secretary dutifully updated then reprinted or sent out electronically, a corrected roster which contained

the new name, placed exactly where that person's name should be placed...
alphabetically.

"Ashcroft... Caldwell... Dyer... Hart..."

Fool Hart needs to stop talking and get off the phone. "Avery? Where's
Avery? Ling... LeBlanc... me... Prescott... Radnor..." *Old woman's red
glasses are bigger than she is.* "Underwood? Underwood! Of course, she
had to be at the end, didn't she?"

Evelyn rolled her eyes in disgust, adjusted her glasses once again, in
order to better focus on the unfamiliar number, and punched the buttons
again. She missed by one digit and got a pizza delivery shop. She hung up
on the guy at the other end, without acknowledging her mistake. She tried
again. This time, she thought, she had the numbers right.

"Avery Underwood here."

"Ah, Avery, just who I wanted to talk to," said Evelyn, in the kindest
voice she could muster. "I saw that *l-o-v-e-l-y* quilt you presented at sew-
and-tell a couple of weeks ago, and I wanted to ask you about it," she lied.

"Who is this?" asked Avery.

"Oh, sorry. This is Evelyn. Evelyn North. I so admired your
workmanship, and I wanted to ask you a few questions. That quilt was
machine pieced, right? And machine quilted? Did you do the quilting
yourself?"

"Uh, I'm sorry, Evelyn. I'm driving right now, but I'm almost to my
destination. Can I call you back when I stop?"

Upon hearing this, Evelyn's eyes grew narrow. She had wanted to
make better progress. This was yet another delay in achieving her goal. She
felt compelled to get things done and felt ridiculously behind schedule,
having fallen asleep and wasting the day away. But she bit her lip, and as
sweetly as she could fake patience, agreed to wait for Avery to call back.

"Thanks. I won't be long." Avery disconnected.

Small frustrations didn't sit well with Evelyn. Knowing there was
nothing she could do to speed up Avery's return call, she stomped into her
sunroom, retrieved the cocktail glass still on the floor and proceeded to the
kitchen, where she intended to make herself another bloody Mary for lunch.
Or was it already dinner time? Evelyn shrugged.

Avery was on her way to the county highway department and had just
turned off U.S. 50 when Evelyn's call arrived on her vehicle's Bluetooth

phone system. Not one to text and drive, she was also averse to talking and driving. Safety first. Business first, too. She'd call the woman back after she finished at the highway headquarters. She wasn't positive, but she suspected Evelyn was the same whirlwind who had thrown the snit that morning at guild. She hoped not. Before she'd call the woman back, she intended to deliver her resume to the office just ahead. Avery wanted to land a part-time job with the county. She guessed she had socked away enough money for six or seven months of idleness. One thing for sure, she did not intend to return to work at Knox Construction.

Avery had quit Knox a month earlier. She put all her belongings into the back of her truck and moved to Athens, where she had gone to college for her undergraduate degree. Unemployed by this decision, she hoped to find work with the county highway department, even if only part-time or temporary. Because her resume listed Knox as her last place of employment, she imagined she would have to explain how she preferred to avoid private workplaces in her future. What she really needed to tactfully explain was not working at any place that allowed the degradation of women, especially a woman like herself, who chose a field considered non-traditional for her gender.

She'd heard too often the sound of snickers behind her back from some of the men who speculated she was lesbian. Then there were the mean tricks they pulled on her. They'd bolted the door once, with her inside, when she had to use the disgusting port-a-john. Sometimes they'd toss all the toilet paper down the hole, then piss all over the seat instead of using the urinal. She also had to rebuke come-ons by tobacco-chewing, married, none the less, Neanderthals. Never did she receive support or defense from her supervisors. Avery hoped there were rules of behavior for government employers, which seemed to be all too absent in certain private companies like Knox. Knox Construction followed no rules against sexual harassment, in spite of working under government contract to repair public highways.

So one day she did resign, collected her final pay and left.

Avery held a degree in civil engineering, a level of education that irked some of her male coworkers at Knox. They were both jealous and spiteful. She was sure they hoped she would quit if they kept up their harassment. But she had survived as long as she could. She 'persisted', as someone said of another woman trying to do her job in the U.S. Senate. Her education, plus a decade of experience building highways and bridges, was all she needed to move on, and hopefully, up. She had reached a point in her life where she was ready to find one place to call home. She finally reached a point where leaving Knox behind felt right.

Road crews spent weeks living out of cheap hotels, eating fast food and never getting the chance to really live what Avery considered a *normal* life. Avery wanted normalcy. That meant the same town every week, the same bed every night, the same decent staff with which to build roads. Normalcy in her mind did not include being mocked for her education or degraded for her gender. She imagined she might have to explain why she'd quit her job just by delivering the resume to the engineer's office. But she was ready to face that question if the subject came up.

Like many members of a road crew, Avery preferred a heavy, four-wheel drive vehicle capable of plowing through mud and rocks, big enough to haul equipment, and well equipped with the latest audio and communication devices. Her bronze F350 was a monster that had never left her stranded or unable to reach a job site. She parked the truck outside the county highway office, picked up her resume off the passenger seat, gave the steering wheel an affectionate pat, then stepped down out of the cab and walked confidently toward the entrance.

A female clerk behind a long counter greeted Avery with a pleasant smile.

Avery handed over the manila envelope that contained her resume and list of credentials. "I was hoping you might have an opening in the next couple of months," began Avery. "This is my resume. I just moved back to the area, and I'm looking for permanent work. Building roads is what I've done since college. I'm willing to start part-time if necessary."

The clerk continued to smile and accepted the envelope. Avery noticed a nameplate on the counter, which indicated the woman's name was Sheila Harper.

"I'll pass this on to our county engineer. If one of the supervisors lets him know they need someone, he'll call you in. You'll have to complete a job application and have a drug test. These are civil service jobs. Your name has to come off a list. You don't need to fill out the job app now, but I'll give you one to take with you. You can also apply online, but only if there's an opening posted. I'll write down the web address for the online site."

Avery nodded and accepted a multipage form and a scribbled note from Sheila.

"What's your name?" Sheila asked.

"Avery. Avery Underwood."

"Oh, what a nice name. I'll remember you."

"And what's yours?" Avery asked in turn, to be sure the nameplate actually did belong to her.

"Sheila. Sheila Harper."

Busy signals and waiting for a callback irked Evelyn. With the Tea Basket roster in front of her and a lovely cocktail calming her impatience, she started dialing other numbers. Evelyn had a good idea who could be easily *persuaded* to join her new guild. She knew which buttons to push for several of the Tea Basket Quilters who would sway their loyalties in her direction. Everyone wanted something. Others had something they wanted kept private. Everyone had a price. She intended to use the Gammill as the lever and individual secrets and desires as fulcrums. She'd tip this mountain of roly-poly gals right over. She'd send them all rolling downhill to her.

Evelyn had just finished her cocktail when the desk phone rang. She felt satisfied to be making some progress, having just concluded a third successful membership phone call.

The caller was Avery Underwood, the new gal — finally.

"Ah, Avery," Evelyn said, her voice dripping with artificial sweetness. "Thank you so much for getting back to me. Yes. Well. I wanted to talk to you about my new guild…"

"I thought you said you wanted to talk about my quilt," Avery said.

Evelyn had forgotten her lie. She'd fix that. She actually did recall Avery's quilt. The pattern was indeed rather intricate. "Oh, yes. I did mention that. Yes. Yes. So sorry. I'm a bit confused. I've been talking for several days to so many about the new guild, that I forgot. Sorry. I thought your quilt was a fantastic piece, actually. Do tell me about it. I believe I heard you're somewhat *new* to quilting." She could hardly say the word new without letting her voice register disdain. "One would never have suspected that fact from the quality of that quilt."

Avery settled back into the meager shade on the driver's seat of her truck, trying to avoid the glare of the day's sun. Once shaded, she proceeded to tell Evelyn some of the details.

"The pattern came from an online mystery quilt. I had no idea what I was about to make. However, the designer gave very precise instructions, so the final assembly wasn't difficult. Not at all. The colors I chose were not those suggested by the designer. I was fortunate — lucky, actually — in the combinations of colors I chose. You see, I'm not that good with color..."

"All beginners say they're 'not good with color,' Avery. That's just rookie fear talking," Evelyn interjected.

The interruption to her story didn't faze Avery. She was used to men interrupting her all the time. Evelyn's rudeness never fazed her. She continued. "The repeated block is cat's cradle. But you probably already knew that. I had the top professionally machine quilted by a woman in Missouri. I shipped the top out to her. She shipped it back after she was done. I thought her workmanship was amazing. Didn't you? Her quilting really made the design 'pop', which, I think is what you call quilting that enhances a project well."

"Ah, yes," agreed Evelyn who, at first, didn't care to hear this story at all. But as she was listening to Avery go on and on about the pattern, Evelyn did recall the quilt in nearly every detail.

Avery had presented it at a recent Tea Basket sew-and-tell, where members displayed finished projects to the group. The quilt was stunning, extra-large, a king-sized bed quilt if Evelyn recalled properly. The fact that Evelyn could remember at all gave her an idea.

"So, just how much *in love* with this quilt are you, Avery?"

Avery was taken aback. She had thoroughly enjoyed making the mystery quilt. She kept it folded and neatly displayed across the back of her couch. She recalled having spent well over one hundred dollars out of her wages for the fabric alone. She paid out more than twice that sum for the machine quilting. Then she spent several hours sitting at her table in the evenings, binding the edges. But if this woman was fishing for an opportunity to purchase the quilt, Avery was not sure she wanted to part with it.

Why would she want to buy a quilt when she could probably make the same quilt on her own?

"Do you? Are you... interested in buying it?"

Evelyn scoffed out loud at such a ludicrous question. "Of course not! Silly goose. But I was looking for a donation that we — that is, us, The Shining Star Quilt Guild — could raffle off. Would you consider donating your quilt to be raffled?"

Avery was stunned silent, yet quite flattered. *Mine? A raffle quilt?*

"I'm thoroughly convinced that a quilt... *your quilt*... could bring in as much as four thousand dollars toward our contribution to the Thimble and Chatelaine's team. You know, the competition to raise a lot of money and win a Gammill? Would you like to be a part of the winning guild? I could really use someone of your talents. I need a strong vice president, too. You might be just the right person for the job. And that quilt of yours is quite stunning. I know we could sell tickets *galore* for it."

Avery sat still and silent. Beads of sweat, caused by the sweltering heat of the day, started to trickle down her temple. She was baking as she sat in her truck, parked in the engineer's gravel lot which, as she looked around, had not one tree nearby to offer any shade. She was forced to shut the truck door and start up the engine so she could turn on the air conditioner. She dialed down the knob as cold as possible and cranked up the fan to high. At that moment, she could think of nothing other than the heat.

Evelyn continued, "Our new guild needs qualified officers. Come join us. Donate that lovely quilt. Help us win the Gammill, and then you won't have to be sending your beauties all the way to Missouri ever again for quilting services!"

As cool air began to blow across her face, her thoughts wandered into a fantasy of becoming second in command of a guild, and of seeing her work as a raffle quilt.

What this Evelyn person offered was another opportunity to belong and contribute both skill and time to a new organization within the community. This was an opportunity to enhance her talents and experience with her newfound hobby. She had no idea if her resume would take her back to work and away from all the free time she now enjoyed. But for whatever time she had left, here was a chance to serve her new community. The mystery quilt had been a learning experience. She considered the time and expense as she would have tuition and classroom time. *Why not?* If this Evelyn woman proved to be habitually nuts, she would just resign from this new group and stick with her current membership with the Tea Baskets.

"Done," she said. "What do I do next?"

Rosie Dyer got the news late that afternoon that Simone and Ximi had not located any place suitable or available for their auction. She was shocked by this report and let her familiar, "Holy moly," register that surprise to Ximi who was on the other end of the line. The girls were sorry, of course, but they had thoroughly telephoned every place they could think of.

"Did you call the community center?"

"Yes."

"Did you try all the churches?"

"Yes."

"What about the schools?"

"Yes, but even the schools are a no-go." This time of year, summertime, most of the schools were having their floors stripped and re-waxed or, as Ximi explained, "Whatever they did to floors nowadays. What are we going to do?" she asked, with an obvious undertone of panic in her voice.

Rosie thought for a few moments, in silence. She'd get back to them. They should sit tight. If they had any further ideas, they were to call her back. Rosie hung up and immediately called her neighbor, Carolyn Ashcroft. She knew this was not going to go over well with poor Carolyn, a woman who struggled hard to do everything right but always seemed to end up almost always doing nothing at all, unless one called worrying needlessly, *something*.

"Ashcroft's," came the voice of the doctor's wife.

Carolyn was a descendant of one of Athens' first families, one Isaac Baker, who had made his fortune in raccoon and beaver pelts, back in a time when the Hock Hocking river valley was covered in virgin timber and Native Americans were the majority. Carolyn never ventured far from her hometown. She chose to attend the university in Athens, majoring in home economics. She had given no thought about a choice of a career. While on campus, she found and eventually married a handsome undergrad, Benjamin Ashcroft, who would later graduate from the university's osteopathic medical school. The young osteopath started his practice in Athens after completing his internship at the local hospital. Thus Carolyn had lived well her entire life within the boundary of one county. When not sewing inside her lovely home in The Plains, she could be found nearby or in its outdoor swimming pool. Ben, who had retired from practice several years earlier, spent a good portion of his time these days out on the golf course.

Carolyn had made many friends over her seventy-some years in Athens, with Rosie being her longest, most enduring friendship. The two women met on the college green one autumn day during their freshman year. Rain poured down that day. Carolyn had thought to carry an umbrella. Rosie had been in a hurry that morning, forgetting hers. She looked like a drowned rat, her hair dripping wet, her skirt streaked with water falling off her slicker. Seeing a fellow coed in need, Carolyn felt sorry for her and offered to share her umbrella. The two scurried under the sycamores toward a lecture hall, where they discovered both were heading to the same classroom.

After class, the deluge had come to an end. As the hour passed in class, Rosie's clothes stopped dripping but remained damp. By the bell, she had started to chill. They decided to walk over to the Oasis, a nearby café. They wanted to chat, and Rosie wanted more time to dry off and to warm up over a steaming cup or two of hot cocoa. The Oasis was a common hangout for students back in their day, located across from the college green. As they enjoyed cups of hot cocoa together, Rosie found Carolyn to be a caring person, though perhaps she tried a little too hard to please everyone. Carolyn decided Rosie was smart but a little bit forgetful, as with the umbrella on a cloudy day. They forged a friendship that afternoon that lasted decades.

Both coeds pledged the same sorority that fall. Carolyn pursued a degree that might allow her to become a home economics teacher or maybe someone's wife and homemaker. She wasn't sure. She didn't care. Rosie was much more career-oriented and focused. She attended the College of Business and never once, after that day on the green, forgot to carry an umbrella on cloudy days. Each graduated with honors from her respective college. When Carolyn wed Benjamin Ashcroft, Rosie was maid of honor. When Rosie opened her own real estate office, Carolyn helped her cut the ribbon.

Telephone introductions were totally unnecessary with these two. They knew each other's voices quite well.

"We have a big problem already."

"Oh, dear. What, Rosie?"

"Ximi and Simone have so far been unsuccessful finding any place to hold the auction." Rosie thought she heard a gasping sound coming over the telephone from Carolyn. "Please don't worry too much. I just wanted to keep you informed. This is the first day the girls have searched. I'm just sure they'll find something. They probably need more time than we thought necessary."

"Oh dear, Rosie. Do you maybe know of a place that's on the market we could use?"

"Holy mole, why hadn't I thought of that? You're a peach, Carolyn! I'll make some inquiries from the office. Nothing comes to mind offhand, but I'll check with other realtors. There may be something out there that I'm not aware of. Good idea! Great idea, actually! Thank you. Now don't go worrying too much, dear. This will work itself out. I know it. But I'll continue to keep you in the loop, OK?"

"Oh, yes, please do. I'm going to fret, but I'll do my best not to let it get me down. You'll call me, won't you? Just as soon as you find a place?"

"Of course. I'll call you... soon... I hope."

Carolyn would not be able to avoid fretting. In the back of her mind, moving quickly forward, was the sound of Evelyn North's voice, repeating her threat over and over.

"You'll have few dollars for all your time, and I'll own the Gammill!"

54

5

 $\mathcal{N}$ora rose early the next morning. She planned to prepare herself a breakfast, high in protein, then spend some quality time in her sewing room before going directly to the Tea Basket hall. She had several UFO's underway and hoped to get at least one finished that day. If no one telephoned, asking her to go open up the hall, she might be able to finish a topper intended for that small round side table sitting bare in her hallway.

Nora always set a proper table for every meal, even when she ate alone — as she almost always did — a lesson learned from her late mother. She spread a clean tablecloth over her small kitchen table. She centered a pieced and quilted placemat to mark the spot where she'd dine, then placed down a neatly folded, linen napkin to the side. She arranged the silverware properly, placed a small glass filled with orange juice above the knife, another glass filled with water beside that, and left an empty expanse on the placemat, where her stoneware plate would go just as soon as an over-easy egg was cooked and two bacon strips were blotted with a paper towel. She had no sooner set the plate of hot food down when the house phone rang.

"Oh, shoot," she muttered, but answered the call before the third ring. "Hello?"

"Hey, baby doll, you awake?"

"Oh, for Heaven's sake, Belle, of course. I'm an early riser. Always have been."

"Well, baby doll, I talked to Vern, and he's looking forward to being at your service. He'll auctioneer whenever you want. He'd hoped, however, you don't want him to work on a Saturday or a Sunday, 'cause that's when my beau holds most of his estate auctions. That's his bread and butter, if you know what I mean. Shoot fire, girl, if you can avoid the weekends, he said he'd do the auction for free. How do you like that?"

Nora was elated and said so. She thanked Belle graciously, hung up and consumed her breakfast in a very cheerful mood. She even listened to the weather report on the radio, not caring one bit that the announcer said the recent heat wave was to continue. She would have to call Rosie and give her the good news as soon as she finished eating, then she'd go to her sewing room to put in a few hours at her machine. Maybe she'd turn off the radio, put an old LP on the turntable and listen to something cheerful. She felt a little like listening to Bing Crosby croon a tune.

'A heat advisory is in effect today. Temperatures in the 90s will continue into the evening hours. The national weather service predicts a high of 98 by noon, with humidity in the 80% range. Use caution when outdoors. It is currently 91 degrees and sunny.'

Avery Underwood rather relished the idea of belonging to two guilds at the same time. With no workload to interfere, she imagined she'd easily be able to participate in programs from both. She wanted to stay busy; actually, she needed to stay busy. Other than her interest in obtaining meaningful work with the county highway department, she still planned to spend a few more weeks relaxing and recreating herself.

High on her to-do list was to practice her new reverse applique knowledge gained from Nora's demonstration. She had seen a pattern she liked at the Thimble and Chatelaine but hadn't purchased. One of the Tea Basket quilters was in the shop at the same time and noticed her looking at it.

The woman, whose name Avery had forgotten, nudged her side and whispered to her, "Don't buy it. I can loan you my copy."

The woman revealed to Avery that she had decided not to make the project, even though she had purchased the pattern. The instructions inside the package looked too difficult for her, after she had had the opportunity to read them over. Avery was welcome to borrow her copy for free, if she wanted. Maybe, given time, the woman admitted, she herself might acquire enough nerve to try 'all that applique.'

Avery accepted the charitable offer and returned the pattern to the display rack in the store. Instead, she purchased all the fabric yardage listed on the supply list from the back of the envelope. A few days after the encounter, she discovered the free copy waiting for her on the counter near the coffee pot in the Tea Basket kitchenette. The donor attached a Post-it note, scribbled with Avery's name, to the front. Avery decided she would cut all the pieces today, since she had the fabric. Then if time allowed, she would begin piecing over at the Tea Basket hall, where she would surely find a helpful pro to talk her through any problems doing reverse applique. Avery was good at organizing her work, setting mini goals, then achieving them. That skill was probably the engineer in her.

Before she dove headlong into the pleasant task of applying a rotary cutter to fabric, she needed first to engage in some work for the Shining Star Quilt Guild. The new guild gave her an opportunity to employ those organizational and goal-setting skills. Her first assignment, as its appointed vice president, other than donating the quilt to be raffled, was to design a plan for selling raffle tickets. Avery opened up her laptop and took a sip of coffee, letting the hot liquid trickle down her throat. She leaned back in her chair to relax and tried to replace thoughts of applique with sales figures.

Evelyn said Lois would make six thousand raffle tickets. So, how many tickets would members need to sell in order to acquire $4,000? Easy: four thousand tickets at $1 apiece. But if buyers purchased a group of six tickets for $5, then how many groups did they need to sell to get $4,000? Hmm. She quickly did the math. Her calculation revealed they needed to sell only six hundred and sixty-seven books. Those figures reflected a wide spread in the number of sales needed. The problem in designing this plan was that she had no idea how many members Evelyn had found to join the Shining Star guild.

If the deadline for submitting their collections to the Thimble and Chatelaine was not until October, then she reasoned they had fifteen weeks to accomplish their $4,000 goal. She thought she'd approach the problem from that angle. Four thousand divided by fifteen weeks came to two hundred and sixty-six $1 sales per week or forty-four books per week. Ah. She decided to present this approach to the group, since she didn't know the size of their sales force. She'd tell the membership, as a whole, that they needed to sell roughly two hundred and seventy tickets or forty books every week. However many members, that figure would have to be divided among them to set personal sales goals.

Evelyn seemed positive they could sell enough to win the Gammill. But to Avery, this sum seemed astronomical. She was so new to the Athens community that she didn't know anyone to sell to, unless she counted Tea

Basket ladies. Avery assumed none of them would care to help out any guild in direct competition for the Gammill. That meant that she and Shining Star quilters needed to sell to groups or individuals unaffiliated with the Tea Baskets, out there in the community… somewhere. Avery hoped there would be members with such connections, because she sure didn't have any. She decided to prepare a one-page report with her projections and print copies, hoping that a dozen was far too few.

How do ladies — people, reminding herself to not be sexist — learn about guilds? Avery found out by walking around town. She'd stopped to admire a Fourth of July display of red, white and blue quilts in a window. When she looked up, she noticed the sign hanging above the Tea Basket Quilters' doorway, that informed her this place was a guild. Avery tried the door, which was unlocked. She entered the meeting room, met Nora Radnor and joined on the spot. Avery hoped that Evelyn was spreading news about the new Shining Star guild who, as far as Avery knew, had no place to regularly meet. Evelyn told her to be prepared to present her report at their first meeting at the Athens Library on Friday. Would there be any interest at all? She would at least be ready. Was the library where they would always meet? She had no idea.

Evelyn rushed through her morning rituals. The night before, she'd created fliers on her computer, then printed copies at her own expense at the big office goods store. The flier was bright yellow to draw attention. Her notice read:

NOW FORMING
SHINING STAR QUILT GUILD
ORGANIZATIONAL MEETING
FRIDAY JULY 13
4:00
ATHENS LIBRARY

She tossed the box of fliers onto the passenger seat of the Prius, parked in her garage, then sped out onto the roadway. Her first stop was to the local newspaper to drop off an announcement she wanted published ASAP. She was in luck. She had just managed to arrive minutes before the deadline for the following day's edition. Her notice would appear the day before their meeting. *Perfect,* she thought. Evelyn handed over the announcement, along with cash to pay the clerk, then quickly left the newspaper office. She failed to acknowledge any thanks to the woman who was required, at once, to hand-deliver the notice to the appropriate desk to meet their deadline.

Evelyn next made the rounds to all the libraries in the county where she planned to distribute fliers. When she ran into the Athens library, the librarian with the braid was again working the desk. He could not avoid helping with her needs immediately.

"I need my flier publicly posted and a stack left on the counter, so interested people can take one home."

Braid understood her demand, but first, he was required to review the content of her flier before he would be able to OK the posting.

This procedure greatly annoyed Evelyn, who allowed the annoyance to register across her pale face. As he slowly read, she crossed her arms and drummed her fingers impatiently. When the librarian was satisfied that Evelyn's notice was appropriate for the general public, he OK'd it. She dropped a stack of fliers in front of him. As she was about to depart, she paused briefly at the door and turned to confirm that he really did set them out on the counter for patrons to take.

Evelyn then drove to the libraries in counties both north and south of Athens, finishing all her deliveries by noon. Her travels included stops at a few quilt shops, which were in the same general areas as the libraries. Getting to all of the quilt shops, however, would take more time. Some were located in a neighboring county that Evelyn had not included for library stops. But with only five quilt shops in a thirty-mile radius, she was confident she could drive to the remaining stores before they closed that evening. She'd just have to drive faster than was normal — for Evelyn.

While Evelyn broke land-speed records in her little Prius, she thought things were looking good for her Shining Star guild. Evelyn let her thoughts travel overseas. Perhaps she would never enjoy a world cruise. Too many rules to follow, beyond her control.

Tea Basket president, Carolyn Ashcroft, had rolled out of bed late that morning, still weary. Sleep had been impossible. Her mind raced with dark, sad thoughts. She rummaged round her closet until she found a cool sundress to toss over her ample body. She barely ate any breakfast and avoided her sewing room completely. As was her habit under stress, Carolyn spent most of the previous evening, and this morning, so far, pacing about her big house, worrying and wearing out the batteries in her little handheld fan.

She had to replace AA batteries in the tiny device which had seen excessive use. *No venue for the auction. What are we going to do? Hold an event outdoors? Unthinkable! Oh, what will the ladies think of me? How will my tenure as president be remembered if this auction is a huge failure? Why, the auction might not even happen. Then what? Will I forever be remembered as a failure, too?*

Oh, the worrisome thoughts she could imagine. And then there was Evelyn...

Though Carolyn hated the heat of this summer, she also loved the serenity of poolside. She hoped spending a bit of time out there might help relieve the stress she felt. She took her little fan and draped its lanyard over her neck. She retrieved a favorite paperback novel off the bedstand and prepared a large plastic tumbler of tea in the kitchen. Laden with these items, and a big towel draped over an arm, she shuffled to the pool located off the back deck. The only shady spot around the big, inground pool was near a feature built to look like a natural waterfall. The stones had been arranged to intensify the sound of the falling water. There she placed the book and tea on a little teak table next to a matching recliner. She spread out the oversized towel across the recliner then, with much difficulty, lowered herself down onto the towel. Not wearing a bathing suit but attired in her loose-fitting, spaghetti-strap dress, with the tiny fan hanging from her neck, Carolyn paused. She inhaled slowly and deeply and then exhaled slowly and deliberately.

Doctor and Mrs Ashcroft's lavish swimming pool provided a calming place to unwind when her unfounded worries got to be too much. Her husband, however, loved its location for entertaining guests at their frequent dinner parties. When darkness fell, he would switch on the party lights above the landscaped jewel. Out there guests could freely laugh, talk and enjoy the night air around the pool. They had, indeed, enjoyed many cocktail parties there over the years. But Carolyn preferred to sit alone and listen to the sound of her waterfall. The sound of rippling water usually brought her a sense of calm and peace.

The portable phone inside a pocket of her dress rang. Carolyn jumped. Her hand knocked over the tea, sending the plastic tumbler flying. It rattled across the stone deck. Tea spread out, creating a wet, brown puddle. The ice cubes glistened in the hot sunlight. An ant that had been suddenly drenched found itself floating toward and finally landing against a slice of lemon. As the puddle diminished, the ant regained footing then marched off on his journey elsewhere, while the hot sun began to melt the ice cubes and evaporate what liquid remained on the hot stones.

Carolyn fumbled to answer the phone with her tea-drenched hand.

The caller was Rosie. "We've got our auctioneer!"

"Bless you, Rosie! Finally, some good news."

"Don't bless me. This was Nora's doing. She asked Belle. Belle asked her husband, Vern. Vern agreed. Simple as that," Rosie said.

"Then bless Nora. That's one problem solved. Any news yet for a place to hold our auction?"

"Sorry. Nothing yet. It's only been one day, dear. They're still working on the problem."

Carolyn's spirits fell back into darkness. The shade from a nearby tree failed to keep the heat at bay. She switched on the little fan and aimed the airflow directly toward her face. Saying goodbye to Rosie, she sat back in resignation. She'd have to give up reclining at the poolside and retreat indoors to air-conditioned comfort. The heat was simply too oppressive outside. Carolyn realized she had reached that age where she was forced to heed those warnings for elderly, who must cope with heatwaves with a certain degree of caution.

Rosie disconnected with Carolyn and slipped her blue cell phone into a pocket of her navy-blue skirt, adjusted her matching open vest over a crisp, white blouse and walked into the hotel lobby. Publicity was on her mind. She passed by the front desk, nodding to the clerks on duty and entered a small office space off the lobby, used by the local Chamber of Commerce. The chamber president was in, his door open. Rosie walked over to his desk, greeting him with a smile and a business-like handshake, and adjusted a vacant chair and sat down.

Two guest chairs in front of his desk were intended to reflect a degree of opulence to the chamber office. The room was warm and inviting. The walls were adorned with framed certificates and glossy photographs of Bob shaking hands with notable figures from local politics, sports and businesses. Bob's nameplate took center stage on the top of his desk. A phone, a few papers and other trappings lay scattered before him. He smiled up at Rosie from his comfortable swivel chair and offered to get her a cup of coffee. She declined, preferring to get right to the point of her visit.

Rosie proceeded to tell Bob about the Tea Basket guild's attempt to put together an auction, and the initial problem they faced so far in locating a place to hold it. She was hoping he could think of a building or a business they might use. She explained their purpose for the auction and also told him that she would call on him when and if their auction did find a place and set a date. In order to be a success, they were going to have to bring in *real buyers* from out of town, not just a few well-meaning locals or tight-fisted curiosity seekers. That was her real reason for the visit. Publicity.

"I can't begin to tell you how much that Gammill means to us," Rosie explained. "For a man who's a car nut like you, I guess it's like you owning your own dealership. As the boss, you could get your work done immediately. You'd be in and out in a jiffy. It's like that for quilters who prefer machine quilting. We have to pay someone else, sometimes out of town. Sometimes out of state. That poses risks, with our quilts traveling by mail. It means getting in line, too. Machine quilting isn't the kind of thing just anybody can do. And it's not something that gets started and finished in an hour. The process can take days. Plus, the cost for professional services can run into the hundreds. So, we've decided to 'kill two birds with one stone', as they say. Well, if we can raise a lot of money, that is. We're going to try to raise funds to help in the fight to find a cure for breast cancer, while at the same time raise enough to win a Gammill. The acquisition of a $30,000 machine will really be an asset, saving our members time and great expense."

Bob knew nothing about quilting. But Rosie's pitch on the subject did make him recall a quilt that had, for many years, adorned his own childhood bed. He remembered being told that the blue and white quilt had been made by his late grandmother, lovingly, and completely by hand. But beyond remembering vaguely the blue and white color of the design, he simply was at a loss to comprehend how a quilt came into being. From what Rosie was telling him, he understood the process took a lot of time.

Sadly, like Rosie, he also didn't know of a place the guild could use, other than Hart's Auction House. Had they tried asking Vern? Rosie explained that, yes, Vern Hart was going to be their auctioneer, free of charge, but the auction had to take place elsewhere. Bob understood Rosie's frustration. Except for Hart's place or the gymnasium at the community center or maybe one of the local schools, there really was no space, to his knowledge, large, open and suitable for her needs. He apologized and said he'd keep his eyes open, spread the word and see what he could find. He'd definitely get back to her if something possibly came to mind.

As for publicity, that was a much different story. Bob prepared a small chamber newsletter every month, which he emailed to all chamber members. Once Rosie had a place and a date, he would be more than happy to write up a story for the newsletter, urging its members to invite their customers and patrons to attend. This offer was the least he could do for a member trying to raise substantial funds for such a good cause. As a matter of fact, he might even seek backing from some of their members so that the chamber could bid on one of their little quilts.

Rosie was pleased to hear this. She thanked Bob sincerely, then took her leave after shaking his hand goodbye. She had an appointment soon, to take new buyers out to view a home for sale. She wanted to be sure her Ford Edge was spotless. She planned to run the vehicle through the car wash up the street before meeting with the potential buyers from out of town. She would chauffer them around, showing them the house they expressed interest in seeing, schools in the district where the property was located, landmarks around the town, and perhaps take them to lunch at one of the local eateries, if they seemed eager to buy. As she left the hotel lobby, the front doors opened automatically. She felt like she'd stepped into a stone-fired oven.

6

By Friday afternoon, Evelyn North had managed to twist the arms of a dozen Tea Basket Quilters to join her guild and attend the meeting. Only a couple of the newest Tea Baskets came willingly and with enthusiasm. The others had to be *convinced* to join, in a manner consistent with Evelyn's tactics of coercion or bribery. The fliers she'd dropped off at libraries brought in half a dozen more recruits. The notice in the paper reached an additional six. She was more than pleased with the number but not certain of all their abilities, except for those of the Tea Basket deserters. Two dozen was an amazing number to show up for a first meeting of a new guild. The number of bodies forced her to dash off to request more chairs from the front desk. The slow librarian with the braid down his back was once again the official she had to speak to.

When he arrived with extra chairs stacked on a special chair dolly, ladies approached to accept one as he lifted them off, one by one. They dragged and arranged them into rows behind the few already in place. Evelyn helped Avery slip her quilt onto a rod through its hanging sleeve. The pair settled the two ends of the rod over the tops of two retractable posts atop opposite stands. They then hoisted the rod higher and higher until Avery's quilt hung in full view, with the bottom edge no longer touching the floor. The room buzzed with quiet but admiring comments. Tea Basket quilters sitting in the front row would catch bits of the questions from women seated behind them. They turned to offer answers.

"Avery was the quilt maker... Machine quilted... Don't know by whom... Thought the work had been done out of state... The block pattern is cat's cradle... Yes, that block is somewhat difficult... No, probably not suitable for beginners..."

As the general volume of conversation died away, Evelyn stepped forward to address the room. "I want to welcome all of you to the new Shining Star Quilt Guild. My name's Evelyn North. To my right is Avery

Underwood. Because this is a new group, we thought we'd start with introductions. Please make them brief, though, as there are many of you here tonight. That's great, of course. Love to see all of you today. Please state your name so everyone can hear, how long you've been a quilter, and what you expect to get out of this guild. We'll start with me, then Avery, then over here to the right at this first chair and go 'round. OK?"

There were no objections

"OK. Then as I mentioned, I'm Evelyn North. I've made quilts for twenty-some years. If you allow me, I'll be your founding president, at least until we draw up bylaws and formally decide when to hold elections and define the terms and duties of officers. My hope is that this group will start out to raise sufficient funds to win us... yes, I said win... a Gammill longarm quilting machine. We can enter a contest to raise the most money for the Thimble and Chatelaine quilt shop's team in this coming October's 5K. If we collect more money than any other guild, we win the Gammill!

"I'm going to pass around an attendance sheet. Please print your name on the paper, as well as your address, both home and email, and a phone number where you can be reached. Again, note to the side what you expect from this guild. Does this hour work for everyone as a general meeting time?"

If anyone had objections, they were not expressed.

Evelyn started the sheet around. "Good. As soon as we can, we'll email everyone a roster. We'll have some raffle tickets ready to sell next week, and hopefully Avery will have her first sales location established by that time so we can begin selling to the general public. Next up, our founding vice president, Avery."

The tall, lanky woman was standing beside her quilt. She smiled, adjusted her glasses and introduced herself. "I'm Avery Underwood. This is my quilt that we will raffle off over the next few weeks. Although this looks really difficult to make, I did all the piecing without even knowing what I was making. I completed the whole top following instructions off the World Wide Web. I started cutting and piecing without knowing what the end result would look like, therefore, it's a mystery quilt. I consider myself new to quilting, as I've only been sewing quilts a short time. I would like to learn more about the Athens community. A decade ago, I went to school here. But I've been away, working, since graduation from the university. It's my hope that I can contribute to the area in some meaningful way. I guess, by donating this quilt, I've started down that path and hope to continue to do so in any way I can."

The first chair to the right was completely covered by Lois Caldwell's expansive print dress, which fell in folds to the floor around her. Lois quickly closed up a small bag of corn chips. She swallowed then licked her lips. With some difficulty, she stood and slowly turned to address the group. Her brown eyes darted from one person to another until they came to rest on the Asian face of Ximi Ling. Seeing someone she knew helped to calm her. She cackled nervously, making the loose flesh of her sagging double chin wiggle. Clearing her throat, she said quietly, "My name is Lois Caldwell."

"Can't hear youuuu!" sang a voice from the rear of the room.

"Ah." Louder this time. "I'm Lois Caldwell. I've been quilting for many, many years, when I find the time. I'm busy with my farm, but I like to sew whenever I have the chance. That's not often though. I like meeting new people. I joined to meet folks."

Lois then held up a single sheet of paper on which she had designed their raffle ticket. As Evelyn instructed, she had made only one sample. She passed her paper over to a woman seated nearby.

"Take a look at the ticket sample. If you see something's wrong, or something maybe needs to be added, make a note somewhere on the paper or just tell me. I'll make corrections before we have any printed, hopefully real soon."

And so introductions progressed around the room, finally concluding with the woman seated in the last chair in the back. Evelyn's hope of acquiring the cream of the crop was dashed. More than half of the women labeled themselves beginners or novices. *I'll have to do something about that in the future. Right now*, she reminded herself, *I need to build an army of ticket sellers and get them on task and ahead of the Tea Baskets.* She asked Avery to explain next what they needed to do to kick-start the raffle project.

"Yes, well, as Lois said, we'll soon have raffle tickets to sell," Avery said. "In order to secure our place as the guild raising the most for the Thimble and Chatelaine team, we need to sell at least two hundred and seventy tickets each week."

A collective gasp came from the assembled women, followed by an increase in noise created by two dozen astounded voices groaning in disbelief.

"I know this may *sound* impossible, but I'm assured it is not. When we divide that number by each of you, the task becomes much easier. The individual number is between eleven or twelve tickets for each of you per week."

The rumble of uncertainty continued, though at a somewhat reduced volume.

"As I mentioned, I'm new to this area. My list of possible contacts is quite limited. So I plan to set up locations around the county where, each week, I can sell to the general public. If you are like me, without connections, then I ask you to join me at these locations until you have reached your personal sales goal. We can draw up a sign-up list to spread the workload around. I also need your help to identify good locations from which to sell — places that have lots of pedestrian traffic. So I'm passing around another sheet of paper. If you know of a good location, then please jot down the name and address of that place for me. I'll try to have a schedule ready next week.

"After you've achieved your sales goal, you can consider your contribution to the cause as satisfied. Please keep in mind, we aren't asking anyone here to pay dues to this guild. This is our first and our only goal for now. We don't even know if we will have dues to pay, since we haven't written bylaws yet. Nor have we any mission.

"Fortunately, if you've been a member of the community for some time, if you're employed, if you belong to other associations, you'll find reaching your sales goal lots easier than I will. You already come with a long list of potential ticket buyers. And not to brag, but this quilt really is well done. I'm sure that whoever sees it, will love to have it. I think this quilt will sell itself."

Avery passed over a clipboard containing a blank sheet of paper for sites, then started to sit down. She paused then turned around, having thought of something. "If I have a location set up before next Friday, I'll email everyone the address. You'll have my cell phone number in the email. Call me if you decide you can sit with me. And call me if you think of other locations that occur to you after today."

"That's all for today's meeting, ladies," Evelyn announced. "I would like everyone to mingle and get to know one another. Please be sure your contact information is on the roster before you leave, and list what you want the guild to do for you. Give the sheet to Lois, who has agreed to act as our first secretary."

By that weekend, Avery had designed a chart using suggestions from the members, who listed four different locations where they might sell raffle tickets. What she didn't have was permission from three of the four businesses to sell tickets outside their front doors. She noted the names and phone numbers of those who agreed to sit with her at the first site where they did have permission. This first Saturday they were going to park themselves at the entrance to the town's largest grocery store. Avery had worked out shifts for each volunteer, so that no one was obligated to stay more than two or three hours, depending on what level of commitment each volunteer cared to offer. Avery was pleased.

Avery loaded the quilt into her truck, along with the stand, an old, white sheet to lay under the quilt so that it didn't get soiled while being put on the display rack, two lawn chairs borrowed from neighbors, and finally, her wooden TV tray for buyers to write their names and phone numbers on ticket stubs. Lois had given her a large antique crock for buyers to deposit their stubs into for the fall drawing. By seven thirty that morning, Avery was excited and happy to be leaving her apartment for 'work', with her new guild. She would have everything set up and ready to sell by eight... sooner, if the first person on her list also arrived early. Avery liked mornings.

Lois Caldwell always rose early, too, but she did so out of obligation, not necessarily out of pleasure. She had chores to do; chores in the morning, and chores at night. The farm made certain demands of her which she always put first. Chickens needed to be released early every morning from the henhouse, where she locked them up every night to prevent fox or raccoons from killing them under cover of darkness. She had cattle that needed feeding at least once a day. They needed water, too. If the pasture was eaten down or the grass was dead from winter frost, she'd have to feed them hay. There was always a fence to mend. Hay had to be cut twice every summer, dried, put into windrows, baled, collected, stacked in the barn and then doled out as needed. There was also her little truck garden, whose bounty she harvested, cleaned and offered for sale at the local farmer's market once — sometimes twice — a week, during summer. Lois stayed very busy. In spite of her robust size, she remained relatively healthy, a fact she attributed to her active outdoor life. Her only complaint was not having enough time in her days to sew. Sometimes that made her cranky.

In the past, Lois had lost many hens to predators, so she stopped 24/7 free-range grazing. One year a neighbor's dog killed all but six of her hens. That happened when winter was coming on and egg production had dropped. She'd planned to bring on new chicks the following spring anyway, so the massacre was not as devastating as it could have been. The hens were old. She'd probably have butchered the old birds, even plucked and dressed them for her freezer, had the dog not gotten to them first.

Then, when a sly fox, in broad daylight, started to pick off her new young flock, one by one, that's when Lois decided to buy a .22 pistol. A neighbor, not the one with the bad dog, but another one who lived nearby, advised her that a pistol was a better option for shooting predators than her ancient .22 rifle. So she went to a local gun store and bought a pistol. They were expensive. She paid the cashier reluctantly and took the gun home, along with several plastic boxes of .22 bullets. She planned to practice shooting tin cans off a fence post until she could shoot with sustained accuracy.

The only time Lois practiced after that week was when she spotted the fox, a raccoon or a coyote. These, however, seemed mostly to arrive at night. Shooting in the dark required an even better aim. Lois found keeping the loaded pistol on hand extremely beneficial for dispatching thieving foxes, or even Copperheads. The snakes seemed to like a certain hill on her farm that she had to drive along to reach one of the cattle pens. If she spotted one or two Copperheads sunning themselves, they were soon buzzard food. Lois' aim was deadly.

Because she drove a four-wheel drive Tundra over the farm as well as to town, she thought maybe it would be a good idea to obtain a concealed carry permit, so her pistol could travel with her all the time. Occasionally, while out mending fences, she might have a need to drive directly into town for supplies. The .22 was always with her, just in case she saw that fox. She was positive she'd get pulled over one day by a highway patrolman. The loaded gun in its canvas holster would be discovered. Then she'd be in a heap of trouble and would most certainly never be able to live the story down. She worried that she might even end up in jail. That thought strongly suggested she get herself a permit. She discovered she'd have to take a gun-safety class before being allowed to purchase the permit from the local sheriff. So Lois signed up for one.

At first, a few of the men in her class snickered at her.

There stood Lois, taking up space, donned in her voluminous print dress, dark socks under old-lady, lace-up shoes, standing next to beefy guys wearing cargo pants and hiking boots, yucking it up between each other. She thought they acted like they belonged to some big badass boys club. They all wore ball caps. Some didn't even know how to wear a ball cap correctly, but spun the bill around to the back of their necks, like a child might if his hat was too large. That defeated the purpose of the bill. It shaded not their eyes but the backs of their necks. Lois wore her old sweat-stained, straw gardening hat. It protected both her eyes and her neck.

Lois ignored the men as much as she could, intently listening to the instructor and even taking the occasional note. She seemed so out of place among them, however, that they could not ignore her. When time came for her to step up to fire her pistol, Lois took slow and deliberate aim. She thought she could hear the faint sound of one of the men whispering to another. Lois took a deep breath, steadied her hand, exhaled and pulled the trigger. Four times she repeated her aim and fired. Four times she hit the bullseye. The men, who thereafter seemed to have a bit of trouble duplicating her good aim, stopped snickering. Lois looked each man squarely in the eye every time one of them turned around holding up his dismal target sheet. In less time than she imagined, Lois presented her certificate of completion to a deputy sheriff to qualify to sign up for her permit.

This morning was one that required Lois to rise early, do chores and then head into town with produce for her booth at the farmer's market. In addition to vegetables for her stall, she carried a few raffle tickets for the quilt. Evelyn had given Lois a color photograph of the quilt and ordered her to take the picture with the tickets to the farmer's market, since Avery would have the quilt and Lois couldn't. Evelyn told her to direct buyers down to the grocery store where Avery was sitting with the actual quilt, if they wanted to be amazed at its actual beauty. So Lois willingly obliged and taped the photo to one of the legs of her easy-up canopy, for all her customers to see. She was a little afraid Evelyn might check up on her to make sure she had done as ordered. She shuddered to think of consequences if she didn't do as the woman ordered.

On Monday morning, Nora had two urns filled with piping hot coffee, one regular and the other decaf, ready for the Tea Basket Quilters. She and Phoebe came down for a cup, from the second floor, where they had been busy in the room with the large design wall. Other members had begun to arrive alone or in pairs. Everyone arriving walked straight to the kitchenette, seeking out their favorite mug from the cabinet. Once retrieved, each selected a labeled urn and drew out the brew of her choice. Talking all the while, they added creamer or sweetener, or both, to their cups, or simply walked off to a seat, carrying a steaming cup.

After everyone found a seat, Carolyn Ashcroft, their president, completed the initial formalities of a brief meeting. Rosie Dyer stood next to give the auction committee's report.

"We are pleased to report that we're making *some* progress on our auction, though not nearly as much as we hoped."

This was met with quiet asides and comments from the assembly. More like the House of Commons than a subdued assembly of Quakers, comments spoken aloud were traditional, fueled by caffeine and the comfort and safety of being among friends.

"First, the good news." Rosie looked around for Belle Hart.

Belle was seated in the middle of the gathering. She was looking intently at a quilt pattern in a magazine which lay open on her neighbor's lap.

"Belle, would you please stand up?"

Belle failed to hear her name being called.

Rosie raised her voice and shouted, "Belle!"

Finally hearing her name, Belle looked up in surprise. "Heavens! Shoot fire! You scared the daylights outta me, baby doll!"

"I just want everyone to recognize you, dear. Ladies, Belle has convinced her husband to be our auctioneer, and wait for it, Vern Hart has agreed to do so free of charge!"

The announcement brought a round of applause. Several women seated around Belle congratulated or thanked her. A few gave her a pat on the back. Belle was deeply touched. She squirmed in her seat, flushed with both embarrassment and pride.

"Now for the bad news," continued Rosie. "As of today, we do not have a location for our auction. That means we still cannot set a date or do any advertising."

A hubbub of discouraged comments followed. A hand in the back of the room shot up. Someone had a question or a comment.

The president, Carolyn Ashcroft, recognized the hand. The hand was attached to the large body of Lois Caldwell, clad in a vast quantity of floral fabric called a dress. She had quietly seated herself in the rear of the group, where she thought a quick escape might be easier if need be.

"Ah, I was wondering, that is to say, how many quilts will you, er, we, be offering up?"

"Excellent question, Lois, thank you," replied the president. "Let's put that to the auction chair, Rosie, to answer."

"Thank you, Carolyn. Well, Lois, based on the replies last week to our secretary's email, which asked everyone what was available at this moment, we will offer almost one hundred little quilts."

A small gasp of delight preceded another lively round of applause.

"I am, like you, quite pleased and stunned by this number. Your generosity to part with lovely, small quilts, which you have enjoyed making and owning, is overwhelming. I understand that all of those quilts are complete and ready to auction off at this very moment. I have also received a few reports that there are some of you out there who have small UFO's, yet to be bound and labeled, that you also hope to donate. We hope they will be completed in time to add to our list. I am so very, very pleased with all of you and your amazing generosity."

One of the new members, seated in front, asked, "What's a UFO?"

Carolyn smiled. "It means Un-Finished Object."

Another hand shot up in the air. This one was from another member seated in the front row. The hand belonged to Nora Radnor, her big, red glasses matching today's red lipstick and solid-red linen pantsuit.

"Phoebe and I and some of the girls have been talking on the phone. We decided how nice it would be for everyone to see some of the auction quilts today. Phoebe and I arrived early and pinned about twenty of them to the design wall upstairs."

A murmur of excitement now filled the room. As anyone, who has labored long hours over the construction of a quilt, knows, one of the pleasures is to have others see and admire it. The makers of the small quilts upstairs smiled with pride, knowing that everyone present would soon see their handiwork. The prospect of this impromptu display created excitement among the novices present. Some of them, out of fear or imagined embarrassment, had not yet offered up a quilt for the auction. They would now judge for themselves if anything they made could even slightly match the quality of those made by quilters with decades of experience. They mumbled comments about the impossibility of creating certain blocks. They were reassured, by more experienced quilters seated near them in the hall, that they would begin to see how block patterns come into being. Gradually their fears and confusion would be turned into love and appreciation for the art form, and quite probably into a passion for it. The old hands apologized, explaining that, once bitten by the quilting bug, there was no known vaccine.

Carolyn asked for and received a motion, a second and a unanimous vote to adjourn. The room emptied quickly, as everyone clamored up the steps to view the little quilts. Lois was the last to go up. She was nervously polishing off a York peppermint patty, worried, yet hopeful, that Evelyn didn't find out she was still a member of the Tea Basket Quilters. She felt like a spy, and she was so afraid she'd let slip her deception, that she barely spoke casually to anyone that day.

The white-carpeted design wall was covered with a collection of wall hangings and table toppers, anyone would have been proud to own. A few tiny doll bed quilts were among them, their tiny blocks capable of pleasing any discerning collector. Lois lagged behind the viewers, making a mental note of the quality. She was impressed. Having gone to farm auctions and seen the prices paid for worn-out, old, raggedy bed quilts, she had a feeling that the Tea Baskets would do very well indeed at an auction, with these excellent offerings. She wondered, though, if the same buyers of old bed quilts were the kind of folks who also bought smaller new versions. Small quilts would never adorn beds, but probably had to be relegated to space on somebody's wall for display. Then she thought, maybe guild wouldn't get much at all for them. But in spite of her guestimates, large or small, all the miniature textiles that hung before her were impressive. She adjusted her glasses and moved in for a closer inspection.

Like grading eggs for a carton, Lois liked to examine similar quilts together as a whole. To her liking, whoever organized this, Phoebe she imagined, the little quilts on the white wall were grouped according to similar blocks or patterns. Samplers hung together. Scrappy quilts made from the repetition of one or two different blocks occupied another section. All the many little log cabin quilts encircled the entire collection. Those that were more unique, like appliques, filled in the space remaining. Lois liked what she saw, liked it very much.

The Tea Basket Quilters were prize-winners, to say the least. They were artisans, quilt-makers who paid much attention to all the steps required to produce quality quilts. The smaller the pieces and the smaller the finished project, the more accuracy required. These seams were undoubtedly perfect one-quarter-inch seams, maybe perfect one-eighth-inch seams. The makers had obviously pressed all those tiny seams to have achieved such crispness. They demonstrated fine examples of hand quilting, or they did excellent jobs of machine quilting. If they didn't do their own quilting, then they knew of professional quilters who were artists.

Samplers included some whose little blocks were named after states in the union. Other thematic collections included a few with Biblical references. The striking differences, other than a mix of different blocks to each, was the variety in color combinations. A few of the quilts were created using batik cottons. Some were created using a multitude of deep, rich colors, with one solid background fabric holding the array all together.

Scrappy quilts, so called because they were often made using hundreds of leftover scraps of infinite colors and prints, hung on the wall, too. Some of them carried the traditional names of Jacob's ladder, Bear Paw, Broken Dishes and Nine Patch.

Log cabins, composed of tiny strips of dark fabrics on one half of a block, and light strips on the other half, amounted to quite a few of the little quilts. Block halves on some were created using diagonal light or dark halves. The placement of dark sides and light sides created the overall pattern.

The appliques were all unique, not one pattern repeated. Lois found a little Orange Peel that had been appliqued by machine using the blanket stitch. Nearby hung a little quilt with a vase on the front, which overflowed with flowers. Its flowers were made of bright yoyos. The yoyos and applique designs had been attached with the tiniest of zigzag stitches. There was a tribute to Valentine's Day in the form of a heart made of men's ties. Upon close examination, Lois was sure it had been executed by hand, using reverse applique. Another quilt was a scrappy collection of pieced baskets. The arching basket handles looked, at first, to have been attached using traditional hand applique. Lois inched closer, her nose almost touching the quilt. She thought the appliqued stem might have been attached by machine on one side. Then perhaps the fabric had been folded back over a machine-sewn seam. She could see only hand-applique stitches on the opposite side of the handles. The fold gave the little handle a bit of bulk.

Very clever.

Lois lingered long, looking at the collection. When her stomach announced time to find lunch, she quietly excused herself. She left the Tea Basket hall, climbed with difficulty into the cab of her Tundra and headed to the nearest fast food drive-through. In her excitement, she thought she would tell Evelyn about all the fantastic little quilts.

But as she later munched on a double burger, large fries and a chocolate shake, she thought better of that idea. Evelyn didn't know she remained a Tea Basket Quilter. Burger juice made its way from her lips to her collar. She licked her fingers, wiped her lips, chin and wattles with a paper napkin and decided to head for the fairground office. The premium book for the upcoming fair exhibitions was almost finished. She wanted all the work done and the task out of the way soon. Seeing so many little quilts had inspired her with ideas of her own. She was motivated with a desire to set aside some precious time to piece a little quilt real soon.

Saturday had been an enjoyable day for Avery. This Monday proved even better. Two Tea Basket Quilters, who were also new Shining Star recruits, Simone LeBlanc, and friend, Ximi Ling, joined her to sell raffle tickets at their next venue, yet another grocery store with lots of foot traffic. Both Simone and Ximi were newbies to quilting as well as guilds. Like Avery, they were eager to learn. Simone and Ximi hoped to make amends to the

Tea Basket guild for not finding a venue. They signed up for Avery's entire ten-hour day. The two justified the effort might somehow make amends for their recent failure, not for the Tea Basket Quilters, but at least to lessen their guilty feelings.

Lots of people bought their raffle tickets. The three women spent some time getting to know one another between ticket buyers. They laughed and made self-deprecating jokes about their sewing skills. They devoured a pizza, which Simone had delivered to the front of the store. It wasn't long before Avery delightedly telephoned Lois, requesting additional tickets. She was surprised when Lois Caldwell, whom she understood lived on a farm several miles outside of town, arrived quickly, bearing a shoebox filled with tickets.

They didn't know that Lois had remained in town after the Tea Basket meeting and impromptu small quilt exhibit. Afterwards she had driven to the fairgrounds to work. Her typing stopped only when the phone rang. She had just finished entering the list of horticultural classes on the office computer for this year's premium book, when Avery's call, requesting more tickets, stopped her progress. Lois kept a box of raffle tickets — just in case — stored in the cab of her truck. She would get them over to the gals 'in a jiffy'.' And she did.

It had been a profitable day for the new guild. Avery and her companions sold three hundred and sixty-one dollars in raffle tickets. Avery's quilt was, indeed, selling itself. Some of the buyers, who stopped by, wanted the quilt for themselves. Some loved the color combination. Some said the quilt was the perfect size for their bed. Others scribbled the name of a relative or friend on the stub they dropped into the receptacle, hoping to win the quilt as a gift. There were those who said they wanted the quilt as a wedding present or a birthday present. A few ticket buyers even asked questions about the new guild.

Avery and her companions eagerly explained everything they knew. They talked about the guild's immediate purpose and what they themselves hoped their group would become after they turned in their donation to Molly Menear's race team in the fall. They invited everyone who asked any questions about their new guild to attend a meeting and join. Most of their buyers were just that — quilt buyers, not quilt makers. They were thanked politely for the invitation. Sometimes a ticket buyer promised to spread the word about the new guild, but definitely they'd tell everyone about the lovely quilt.

Several lookers asked the women where their next location would be to sell tickets. Avery imagined that perhaps this question meant they didn't have extra spending money at the moment, or they couldn't really afford to spend money on a raffle anyway, and were trying to cover up their lack of funds and thereby save face. She quickly dismissed the assumption. But being unfamiliar with some of the locations recommended to her, Avery felt she needed to explain the problem.

Avery pointed out that their schedule was as yet incomplete; exact hours and days at future places not yet confirmed. Therefore she was hesitant to say anything which might be wrong or later changed. She was sorry. But she thanked them for pointing out something she needed to remedy. She made a mental note to start carrying a copy of the schedule to all of the guild's upcoming sales locations.

Over the phone, Evelyn sounded uncharacteristically pleased with Avery's report about their sales. She was curious when Avery mentioned how fast Lois had arrived with additional raffle tickets.

"Ten minutes? That's how fast she got them to you?" she asked.

That didn't sound like the Lois Evelyn knew. Lois was slow, partially due to her bulk, partially due to her nature. Lois only hurried if there was food to be had. *Where the devil had she come from? The local donut shop, havin' a dozen for a snack?* Evelyn knew where Lois lived, and she knew that driving from the farm to town would have taken Lois twenty minutes, at minimum, to reach Avery in front of the grocery store, if home was where she had driven from. Evelyn had traveled to Lois' farmhouse once. She vowed never to drive out there again. The county road was a twisting nightmare in her Prius, only partially paved, riddled with potholes in valleys and washboard on the hillsides. Evelyn would never live in such a remote place, even if her life depended on it. Surely Lois must have been in town to have gotten those extra tickets to Avery in ten minutes.

Probably, Evelyn thought, *she drove from the fairgrounds. Yeah, she could have popped over to the east end, on the bypass, in ten minutes. Good for her. Never thought she was so efficient. I might thank her. Might as well go do that and get it over with.*

Evelyn hung up the phone with Avery and trotted out to her Prius to make the short drive across town to the fairgrounds, where Evelyn assumed Lois could be found. But when she arrived on the hilltop, Lois' Tundra was not out front of the fair office. In fact, there were no cars parked anywhere near the fair office. *Blast it. I guess I'll have to call her, 'cause I'm sure as heck not driving out to her place,* Evelyn thought.

Just then, the gray Tundra, with Lois at the wheel, rumbled up to the top of the hill and pulled into the spot where Evelyn remembered the truck had been parked the day she first approached Lois about the Shining Star Guild. The door opened wide. Lois, in her tent dress, slowly emerged and slid to the ground. After retrieving her bag off the bench of the truck, she turned and shut the door. That was when Lois spotted the black Prius in the shadow of a nearby tree. A hot-pink jog suit and mass of orange hair emerged from the driver's side and was now trotting toward her. Lois felt suddenly faint. She had been so engrossed in thoughts of small quilts that she had not noticed Evelyn's car.

"Lois!" shouted Evelyn, as she quickly approached.

Oh, God, she's found out.

"Hey, where were you…"

"I can explain," Lois began to sputter. "I just didn't want to give up my membership just yet. I'm sorry. I really don't mean anything by it."

Evelyn came to an abrupt stop in front of the tent dress, blocking Lois' path to the office. "What?" Evelyn asked. "What do you mean, 'you're sorry'?"

"Really, Evelyn, I'm sorry," whined Lois, who was now starting to feel even fainter in the heat of the afternoon's sun, with Evelyn holding her at bay. "I really want to be your secretary. I'm trying to do a good job. But I like the Tea Basket ladies, so I went there. I really don't want to give up my Tea Basket membership like you. I want to belong to both. I want to be your secretary. I want to do a good job, and I want…"

Evelyn held up both hands to stop Lois from going on any further. She wasn't exactly sure what she was hearing.

"Lois, you idiot, I think you *are* doing a good job as secretary. Saying so annoys me. But Avery told me how fast you got extra raffle tickets to her today. There's nothing to be sorry about. You did do a good job. What's this all about, this liking the Tea Basket and giving up your membership…"

The picture became suddenly very clear to Evelyn. Today was Monday. Lois had been to the Tea Basket's regular Monday meeting. Lois was retaining her membership with them, in spite of accepting the secretary's job, the job Evelyn gave her, the office of secretary being the bait to bring Lois into the Shining Star Guild.

"Oh. Oh, you thought I was here because you went to and still belong to the Tea Basket guild!"

Lois hung her head, shuffled her old-lady shoes and fidgeted with her tote bag straps which hung in her sweating hands. She had been caught. She had nobody but herself, and her own big, fat mouth, to blame for revealing her deception. She was caught like the fox in the henhouse. No, she was the hen in the henhouse, and Evelyn was the red fox who had caught her.

"I just couldn't give up my membership," Lois whined. "They don't know anything about me being in your guild. Honest! I just couldn't quit them. And I got to see some of their auction quilts today. They're really nice, too. All kinds: applique, log cabins, samplers. All kinds. Rosie said they had…"

But then Lois decided not to reveal the exact number. Evelyn was standing way to close to her to reveal such news. Better Evelyn heard that news from someone else, someone far out of reach.

"They displayed twenty, to show all the ladies today. They still don't have a place to hold the auction, though. But Vern Hart, Belle's husband, he's going to be their auctioneer. And well, I just thought if nobody, if you didn't find out about me, about being in both guilds, that nobody, that you wouldn't be hurt, or care, but then you did and…"

Evelyn's thin lips tightened into a crooked smile. She wished she had thought of this. This was perfect. "Tut, tut, Lois. I have no problems with you remaining a member of the Tea Baskets, as long as, since you are an officer of the Shining Star guild, as long as you don't share any of *our* information with them."

Lois let out a long, slow breath then relaxed in disbelief. This was not like Evelyn to be forgiving. Lois was extremely relieved to find herself not about to face the wrath of the woman.

"As a matter of fact, I think your continued membership in the Tea Basket Quilters will come in quite useful. Yes, indeed, quite useful. Now what were you saying about Belle?"

Lois gulped. "Well, Belle's husband, the auctioneer, he's going to do the auctioneering after they find a place to hold it. Rosie said that he'd even perform the auction for free. She thanked Belle, in front of everybody, for getting his commitment."

Evelyn's complexion faded more than usual. *Belle!* She had intended to phone Belle days ago. She recalled making herself the cocktail, then falling asleep, then the busy signal when she first telephoned. She made all those other calls to members of the Tea Basket Quilters, but she had completely forgotten all about calling Belle again.

"Crap!"

Lois' heart gave a start. Was Evelyn changing her mind and working up to a snit?

Evelyn pointed a boney finger at Lois and tapped the woman's chest with each word. "You just stay a member of the Tea Basket, Lois. But like today, you keep your eyes and ears open. You hear me? Anytime you hear something I should know, anything at all about their auction, you tell me. OK?"

"Ah, OK, I guess."

"Great. Now you go on and do whatever you do here. I have to go fix something."

Without a word of farewell, Evelyn spun quickly around. The spin let fly a bobby pin from her orange curls, which fell to the hot, dusty ground where she had just been standing. She jogged back to her car and jumped behind the wheel. An errant curl, no longer in control, fell over her eye, forcing her to clamp the annoyance behind an ear in exasperation.

Lois stood sweating profusely in the sun, staring blankly as the silent Prius spun its tires and churned up dust that drifted upward in the hot air. She watched the car grow smaller as it traveled down the hill. She finally sighed in relief when the Prius disappeared onto Union Street. She fumbled in the tote bag she had been holding and withdrew a large bag of barbeque chips, ripped open the top and stuffed a large potato chip into her mouth. So fortified, she labored up the steps and into the fair office. The premium book still needed more work. She now felt a great sense of relief.

What Evelyn planned to do, had to be done in person. It was vital that she catch Belle Hart alone. A phone call would prove unsuitable. *I don't want her escaping. I need a direct in-your-face approach.* Evelyn decided the coffee shop was where she'd try to catch Belle. Belle was known to frequent the shop after her regular visit to the salon following Tea Basket meetings.

Donkey Coffee operated out of an old, two-story, shotgun building on Washington Street. The narrow shop was beside an attached office-goods store on one side and a darkened, narrow, dead-end alley on the other. The Sheriff's department stood across the alley, with black and brown cruisers usually parked out front. The owners of Donkey employed young baristas, both men and women, some of them attending the college and most of them abundantly adorned with tattoos.

Nasty kids, thought Evelyn, as she entered the coffee shop. *The Judge never approved of tattoos. He'd never have darkened the doorstep of this place if he'd known about these upstarts. Imagine, hooligans making coffee for officers of the court! Geez, what is this world coming to?*

In spite of Evelyn's misguided opinion, Donkey baristas were a hard-working, efficient staff. With long hours of practice, they quickly filled complex coffee orders for a steady flow of patrons coming into the comfortable shop. Even when the line stuffed the small front room to overflowing, these young people rarely lost their cool or messed up an order. They knew their regulars by name, and the regulars knew them.

Attorneys, as well as an occasional local politician, stopped in from time to time from the courthouse around the corner. The politicians pressed the flesh with voters. Uniformed deputies, as well as plainclothes cops, stopped in for large cups to go. The officers in plain clothes might expose badges looped over belts, dangling cuffs and sometimes a holstered pistol, when they pushed a jacket aside to extract a wallet from a hip pocket. Young students laden with backpacks, and older faculty from the nearby college, created a regular ebb and flow with each hourly class change. Downtown businessmen and women stopped by before shops opened or during their short mid-afternoon breaks. An occasional out-of-town visitor wandering in off the street would be pleasantly surprised by Donkey's popularity.

The coffee shop consisted of two floors, each being one room wide and stretching back to the end of the building. Coffee was made and sold at street level near the front. The rest of the first floor provided seating to the rear, where a small stage occasionally presented live evening music. There were two rooms on the main floor, mostly always filled with college students. They sat at little tables lined against the walls, with access to electric outlets. There some typed, intently bent over laptops. Others scrolled through iPhones while seated at a mismatched collection of small tables and chairs arranged haphazardly in the center of the room. And others chatted with friends, lounging about the overstuffed, secondhand couches and chairs tucked into corners. The coffee shop's second floor contained several smaller rooms located up a narrow set of stairs near the front. People could find a quiet niche to sip a hot beverage and escape the heat of the day, while reading an exciting novel or a dull textbook in one of Donkey's alcoves.

Evelyn had no idea if Belle preferred the oft crowded first floor or the secluded spaces on the second floor. So she arrived at ten a.m., queued up in the line and placed her order for an expensive, flavored latte from one of the tattooed kids working behind the counter, whom she considered unsuitable. A hot cup in hand and determined to wait as long as necessary, Evelyn planted herself in one of the vacant overstuffed chairs by the front window and pretended to be reading a free newspaper left behind by an earlier patron. From that vantage point, Evelyn saw everyone entering or exiting. There, in a quite comfortable overstuffed chair, she lay in wait for Belle.

Belle gushed with the day's news while her manicurist removed her old polish with a file, tidied up the edges and dotted adhesive on a few loose spots on her acrylic nails. Belle was chattier than usual and babbled on while the manicurist began to fill in the space between Belle's cuticles and where the nail had grown out. The manicurist, for the most part, remained focused on her work but smiled politely and nodded when appropriate.

"I was so surprised, baby doll. My gosh, to be acknowledged in front of all the members for doin' something' so easy. Why, I woulda asked Vern to be their auctioneer even if they hadn't approached me. I thought of him the very moment we voted to have an auction. But my, the response! Everyone seemed so pleased. My Vern! I guess he's well-liked by many; maybe more people than I ever realized."

The manicurist continued her careful application and evening out of the acrylic filler.

"You know, someday I'd love to be one of the officers of that guild. What an honor that would be. You know? It's a big group, nearly a hundred members. So to be recognized publicly like that really means something. Now all the members know my name. Shoot fire, they probably already know me anyway, because I have such a loud mouth. But if I can get nominated for an office, like maybe, for the office of secretary, or maybe treasurer, they'd remember how I helped get our auctioneer, and for free. Did I tell you that? Vern's going to auctioneer free of charge. They'd surely vote for me now that they know how generous my Vern is."

The manicurist continued forming yet another perfect nail, while bobbing her head.

"Yes, my Vern, he said he'd do the auction for free, as long as we hold our event on a weekday or evening. He's very busy on weekends, you see. That's our bread and butter — weekend auctions. That's when Vern makes the most money. The rest of the week he's usually busy getting ready for the weekend auction.

"Gosh, I'd love to be the guild's treasurer. I don't know if Rosie Dyer will run again. She's good. But you know, holding an officer's position can sometimes be a drag, after a while. I think Rosie's been treasurer for several terms. She's a real estate agent. Do you know her? No? Oh, well."

As Belle continued to ramble on, the manicurist finished shaping the new nails, buffed them down and finally reached a point where she could give her ears a break and sent Belle off to scrub her new nails clean.

Belle's new fingernails were as lovely as she had expected them to be. In her own cosmetology training, she had studied and earned a license to do nails, as well as hair. But after Vern came into her life and swept her off the salon floor, she left behind her day job to become the wife of a well-to-do auctioneer. Nobody in Athens knew anything about Belle before she came to live with Vern as his new bride. She realized her marriage, her new name and the move provided a perfect opportunity to remake herself, an opportunity that was not to be lost.

Vern didn't care if she worked or if she didn't work. He loved her no matter if she earned a wage or simply spent his money. He just wanted her to be happy. She was sure he loved her in spite of her flaws and the skeletons in her closet. So Belle became a stay-at-home wife. She engaged her talents making his home beautiful. But she worried how his associates would see her if they knew the truth about her past. She thought that truth might hurt his standing in the community. His business might suffer if Athens was the kind of place where gossip ruled.

So Belle assumed her new identity as a dutiful wife and homemaker. A belle, if you will, of the Old South. Good taste. Well dressed. A beautiful trophy wife. Not a very young trophy, but a shiny trophy, none the less. Her secret and her past employment as a hairdresser were soon covered up, just like glossy, acrylic nails covered weak and imperfect natural nails underneath.

Vern seemed happy to come home to her every evening, attired in his trademark bow tie and ball cap. He would give her a kiss on the cheek and a big bear hug that almost always ended up with him hugging her right off the floor. Then he would pour her a glass of her favorite Moscato white wine, while he enjoyed a cold Jackie O's Mystic Mama India pale ale. He'd talk to her about his upcoming auction or who he'd seen during his day, while she put the finishing touches to their dinner. If he couldn't arrive home at his usual hour, he'd always call her. Sometimes they'd eat out if he had to be late. They'd have a rendezvous. Vern would arrive in his black Escalade and she in her white one, at their favorite steak house.

Vern was such a pushover for anything Belle wanted, no matter what that might be. When she had arrived at his home, the first thing she wanted to do was change the color scheme of the house, both inside and out. So Vern hired painters and let Belle select the colors. He had to admit, when the work was done, that Belle had an eye for color. The house looked larger on the outside and more welcoming.

Inside, Belle had selected paints to enhance the mood each room was to convey, cool blues and greens for the dining room, warm reds and oranges for the living area, exciting colors for the family room, and rich, serious browns and tans for his study. One light, neutral tone of tile had to be special ordered and laid by experts over all the floors before she was satisfied her decorating was finished.

Belle did little, however, to alter the look of Vern's '*Mistress*', Vern's only extravagant toy, a houseboat moored at the Gallipolis Yacht Club, fifty miles away. On occasion, during summer months, they'd drive down to the marina and take the sternwheeler out for leisurely cruises up and down the Ohio River. Belle always laughed when Vern replaced his trademark ball cap for the captain's hat he kept on board. Vern always got a chuckle from anyone he'd tell about taking Belle for the first time to meet his *'Mistress'*. Everyone drew the wrong conclusion, which always left Vern doubled over with laughter at their looks based on faulty assumptions.

After she joined the Tea Basket Quilters, Belle acquired an expensive sewing machine and some of the best tools available. She turned a spare room in their house into her studio, and there she assembled a stash of fabrics any quilter would envy. If she saw a bolt of fabric she absolutely adored, she bought the entire bolt. Several such bolts were stacked on a long shelf along one wall. The remainder of the bookshelf wall was filled with fat quarters and half-yard cuts of every color and print manufactured. Vern often teased her good-naturedly that one day she'd be able to open her own shop with such an extensive collection of fabrics. No, Vern never refused her anything. Maybe that was his only fault. His generosity toward Belle gave her too much influence over him. But Vern bestowed gifts on his wife based on his own secret fear.

Thinking only of purchasing her favorite hot beverage, Belle Hart walked through the front door of Donkey Coffee a few minutes past eleven. She pulled opened the door without looking around and therefore failing to notice the thin head of wild, orange hair on a woman seated by the door, dressed in a matching pink running tee and spandex exercise pants. Had she been more aware of her surroundings, she might have thought twice about needing coffee at that moment.

Belle walked straight up to the counter and placed her order. She paid for her coffee and carried the hot cup up the stairs. She planned to sit outside on the little second-floor balcony where she might catch a breeze this warm day, if there was one, and savor her beverage alone and gaze admiringly at her new nails. Evelyn followed close behind, so close that the door to the balcony had not even shut before Evelyn walked through, right on Belle's tail. Belle hooked her purse over the back of a chair and took a seat. She was just about to take that first sip when the shadow of Evelyn hovering nearby finally caught her eye. With a start, Belle looked up.

Evelyn wore a thin-lipped grin. Belle's mouth fell open.

"Belle," Evelyn crooned.

"Evelyn! Baby doll, you gave me such a start. I didn't know you ever came here!"

"I don't."

Belle's expression changed. "Then why are you here?"

Evelyn pulled an empty chair close to Belle and sat down beside her. "You probably don't remember me, do you?"

"Of course I do, baby doll. You've only been gone from the Tea Basket Quilters a couple of weeks, for heaven's sake."

"No. You don't remember me from Ironton, do you?" Evelyn said, letting the question take Belle back in time, back to her past she imagined had been buried.

"No... I don't think... I'm sure you have me confused with somebody else, Evelyn."

"Really? You didn't work at the Clip Joint beauty salon near campus? Weren't you Isabel Williams back in the 60s? A beautician? Used to cut hair? You used to cut mine for ten dollars, and I always gave you a one-dollar tip. Good wages back then, I'd say, for a working girl such as yourself. I'm sure you remember me now?"

Belle remained stone-cold silent, her coffee cup still raised in midair, as yet untouched. The red mass of curls. The thin frame. The pale complexion and slate-gray eyes. The one-dollar tip. Oh, god. She did remember a college student. That was years ago. That student used to complain the whole time she sat in her chair. Used to go on and on about her miserable father. A judge. Never satisfied with the cut either, in spite of giving a decent tip. Her hair, uncontrollable then, just like now. Evelyn North.

"You don't come from the Deep South like you pretend, do you, Belle? You weren't always rich either, like you are now, thanks to your well-to-do husband. I thought everybody knew you came from Ironton — from the poor side of town, I might add. Surely everyone knows how hard you worked back then in that little beauty shop. The local paper even did a feature on you. I read how Isabel Williams, *parolee*, had studied long and hard during her *incarceration*, got herself a cosmetology license and was now working to put that nasty *grand theft juvie record* behind her. There she was, slaving six days a week in that cheap salon, trying to overcome a sorry indiscretion. You've done quite well for yourself since then, haven't you, Isabel Williams?"

Evelyn spoke her name like she was saying something obscene. Belle got the implication. Everyone *would know* about her past — all too soon, if Evelyn, in fact, decided to tell.

A long, painful silence separated the two women on the balcony that hot and uncomfortable morning. Belle knew her past was about to be exposed. She would pay, once again, for a stupid decision made as a fifteen-year-old. She would find herself being labeled *bad* once again. Perhaps ostracized. A felon. Why had she ever, ever agreed to be interviewed? Talking to that reporter was as stupid as taking her aunt's car without permission and without a license. She saw clearly now. Our histories, good or bad, stay with us. Follow us. Lurk in the shadows. Sooner or later they reveal themselves. If she thought it embarrassing to be locked up, she was about to find out there was still more embarrassment ahead for the cover-up. Her stupid past would tumble out like stinking puke. Belle felt a cold ball of fear form in the pit of her stomach.

The fact that she took a joy ride in someone's car, with keys left in the ignition, was wrong. But stabbing her in the back with this history was also wrong. Only problem, Evelyn had every right to blab. Belle had had no right to take that car. No right to hide the indiscretion. Belle remembered the struggle she endured as a young parolee. She was nothing more than a poor working kid with less than nothing to her name. Learning to be a beautician was her only pathway to some kind of life after prison. Then came her amazing good fortune to find a man who, when she confessed her checkered past to him, still loved who she was.

But that past... if Evelyn talked... that dreadful account would be revealed to all: to Carolyn, the doctor's wife; to Phoebe, the college instructor; to Rosie, the agent; everyone in guild who she had led on to believe she was so much more than what she really was. Belle was in fact, just a felon from Ironton. She saw no hands raised in votes for her imagined guild office. Then she thought of Vern. What might this public revelation mean for him, or to his business?

"Oh, no. I do remember you now... such a long time ago. Oh, please. Please, don't tell anyone. I don't want folks to think of me like that... as a f... as a f... as a fake. I just couldn't bear to face them... not if you tell."

Evelyn's thin lips curled up in an evil grin. "Really?"

"Oh no, *please.* My life here means so much to me. I'm so happy here with Vern. I love guild. The girls are so sweet. They'd never look at me the same way ever, ever again."

"No… I suppose they wouldn't…" Evelyn said, quietly pretending to consider the serious implications to Belle if someone were to expose the woman's pitiful past.

"Please, Evelyn… I'll do *anything.* Anything you ask."

Evelyn couldn't believe the opening Belle had just handed her. She could not have asked for a more compliant victim if she had created one herself. She laid a cool, bony hand over Belle's arm, slowly pushing the hand and its coffee cup down to the tabletop.

"*Anything,* you say?"

"Anything," Belle begged.

"I suppose I can be convinced to keep my mouth shut. But you have to promise to do one thing. Something that you and *only* you can do."

"Oh, baby, just name it."

"I need you to convince Vern to pull out of his agreement to auctioneer the Tea Basket auction."

Belle was stunned. Evelyn had asked the impossible. Vern had given his word. He would never agree to go back on it. He was a man of principle, a man who was honest and forthright, unlike herself. Though Vern knew her past, he vowed he loved her for who she was, not where she came from. He wouldn't hold what she had done four decades earlier against loving who she had become. Her big fear was not that Evelyn would reveal anything to Vern that he didn't already know, she feared the knowledge of her past might damage his business.

When Belle met Vern, she was clipping hair in the salon. He had walked in for a trim before he was to auctioneer a large estate sale the next day. He sat in her chair as she snipped his hair. They chatted while she worked. She liked Vern Hart. Apparently he liked her, too. Afterward he asked her out on their first date, and they were forever after an item. She told him about her sordid, youthful past on that first date. That didn't change his mind about her. Months later, when they married, Vern embraced the older woman he had come to know and openly accepted her family and her poor relatives. Vern wasn't the type of man who measured people based on labels or levels of financial standings. Vern had worked very hard to get where he was, harder maybe than most, and he never looked down on anyone who had less or who had made mistakes. Not then. Not now. But Vern would never go back on his word.

What worried Belle most was what the revelation of her past would do to his business. How would he survive financially if everyone found out Vern Hart was married to a woman with a felony record?

"Well? What do you say?"

"Baby, I can't ask Vern to renege."

"Then I'll be sure your quilting buddies learn the truth about Isabel Williams, old' girl."

"Oh, please, no!"

"Sorry," Evelyn scoffed.

Belle felt her entire world about to vanish. Friends would learn about her past and would soon thereafter avoid her. She was sure of it. They would find out she was nothing but a felonious fake. She loved Vern. She loved the guild. She loved the life she had fabricated for herself.

"I'm not sure I can."

"Well, you better try. We'll have another little chat in a few days. If I don't hear that Vern has withdrawn his services soon, then your disgraceful past will be out."

Having delivered her message, Evelyn rose and shoved back her chair. She quickly exited the little balcony, pulling open the door and disappearing to the other side. Her departure left behind a sad and worried Belle, more alone than ever, alone to reflect on her predicament, still holding a cup of coffee which was growing colder by the minute, having left a bitter taste in her mouth.

7

Avery Underwood decided to scout locations to sell tickets. She wanted to check with the potential sites Shining Stars members had recommended. Having been away from Athens more than a decade, she was no longer familiar with the county. She liked the idea of a road trip to reconnoiter. While out, she planned to approach managers of each place, asking, in person, for permission to display their raffle quilt. One by one she would confirm all the places they could use over the weeks ahead. Since Ximi volunteered to go with her, Avery decided her first stop would be there, to pick up her companion. Avery, however, was not prepared for the road conditions she was about to experience on this first leg of her day's travels.

Ximi lived in northern Athens County, an easy fifteen-minute drive from Athens by the four-lane. Avery discovered that was followed by an additional fifteen minutes on back roads. As soon as Avery turned off the highway, conditions immediately began to deteriorate. Four lanes of well-maintained concrete gave way to crumbling chip and seal and loose stone. The farther she drove, the worse the conditions.

She slowed to negotiate her truck along a narrow path, barely one lane wide. The surface was interspersed with stretches that might once have been covered with gravel, worn down to bare clay in many stretches. Huge clouds of impenetrable dust billowed high in the air in the wake of her truck. Dust had settled over brush, flanking both sides of the road, turning once-green foliage into a sickly shade of gray. Obvious to Avery, months had passed since a grader had pushed gravel back onto the crown. The wheels of vehicles had shoved all the loose stone off to both sides, which served only to mulch the uncut grass along the banks.

She came suddenly face-to-face with an approaching vehicle flying recklessly over the top of a hill, trailing behind him a great billowing cloud of dust. Washboard rattled her nerves as well as her truck, as she tried to veer quickly out of his way to avoid a head-on. The driver saw her in time and had difficultly controlling his car in the attempt to avoid hitting her. For several feet, her truck traveled through his wake of dust, making visibility impossible beyond the hood. On another occasion, she was forced to swerve left of center, if there was a center. Had she not swerved, she would have rolled her truck down a ravine at a dangerous blind curve where the roadway had slipped down a hillside on its way toward a dry creek bottom. And yet on another stretch of washboard, her big Ford bounced so badly it fishtailed. The bounce caused her head to smack against the roof of the cab, this in spite of wearing her seatbelt.

Avery was unable to stop herself from judging the pathetic road conditions. She noted every point of degraded surface, every ditch that should have been dug out and every location worn away by erosion or neglect. Water runoff sliced deep gouges into the road surface, or it had filled in former drainage ditches with loose soil and gravel. In some areas, she noticed that the roadway was actually below the level of the ditch beside it. Avery wondered how anybody could drive safely on this road at all. What was the county engineer doing? Certainly not his job.

However, the trip to Ximi's place wasn't all bad if she managed to divert her attention ever-briefly to enjoy the rural landscape beyond the right of way. Once or twice she was successful. She spotted a large flock of turkey hens with a dozen half-grown chicks in tow, grazing in a field. Around a bend she came upon a cow and calf that had escaped from a poorly fenced field. The cow was grazing alongside the road in uncut grass. The heifer swatted flies with a manure-stained tail while a calf slept in the hot sun, nearby on the bank, its neck folded back, resting its head against its flank. Neither cow nor calf seemed at all concerned by a passing pickup that would soon dust them in its wake. By the time Avery arrived at Ximi's, according to her GPS, the once-clean bronze truck was covered entirely in a fine layer of dust.

Ximi had been waiting on Avery's arrival. She came out of her house as soon as Avery stopped.

"Whoa, I didn't know you drove such a big truck!" said Ximi, as she opened the passenger's side door and failed in her first attempt to climb up, due to her four-foot-eleven-inch frame.

"Yeah. I work on roads," Avery said. "Usually find myself driving off-road a bit, to a site. Can you get in OK?"

Ximi tossed in her purse. She took hold of the door handle and the door jamb and made a successful vault on board.

"Oh, sure. No problem. Just not practiced at climbing up into a vehicle. I've got a little car, not a truck."

"How's the suspension? Have your tires aligned often? Gads, this road out here is a mess! I nearly lost control back there on a hill. Back end of my truck got bounced around like a ball on a basketball court!"

Ximi giggled. She was one of the youngest Tea Basket Quilters, an architect in her early fifty's with a flair for drawing, who wanted someday to design her own quilt patterns. Simone LeBlanc was her best friend. The two were almost always together at guild functions. Simone lived a few miles away; 'just around the bend', she told people. But on this particular day, Simone had a conflicting appointment to keep. Being self-employed, Ximi could set her own schedule. She had enjoyed her day out with Avery when they sold raffle tickets together. She was delighted to join Avery once again, minus her sidekick, on this little excursion.

"Yeah, the roads are pitiful. You should try to drive 'em right after a snowstorm." She snorted at the thought of snow. "I guess a snowstorm's nothing to worry about in this heat."

"What does the county engineer do? About snow, I mean."

"Well, yes, they plow. But we live so far north in the county that the snowplow, which is really just a pickup with a blade on the front, doesn't usually get here until noon."

"What about regular road maintenance?"

"Huh? Regular? Are you kidding? You *are kidding*, right?" Ximi buckled her seat belt. "God, we haven't seen a grader in years. Last time they did the chip n' seal thing, you know, when they pour oil all over the dirt and then spread little pieces of gravel on the top of the oil. That was, let's see... I think three... maybe four years ago. Every winter they scrape off a little more until it's gone. Then they wonder why people complain. When they put that stuff down, my car got covered in tar every day for a solid week. Then every time the sun came out, like now, and the temperature rose above ninety degrees, the road oozed tar and my tires threw the stuff up all over the paint again. God, what a mess. You have no idea how difficult it is to get tar off a car. But hey, the county engineer's elected, so he's the boss of the department. Isn't any point complaining.

I've lived here for years and I'll tell you, it doesn't do any good to call his office. I think requests get tossed into the trash bin the second they hang up the phone."

"Really?" Avery was beginning to think maybe trying to land a job with the county highway department might have been a mistake. "I just gave them a copy of my resume. I'm trained as a civil engineer."

Ximi looked at Avery with surprise. "Well, if you get hired, maybe you can get them to come out here and fix my road. If you did, I'd owe you, big time."

Avery maneuvered the truck around in a smooth three-point turn in the roadway and drove slowly back toward the highway. She indicated to Ximi a clipboard wedged between the passenger's seat and the center console. Ximi pulled out the board and looked over the attached sheet. Avery had prepared an excel spreadsheet with all the places recommended by their members.

"Where should we start first? You tell me," Avery said. "You're the navigator."

Ximi looked over the list and decided they'd begin in Nelsonville. "Let's go to Stuart's Opera House first. Go three miles and turn right," she said, pointing back down the dusty road that Avery had just traveled.

Avery smiled. She wondered if she'd get another opportunity to see the cow and calf up close.

The former Isabel Williams of Ironton was in a dark mood when she arrived home. Vern was at work, for which she was thankful. She was torn emotionally, and fearful. On one hand, she feared her past was soon to be known to the Tea Basket women and Vern's customer base. She also felt a desperate fear of putting Vern into the position of having to go back on his word. She could not think of a way to continue hiding her past any longer, thanks to Evelyn's threat.

She went into her sewing room to work on a project, any project actually, to distract herself from the problem Evelyn had dumped on her. She selected a half-finished block and sat down, turning on her sewing machine. A small light came on over the feed dogs, and the mechanism hummed to life. Needle was up. Thread was through the eye. The sewing machine stood at the ready, but Isabel Williams faltered.

The block she had selected from a small stack beside the sewing machine only needed corner pieces to be complete. She finally slipped a triangular cut of fabric into her machine, over one corner of the block, right sides together, and lowered the presser foot. She touched the control, and the machine stitched a perfect little seam for her. She snipped the thread and stood up. Only after she finger-pressed the seam open, did she realize she had just sewn the triangle to the wrong corner.

With a heavy sigh, she sat back down and picked up a seam ripper to remove the triangle. In the process of ripping the seam, she cut into the block fabric with the sharp end of the tool, making an irreparable hole. In fury and frustration, she threw the block and seam ripper into a nearby trash can and began to sob.

Belle found she was unable to concentrate on anything. She could no longer see through tears to sew a straight line. She couldn't think about anything except her dilemma. Questions swirled around her head in non-ending circles, like vultures over a corpse, circling, circling, but never stopping with answers. Evelyn truly had her where she never imagined she would find herself. She was sure that any guild member who might have considered her to be a good soul, would from that point forward always know her as a felon. Even if she convinced Vern to back out of his commitment, which, too, would greatly reduce her stature with them, she'd be considered unreliable. Surely no one would ever, ever want her as an officer of the Tea Basket Quilters.

Then there was Vern to think about. If she asked him to withdraw his offer, surely he would want to know why. What would she say? Make up lies? Hide the fact that she had presented herself to her friends as someone she was not? Or should she just confess to Vern that she had been caught in a huge omission of facts about her sorry past? If he did agree to withdraw his services as auctioneer for the little quilts, what would that do to his reputation? Would he be considered the kind of businessman who put himself or his business before a benevolent commitment? With no answers to any of her questions, she walked out of her studio and into their bedroom, flung herself across the bed and continued to sob until she finally cried herself to sleep.

This day continued to be as oppressive as the unusual weather pattern had been for weeks. At eight in the morning, high heat and humidity made Phoebe Prescott's gardening work miserable. Every pore in her old body was sweating. Her grubby dungarees weighed heavy and clung to her legs, soaked through around the waist. Wearing leather gloves had become unbearable. She had worn them to protect her manicured hands as she cut a furrow with a hoe. As was her OCD need to be exacting, she had carefully followed a string tied between two stakes to dig a straight row. But now that she had to drop seeds into place, gloves were useless and exceedingly cumbersome. They, too, had become damp with sweat. She cast the gloves aside with the hoe and picked up a small paper bag.

Phoebe wiped sweat from her face and neck using the bottom edge of her wet, grimy T-shirt. In all of her years, she never liked to sweat. There was a time — back in her youth, she remembered — when she hated planting beans too. Yet here she was, planting beans and sweating.

Time has a way of changing what one is willing to tolerate, she thought. She retrieved her garden hoe and leaned on the handle, pausing to cool down. Here in her small vegetable garden, she found pleasure these days in beans, both in the planting as she was doing that day, and in harvesting, which would come soon, and definitely in the eating. She smiled to herself, remembering her late mother frying up fresh green beans in bacon fat in an iron skillet. She now owned that same skillet — a spider, it's called — and she was now the cook. She hiked a shoulder to catch another stream of sweat that ran down her temple and into an eye. No, she would never find sweating in sun and heat pleasurable. *Never.*

Setting aside her hoe once again, she felt heat radiating upward off the soil even at this early hour, as she stooped to place round, white seeds precisely four inches apart along a yardstick laid into the furrow. Carefully, she set eight seeds where they were to grow. She slid the yardstick over to drop eight more seeds along its edge. Phoebe repeated this process over and over until the forty-eight-foot row was *precisely* seeded. She stopped only on occasion to wipe away trickles of sweat running down her temples.

After the furrow was lined with small, white dots, she stood. She tossed aside her yardstick, folded up the bag of remaining seeds and dropped the sack into a wicker basket waiting on the ground at the end of the row. She picked up her garden rake and walked back along the row, carefully pulling loose soil over the seeds. When finished, she wiped more sweat from her face and neck, then stood back to admire her morning's accomplishment. At that moment, the cell phone in her back pocket rang.

"Hello?"

It was Nora, breathless with excitement. "Phoebe, dear, I do think the Historical Society might be able to help us! Can you come over to accompany me to meet with their director? Yes? Wonderful!"

Phoebe Prescott lived alone at the edge of the woods in a new, modern log cabin. She loved the peace and quiet, her flower gardens, planting seeds, harvesting vegetables, and especially, the absence of people. At least that's what she always said. She sighed and hiked up her dungarees, gathered up her basket with the bag of seeds and her damp leather gloves, and leaned the rake and hoe against the garden fence. She shoved opened the gate and walked toward her cabin with basket in hand. She planned to shower off the sweat and dirt then drive into town to join her good friend, Nora Radnor.

Nora hung up the receiver and did a little jig. Why she had never thought to call the Historical Society was beyond her full comprehension.

Maybe I'm just getting too old.

It took a TV show to make her think of the Historical Society. Watching a PBS documentary late the night before, she saw historical photos on the screen. One photo of an old quilt sparked racing thoughts, which quickly formed an idea.

Old quilts... History... Historical Society... big building... big, new building... new quilts... auction!

She had refrained from immediately calling Phoebe, only because of the late hour. But the next morning she telephoned the society, got the director on the other end and boldly asked him if he would see her. She wanted him to consider hosting an auction of their guild's small quilts.

To her surprise, he said, "Yes," and suggested a meeting to discuss the idea. "Stop by anytime."

Finally, maybe, this would be a place to hold their auction. So she did that little dance of glee, now that her friend, Phoebe, would accompany her to his office to find out for themselves if this possibility was at all as real as she hoped it to be.

The hour Nora waited for Phoebe to arrive was agonizing. She was frustrated waiting for Phoebe to take a shower first. *Why?* Nora felt certain that the Historical Society director had seen honest dirt before. But no, Phoebe insisted. Being sweaty, smelly and dirty, she simply had to have a shower before she could possibly present herself to the public. *For heaven's sake!* Then there was her slow, ten-mile drive on county roads to get from her cabin into town to Nora's house. *She never drives faster than twenty miles an hour,* Nora imagined, antsy to move forward on this possibility as quickly as possible.

Nora's new, red Buick was parked inside the attached garage of her house, with the garage doors up. Nora stood waiting beside the automobile, with keys in hand and a purse dangling from an arm like the queen. As Phoebe parked her yellow VW Beetle out of the Buick's path, Nora switched off her cell and dropped the phone into her purse.

Phoebe could see Nora planned to drive and that they would be departing *immediately.*

The director of the Historical Society met Nora and Phoebe in his small office, offering his hand. Unlike some men who were known to crush women's fingers against their diamonds, pressing flesh and bone into metal, the director's handshake was firm but quite gentle. This kindness gave him immediate points, in Nora's estimation. She had never met him, but now considered him to be a gentleman. He was tall, graying at the temples and wore wire-rimmed, round glasses. He was dressed in business trousers, a crisp, white shirt and a blue tie. His suit jacket was draped across the back of his swivel desk chair. Phoebe was reassured that having taken time to clean up before coming to town had been the right decision, in spite of her friend's impatience with her for having taken so long to do so. The director indicated the women should take seats across the desk from him. He did not take his seat until they were settled. Another courtesy noticed by Nora.

"Well, Mrs Radnor, you mentioned on the phone you needed a place to hold a quilt auction. Please tell me what exactly you need from us."

"Please, call me Nora. This is my friend and fellow guild member, Phoebe Prescott." Nora adjusted her large, red-framed glasses and indicated to Phoebe, with a nod and smile.

Nora wore a white blouse this morning, with navy-blue slacks and navy pumps. Around her neck hung several strands of peach-colored beads. Her earrings were the same shade of peach. Beads and earrings matched her lip gloss this day. She ran her tongue nervously over her peachy upper lip and began to tell the Historical Society director about the Tea Basket's needs.

"Our goal," she explained, "is to raise funds for the upcoming 5K, which is scheduled for October. The guild hopes to raise more money than any other guild for Molly Menear's team. All funds are to be donated to the team and the team total donated to fight breast cancer. If the Tea Baskets can raise the most, we will be the recipients of a used, but very expensive, Gammill longarm sewing machine, as a reward from Molly's quilt shop. All our members would have access to the quilting machine at our hall. A longarm like that would save us hundreds of dollars in no time at all."

The director kept his focus on Nora, with his hands folded on top of the desk. He listened to her explanation.

"That's a challenge that we simply have to accept," she said. "Fighting breast cancer is a cause very dear to many of our members. Some of us have lost sisters, mothers, even daughters, to breast cancer. Some are breast cancer survivors themselves. Donating is important to us. We hope others might someday not have to suffer with cancer.

"So our guild voted and decided to donate to Molly's team and to hold an auction to raise the money. Over one hundred little quilts are promised," Nora continued. "Everyone agreed to donate at least one, some more than one. All handmade. Every dollar our auction raises, less whatever expenses the guild has to pay, will go directly to The Thimble and Chatelaine Team. There will be other guilds making contributions, also to Molly's team, of course, and all the money would be given to the cause."

"And you came to me because...?" the director asked.

"Because," Phoebe explained, "we cannot find a place to hold our auction. Nora and I are on a committee to locate a suitable venue and an auctioneer. So far, every place we've asked is unavailable, unsuitable or too expensive. We've tried churches, schools, the community center — you name it."

"Then I thought of the Historical Society!" Nora said. "You have this nice old church building which might have room; that is, if you think our little auction would be something you'd let us hold here."

"I see," the director said. "And this little auction of yours is entirely to raise money for cancer research and nothing at all for yourselves or your guild?"

"Yes," Phoebe said. "Our guild is doing quite fine financially. We even have our own place over on Shannon. But even our own building — a house actually — is not large enough to both display the quilts for early viewing or to use as an indoor auction site."

"Well, ladies," the director said, rising to his feet. "Come with me. I'll show you what we can provide, then you decide if the Historical Society is at all suitable."

Nora looked at Phoebe with excited anticipation as they quickly rose to follow the director out of his office. He led them down a small corridor and into a large, open area that had once served as the church sanctuary. The former church now served as the new home of the Historical Society. The pews had been removed, leaving a vast open area. At the back, where the pulpit had once stood, an elevated platform still remained. Nora could barely control her joy. The space was perfect! But then, she thought about the cost.

"Oh, sir, this is wonderful! But how much would you charge us?"

"Well, Nora, I'll present your request to our board at our next meeting. They can discuss your request and decide if they'd like to help. After they meet, two weeks from now, I'll call you with their proposal. How does that sound?"

"I see…" Nora started to say. "So you don't decide? Your board will?"

"Yes. They should have input on this request."

"Uh huh. Well then, I will simply have to wait for their decision. If you think I should talk to them, to present our need in person, I can make myself available. If I won't be needed, then I'll leave you to submit our case. I'll wait by my phone until I hear from you."

"I can take care of your request. You should expect to hear from me in a few weeks. The board meets in the evening, so my call to you will be the following morning, with news of their decision."

Nora thanked the director. Both women shook his hand goodbye, and the two left out the same front door by which they had entered.

The two friends stood for a time beside Nora's Buick. The meter where they had parked along the street still had time on it. Nora was no longer in a rush. Her excitement had waned. She felt an uneasy mixture of hopefulness coupled with dismay. The director was not the one to make any decision on their behalf. Nora muttered something under her breath that Phoebe didn't quite hear.

"What was that?"

"I'm worried. At ninety, I don't like to wait. I may not have two weeks to wait."

"Oh, Nora, you're such a worrywart," Phoebe laughed, poking Nora on the shoulder. "You'll live. I know waiting won't be easy on you. But you'll live."

"I just get the feeling that the director was hinting that his board's decision might not please us. And we won't know anything for two solid weeks. Will we, or won't we, have a place?"

"Then stop letting the unknown get you down. What do you say? Since there's still time on this meter, why don't we walk over to Donkey Coffee? I've got a thirst for a fancy pants coffee that I don't have to make myself."

Nora shrugged in resignation. "Why not? We can kill the first thirty minutes of the next three hundred and thirty-six hours that I have to wait."

Phoebe laughed, took Nora by the arm, and the two women walked the block and a half to the coffee shop.

Vern Hart arrived home, hung his trademark ball cap on a hook by the door, loosened his bow tie and called out for Belle in his booming voice.

"Hey, toots! I'm home. I'm going to get your favorite wine! How would you like to go out for dinner tonight? I feel like going to Lake Hope Lodge. You wanna go?"

Vern began pouring Belle's favorite wine, Moscato, popped open a bottle of Mystic Mama Ale for himself, taking a sip, then called out for his wife again.

"Belle, honey! You home?"

It wasn't like Belle to go off without telling him she'd be away. He decided to look for her. Probably she was sewing. He peeked into her sewing room, carrying his Mystic Mama in one hand, her wine in the other. Belle wasn't there. He went to the back door and looked out. She wasn't lounging by the pool or gardening.

"Hmm?" he muttered, beginning to feel the tiniest bit edgy.

His next stop was the master bedroom. There, bundled under the covers, he noticed a large lump that was probably the pretty woman he had married. After she finally roused and pushed the covers off her head, he noticed her puffy face. As her eyes fell upon him, she burst into sobs. In his memory, Belle had never wept like that before. She was scaring him. Rushing over to her and putting the drinks on the bedside table, he took her gently by the shoulders and looked into her blue but bloodshot eyes.

"Hey. There, there. What's wrong? Tell me? Are you OK? Are you sick? What's happened to make you so unhappy? Oh, god, who died?"

Struggling to stop sobbing but being only half successful, Belle managed to find her weak voice. "Oh, baby doll, nobody's died. But I wish I were dead."

"Oh, Belle, don't say such a thing. What would I do without you? Now you just tell me what's wrong. I'll fix it. Yes, sir, I'll make everything right again."

Having struggled with thoughts of every kind of evasive explanation, Belle resigned herself, in that moment, to doing one thing right. She would tell Vern the truth. She would confess that she'd been less than truthful to her friends, had kept her juvenile record a secret, and that now her past had finally caught up with her. She decided to beg his forgiveness and accept whatever repercussions came her way, from her guild friends, and from the one person in the world who meant the most to her, Vern.

"Talk to me, Belle. I can't help if I don't know what's wrong."

Belle sniffed, blew her nose, wiped away the tears that seemed never to stop, and began.

"Baby doll, I've done something I should never have done. I've been a liar and a fake to my friends and to the community. Now those lies are going to hurt you. I never, ever meant anything like this to happen. I never, ever intended this."

"It's OK. Whatever you did, we'll face the storm together. Now come on, tell me. What makes you this liar that you think you are? Why, to me, you're the sweetest thing in my life. I can't imagine anything you've said could ever come 'round to hurt me."

Belle's nose continued to drip, and tears streamed down her cheeks. As she chased them with another tissue, she began her confession. "I've been leading a life that's a lie, Vern. All the girls think I'm some sort of Southern belle; that I came from money, like maybe I was a debutante or something. Nobody knows I was convicted of grand theft. Nobody knows that I spent time in lockup. Nobody knows I was just a hairdresser, or that I learned the trade while incarcerated. Nobody knows anything about my life before you.

"I'm no debutant. You know that. I'm nobody. I'm a stupid fraud who got lucky one day when somebody wonderful and kind found me and made me his wife. I never imagined that my past would follow me here. I let on to all my friends, to people you know, that I was somebody better than I really am. And now, someone, who does know about my past, is promising to bring my awful history crashing down around my ears... and around yours too, in the process."

Vern gave his wife a bear hug. He cupped a burly hand under her damp cheek and turned her face up so that she looked him in the eye. "You are somethin', girl. You really are. And I mean that in a nice way, 'because you *are* my perfect Southern belle. That's all that matters to me. And if I know your friends like I think I do, and I'm a very good judge of character, then you're their Southern belle, too, no matter what happened when you were a kid. Honey, it never matters where a person comes from. I heard in a song, once, that it only 'matters where you're going'. Your friends don't care if you came from Ironton, Ohio or Nashville, Tennessee, or what you did forty years ago when you were a misguided teenager. Hell's bell, sweetie, some of your friends probably did stuff in their youth that they're not proud of, too."

"Oh, Vern, you don't understand. This woman, she's threatened to tell everyone what a liar I am. You don't know her. She's... she's... evil. She's ready to twist my lie around my neck and hang me with it. She'll figure a way to drive a wedge between me and every friend I have."

"Bull crap!"

"No, I'm serious. She threatened to bring down my world if I don't get you to withdraw your offer to auctioneer our little quilts. Please, Vern, you gotta help me. I'm so sorry to ask you, but you gotta withdraw your offer."

The tears fell freely once again, no matter that Vern still held her close.

8

Avery and Ximi drove north to Nelsonville. There they received the OK to hawk raffle tickets on the sidewalk in front of Stuart's Opera House. The young staff of the old, renovated building told them they'd have a good day.

On the evening the women wanted to sell tickets, Ralph Stanley would be making a return performance to the opera house stage. Stanley had a loyal local following. All seats were sold out. If the quilters were lucky and the weather was good, they'd have four hundred Stanley fans pass by their quilt.

Their next stop was at the technical college on the other side of the Hocking River. There they struck out. Soliciting was prohibited on campus. Avery drew a line through that option, with a sigh. They climbed back in the truck and headed south on the highway, stopping off in The Plains, the small village located between Nelsonville and Athens. Shining Star members told them of three possible sales locations there. Avery suggested to Ximi that they make their first inquiry at the grocery store. Her experience in Athens gave her hope for finding another lucrative venue. Grocery stores attracted plenty of people carrying cash. If this place was like the store in Athens, they would have a steady flow of potential customers seeing their quilt. Avery and Ximi had also learned the value of chatting up those who passed. Engaging someone in conversation, more often than not, made the person decide to buy a ticket.

The manager at this store, like the one in Athens, was most helpful. He agreed they could set up the quilt stand at the entryway. But they weren't allowed to block pedestrian traffic coming or going through the doors. Avery and Ximi agreed. They would place themselves under the awning, with the big, plate glass windows to their back. Avery penciled in dates that the manager had agreed to, on the spreadsheet. They would sell tickets once this month and two weekends the following month.

A mini mall was adjacent to the grocery store. There was no way to enter the mall from the store except through a separate entrance at the far end. They had to talk to somebody in charge by walking to the end of the complex. Avery found the manager's office in a small alcove. The manager, a woman, was in. To Avery's delight, she gave them permission to sell inside the mall. The manager assigned them to a central location where it looked like foot traffic might be high.

Avery asked to hold off setting specific dates. Being able to sell under cover meant this was a great backup location for a rainy weekend, but of course, Avery had no way to know when rain might arrive. To her mind, every day seemed forever sunny and unbearably hot. The mall manager agreed. But there was one stipulation. They'd have to call the day before to confirm. Avery agreed, figuring a twenty-four-hour weather forecast was all she'd need. She wrote down the manager's phone number, again making notes on her clipboard. Their last stop was to a feed store, a strange place she thought to be selling raffle tickets, but one of their members insisted she try. The owners objected. She crossed that business off her list.

Avery and Ximi climbed again into the truck. They turned southwest, opposite from U.S. 33, and drove through the village on the state highway serving the town as its main artery. Her radio was on, and they had been listening to the local station's airplay of top ten teen songs. An announcer gave the latest weather report:

'This heat wave will continue, with today's temperatures soaring into the 90s once again. There is no relief in sight, with a zero percent chance of rain for the rest of the week.'

Beyond the town limits, the truck dropped down off the plateau and entered the lowlands along 682. Modest homes, spaced far apart, dotted both sides of the road. A few houses stood near the highway, with short, gravel driveways, and old mailboxes out front. Others appeared to be newer structures, set farther back. These had poured concrete drives that led to two and three-car garages. They passed homemade signs offering computer repair, small engine repair and other home-based enterprises. The road delivered them to a traffic light six miles later. They stopped for the light, having reached the edge of Athens. Ahead of them, Union Street, to their left, crossed over a highway bridge above the meandering Hocking River.

Their destination was straight ahead, to seek permission from two places near the intersection: the convenience store at the crossroad, and White's Mill just beyond the light. Both busy businesses agreed to allow the women to sell tickets. The staff at White's insisted they set up and sell indoors. The owners welcomed them to come back anytime they wanted. They had to set up outside though, at the convenience store. Avery and the manager on duty picked a Saturday both agreed upon. She scribbled down his phone number in case the weather turned to rain. They would have to set up to the side of the paved lot, away from traffic. The location was not the best. They would be in the open, several yards away from the pumps and the entrance into the convenience store. Avery thanked him, shook his hand and once again returned to her truck, with Ximi in tow. The women made a few more stops around Athens, until they finally realized they'd scheduled enough places, rain or shine, that they'd be selling tickets every Saturday for the next eight weeks.

"I say this calls for a celebration!" said Ximi. "Have you ever been to Donkey Coffee?"

Avery had not.

"Do you drink coffee?"

Avery did.

"Then you have to check this place out. It's downtown. I'll direct you."

Ximi proved a good navigator, giving clear instructions where to turn. Many of the streets in Athens were one-way. Traffic became heavier once they turned onto Court, a two-lane, one-way brick street, lined on both curbs with parked cars. Avery maneuvered the big, bronze 350 around several double-parked delivery trucks, some in the right lane and some in the left lane. Pedestrians, mostly college students, jaywalked randomly along a two-block stretch congested by the slalom of parked vehicles. Pedestrian carelessness added to the hazards, as did the occasional scooter maniac.

The real challenge was finding a parking space. The big truck didn't exactly maneuver well into spaces designed for cars. They got lucky on the fourth lap of the courthouse block. Someone on an end space pulled out just as Avery turned the corner.

"Grab it! Grab it!" shouted Ximi.

Avery whipped the truck into the spot with ease, much to her passenger's delight.

"Awesome! Now let's feed the meter and grab some coffee."

Avery had never been to Donkey, but she liked the place even before she entered through the doorway. There were students and townspeople seated at chairs with small tables out front on the sidewalk. More people sat in overstuffed comfortable chairs just inside the door. The place seemed well worn, casual and busy. The line at the counter moved quickly, and they arrived at the counter in short order.

It was obvious that Ximi was a regular. The tattooed barista seemed to know her. He took a plastic card, bearing the coffee shop logo, she offered. Ximi told him what she wanted and instructed him to put Avery's order on her card. After the barista had filled their orders, they walked into the back rooms.

Small tables and chairs were scattered all around creaky, wooden floors. There appeared to be no order to their arrangement. Patrons moved light tables into any configuration that suited their purpose. A pair of couches formed an L around a well-worn coffee table, against two intersecting walls. This created a small and relatively quiet conversation pit. One couch was already occupied, so the women took the other vacant couch.

Nora Radnor, with her big, red glasses, and Phoebe Prescott, the black member of the Tea Basket Quilters, were comfortably chatting on the first couch. Avery walked over and sat down, followed by Ximi, before either Nora or Phoebe recognized them.

Phoebe Prescott looked up from her coffee to see Ximi, the only Asian in their guild. Then she realized that the tall person accompanying her, who she thought at first to be a man, was, in fact, a woman. Phoebe thought she was a new member to their guild. She thought she had been one of Nora's reverse applique students, if she was not mistaken.

Phoebe paused mid sip of her coffee cup. "Ximi? And Avery?"

The younger women laughed for having not recognized Phoebe and Nora.

"Oh my gosh," said Ximi. "How nice to see you. Sorry we didn't recognize you two right off."

"What brings you gals downtown?" asked Phoebe.

Avery and Ximi looking to one another for an answer. Both suddenly realized potential repercussions. They were about to be caught working against the Tea Baskets. Neither Avery nor Ximi had intentions of resigning from the Tea Baskets, but they also looked forward to participating in the new guild, too. How could they explain to Nora, a founder of the Tea Baskets and its oldest member, that they were making money selling those raffle tickets?

"Uh…" stumbled Avery. "Well… Phoebe, Nora, it's been a good day for us. However, I'm not sure how you'll take it."

"What do you mean, child?" Nora asked seriously.

"We've been out, you see… we've been securing places to sell raffle tickets."

Ximi put down her hot beverage. Leaning forward and laying a gentle hand on Nora's knee, she tried to explain in the kindest way she could. "Nora, we adore you. Avery and I are new to the guild, the Tea Basket Quilters, and we love all things related to quilting."

"Thank you, Ximi. I like you too," Nora replied, patting Ximi's hand.

"We joined another guild, too," she said, apologetically.

"Oh! I see," said Nora.

"Have you left us?" asked Phoebe, rather curtly.

"Oh, no. No! Of course not," Avery said. "We love the Tea Basket Quilters. But we want to do more, to belong to more than just one guild." As an afterthought, that perhaps belonging to more than one might seem unethical, she added, "Belonging to two is OK, isn't it?"

Nora laughed at their innocence. "Of course! You can belong to as many guilds as your time and interests allow! What new guild did you join?"

It was only a matter of time until Nora found out anyway, so Avery confessed.

"We joined the Shining Stars. I donated my quilt as a raffle quilt. We've had one outing to sell tickets. Now we're setting up new locations around the county where we can sell more as the weeks go by."

"The Shining Star guild? I've not heard of that one before," Phoebe said.

Ximi explained next. "Well, yes, you have… sort of… It's the guild Evelyn North started."

Phoebe paused mid drink and snorted in disgust. Nora gave a little gasp. Both older women looked to each other, a little shocked.

The younger women wore expressions of chagrin.

"Look, I know Evelyn can be a holy terror," said Avery. "I'm, of course, keeping my options open. If she behaves badly, I plan to distance myself from her and her new guild. I'm not much for her kind of drama. But she offered me the opportunity to be the new guild's vice president. I couldn't refuse. In that position, I'll be able to influence the direction of the guild, get programming established in areas that interest me and others. Now, I'm not saying that the Tea Baskets aren't sensitive to us newcomers. I'm simply saying that I personally need *more* than one guild offers.

"As you know, I'm between jobs. I have a lot of free time on my hands at the moment. I want to be busy. I need to be productive. This opportunity to serve others means a lot. So I donated a quilt to raffle off, and now I'm working to secure locations to sell tickets for it, for the Shining Star guild. You do appreciate my need to be active, I hope? I mean no reflection on the Tea Baskets. I have no displeasure toward it. I truly don't mean to disappoint you or anyone. I enjoy guild, immensely. But I have so much more to offer. I want to learn and do all I can while I have this free time. At some point, in the not-too-distant future, I hope, I'll probably be back in my traces, as they say. My free time will be limited and I'll have to devote my time to work."

"I see," Nora said, while her mind raced with thoughts for her beloved Tea Basket Quilters. *So, Evelyn is raiding our membership! As I suspected she would. Here sit two perfect examples. Who else has she bribed away? How will we survive if all our new young members leave us?*

Phoebe, whose dislike for Evelyn North transcended good reason, was inwardly livid. Her stomach churned. Her hands were beginning to tremble ever so slightly. She put down her coffee cup, noticing the tremor, and folded her arms across her chest to hide them. She brought to mind every mantra of kindness she could remember, to recite silently to herself, attempting to hold her tongue in check. She had no intentions of blowing up in public, of becoming someone like Evelyn. Phoebe struggled in silence to keep her temper under control, while Nora continued.

"So, you're selling these raffle tickets for *them*. But what about the Tea Basket Quilters?"

"I've promised three small quilts for the Tea Basket auction. I'm certainly not abandoning it," said Avery.

"Me, too," added Ximi. "I'm donating two little quilts I've made. And as you know, I was on the auction committee. I just failed in my assignment, though. Simone and I couldn't find a single place to hold the auction. I feel awful about that."

"Well, don't, dear," Nora said with kindness. "Phoebe and I have just come from the Historical Society. If their board agrees, we might be able to hold the auction on their premises."

Ximi was relieved to hear this news. "All right, Nora! That is good news. Why didn't Simone and I think of them? Oh my gosh, I'm so pleased."

"Though we seem to be at odds with each other over separate fundraising efforts," Nora said, "let's remember that Gammill is really not the purpose of our fundraising. We're all doing this to fight breast cancer. Both guilds will make donations to Molly's team for the cause."

To that end, Phoebe could agree. "Amen."

"I hope you don't think less of us for being in both guilds," said Ximi.

Nora sighed. "No. I understand. I'm fine with it." Then added, "As long as you don't leave the Tea Basket Quilters. You girls are exactly what we need. You're talented, and you aren't afraid to work. We need young people in order to survive. Some of us are getting older by the minute."

Phoebe glanced at her friend, rolled her eyes and jabbed Nora once again in the arm. Everyone smiled, even Phoebe, as Nora raised her cup for a toast among the four of them. "To the fight against breast cancer. May every *woman* win!"

"Here, here," everyone chimed in, clinking coffee cups together.

9

Vern Hart, their auctioneer — their ex-auctioneer — telephoned Carolyn Ashcroft with the news. Vern was afraid he would have to back out on his offer.

"It isn't a matter of money," he'd stammered apologetically. "The auction house is understaffed. A lot of the physical work required to ready items for weekend auctions now falls to me. I'll have to be out there at the auction house, most days, doing time-consuming manual labor, categorizing and arranging items before auction days." He was very sorry to have to do this to them, after all he had promised. But he was the boss, and now the boss was needed on site during weekdays, too.

Carolyn was devastated. She hung up from the call and immediately entered fret mode. *No site. Now no auctioneer. What more could possibly go wrong with their plan? I'll call Nora. Then Rosie.*

Carolyn was unable to reach Nora. A disembodied voice said, "Your call cannot be completed at this time." She punched up her friend Rosie's number.

Rosie Dyer was driving her blue Edge back to the real estate office, after having shown a young couple a house for sale in Amesville, a small town ten miles east of Athens. Amesville was built along Federal Creek, which fed into the Hocking River. The deceptively small stream at the lower edge of town overran its banks regularly. Rosie was honest with her buyers about that fact. She assured the couple that the stream had never risen high enough to endanger the house they were interested in, which was located on a hillside overlooking the town.

This couple was new to the Athens area. They liked the lower tax rate in the Fed Hock School district. Even more, they liked the lower price of the house in Amesville. They asked why. She told them. It was because Federal Creek always overflowed its banks after heavy rainstorms, and flooded the valley. The swollen creek would cut the village off with rising water across the highway, leaving the town isolated until the water receded. This was of concern to them. Both worked in the city of Athens. He was a new professor at the university. She was a nurse at one of the medical facilities. Getting to Athens and their jobs every day was vital.

Rosie understood. She recommended they look, instead, for a place close to their jobs in Athens and not along the many creeks that comprised the Hocking River watershed. Yes, she pointed out, they'd either have to lower their expectations on the size and quality of a home, or they'd have to reconsider paying much more to get exactly what they wanted. As she drove down the roadway, Rosie wasn't sure she'd ever hear from that couple again, but flooding was a factor to consider when buying property in the hills and hollows of Athens County.

Rosie's car cell phone connection announced an incoming call from her friend, Carolyn Ashcroft.

"What's up?" Rosie asked.

By then Carolyn had worked herself up near tears. Rosie heard the despair in Caroline's voice.

"We've lost our auctioneer! I don't know what to do. This is dreadful news."

"Whoa. Oh, no," Rosie said, stunned by this development. "I'm on 550, Carolyn. I'm going to find a place to pull off the road. I'll call you right back."

This state roadway was a winding and hilly two-lane. She never took chances on it. Several people, probably careless and speeding, had lost their lives on this highway over the years. So she was extra cautious whenever on it. She found a wide gap ahead, on her side of the road, and pulled the Edge completely off the highway. She came to a stop at the entrance to a private gravel drive. She put the crossover in park and punched a button on the steering column. "Call Carolyn Ashcroft," she said.

When Carolyn picked up, Rosie asked, "What's this you say? No auctioneer?"

"I'm worried sick, Rosie. Vern called and said he had more work to do than he'd expected at the auction house. He's not free any longer during the week, so he can't be our auctioneer. What are we going to do?"

Rosie almost swore. "Da... ng! Can anything else go wrong?"

"Exactly my sentiment. Is our project doomed? Was Evelyn right? Are we fools for thinking we could hold an auction, let alone raise money at one?"

"Did you tell Nora the bad news?"

"I tried calling her. Think I misdialed or something."

"Well, keep trying. I'll stop by soon. I have to go to the office first. I'll see you within the hour. We'll talk then."

Rosie disconnected. She had the sinking feeling that she'd let down her guild. Was her idea of an auction indeed stupid and foolhardy? Was she indeed the fool that Evelyn accused her of being?

Nora eased her Buick slowly into her garage and turned the engine off. Phoebe climbed out from the passenger's side. Nora climbed out from behind the wheel, shut the door behind her and locked the car with a press of the fob. Phoebe said her goodbye and climbed into her VW, left parked off to the side of Nora's short but wide drive. Nora waved farewell to her friend then pressed a button to close the garage doors between them. Once inside her kitchen, she retrieved her phone from a side pocket in her purse. She plugged the cell phone in to recharge the battery. Only then did she noticed she had missed some calls.

Having lived alone for many years since becoming a widow, Nora picked up a habit of talking to inanimate objects around the house. This time she held a one-sided conversation with the cell phone. She noticed on the display that Carolyn had been trying repeatedly to reach her. "Oh drat! I forgot I had you on silent for our meeting. Well, you charge up a bit, while I call her on the house phone." She dialed Caroloyn's number. "Hello, Carolyn. Did you want something?"

Carolyn was brief and to the point. The news hit Nora so hard, she found her legs a bit unsteady and felt the need to sit down. From her new position on the edge of her bed, she gathered her thoughts in stunned silence.

"You still there?" Carolyn's voice on the receiver asked.

"Yes. Just in shock."

"I know what you mean. I'm devastated. This news is just awful. We have no place and now no auctioneer. I'm going to end my term as guild president as a total, total failure."

Nora was thinking about the meeting she had just had with the Historical Society, about Avery and Ximi, about raffle quilts and this new Shining Star quilt guild. "I'm afraid I have even more bad news." She paused long enough to hear Carolyn's little gasp. "Evelyn has been bribing some of our members to join her new guild. Phoebe and I had coffee a few minutes ago. Ximi and Avery came in to Donkey while we were there. You know them — the Asian and the really tall woman. Well, Evelyn made Avery her vice president. Avery *donated one of her quilts,* and they've already been selling raffle tickets for it."

"Oh, no... Oh, dear... Oh, my."

"Phoebe and I just finished talking to the Historical Society director about a venue. But we won't know if their board will allow us to hold an auction at their facility, for at least two weeks. The director said that his board has to vote on our request. I guess I should probably contact him about this. Maybe we should just cancel the whole thing."

"Whatever you think best, Nora." Then Carolyn had another thought. "Maybe Rosie should really make the final decision. I just told her about losing Vern's services. You know, I depend on you and the others to guide me. Rosie said she'd call me again when she gets back to town. Maybe we should all meet. We need to decide what's to be done. I'll call her back, tell her to meet us at the Tea Basket hall. Maybe in an hour and a half?"

"I'll unlock the doors," Nora said.

Nora set her receiver down. Her first inclination was to call the Historical Society to cancel their request. But she knew Carolyn was right. The original idea had been Rosie's, and Rosie was chair of the committee. Rosie needed to make that decision. Nora sighed wearily. She liked to get things done quickly, but eagerness to throw in the towel wasn't her decision to make.

"I'm not gettin' any younger, people!" Nora shouted angrily at the phone.

The red Buick of Nora's was parked on Shannon, in front of a sparkling, white S Class Mercedes sedan belonging to the doctor's wife. A blue Ford bearing a real estate sign on the side door panel parked behind the Mercedes, and a dusty Maxima belonging to Ximi, behind that. Bringing up the rear line of parked cars belonging to Tea Basket friends was a dust-covered, yellow Beetle. Inside the hall the women sat around one of the tables in unusual silence, as Nora served them hot coffee. She had cups waiting as they arrived. Hovering over their coffees, no one seemed eager to talk, the bad news having dampened everyone's spirit.

Carolyn, as guild president, thought she should speak up first. Rosie, as the committee chair, thought she should speak. Both spoke at the same time. Rosie acquiesced to the president.

"I'm at my wits end. This little idea of ours…"

"Of mine, I'm sorry to say," corrected Rosie.

"No. No, dear. We all agreed. We all liked your idea. But we seem to be stymied at every turn. You've all tried so hard, but we keep coming up empty-handed. The question is, should we continue to work on this plan? Or should we abandon our hopes for the Gammill?"

Phoebe spoke up. "When we were at the coffee shop, we were reminded that the Gammill was not the real purpose of this auction. The real reason was and still remains to raise funds to fight breast cancer. We wanted to donate to the race team even before word came about the possibility of winning a quilting machine. I'd like to remind everyone here at this table, again, that a donation for that cause still remains our primary goal. The Gammill was only a dream. Maybe just a fantasy. I say we continue to seek solutions to the problems we face. It's important that we focus on trying to raise funds for the Thimble and Chatelaine team and the fight against breast cancer."

"But without an auctioneer? How can we hold an auction?" Carolyn asked.

"Surely there are other auctioneers in this corner of the world. We only thought of Vern because we know him. He's family, so to speak, since Belle's in our guild," Rosie thought openly.

"Well, there still remains the problem of a place, in addition to not having Vern," commented Nora, adjusting her red glasses. "We won't hear if we can use the Historical Society, for two weeks." An eternity in Nora's estimation, though she didn't openly say so.

Rosie spoke next. "Personally, I don't want to give up. Not yet. Let's look for an alternative auctioneer before we do. Please? Since we don't know if we can have the Historical Society yet, that gives us time to make inquiries. I'll ask around my office. There's bound to be someone who knows of other auctioneers in neighboring counties. There has to be auctions Vern didn't handle. It only makes sense."

"I agree," said Ximi. "I'm so sorry that Simone and I couldn't find a venue. But I hope we don't just give up on the little quilt auction idea. Things will all work out. Maybe we just need people other than ourselves, people not in our guild, to offer guidance and suggestions. Maybe even the Historical Society knows of another auctioneer."

That thought had not crossed Nora's mind. She had so resolved to quit that she had failed to think about asking for help. "Well, since the director hasn't yet put forth our request to his board, I could call him back. I could tell him we've lost our auctioneer, but we're searching for another. I can say that we still want him to ask his board for permission. But maybe he should let them know that if we don't find a new auctioneer, our request cannot be acted upon."

Carolyn's hands remained folded, as if in prayer, on her lap. As usual, she froze with uncertainty, while very quietly humming a worried tune under her breath. She looked desperately to her friend, Rosie, for any answer.

"Well, ladies," Rosie said. "If we all agree, then let's not abandon all hope. Not yet. Are you all willing to try to locate a substitute auctioneer?"

Heads nodded.

"Then let's get our auctioneer problem solved while we wait for the Historical Society board to meet and decide. We have two weeks. Nora, did the director say he would contact you once the board made a decision?"

Nora nodded.

"Then we all put our efforts on the auctioneer problem until Nora gets the word on a venue."

Ever the optimist, Ximi smiled and stood to leave, saying, "I just know this will all work out. You'll see."

10

$\mathcal{T}$he following fourteen days were filled with disappointing phone calls, empty trips to various offices and unanswered email inquiries. Everyone on the committee suffered a large dose of worry.

Rosie called on Bob at the chamber. She telephoned her competitors in the real estate business, brokers and appraisers. Finally, the banks gave her leads on three possible auctioneers. She finally felt somewhat upbeat, holding this short list of prospects in her hand. She telephoned Carolyn immediately, so that her longtime friend might also feel somewhat less anxious.

One auctioneer, a local she was not acquainted with, was tied up with his work at the produce auction house near Chesterhill, near Amish communities in neighboring Morgan County. Rosie had never been to the auction house but understood the place was bustling on auction days. When this man was not calling the produce auction, he had a hog farm to run.

The next prospect specialized only in real estate property auctions. He was sorry he couldn't help, but he hoped the ladies understood.

Finally, the third possible alternative to Vern Hart turned them down, arguing that Athens County was too far from his home to travel. Rosie had struck out.

Ximi used the Internet to do her search. In the entire World Wide Web, there were no auctioneers willing to respond to her request. She even tried flipping through various yellow pages in phone books in the university library, looking for one in some of the larger towns in the region. She was finding the same issue that had come up for Rosie. Many of the auctioneers specialized. None of them seemed willing to travel to Athens.

"God, Rosie, it's just as bad as finding a doctor around here!" she said, when she finally decided to quit her search, and once again, report failure.

"Tell me about it." Rosie replied. "These guys have probably settled where the money is. I guess they don't think southeast Ohio has two cents to rub together."

Rosie, of course, accomplished little to nothing toward solving the problem of an auctioneer. But she did answer her phone every time one of the Tea Basket Quilters on the auction committee called with bad news. She would then throw herself into bemoaning the loss and worried herself into a hot flash. She wore out several batteries in the little fan hanging from the lanyard around her neck.

Phoebe had no contacts to call. She worked off her frustration by sewing down binding at night on a queen-sized quilt just back from a professional longarm quilter. She assumed none of her ex-coworkers back at the college could help. She didn't recall any of them being the type to attend quilt auctions or even use an auctioneer. Nevertheless, on a whim, she called one of them. That conversation was half-hearted in her attempt. Her call simply spread the word about a possible auction of little quilts, maybe. She rather enjoyed reconnecting with the guy who had been a financial aid advisor during the time she worked there. To that end, she surprised herself. She learned that he had been promoted to a dean, or perhaps vice president, over financial aid. The college had always been top-heavy when Phoebe worked there. Seemed like nothing had changed in that respect, according to her friend. But he offered to spread the word among the staff about their possible auction of little quilts.

Phoebe needed gardening supplies, bags of organic fertilizer and maybe some peat moss. So she left her little VW bug parked in the garage and grabbed the keys to her truck. The bug didn't hold much, and she was never sure what plant she might find at the garden store that needed a new home. So she drove the truck to White's Mill, just in case she needed the bed to haul something large back home. While looking around at their potted trees for sale, she mentioned the need of an auctioneer to one of the owners. The man gave her Vern's name as a referral. She thanked him, wrote a check for five dwarf fruit trees she didn't need and had the guys load them into the bed of her truck, along with a bale of peat moss and a few bags of fertilizer. She drove off, wondering why she had spent money on trees that would probably die this late in the season and in this heat wave.

Pulling and dropping the trees out of the bed of her truck was almost more than she could do. She could only manage to plant one in the day's heat and humidity. To avoid the worst of the heat, the following day she dug a hole early in the morning then set a tree that night. Five trees took five days to plant. She worked outside even less the following week. She mostly stayed indoors to finish binding the big quilt.

Nora reluctantly telephoned the director of the Historical Society. She told him their tale of woe to let him know that the future of any auction, even if his board approved, looked very bleak without an auctioneer. The following two weeks she managed to finish two of her small UFO's and tidy up her sewing room. She looked at the clock on the wall, every hour, while working. One moment she wished time would speed up. When she'd realize that only one hour might have passed, she'd sigh then scold a piece of furniture in frustration. There were other days Nora would catch her reflection in a mirror. She'd adjust her red glasses, smooth her hair and attempt to ignore a nagging thought creeping up, that her time on earth was limited. In those moments, she'd wish time would slow down.

On one occasion, she berated the ivy hanging in her sewing room for not having feelings for her situation. She told it, "I don't know what you think you'll do when I'm gone. I water you. I feed you. I give you light. And what do you do to me? You drop your leaves all over my clean floor! That's what you do. I'm getting tired of cleaning up after you! When I'm dead and gone, who's going to look after you then? Huh? You're just like guild. Do you think just anybody will care for you like I do? I won't be around forever, you know."

And so two long weeks passed for Nora. The hours seemed to drag, but the days flew by. Then one evening, Nora's telephone rang.

"Hello?"

"Mrs Radnor, This is Tom Fox at the Historical Society."

Nora's heart gave a little jump. "Oh! Yes. Hello. Thank you for calling me back... I guess. Do you perhaps have news for us?"

"Indeed. The board met, and I presented your request to them. They voted..."

Here it comes, Nora thought to herself. *He's going to say no.*

Nora missed what he said. "I beg your pardon?"

"I said, the board will be honored to host your auction. And Mrs Radnor, they have found an auctioneer who will be available to you. You can tell your members the good news, and put your plan for a quilt auction into motion. Be sure to let me know the date you select, so I can tell your auctioneer. His name is William Evergreen. He's a retired textile curator from the State Historical Society. Auctioneering is his retirement pastime. He's absolutely thrilled to be a part of your efforts, and he looks forward to coming down to Athens, from Cleveland. We're delighted to welcome him. You should be prepared to bring your quilts to our own curator here at the Historical Society, one week before the auction. She will prepare them for display and have all of them hung by the time your bidders arrive."

There was silence on the line.

"Mrs Radnor? Are you still there?"

Nora was speechless. "Oh, my dear, Mr Fox, you have made my day, sir! You have no idea how I — how we — have all been so worried. I will tell our members at once! Thank you. Thank you! I don't know how to express my gratitude enough."

"Well, we're pleased that we can be of assistance. And once you have a date, we'll be sure to get the word out to our members, too. And I'm sure Bill will also want to inform people whom he knows have a keen interest in fiber arts. I'll be waiting to hear from you. OK?"

Nora was breathless in her jubilation but managed to repeat, "OK", and thanked him once again.

Nora ever so gently hung up her phone, disconnecting the call. In a semi-stunned and semi-euphoric state, she punched up Rosie's number to share the news, while performing several quick rhumba steps. Next she called Carolyn. Then she called Phoebe. Then Ximi. Then a number of Tea Basket Quilters to share the good news. Her phone got a workout that day. She was sure, by the time she went to bed that evening, that she had called every member of the Tea Basket Quilters. She thought once that she might even call Evelyn out of spite, to gloat, but of course she did not.

Evelyn found out through Lois.

Carolyn didn't need to make any meeting announcement at the Tea Basket's the following Monday, thanks to Nora's hotline. Instead, she immediately turned the short meeting over to Rosie, who was eager to set a date and get their little quilt auction finally underway. The membership pulled small calendars out of purses or checked iPhones. After several dates were suggested but rejected for their conflicts with other big events in Athens, the group settled on a date that finally seemed void of competition from either the college or the community. They would hold the auction in four weeks.

"In the meantime, ladies, all who are donating a little quilt, need to have a hanging sleeve on the back. Our secretary has a sheet for you with dimensions for minimum depth of the sleeve, that the Historical Society curator explained she needs in order to display your quilt. All the quilts need to be delivered to them by Friday at the latest, one week before the auction. Let's see." She glanced at her business calendar laying open in front of her, to confirm the date. "Yes, they need to be delivered to the society before four thirty the afternoon of August 14. Please invite everyone you know to attend, and encourage them to bid. Remember, this is to raise proceeds for that 5K, less any expenses to the auction event."

Several hands shot up in the air.

"Yes?"

"If we didn't have a little quilt to donate when we first talked about this, can we still donate one?"

"Oh, of course! When we surveyed everyone, there were a few out there that weren't finished. So yes, of course! The more we can sell at auction, the better! Maybe I should pass around a sheet before anyone leaves today." She rummaged among the pile of papers in front of her and removed a yellow pad from the clutter. She handed the pad to the first woman seated in the front row. "Write your name down on this if you're going to donate a quilt. Then note the number of quilts you'll be delivering to the Historical Society."

"Do we need to have a label on the back of each quilt?" asked another member, whose waving hand Rosie recognized next.

"Well, of course! Every quilt you make deserves a label, not just these. But that reminds me. I should tell you that the Historical Society will want you to fill out an information form for each of your quilts. You'll be asked to attach this form to the front of each quilt you take in. But we don't have the forms yet. I'll be sure a stack of them are left here in the hall very soon. I understand that on one side you write information about your quilt to give the auctioneer, and on the flip side will be a release so that your quilt can be held by the Historical Society until the auction."

"Does anyone else have another question?"

There were no more hands.

"Don't leave the building until you've signed your name on the yellow pad going around," she instructed.

Rosie turned the brief meeting back over to Carolyn, who called for a motion to adjourn. After the second and subsequent declaration that the meeting was adjourned, the noise level in the hall rose. Everyone talked excitedly at once.

Rosie, now armed with a date, an auctioneer and a place to hold their auction, knew she next had to get the word out to the public. She was dismayed that four weeks offered no time to get anything posted into quilt magazines. Another thought occurred to her. What about all the quilt shops in the area? She began scribbling ideas in her calendar. 'Q-shops newsletters' was her first goal. Knowing most shops issued a monthly email to their patrons, she figured this would be just as good as any magazine announcement. She decided to compose a short blurb that evening and email it to local shops.

Rosie looked up from her calendar and glanced around the room. The yellow pad was making its way up and down rows. She noticed most of the ladies hadn't left their seats. They were waiting patiently for the list to reach them. That seemed like a hopeful sign. Did that mean most of the members were going to donate? She hoped so. She continued to scan the membership until finally locating the only naturally black head of hair amidst the sea of gray tresses.

Rosie approached Ximi, who was engaged in conversation with her friend, Simone. She tapped her on the shoulder, and Ximi turned around.

"Could you possibly use your artistic skills to design a flier for the auction?"

"Wow, sure," Ximi said with surprise and pleasure. This, at last, was something she could do that she wouldn't fail at. "What do you want? How soon do you want it?"

"I don't know what I want, to be truthful, artistically. But the flier needs to contain all the information anyone needs to locate and attend our auction. Who, what, when, where, why. You know."

"Of course. I'll get on it right away. Is this for an advertisement?"

"Quilt shop newsletters. If you can email an attachment to me, I'll send your copy out as an attachment with my write-up."

"Oh, you could post the flier on our guild Facebook page, too!" Ximi said.

Rosie hadn't thought of their little Facebook page. "Great. Send me your draft as soon as you can. If I like your copy and the work doesn't need edits, I'll forward the flier to our guild secretary. I'll let her know right now before she leaves that she's to post the flier onto our page when she gets the document. That's a great idea. Thanks."

"Ximi and I are going to make a little quilt together for the auction," announced Simone. We have four weeks..."

"Three," corrected Rosie. "All auction quilts have to be at the Historical Society the week *before* the auction."

"Oh, yikes. I didn't think of that," Simone said.

"It's OK, Simone," said the ever-optimistic Ximi. "We'll give this endeavor our best shot. I'll email a draft to you tonight, Rosie."

11

Evelyn shut the door to her kitchen, after having returned from a run. Her house phone rang. She was still wet with sweat and slightly out of breath. Picking up the receiver, she listened silently then hung up without saying a word. Inside she was boiling with rage. Lois had just informed her about the Tea Baskets' progress. Lois revealed the Saturday date they had picked for the auction, and also the news of William Evergreen, the auctioneer. Evelyn flung her towel to the floor and kicked it across the kitchen floor, out into the living room, while shouting a string of epithets.

When her tantrum subsided, she retrieved the towel. It had sailed to the top of her big screen TV mounted on the living room wall. Evelyn finally paused to process the news.

So, Belle did get Vern to withdraw. Lucky her. Still, we're miles ahead with our raffle. See what good it does them to have this auction. Nobody's going to show up.

Evelyn's temper under control, she needed something to assist her return to a feeling of calm. She mixed up her go-to favorite, a bloody Mary. As she sipped the bitter cocktail, she grew strangely pleased with her crew. Lois was proving to be a beneficial spy. Avery's organizational skills seemed excellent. And so far, her guild had already banked over $1,300 toward that Gammill. In Evelyn's thinking, that was exactly $1,300 more than the Tea Basket Quilters had, and probably $1,000 more than they would have, after their foolish auction came and went. She was confident that the Gammill was as good as hers.

But she had a nagging suspicion, too. Avery.

Avery's success might mean too much to her Shining Star ladies. Evelyn decided she needed to take control of the raffle — reassert herself as leader. So she picked up the telephone and called Avery.

"I'm sure it's been difficult for you to carry the whole workload for this raffle," Evelyn said. "Let me take some of the burden off."

Avery wasn't sure what Evelyn meant. Avery had never mentioned anything as being difficult or burdensome. As a matter of fact, Avery rather enjoyed all the activity that spearheading raffle sales provided her. This task had been easy to plan. The schedule of sales sites was time consuming but simple. The efforts got her out of the apartment and exploring parts of the county she had not visited since, or even during, her college days at the university. She enjoyed meeting each member of the new guild as she spent time getting to know them all. They, like members of the Tea Basket Quilters, shared quilting knowledge freely. As a bonus, Avery had picked up several useful tips just from chatting, while passing time as they sat with the raffle quilt.

Neither was caring for the quilt difficult. The big F-350 provided adequate storage space for their little table, the ticket receptacle, two canvas, fold-up camp chairs and the big bag containing the metal quilt stand. She never left the raffle quilt unattended in her vehicle, but always took it inside to keep it safe at night. She realized, in a sentimental and silly way, that one day *her quilt* would belong to someone else. Any amount of time she could have it nearby seemed precious. After all, these were the last days she'd own it.

Avery turned over sales money for deposit, every Sunday night, to the Shining Star treasurer. Also easy to do. And reporting collections to Evelyn, by phone, after each day's outing was nothing. So why was Evelyn trying to be so helpful now? Avery doubted *being helpful* was typical of Evelyn.

"Well, I think you're shouldering too much responsibility," Evelyn said. "I feel like I should take part more — be more responsible — myself. Why don't you let me keep the quilt and the stand? Both are quite heavy and cumbersome. I'll meet you with them every weekend to get set up. I'll even help you set up. I can spend a little time selling tickets, too. I can also take the collections to the treasurer after you tear down. How does that sound?"

It sounded odd to Avery. She was sad to think of her quilt spending time in someone else's care. However, Evelyn had not yet volunteered for any work hours. Avery shrugged off her doubts. Why not? Though both collapsible stands, together with the rod spanning between them, were heavy, when stowed together inside the nylon carrying case, they added up to a lot of weight. She didn't really think skinny Evelyn would be toting the heavy stand around for too long, even if she did offer to do so today. *A little break from that chore might be nice,* she thought. Though reluctant to part with her quilt, she rationalized, *It isn't my quilt, any more.* Her quilt now belonged to the Shining Star Guild. So Avery agreed.

"OK, sure, Evelyn. That would be nice," Avery finally said.

They were to sell outside the grocery store in The Plains, next. Evelyn arrived on time. The black Prius zipped into a parking spot near Avery's big Ford. Evelyn brought the car to an abrupt halt, squealing rubber on asphalt with her sudden stop. The redhead went over to Avery's truck and tugged the nylon bag containing the stand, out of the truck, with difficulty. She strained to maintain a straight line as she wobbled with the burden over to Avery, who was already setting up the camp chairs and small table near the store's entrance. Evelyn dropped the bag. A loud, metal clatter rang from within.

Avery unzipped, then removed the three components. She unfolded one of the legs and pulled the pole upright. Evelyn copied her movements to set up the other leg. Avery spread a sheet on the sidewalk, between the uprights, to protect the pristine quilt from picking up dirt from the ground while being hung. While Avery smoothed out the sheet, Evelyn returned to Avery's truck for the quilt.

Getting a good hold on the bag containing the quilt proved troublesome for little Evelyn. Clutching the very large, clear plastic bag with its handle, she pulled the quilt out of the cab. But once the slippery bundle was out, the handle was useless. Evelyn was too short to keep the bag from dragging on the asphalt. She tried to hug the plastic to her chest. With the heavy quilt inside, the plastic bag proved to be slippery and impossible to control. If she squeezed the bag tight enough, she could just barely prevent the quilt from shifting about inside, but then she couldn't see over the top to where she was walking.

Evelyn managed to stumble her way to Avery. She dropped the plastic bag and glared down, as if the object were a bad dog she was about to scold. Avery caught the look of frustration on Evelyn's face. She hid her own face from Evelyn, as she stifled her own grin of amusement. Avery proceeded to unzip the bag to remove the quilt from within. Evelyn accepted one end of the quilt then helped Avery slip the stand's rod through the hanging sleeve on the back. Together they each placed their end of the rod atop the pair of stands and hoisted the quilt like a banner, as high as the two rods allowed.

Evelyn noticed the label on the back while hoisting the bar holding up the quilt. Lines of machine quilting ran over the label. So the little patch of information had to have been on the backing before the quilting was performed. That insured the label could never be removed, at least not without destroying the quilt in the process. The label was therefore guaranteed to stay put as long as the quilt survived. Briefly she wondered how Avery, or maybe the quilter, knew exactly where to attach the label to line up so perfectly to both bottom and side edges. Evelyn opted, however, not to ask. She had pulled a muscle carrying items from Avery's truck. The pain concerned her more. She wondered how Avery, as tall as she was, could have done this job of setup alone, all these weeks.

With the quilt hoisted, little table in place, the collection receptacle out and tickets at the ready, Evelyn sat down beside Avery. No one came by in the first five minutes.

"When do you wrap up here?" she inquired.

"Six or seven. Depends on traffic. If people are still buying, we'll hang around the extra hour."

"Well, then I'll see you later." Evelyn abruptly rose from her chair and left for her Prius, leaving Avery behind, alone and blinking in wonderment at her guild president's sudden and strange departure.

A woman just then approached the little table where Avery sat alone. The woman carried a jug of milk obviously just purchased inside the store. She asked how much raffle tickets cost for the 'beautiful quilt.'

Avery dismissed further thoughts of Evelyn to attend to her first customer of the day. "One ticket for a dollar, or a book of six tickets for five dollars."

The woman standing before her was seriously interested in her quilt. "I have a twenty. I'll take four books." The woman handed Avery her jug of milk, while she lifted a wallet out of her shoulder bag and withdrew a twenty-dollar bill.

After that sale, Avery was approached by a slow but steady string of interested buyers, although none of them bought four books at once.

Avery soon forgot all about Evelyn's abrupt departure. Later that morning and throughout the day, she was joined by a string of other Shining

Star members who had signed up for a shift. Avery was glad she hadn't excused anyone, imagining that Evelyn might have actually stayed longer than a nanosecond.

Evelyn was a very peculiar woman, in Avery's opinion.

Rosie looked at the yellow pad after it finally made the rounds among all the members. As she scanned down the list of handwritten names, some in cursive and some printed, she began to notice most had written the number '2' following their signatures. A couple wrote '3'. Nora Radnor clearly wrote '4' after her name. Rosie felt her heart give a joyful leap. She withdrew a small calculator from her blue handbag, which she normally used to calculate estimated monthly mortgage payment amounts for prospective home buyers. This time she tallied those twos, threes and one four. When she reached the end of the list, which included names on a second sheet of yellow paper, she was left awestruck. The Tea Basket Quilters were going to auction two hundred and seven quilts! Rosie walked over to her friend Carolyn to show her the figure on the calculator display screen.

Carolyn looked at the pad that Rosie held up in one hand. She then looked at the number on the calculator in Rosie's other hand. Her eyes darted back and forth several times, until at last she understood. "Oh, my goodness! We're going to have over two hundred quilts in the auction?"

Rosie smiled broadly and nodded.

Carolyn smiled widely. This number meant their auction of little quilts was likely to be a success. Every member seemed to have climbed on board the project. Everyone was contributing and participating to raise funds to fight breast cancer. Carolyn's smile slowly faded. She was imagining an auctioneer standing in front of the room at the Historical Society, holding up her own donation. He was looking toward the big room where the buyers stood. And there they stood; three, and only three, miserly bidders dressed in rags in an otherwise vast and empty hall, holding bidding cards in their hands. #1. #2. #3.

"Oh, my. What if nobody shows up to bid?"

Carolyn, as usual, had found a topic of worry. Her hands assumed their all too customary prayerful pose in front of her. She started to hum. She felt a hot flash coming on.

"Carolyn, you're something else!" her friend Rosie laughed. "Stop worrying. Ximi is drawing up our poster. The Historical Society said they'd be getting the word out. I have assurances from Bob that the chamber members will be notified. If you are worried, which I think is for nothing, ask all our members to spread the word among their other affiliations: their churches, clubs, neighbors. You could ask your husband to tell his golf buddies to pass the word on to their wives. Maybe some of his old hospital and clinic staff might like an invitation. I'm going to ask other brokers to invite their buyers. How nice to hang a little piece of local fabric art to the wall of their new home?"

Carolyn nodded, but not convincingly. She would definitely ask her doctor husband. She would also instruct the guild secretary to email all the members, urging them to spread the word far and wide. But she couldn't help herself. Until the day of the auction, until she actually saw more than three bidders walk into that room, there was no way her vision of failure would leave her in peace.

Rosie gave her friend a big hug. "Who knew to carry an umbrella that day we first met? You did. Stop fretting so much. You were prepared then, and you've done all you can do to prepare guild for the upcoming auction now. If this is a bad decision, I'll be the one getting soaked again. This event was, after all, my idea. And Carolyn, I'll dry off, even if I do get drenched."

The email hit every member's inbox the next day. At that point, there really was nothing left for Carolyn to do. So she worried. She'd shuffle outside and try to relax by the pool. The heat of the day drove her back inside. She wore out two more pairs of batteries in her little portable fan. Dr Ashcroft visited his old haunt at the hospital where members of the staff expressed pleasure at seeing him looking so fit and tanned. Many agreed to attend his wife's event. He then told his regular golf foursome, who in turn told their wives, who in turn told some of their friends. And so Dr Ashcroft did his part.

Rosie convinced several competitors in her real estate world to invite potential buyers. They all had a few parents of incoming freshmen looking for temporary housing for their progeny. The invitation seemed like a nice perk to lure those parents back to Athens, one more time, to sample a bit of local flavor and then, of course, to visit a few properties newly listed on the market.

Ximi's poster was professional, colorful and to the point. No editing had been needed. Rosie sent an email with the attachment to several local quilt shops, including one copy to the chamber. She followed those up with phone calls. A day later, she followed up the call to the chamber with a visit to the office. Bob appreciated only having to cut and paste her entire document into his newsletter. That reassured Rosie that every detail would be correct.

Friday, the week before the event, members of the Tea Basket Quilters began to arrive at the Historical Society, delivering little quilts with the required release and information cards pinned to the front of each. Volunteers manning the front desk took the quilts as they arrived and carried them into a room out of sight in the back. In that room, the curator soon regretted having ever volunteered to do the display all by herself. Quilts finally stopped arriving after Ximi Ling dashed through the door just before closing with the two hundred and tenth little quilt for the Tea Basket's auction.

The curator put her hand over her forehead as she gazed over ten eight-foot tables covered with small quilts of every color. She was the next woman to start worrying about the approaching auction. Not that she imagined no one would attend — she was worried about the work involved beforehand. Maybe she alone couldn't get a catalog finished and the quilts all hung in time. She dashed into her office and stopped her assistant from leaving for the evening.

"Put out a call for volunteers, will you? Send an email before you leave. Sorry to do this to you at the end of your day, but have you seen how many quilts those ladies brought in?" There was a hint of panic in her question. "I need able-bodied people, Wednesday evening, to help me hang all of them. I don't think I can get all these cards transcribed by myself, either. So ask for a couple volunteers with word processing skills, starting Monday morning."

Ximi felt a sense of relief and pride as she smiled and handed over her donation. She and Simone had finished the small but easy wall hanging, only that morning. They had pieced puffy, pleated three-inch squares of pastel fabric, acquired from their own collection of scraps, to the top. The patches gave their small quilt a three-dimensional look and feel. She bounced down the front stairway with a light spring in her step, as a volunteer locked the Historical Society door behind her.

Ximi thought maybe she'd take the slow way home that evening. Maybe she'd drive through The Plains. Maybe she'd celebrate. Stop by Larry's Dog House and buy a cold ice-cream cone to chase off the day's heat. Or maybe she'd splurge on calories and buy a milkshake instead. Chocolate. Once in her car, she turned on the radio which was always tuned to her favorite local station. A weather report was being broadcast:

'The Midwest continues to suffer in heat, with a slow-moving high pressure system over Indiana. Two systems in the western Plains may bring relief later in the week. A storm system, developing in Colorado, northwest Kansas and southwest Nebraska, may bring much-need relief to the central Plains. Another system in northern Michigan may also bring rain to our region. Until then, we remain under a heat advisory, with temperatures to remain in the upper 90s.'

Lois Caldwell finished typing up the fair premium booklet at the fair office. She copied the document to a flash drive, to be printed. Satisfied, she, too, felt like celebrating that day. She dove into her tote bag sitting on the floor beside her desk, to retrieve a bag of Fritos. Pulling open the bag for a handful of crunchy, corn chips, she remembered she needed to report to Evelyn. She felt hesitant. Lois had overheard Carolyn and Rosie talking about the total number of quilts for the auction. Evelyn was not going to be thrilled to hear how many had been promised and donated. Lois decided that if Evelyn asked her how many she personally had donated, she'd lie and say, 'only one'.

But Lois had been as generous as Nora and had donated four: two older little wall hangings she'd made a decade earlier, and two relatively new ones. She had decided that her tastes had changed, and time dictated that someone else should enjoy her older ones. She made the two newer ones in classes taken at the Tea Basket hall. She enjoyed learning new techniques; paper piecing for one, and reverse applique for the other. But she wasn't thrilled with their colors. They were well done, of course, but they didn't fit the country décor of her farmhouse. They were simply too bright. One was made of Oriental prints, with metallic threads running throughout. The other one was done in pink fabrics. Lois was definitely not a lover of pink. So Lois had scribbled on Rosie's paper a '4' at the very last minute, overtop her previous '2'.

After a few more fortifying fists of corn chips, Lois finally got up her nerve to call Evelyn. The reaction was worse than she imagined.

"What?" Evelyn screamed over the phone, as if Lois had contributed all two hundred quilts by herself.

Lois cringed. She stuffed a corn chip into her mouth and tried to munch quietly, as she moved the receiver away from her ear as the tirade continued.

"Those damn women! Do you have any idea what this could mean? Two hundred? Are you sure? That's ridiculous! How in the name of God did they find that many?"

Lois, of course, had no idea how they found or made so many little quilts, so she didn't try to answer. She took, instead, another corn chip to munch on.

"I can't believe it! And the auction is next Saturday?"

"Mmm hmmm," Lois replied, her mouth stuffed with salty, soggy Fritos.

"I've got to call Avery. We need to be sure we're selling our raffle tickets far and wide. I'll have her set up spots in Meigs and Hocking County, maybe even Vinton County. Two hundred?"

"Two hummbrd 'n tn," Lois corrected, shoving more chips into her mouth.

"Crap!" Evelyn disconnected.

With a satisfied sigh of relief after Evelyn hung up, Lois leaned back in her office chair that was hidden under her long, floral dress. She sat several minutes in the fair office, chewing contentedly, thinking about her four donations and wondering how much somebody might bid on them next Saturday. Eventually, the Fritos were gone. She tipped the bag up, over her open mouth, to catch every last salty crumb spilling out. She tossed the bag into a nearby trash receptacle. Gathering up the pages she'd printed out, the flash drive, her tote bag and purse, Lois drove from the fair, heading next to the printer's office downtown. She figured Saturday would be fun, maybe even exciting. Yes, exciting *and* fun. Especially fun if Evelyn stayed far, far away.

12

Saturday morning, Carolyn, Rosie, Nora and Phoebe met with auctioneer, Mr William Evergreen, and the staff at the Historical Society. They arrived promptly at eleven as arranged.

Before Rosie could get herself ready that morning, she had to answer her phone numerous times. The calls were not for real estate. Carolyn was stressing out, calling her no less than three times. Rosie assured her that all would be well. After all, they were supposed to be treated to a tour of their auction quilts. What was there to worry about that?

It seemed that Carolyn fostered an irrational fear for how much money the Historical Society and the auctioneer would want in payment for services rendered. Rosie assured Carolyn it was to be what it was.

Rosie was dressed and ready to head out the door to pick her up. She felt jubilant and was not in the least worried about imagined expenses. She turned off the phone and hoped she could get into her car before her friend called one more time.

Carolyn did not telephone Rosie again, but instead she darted to her front window and peered anxiously down her street. She watched the blue Edge leave a garage two doors down, back into their street and turn into her place. Carolyn grabbed her purse and her lanyard with the tiny fan and shot out the door, feeling as anxious as ever.

"But what if the fee is exorbitant?" was her first question, as soon as her passenger's side door closed. "What if this guy wants a huge percentage of each sale? What will I tell members? That we forgot to ask when the society director told us about this guy? We even forgot to discuss fees for the facility!" Carolyn was beside herself now that she realized their omissions. "How could I have forgotten such important things?"

Rosie failed in every attempt to comfort her during the drive down Route 33 to Athens. She had not succeeded during any of the earlier phone conversations and not now that Carolyn sat by her side, rambling on and on. Obviously, she was not easing the woman's tensions one bit. Rosie had turned on the air conditioner back in her driveway. She now dialed down its temperature as cold as possible. But while cruising down 33, fretful Carolyn's little fan ran full tilt, adding to the frosty breeze that was blowing her friend's curly, gray hair away from her face.

"You have got to stop all this worrying, Carolyn. It's of no use. Whatever will be, will be. That we never thought to ask was an error, yes. But it's too late to fret. Please, just try to relax and enjoy this outing. I'll get you there, then we'll get all the answers to your questions."

Carolyn looked rather pale and not at all reassured.

"Listen, I'll do the asking. Now stop worrying. Everything will be OK."

Rosie rounded the block three times before she found a vacant spot to park near the former church building where the Historical Society had made its home. She saw Nora's red Buick during her first trip around. She then spotted Phoebe's dusty, yellow Beetle on the opposite side of the street on the second lap. She and Carolyn were the last to arrive. A quick check of the dashboard clock reassured her they were not late. Nora had no doubt been early, as usual. After parallel parking the Edge on her first attempt, Rosie led a nervous Carolyn by the elbow, up the steps and into the old church.

In Carolyn's mind, the climb upward was ushering the condemned to the gallows. Surely her demise was near. The stained-glass windows made Carolyn think that perhaps now was the time to repent of all her sins.

Tom Fox, the society director, was waiting for them inside the door. He shook their hands graciously, welcoming them. "I think you'll find that our curator and a company of eager volunteers have displayed your collection of little quilts with quite an eye for their beauty and variety. You'll be meeting your auctioneer in the hall, where your quilts now hang for inspection. Other members of your party are already inside. Are you ready to see your auction quilts and meet Bill?"

Carolyn swallowed with some difficulty, her nervousness apparent. She was impressed by Rosie's calm outward demeanor. Reluctantly, she assumed the guild president's responsibility. She spoke aloud in deference to her nervousness and forced her fears into words.

"Yes... let's see. I'm on pins and needles."

Fox took a position between both women, offering each an arm. In this manner, he was able to escort both into the exhibit hall simultaneously. A stunning sight greeted them beyond two swinging doors, which were opened by attentive volunteers standing by to admit them. Carolyn and Rosie felt their jaws drop. They saw two hundred and ten colorful little quilts suspended midair around the open former sanctuary. The quilts created a temporary wall, suspended five feet off the ground, running all the way around the perimeter in a horseshoe configuration. The long row of little quilts was aglow in an explosion of patchwork colors and designs.

Rosie was drawn instantly to all the quilts made in blue. She spotted her own instantly — a small Bear's Claw pattern in multiple shades of dark and light blues.

Carolyn loved the pastels. There were paper-pieced whimsical houses, appliqued flowers, traditional patterns and so much more.

Unseen rods, hooked to pairs of fine wires, held each quilt aloft. The thin wires dropped down from the tall ceiling to both top edges of each quilt. These were attached to the unseen rods hidden inside each quilt's hanging sleeve. The former sanctuary was filled with every imaginable variety of colorful cloth, all made by members of the Tea Basket Quilters. Batiks, Civil War reproductions, 1930s prints, and the latest designs from all the fabric manufacturers.

Quilts were arranged in two long rows along each side of the former sanctuary. One row that hung parallel to the front wall of the great room was split into halves in the center, leaving a large gap between. In the space stood the auctioneer's block at the former alter. The manner in which the rows had been set — ten feet from each outside wall — created temporary hallways. The arrangement made for ease of viewing of backs from one side, as well as colorful tops from the center of the room.

From the back side of each row, this hallway allowed viewers to read labels and view the hand or machine quilting against whole, cloth-backing fabric. Inside the circle of quilts, beams of light from high above had been strategically focused on each quilt front. The lighting accentuated their colorful blocks, as well as the quilting. Bright rays of light also served to enhance the multitude of patterns, fabrics and techniques. The impression was breathtaking in its overall professional appearance.

"Oh, my," were the only words Carolyn could muster.

Rosie could only nod her approval and smile. The presentation was more than she could have hoped for.

Nora had been standing with Phoebe. A tall, black man in a business suit stood beside Phoebe. The trio approached as the newcomers continued to scan the quilts, walking deeper into the room. Nora led, followed by Phoebe who was still engaged in conversation with the man who was, no doubt, to be their auctioneer.

The director made the introductions. "Carolyn, Rosie, I present to you your auctioneer, Mr William Evergreen, from Cleveland."

William Evergreen was as different from Vern Hart as anyone could possibly be. Vern was a stout old boy with rosy cheeks and usually wore his ever-present ball cap with the Hart heart emblazoned on the front. This man was tall and fit. He wore a pleasant smile on his dark-brown face. His salt and pepper hair was close-cropped. Vern was a casual dresser, often attired in faded jeans and a short-sleeved shirt. William Evergreen wore a crisp, white shirt, the sleeves of which extended the perfect distance beyond the cuffs of a tweed jacket. Both shirt and jacket coordinated with a striped tie. Evergreen's hands were constantly in motion as he spoke to Phoebe in animated conversation. On one wrist he wore an expensive watch that would occasionally catch and reflect a beam of light meant for one of the quilts. He wore a gold ring, with an inset stone, on the other hand. By every female's standard in that room on that day, William Evergreen was a very attractive man.

"Ladies, I'm honored to meet you," Evergreen said, as he took first Carolyn's and then Rosie's hand, shaking each one in turn. "My, what excellent workmanship your guild members produce. I was just telling Phoebe that I'm going to enjoy, so very much, selling off these fine examples of pieced and appliqued quilts. You're offering a very wide range of block patterns, too. Both the machine and the hand work on the quilting are impeccable. You have something, I'd say, for every possible buyer. Well done, ladies!"

Nora beamed. Phoebe, still by Evergreen's side, seemed pleased as well, though somewhat quiet and reserved. This reticence was unlike Phoebe. She was one to offer up commentary on most subjects, but this day she seemed distracted with other thoughts.

Rosie, the last to accept the auctioneer's congratulatory handshake, was never at a loss for words around anyone. Once she had his hand in hers, she immediately thanked him for driving all the way down to Athens from so far north. She asked, "How long was your drive?" But before he could respond, she shot forth a barrage of other questions, eager to learn as much about him as she could in as little time as possible. "Did you have an uneventful journey down? Where are you staying tonight? What are your plans for the day until the auction begins? What do you have planned for afterward?"

Evergreen hastily intervened before more questions could assault him. "Well, I must say I had a rather long trip. The drive took five hours. I arrived around six yesterday evening. I'm staying at a hotel on the edge of town, and I'm visiting with some old friends here in Athens. They were another reason why I was eager to come down. I haven't been able to visit with these friends in ages. This opportunity made that visit possible. Thank you for that. They've invited me to join them for lunch today. I'll return here to the Historical Society to get ready for your auction, by two. I hear the doors will open so the quilts can be inspected at that hour. Two o'clock, right?"

Fox nodded affirmative.

"We'll begin the auction promptly at three. Should be finished up by six, I'd say. And then, I would love to have you ladies join me for dinner afterward. How does that sound?"

Nora was always ready for any social event. Dinner sounded perfect to her. She had planned only to make herself a tuna salad sandwich that night.

Phoebe said, "I do appreciate the offer of not having to drive home on an empty stomach."

Rosie also agreed that dinner with Mr Evergreen sounded delightful.

Carolyn said, "I'll let my husband know not to expect me."

"Then it's settled. Where's a good place to dine in town?" Evergreen asked.

Carolyn spoke up. "Mr Evergreen, the Tea Basket Quilters would like to treat you. Dinner should be a part of our fee to you. And speaking of fees, we have been remiss. We never had an opportunity to ask what we will owe you for your service."

The auctioneer chuckled. "Well, I never argue with a lady. So, if you wish to pick up the tab, then by all means, I accept your offer. Thank you.

As for a fee…" He glanced dramatically upward, brought his hand to his chin in a thoughtful pose, pretending to ponder the subject deeply, then glanced briefly at Phoebe before answering.

Carolyn held her breath.

"Allow me to choose one of your little quilts as my fee."

The four Tea Basket Quilters looked to one another in pleasant surprise.

"That's *all* you want? One little quilt?" Carolyn asked, dumbfounded.

That's all I want," he replied.

"Sold!" exclaimed Rosie, making everyone laugh. "And now, sir," she said, turning to the Historical Society director. "What do we owe the society for the use of your building and for all the work your curator and staff have done for us?"

Director Fox smiled. "If you would make a donation to the society in any amount, we will consider that donation fair. We're happy to host your event. The auction will bring people into our facility, and hopefully, they will return again in the near future to see other displays. We're promoting an antique quilt display this month, located in another smaller room downstairs. When your buyers come through the door today, we'll announce that our exhibit is open and free for them to enjoy today while they're here. Who knows, they might return later in the month to see it."

Rosie, as Tea Basket treasurer, thought about his modest request. "Would a percentage of whatever Mr Evergreen raises for us be sufficient? Say, ten percent?"

"Oh, my, yes. That's very generous. Any amount you offer will be sufficient. Thank you. Now, I must leave you. Please stay as long as you wish. I have dull administrative duties to attend to. I'll see you all back here for the auction then? Three o'clock or before."

The director departed through the set of doors where they had all entered. The small group of four women and their handsome companion turned back to the display hanging around them. Rosie and Carolyn had not seen all the quilts in one location before. They decided to walk around the room once, or maybe twice, before leaving, just to view them all. This would be their last chance to see all these quilts together. Soon, they hoped, every little quilt would go to a new home where each would be appreciated and cared for lovingly.

Nora, acting as the tour guide, accompanied her friends, chatting excitedly about several of the quilts as they slowly made their way along the first wall. "This one was made by Lois Caldwell during a class. You remember. The one taught by Molly Menear? Lovely paper piecing, don't you think? This was Lois' first time to try this technique, too. Here. This next one's by those two new girls, Ximi Ling and Simone LeBlanc. Those two are showing promise, aren't they? Oh, and here's that county fair winner of Belle's. Isn't she good with color?"

There was little need of conversation between Carolyn and Rosie. They walked quietly behind chatty Nora and simply admired each little quilt as they paused briefly before it. Their *quick* tour ate up an hour before they circled the room and returned to the start. Phoebe and William Evergreen talked quietly to each other, lagging behind the three women.

As the small group finally reached the last of the two hundred and ten little quilts, William Evergreen spoke up. "Ladies, I must excuse myself now. As I mentioned, I have to meet my old friends. Phoebe has agreed to accompany me. She offered to drive me to the OU Inn. She thinks I can fit inside her little Beetle, in spite of my long legs."

Evergreen had the ladies' full attention the moment he announced that Phoebe was going to lunch with him. Phoebe had so often expressed her dislike of people in general, that this piece of news was most intriguing to hear. Most intriguing.

"Oh, *really?*" Nora said mischievously with a grin on her face, looking at Phoebe and adjusted her red-rimmed glasses in order to better observe her friend's eyes.

Phoebe smirked back, but carefully so as not to be seen doing so by William Evergreen. "Yes. I think I may know Bill's friends from college. Meet me right here when we get back?"

Her friends agreed.

After the museum doors closed solidly behind Evergreen and Phoebe, Rosie looked to Nora, and both burst out in giggles as if they were once again teens.

Nora was the first to utter what all were thinking. "Oh my God! *Bill?* Did Phoebe actually call him *Bill?* I think Phoebe's found a *b-o-y-f-r-i-e-n-d,*" Nora sang.

All three again laughed happily. To everyone's knowledge, Phoebe Prescott had never had a boyfriend. She almost always made a point of saying how much she disliked people. Not once had she ever mentioned a boyfriend, a lover, or even one single interest in a man, to any of them.

Nora capped their giggle fest with a new thought. "A boyfriend. Now wouldn't *that* be something?"

13

*E*vergreen and Phoebe returned to the museum at two o'clock sharp. As the couple walked in, they saw a dozen people already milling around the room, viewing quilts. Evergreen noticed bidding cards clutched in several hands. That was a good sign.

"I think I'd better get my fee down from this display, before anyone decides they'd like to bid on it," he said to Phoebe.

"Have you decided which wall hanging you want?" Phoebe asked.

"Yes. I want that Broken Star Log Cabin of yours. Over there," he said, nodding his head toward the far back wall.

Phoebe looked to him with surprise. Though the quilt was a lovely piece, in her opinion, the quilt was far from the quality she would have expected a textile curator to have selected. She suspected there was another reason for his choice, which gave her hope, and simultaneously, some unease. She looked across the room toward his selection. He stood in front of the quilt she had pieced three years earlier. The small log cabin was composed of sixty-four four-and-a-half-inch blocks, each containing seventeen one-inch strips of fabrics. These were arranged in a pattern creating a dark sixteen-point star in the center. The entire quilt was then bordered with a different dark fabric on each of the four sides. Phoebe had selected the border fabrics from one of the fabrics among the darks.

"It's not an original design," Phoebe objected. "I bought a commercial pattern years ago to make that. And how did you know that thing was mine, anyway?"

"I don't care that it's a commercial pattern," he confessed. "I want to take something home that reminds me of you. Earlier today, I noticed the label on the back; that's how I know it's yours. What I didn't know at the time was if the Phoebe Prescott on the label was the same Phoebe Prescott I once knew here at OU."

Phoebe smiled with some embarrassment. Of course, the label. She found herself, once again, liking this man, more than she knew she should. She also knew she'd have explaining to do to Nora and the others as soon as he was gone. That thought gave her pause. He'd return to Cleveland. She'd be here in Athens. She tried not to think about Bill Evergreen beyond this day. She felt irritated with herself for having entertained, even fleetingly, the thought — the fantasy — of being a couple. Phoebe shook her head to toss the idea out of her mind.

Evergreen was looking toward her quilt, not at her, and so he missed her shudder. "I'll see you after the auction then?" he turned toward her and asked. "For dinner?"

Phoebe nodded.

People continued to file slowly into the hall, singly or in pairs. The noise level increased with their conversations. Some proceeded to examine specific quilts they'd spied in the program leaflet. Others ambled along the walls, viewing little quilts as they walked. Evergreen had excused himself to find the curator. He wanted to collect the information cards that Tom Fox said he could use to introduce each quilt. As he walked out of the hall, Phoebe caught sight of her friends walking in. They greeted him in passing with friendly hellos. Evergreen returned their greetings with a wave and a smile. Phoebe noticed, at once, the amused look on their faces when they caught sight of her. She had been caught red-handed today, in the company of... a... man.

"Soooo," Nora began, "How was your lunch with *Bill?*"

"Oh, for heaven's sake," Phoebe scolded. She sensed there would be no escape from their teasing.

"Oh, yeah," joked Rosie. "Phoebe can't *stand people*... unless the person is the very tall, very polite, very interesting and the *very handsome*... *Bill*... Evergreen."

"I knew you'd make fun of me. Just stop, please. We simply happen to know the same people," Phoebe tried in vain to explain. "It was *just* lunch."

Carolyn had gotten over most of her uneasiness about event expenses. She had since substituted that worry for whether anyone at all would show up to bid. She was, however, able to shed her nervousness in order to offer a congratulatory sentiment Phoebe's way. "Well, Phoebe, I, for one, am very happy to see you going out with..."

"Going out? *Please!* I just had a friggin' lunch with the guy… *and his friends*. Will you all just drop it?"

Carolyn smiled and changed the subject back to her new preoccupation. "There aren't many people here, are there?" She was indicating the small crowd that had already grown to thirty.

Rosie looked around, checked the watch hidden under the cuff of her blue jacket and then caught a glimpse of more people entering the hall. "I think we're going to be OK. Look." She nodded her head toward the double doors, now propped open to admit a constant stream of potential bidders. A line formed at the table where some were verifying their method of payment and signing up for bidding cards.

Nora's attention turned to a small booklet she held in her hands. She was thumbing through its pages. Someone had transcribed their handwritten descriptions alongside a small black and white photograph of each quilt. Their entire collection was printed up in the booklet. Nora was impressed. The museum staff were handing these out to buyers at the table where the queue formed. Nora had picked up one of the booklets out of curiosity as she passed by. A small blank line below each photograph provided a place to record the winning bid for each. Nora fumbled in her purse for a pen.

"Did you all see this?" she asked. "These historical people have been working overtime for us. I think we should give the Historical Society at least fifteen percent of our sales, as a donation. Don't you, girls?" She finally located her favorite pen at the bottom of her bag. She then held up the booklet for the others to view.

"We've already promised ten percent," Rosie said, looking at the image of a familiar quilt on the page Nora held out for inspection.

"Yes, they have done a remarkable job, but Rosie's right. We've already committed ourselves to ten percent," Carolyn said.

"Ten percent is a fair amount. But I have no idea what the quilts will bring," Phoebe wondered aloud. She was relieved her guild friends were no longer preoccupied with the subject of her and Bill Evergreen.

"This crowd doesn't look to me like bargain hunters," Rosie observed.

The four took notice of the people milling about the big room. A few were pointing to this or that quilt, some were getting up close to inspect a tiny element. Others had made their way to the back side of the quilt wall for another angle of examination, only the lower half of their bodies visible.

Some of the women wore painful-looking but stylish heels. Others had slipped painted toes into sandals. Some of the legs behind the quilts wore blue jeans, as expected of a younger generation. The men wearing jeans dressed them up with expensive running shoes or well-polished oxfords.

The hall was filling up with people milling about who dressed like people with money to burn. Young men sporting stylish haircuts wandered about, a few of them in suits. Older women strolled along, wearing clothing that could have come from Nora's own closet: silk tops, linen slacks and tasteful accessories. Older gents wore the occasional tie. The crowd ambled along the quilt walls in quiet conversation, often jotting down notes in their booklets. There were younger women among them who squeezed themselves into upscale skinny jeans and silk tees. Their necks were adorned with gold necklaces. Very expensive-looking earrings dangled from their ears. The gold definitely did not come from a big box store.

Rosie was impressed. This crowd smelled of disposable cash. She thought maybe she should leave a few of her business cards out on the table, if the museum staff would allow it. She excused herself, saying she'd get a copy of the bidding program for each of them, and then she left, promising to return soon.

Phoebe saw the museum curator walk in and go directly to her quilt, which hung at the back. With efficient and quiet movements, the woman attached a printed sign on Phoebe's Broken Star Log Cabin .This confirmed that Bill had made his selection official.

Nora saw what had taken place, too. She knew the quilt's maker was her friend, Phoebe. Nora arched her eyebrows at Phoebe, in mocked questioning, and nudged her with a friendly elbow.

Phoebe sighed heavily and rolled her eyes in exasperation.

By three o'clock, the hall was jammed with people eager to start the bidding. A few stragglers were still trying to make up-close examinations of the offerings. They were having difficulty now that the crowd filled the empty space in the center of the former sanctuary. The latecomers had to inch their way between the walls of quilts, trying not to touch them, while at the same time avoiding collisions with the back sides of other bidders.

Evergreen stepped up onto a small, portable stage in the front of the room where he could be seen. He clipped a small microphone to his lapel. In his hand he held a wooden gavel. Somewhere, someone turned on a sound system which crackled to life. Speakers in the hall hummed briefly. Then Evergreen spoke to the assembly, using the wireless public address system. His voice was loud and clear, filling the room over the PA.

"Ladies and gentlemen." He waited for conversations to subside, and then he resumed his introduction. "Today's auction of little quilts, by members of the Tea Basket Quilters, is about to commence. I am today's auctioneer, William Evergreen. Welcome, everyone."

The people who had failed to make their way around the hall to examine quilts stopped where they were. The gathering quieted. Carolyn, nervously standing in the back of the room beside her guild sisters, switched on the quiet little fan that always hung from a lanyard around her neck and directed the flow of air across her face.

"Your winning bids today will be donated to the Thimble and Chatelaine 5K team, this fall, by the Tea Basket Quilters. Your money will then be donated by the Thimble and Chatelaine for breast cancer research. A small percentage will be donated here to the Historical Society and Museum, as a thank you for their hard work in putting on this beautiful display you see before you, and for providing the space for this very unique auction. I'd like to point out to everyone that all these quilts are listed in today's program. However, please remove number one hundred and forty from the offerings. I, myself, have selected that quilt as my auctioneering fee for today. I apologize; *you* will not be bidding on *my* selection."

A quiet buzz of laughter rose from the audience, accompanied by the sound of pages being flipped in program booklets. An occasional disappointed moan escaped from a few who had designs on Phoebe's broken star log cabin.

Evergreen continued, "Members of the Tea Basket Quilters have made and donated all of the quilts you see here today. Not only will you take home today a unique, handmade piece of American fabric art, but your bids will go to support a very worthwhile cause. So, please everyone, be generous with your bidding and your support. Shall we begin? We'll start with lot number one."

While Evergreen made this announcement, the curator had taken down the first little quilt from the wall. She handed the quilt over to a museum staffer wearing white gloves. The tall, lanky volunteer took a position standing next to Evergreen, holding over his head the small, red, appliqued heart quilt. Evergreen read what was printed on a card.

"Heart applique. One hundred percent cotton. Hand quilted. Blue ribbon winner at the Athens County Fair in 2017." He then looked out onto the room filled with eager buyers. "Do I hear one hundred dollars? One hundred dollars to start today's bidding."

"Yo!" came a shout from somewhere far in the back of the room. A short man waved a bidding card high over his head.

The little quilt auction was underway. Evergreen nodded to the first bidder and began to sing the auctioneer's song.

The heart quilt went for one hundred and thirty-three dollars. Nora made a note in her booklet. Never in her wildest dreams did she imagine such a price would be paid for it. The heart was her quilt. She saw the buyer being congratulated by those around him.

Evergreen turned back to someone to say something not broadcast over the speakers. Nora assumed the bidder's card number and the winning bid amount was being recorded by a museum staffer seated behind Evergreen. The woman seemed to be writing down what Evergreen said.

The volunteer, who had held the little heart quilt aloft, now carried it toward the woman who made notes for Evergreen. The volunteer took a piece of paper from her, then crossed behind Evergreen and left the stage with both red heart quilt and the paper. Nora continued to watch the man as he made his way out a side door.

While he left the stage, another volunteer had taken his place and was holding aloft the second quilt for bids. Evergreen read the story of this little quilt, a colorful applique basket with embroidered flowers and an abundance of embroidery in the border.

"Let's start the bidding on lot number two at one hundred and fifty dollars. Do I hear one fifty?" Evergreen asked.

A bidding card in the front row shot into the air.

"My!" was all that Nora managed to utter.

The Tea Basket Quilt auction ran from three o'clock that afternoon until nearly six p.m. Their quilts brought so many high bids that Carolyn felt weak in the knees with excitement and relief. She needed to leave the hall at one point to sit down. All of her worries had been for nothing. She felt a huge weight lifting. That, in turn, made her feel faint. Nora never once left the floor, keeping record in her program booklet. She scribbled down the amount of each winning bid for every little quilt. Only after the final 'Sold!' rang out, did she leave the hall in search of her friends.

She was impressed that so many bidders remained to the end of the sale. This made crossing the room somewhat difficult for her. She had to snake her way past people to get out of the sanctuary. Though some had already paid for and departed with their treasured quilts, the entrance hall was crowded with other winning bidders queueing up at the desk to settle their accounts. Several minutes passed before Nora located her friends in the vestibule.

"Girls, can you believe this? I had absolutely no idea we would get so much for our quilts!"

Rosie was beaming with pride. Carolyn, seated beside Rosie, the little fan dangling unused around her neck, was smiling ear to ear. Phoebe, too, looked happy.

"How much do you think we made?" asked Carolyn.

"I've been keeping a running total," announced Nora. "I have a total of $21,126.00!"

"Oh… my… God!" gasped Rosie.

Jaws dropped on everyone's faces.

Rosie began to work a mental calculator. "We'll be giving the Historical Society two thousand, one hundred and twelve dollars. That'll leave us nineteen thousand for the Thimble and Chatelaine team." She paused while digesting the full meaning of that enormous sum. "Girls, I do think we might very well end up with a Gammill."

"Well, ladies? What do you think? Are you pleased with your sale?"

It was William Evergreen. Tom Fox, the museum director, accompanied him. Both wore smiles on their faces.

"Oh, Mr Evergreen, how can we ever thank you?" Nora asked.

Evergreen chuckled as he held up the broken star log cabin quilt, which he carried under his arm. "No need, ladies. I'm just delighted that I could be of assistance. It's been a real pleasure to meet you all," he said, looking directly at each of the Tea Basket Quilters in turn, but stopping longer to look into the eyes of Phoebe. "Shall we wrap up here and have our dinner? I believe you all promised me a treat. I'm dry as a desert and hungry as a bear."

Everyone smiled more, as if that were possible.

"After the last of the buyers has paid, I need to make a lovely deposit at the bank," Rosie beamed. "And I have a check to write for you, sir," she said to the museum director. Then she asked, "Would you care to join our party for a celebratory dinner?"

The director smiled graciously. He was just as pleased by the outcome of the auction as they were. He was proud of his staff's efforts and their performance, too. He also realized the donation that Rosie would offer from the auction was going to amount to a tidy sum indeed.

"I would be honored to join you. Where are you going?"

'Where are you going?' was a phrase that normally sent the friends into a ten-minute non-debate of 'I don't care; where do you want to go?' replies. But this time Nora took the lead, deciding for everyone.

"I say we all go to the steakhouse down on State Street. Plenty of parking. Easy to get to. It's a loud and raucous establishment, quite suitable for our celebration. They even have *alcohol!*"

Everyone laughed and agreed.

"I'll meet you all there," announced Rosie. "I won't be long. Won't take but a jiff to drop off a night deposit at the bank. And I'll write out that check for you, sir, right now, if you care to wait with me," she said to the director.

"I'd be pleased to wait," he said.

"Then we'll get a table for six," Carolyn announced. "I'll go with Nora. See you there."

"Missus Prescott," called out Bill Evergreen. "Would you care to ride with me?"

Phoebe smiled. "Actually, I'd better drive my Bug so I can get home after dinner."

"Oh," Evergreen said, with a slight hint of sadness in his voice. "I was hoping you and I could linger in town a while longer after dinner. Seems like a lovely night for a stroll on campus or somewhere."

Phoebe was flattered. She sighed. "Maybe," she hinted. "But I still need to drive to the mall with my own car, if you don't mind."

Bill grinned and nodded.

Phoebe always liked that smile. It seemed genuine. Her heart made an extra little beat.

14

$\mathscr{P}$hoebe's radio was tuned to the local station. She barely listened as she drove the dusty Beetle down State Street to the mall parking lot where the freestanding steakhouse was located. An obnoxious buzzer preceding a National Weather Service advisory got her attention. She turned up the volume.

'The National Weather Service in Charleston predicts a line of severe thunderstorm cells that could produce strong surface winds in excess of sixty miles per hour, across the region, this evening. Heavy rain will accompany the system, which may cause small stream flooding.'

"At last, some rain," she muttered to herself, thinking only of her vegetable garden soil that had nearly dried to rock in the heat and sun these past weeks. The cracked clay begged for a good rain. Her attempts to water, by stringing several very long garden hoses in a line out to a sprinkler head, was the only thing that helped. But that wasn't the same as a good soaking rain from above. Her plants, and the soil under them, really needed water; hours and hours would be perfect.

She found a pull-through parking spot and slipped the yellow Bug in. Those were the only kind she liked. With the top up, rear visibility was greatly restricted in the convertible. That made putting the car into reverse risky. She feared hitting someone trying to back up. Phoebe preferred a clear line of sight ahead, allowing her to see anyone as she pulled away.

Bill Evergreen drove his car into the parking space right behind hers. She saw that maneuver all too clearly from a side mirror. She fumbled with the buttons on the dash to switch back to satellite radio for a channel that played fifties music. Then she punched off the engine.

Evergreen's Mercedes was sparkling clean, in spite of making the long drive down from the Interstate a few days earlier. In a way, just for one moment, Phoebe missed being near a large metropolitan area. But she quickly dismissed the thought. She could think of nowhere else she liked better to live than in Athens County, except for one thing. She did not like shopping in the town. White's Mill was her one and only favorite place to spend money. She boycotted the big box store. In her opinion, too many people crowded the isles. They zipped up and down the parking lot, without a thought to anyone else's safety. The big store also attracted too many uninsured cars and too many unsavory looking people.

Even when forced to grocery shop, Phoebe avoided the crowds. Her ideal time to buy bread and milk was late summer nights or early winter mornings. Early yes, but not too early.

She knew workers stopped by the big grocery store in town to grab a Starbucks coffee or a newspaper on their way to the office. So she never arrived before eight in the morning. By eight, most offices were open and their staff in place. Phoebe didn't care much for people. Not any more. At least, that's what she told her friends. She'd had her fill of the masses when she worked. Since her retirement a decade earlier, she had practiced the life of a hermit, with one exception — her Tea Basket quilting friends. With that bunch, she found a friend in Nora Radnor and a few select others. The rest she politely tolerated.

Affiliation in this group of women gave her all the human contact she thought she needed for a happy existence. The balance of her time she spent alone, toiling in her garden or sitting indoors at her sewing machine, accompanied by her two pugs, Stitch and Medallion. The dogs usually spent their time snoring on nearby cushions as she occupied herself piecing a quilt.

Phoebe felt a stirring of unease seeing that Mercedes and Bill Evergreen so close at hand. She wished to avoid any complications to her life of solitude; a complication like one Bill Evergreen, who was just then getting out of the Mercedes parked on her bumper.

"Phoebe," he acknowledged, as he locked his car door.

Phoebe smiled back. "You found the steakhouse, I see," she said.

"Just followed your bright-yellow Beetle," he indicated, nodding toward her dusty Bug.

Phoebe smiled. She didn't know why. She was beginning to feel self-conscious about herself. "Shall we go in? Nora probably has a place for us by now." Phoebe wanted to get out of the heat and stifling humidity. She smelled the rain that was on its way. But a glance skyward revealed only a blue expanse.

Not a cloud drifted over the Hocking meandering along a wide valley between tall, wooded hills on both sides. The Hocking was very low, the water level reduced to little more than a stream in places; so low that a person could walk across the muddy bottom. What water did define the river, meandered casually eastward. The town of Athens lay quietly in the valley. Most of the houses and businesses nestled up against wooded hillsides along the northeast bank. That's where the mall was also located, and where Phoebe and Bill Evergreen walked together toward the restaurant door.

"After you," Evergreen gestured.

Oh, god, Phoebe thought. *He's being a gentleman.*

At the steakhouse, Bill Evergreen did, in fact, open and hold the door for Phoebe, allowing her to enter first. Nora had obviously alerted the hostess on duty, who seemingly recognized the pair and took them immediately to a large table set with service for six, located in the back of the bustling steakhouse. Nora and Carolyn were already seated side by side. Each had a beverage in front of her, alcoholic by the appearance of the glasses.

"Over here, you two," Nora called out, waving a hand.

Evergreen pulled a chair back for his companion. Phoebe caught an unmistakable twinkle in Nora's eyes and a grin on the older woman's face, which only Phoebe recognized as amusement. Evergreen failed to catch the look, his eyes fixed on Phoebe. He took the chair next to hers and sat down.

Carolyn took a sip of her cocktail and looked, for once, to be at ease. "Mr Evergreen, again I thank you for what you've accomplished for our guild. I had no idea our little wall hangings would bring so much money," she said, with genuine gratitude in her voice.

"Mrs Ashcroft, they were beautiful examples of your members' skill at quilt making. The auction's success had much more to do with the wherewithal of your customers than my efforts. I believe there was a concerted effort to advertise to a population of fiber art connoisseurs who understand the number of hours required to create such works of art. Those people know that it takes much more than a few dollars in fabric and thread to produce a quality quilt, large or small. You owe your thanks to whoever did your publicity."

A waitress arrived to recite the day's specials and take the couple's drink orders.

A few minutes later, Rosie and the museum director arrived to take the last two seats at the table. For the next ninety minutes, the six of them enjoyed each other's company, shared interesting stories of family and work, downed several rounds of wine, beer or cocktails, as each preferred, and collectively ate far too much food.

After the wait staff took away empty plates and everyone had finally finished their last round of drinks, Rosie called for the check and pulled out a credit card to pay the bill.

They all rose together, dropped generous tips on the table and headed for the door to leave. But no one ventured outside.

The storm that had been predicted by the weather service had arrived. The sky, once clear, had grown dark with angry, swirling, ominous clouds. Rain fell in sheets. Quickly, this storm intensified violently. Huge droplets pummeled the earth, drenching everything in waves. Wind blew great sheets of water sideways, slamming it against the door of the restaurant, blocking their exit. Anyone who dared push open the door to leave was met with stinging pellets of ice-cold, wet projectiles. The Tea Basket Quilters and their guests wisely opted to retreat from the doorway, to wait out this storm from inside the restaurant's confines.

Those with a view out the windows on the door, saw buildings on the far side of the parking lot, a mere thousand feet away, disappear from view behind wave after wave of falling water. William Evergreen, the tallest among the group, observed and commented on the rain thrown against the door glass.

"It runs down as if it's a waterfall," he said.

Cars parked out in the lot disappeared from his view, hidden behind this deluge. Just then the lights in the restaurant went out, throwing everyone inside into sudden darkness. Music stopped. Patrons let out a collective gasp. Workers groaned. Thunder rumbled loudly overhead.

The sound of wind surrounded the structure. It increased in intensity. The windows rattled, and rain thumped on the roof as if it were beating a drum or attempting to find a way inside. The fury of this storm had everyone's attention. A collective unease permeated the darkness. Lightning strikes accompanied intensifying thunder. Booming from the thunder shook the walls, the floors and everyone inside.

"Oh, my gosh!" Nora said. She was worried only about the loss of electricity. If the power went out in this restaurant, that meant the power was probably also out at her house, less than a mile west. State Street was known for having frequent power outages, as was most of the county. There were so many trees and so very little attention paid to keeping the rights of way cleared, that the power company was constantly tasked with restoring power after every little storm. The smallest of rains caused trees on the hills to loosen their grip on the earth and topple across power lines somewhere, every time. This storm, however, was accompanied by an unusually intense straight-line wind. The fury of this storm seemed angrier than any Nora could remember in all of her ninety years. She was positive no tree could withstand the beating this wind was throwing at them.

Each new clap of thunder and accompanying flash of lightning brought sudden gasps and shrieks from trapped and nervous patrons in the darkness. The Tea Baskets were growing uneasy themselves, standing, as they were, so close to glass. They pushed back against the wall of bodies who had also planned to depart, but were now trying only to catch a glimpse of the raging weather just beyond the window pane of the door. Bill Evergreen and the museum director were doing their best to clear a way for the women to retreat. A particularly loud and unmistakable snap of electricity, followed immediately by an explosion of thunder directly overhead, made everyone jump, including the men.

Carolyn, standing at Nora's side and always one to worry over nothing, collapsed to the floor in a faint.

"Carolyn!" Nora shouted at the crumpled form now sprawled on the dirty floor amid the feet and legs of friends and strangers.

Everyone who had stood frozen in the restaurant's dark entryway, gawking at the wall of water pummeling the door, pushed away from the form of the woman sprawled on the floor. The building, which offered a dry but very dark refuge, suddenly seemed more crowded by Carolyn's horizontal body. Patrons pushed each other together, even more tightly than they had been before her collapse.

Evergreen was the first to kneel beside her. He laid his fingers under her jaw to check her pulse. He then removed her glasses and pushed back an eyelid. "I think she's just fainted," he announced.

Her friends had shuffled around forming a circle, forcing strangers back. Bill handed Carolyn's glasses to Phoebe for safekeeping. The restaurant manager soon arrived, squeezing through the crowd. He carried a cell phone, ready to call for aid. He worried he'd have to make an accident report to his supervisors, praying all the while that the hubbub had not been a shattered window that struck this patron down.

"I think she's just fainted," Evergreen told the manager.

"I'll call 911 to be sure she's OK," the manager said. He punched the numbers into the phone then held the phone up to his ear.

Nothing. The manager cancelled and tried again. Still nothing. He tried calling a third time. Again nothing.

He then looked at his phone and realized he had no bars. "I'm afraid my cell phone doesn't work," he said.

Everyone who kept a cell phone in their pocket or purse, pulled them out and tried their own phones.

They, too, got nothing.

"Cell phones are down," a voice in the crowd confirmed.

Carolyn, sprawled out on the cold floor, began to flutter her eyelids.

"Here she comes, back among the living," Evergreen announced, still kneeling by her side.

Evergreen slid a hand under her neck for support, as the woman began to regain consciousness. She slowly became aware of her rather awkward and embarrassing position, stretched out as she was at the feet of friends and many, many strangers.

"Wh... what... happened?" she muttered.

"I think you've fainted," Nora told her from above.

"Oh, dear," Carolyn muttered, raising a shaky hand to her head.

"Can she stand?" the manager asked. "Can we make room for her, people?" he ordered, trying to part the wall of bodies surrounding the scene.

"Give her a few minutes," Evergreen cautioned. "When you feel ready, Mrs Ashcroft, I'll help you sit up."

"Oh... OK," came a weakened and confused response.

Carolyn's unexpected trip to the floor, temporarily diverted attention from the storm raging outside. The Historical Society director came to Evergreen's aide as Carolyn managed to right herself with difficulty. A moment passed, then she nodded to them that she was ready to get to her feet. With men on either side to support her, she walked unsteadily forward, parting the crowd of strangers on her way to a bench against the wall which had been vacated for her by a man she did not know. She sat down carefully then accepted a damp linen napkin from one of the hostesses who had squeezed through people, carrying the cool cloth to her. Carolyn dabbed cold sweat from her forehead, cheeks and neck. She tried to calm herself and regain some composure.

Phoebe and Nora stood in front of her. "You scared the daylights out of us, Carolyn," Phoebe said, handing over the glasses Bill Evergreen had passed to her.

Carolyn accepted them and put them back on.

Nora handed the purse over to its owner. "Are you going to be OK?"

"What happened, dear?" questioned Rosie, with concern in her voice.

"Oh dear," began Carolyn. "I'm deathly afraid of big storms. Have been since I was a child. My mother got caught, driving home one day, by a tornado. I was in the back seat... The funnel came right for us! The sky got darker and darker... I'll never forget. Momma had to drive the car off the road, down into a ditch. I was petrified. The noise was just like now... Momma yelled, 'Get on the floor!' I tried to hide as best I could. She couldn't get to me. She was up front. I was alone on the back seat floor. The roar was deafening, like a locomotive bearing down on us... I thought I was going to die. The car rocked terribly. That sound... the wind... lightning... like now... dreadful... that memory came rushing back, I think... that frightening ordeal. I couldn't bear the nightmare again."

Through this telling, fierce wind and pelting rain continued to rage just on the other side of the restaurant walls. Strangers, as well as friends, strained over the noise to hear Carolyn's tale. Carolyn's mention of a 'tornado' infected several nearby with a sense of dread. As their interest and concern over this woman waned, fear for their own wellbeing increased.

A sound like something falling on the roof above preceded another tremendous explosion of thunder. Once again, this was accompanied by the electrifying snap of a lightning strike. Together the effect was like an exploding bomb. The lightning lit the entire waiting area with an eerie, blue-white flash. Carolyn was sure she could feel the hair on her head shift with static.

"Oh, my lord!" shrieked Carolyn. "It's on top of us!"

If they had only known how lucky they were to be where they were when this storm descended upon them. Even though they were trapped inside, forced to hear and endure this storm's fury, they remained safe, unharmed and dry. Nerves were on edge for many, if not most, in that darkness. But this particular storm was blasting its way down the valley, plowing eastward on a devastating rampage.

High winds rolled over farmland and forest, barreling toward Marietta, Ohio and Parkersburg, West Virginia and beyond. The tall foothills that separated Athens from The Plains, to the north, served as a ramp, of sorts, tossing the tip of the storm upward like a stone skimmed across a pond. When it slammed back down to earth again and again, it did so in a long and destructive path. The restaurant with patrons inside, and the town of Athens, were more fortunate than most other places this storm was to visit. The hills, now shrouded in darkness, had protected Carolyn and her friends from the worst.

When the storm fell again to earth, not half a mile to the east, wind gusts smashed headlong into everything in its path. High winds peeled shingles off countless rooftops. The force of the gale slammed an entire commercial structure to the ground. Gusts ripped metal siding off walls, sending panels swirling upward into the darkened sky like giant leaves. The electric grid fell like dominoes, weak wires snapping in its fury, like old strands of cotton thread.

This was no gentle and soaking summer rain, the kind longed for by Phoebe Prescott. This was what the National Weather Service proclaimed a derecho, a devastating straight-line wind, a land hurricane. Athens felt only the edge of its rampage across the Midwest and eastern U.S. Before this storm dissipated out to sea, it blocked roads across ten states from Nebraska to Maryland and destroyed several small towns on its journey. In a single day it toppled and uprooted thousands of trees, downed power lines and damaged homes and businesses in a swath hundreds of miles wide. Property damage climbed into the millions. Many people, like the Tea Basket Quilters, suffered without power in one hundred degree heat for weeks.

15

Avery and a Shining Star member had returned to the sidewalk in front of Stuart's Opera House to sell raffle tickets. Avery was hoping for a repeat of their previous success there. The two women sat with the quilt, chatting with patrons. Some stopped by to purchase a ticket, others to admire the quilt on display before they entered the historic opera house. Avery tallied up another three hundred dollars in tickets sold just before her cell phone emitted an alert tone.

'This is a weather advisory from the National Weather Service in Charleston. A rapidly developing squall line will bring heavy rain and strong, damaging winds to the area. This alert covers the counties of Athens, Hocking, Morgan…'

She and her sales companion agreed to quit before they got caught in the approaching storm. Avery didn't want anything bad to happen to the quilt. She punched up Evelyn's number on her cell to come by for the money, stand and quilt.

"Storm's coming. We have no protection out here on the street, so we're quitting early."

Evelyn announced that she was in Nelsonville anyway. She would stop right over. Avery wondered why the woman hadn't bothered to lend a hand selling tickets.

She shrugged off her wonder as the two workers busied themselves taking down the quilt from the stand. Avery insisted each time that they alter how the quilt was folded. She instructed her helper this time to fold it with the back facing out. First, they folded the heavy quilt into thirds, turned it around long way and folded it in thirds once again. They then stuffed the bundle neatly inside the large, clear, plastic bag and zipped the protective bag shut. When finished, Avery's quilt label could be read through one side of the bag. Avery liked that label a lot. She gave the bag a little pat of affection. They packed up the table and chairs and carried everything to Avery's truck parked nearby, where she would wait for Evelyn.

Evelyn, as promised, soon drove up. She double parked the Prius on the one-way single lane street and climbed out, leaving the engine running. She gathered up the Shining Star raffle quilt and lumbered with the bag back to her car. She returned to take away the day's collections, along with the nylon bag containing the heavy, metal stand. She wobbled to her car again, and with much difficulty, propped the long bag against her little car. By now, a queue of frustrated motorists were stacking up behind her car. Having collected the things she agreed to take, Evelyn shoved the black bag, with the heavy stand, onto the seat. When someone blasted a car horn, she looked up at the line of cars with disdain. The redhead, dressed in her usual running attire, flipped off the offender and walked around to the driver's side of her Prius, then drove off.

Avery's helper blinked in wonder. "Doesn't she ever say 'hello' or 'goodbye'?"

"Nope. She's the funniest person I know. She never takes a second to say thanks, either. Seems she's always on the run." Avery mused, "Hmm, maybe that's why she's always in running gear."

They both snickered. Her sales companion did have good manners. The woman bid Avery farewell and said she looked forward to another day soon of selling more tickets with her. Her departure left Avery standing alone beside her truck with nothing more to do. The weather alert suggested a soggy evening on its way. She thought she might take advantage of this early release. She planned to drive down the highway to Athens, grab a bite to eat and watch a matinee at the local multiplex.

Once on the four-lane, she set the cruise at fifty-five then tuned in to a local radio station to hear perhaps how far away the approaching storm might be. She then noticed that her fuel gauge indicated the truck was down to the last quarter tank of gas. She decided to stop in The Plains to top up. The town was on her way, and she knew the station there was rarely busy. She imagined she'd find an empty pump without a line. Maybe if lucky, she'd fill up before it rained. As she drove, she could see clouds over the hills, rolling in from the west. Ten minutes later, Avery steered the Ford alongside the pumps. Wind had picked up by then. Did this promise cooling rain and a break from the heat and humidity? She hoped so.

Avery gripped the handle on the gas nozzle. A little bell in the pump chimed with each gallon that flowed into the truck's big tank. A rotating display indicated how much this fill-up was going to cost. Avery's mind wandered. Her stomach growled. *Maybe I'll get a pepperoni pizza with extra cheese… Maybe a hot, spicy Italian sub… No, maybe a footlong hot dog with everything, from Larry's Dog House… and a chocolate shake!* By the time the tank was full, the hot dog and chocolate shake at Larry's was all she could think about. Her hunger had grown exponentially.

Instead of backtracking to the highway, Avery drove west on 682 through The Plains, an alternative road that would let her enter Athens from the northwest side of the town, closest to Larry's Dog House. Six miles later, she turned left onto Union Street and left again, into Larry's. There were two cars queued up in Larry's drive-through. Avery parked the big truck in a side lot and walked inside to get her carryout footlong and shake.

The air-conditioning inside Larry's was set to winter. She felt the cold air against her sweaty back. Stepping right up to the counter, Avery ordered her footlong, with everything, and the chocolate shake, 'to go', opting to devour the dog behind the wheel where she wouldn't shiver. The wind was picking up in Athens. Gusts sent dust and debris on the lot flying across the asphalt. Small pieces of litter and dried leaves along Union Street swirled in clouds of dust and dirt. Dust devils danced down the long street.

Avery dashed back to the truck, carrying her drink in one hand and a wrapped footlong in the other. She wanted to get out of the blowing dust as quickly as possible. She opened the door, set the shake in the center console beverage holder and jumped in. Once the door to the truck was closed, the delicious odor of fresh cut onions and coney sauce filled the cab. She rolled down the passenger's window which was away from the wind, so as not to admit airborne dust. Wasting little time, she unwrapped the long bun and bit into her hot dog. As the footlong grew shorter, she idly watched the traffic go by. She let her gaze follow some of the litter blowing along the roadway. Flying leaves matched the speed of vehicles. *Thirty-five mile-an-hour gusts,* she thought absent-mindedly. She polished off the dog and thought that she'd sip on the shake while she drove across town to the movie house.

Avery had learned to eat fast, like one of the guys, after spending so many months working with them on highway jobs. Back then, lunch zoomed by fast. Time was money. Avery had lots of time now, though her money was drying up. She didn't know why she'd gobbled the hotdog so fast. Habit, she guessed. She had only the wrapper and a lingering odor of onions to remind her of its former existence. That and a sudden oniony burp.

Torrents of rain fell just as she wadded up and tucked the wrapper into Larry's brown bag. Avery belched onions again. She hastily put the truck window up, staring out in disbelief. Trees on the hillside, only a quarter of a mile away, vanished one after the other behind a solid approaching wall of blowing water. The rain came fast and hard, straight for her.

Only a second later, Larry's Dog House, mere feet from her parked truck, vanished from her view, behind sheets of water. Huge droplets crashed against her truck. The rain plummeted not downward from the clouds swirling above, but sideways, slamming against the big truck like hammers against nails. Avery's heart jumped at this storm's sudden ferocity. Would the paint on the side of her truck survive? Her truck rocked in the blowing winds. Was that hail? She couldn't see beyond the window to know for sure, the hood having disappeared too, under blankets of a solid, gray waterfall. The rattle against the cab intensified. The huge droplets sounded like a falling stones.

Evelyn drove away from the bank drive-through in The Plains, where she had just made the raffle deposit. She was absorbed in thoughts about Shining Star's financial success and felt quite satisfied with that day's deposit, short though, the sales day had been. She examined the teller's receipt and noted that this put them over the $3,000 mark. She was positive that the Gammill was theirs, as sure as she was Evelyn North. Distracted in thought, she failed to notice Avery's brown Ford parked across the street at the gas station pumps. She zipped quickly away from the bank, out onto the main street and aimed the little black car toward home. She slipped her Prius quickly into her garage while failing also to notice another sight — dark, swirling clouds overhead that were bearing down on her little community. As the garage doors descended, she jumped out of the car and hauled the heavy quilt in its clear bag into her kitchen. Branches on the trees outside swayed wildly, as the first hint of the storm's power was just reaching The Plains. Leaves began to fly past her window, propelled by a growing wind ahead of an unprecedented low pressure system.

An airborne twig rapped against a kitchen window pane. *Must be the storm Avery mentioned,* she thought, at last taking notice. Evelyn dropped the heavy quilt onto a kitchen chair, her purse onto another. She needed a drink. Spying on her guild workers was tedious and hot work. She mixed up her favorite cocktail of vodka, tomato juice and lemon, topped off the cocktail with a single ice cube then trotted off to the sunroom. There she intended to kick back, let her mind wander, think thoughts of a quilting machine and watch some much-needed rain arrive.

Evelyn didn't have long to wait. She had no sooner loosened her running shoelaces and curled up on the floral cushions when the little wind transformed into a huge gust. From her comfortable perch in the sunroom, she had a front row seat to this storm's approach. She took a sip in calm anticipation when the storm threw its first punch. Evelyn was about to feel the sting.

Her favorite tree, on the western property line, toppled over and crashed to the ground in front of her eyes. The big maple had shaded Evelyn's sunroom every afternoon. Its roots and the sod around them now projected upward in a twisted vertical plane. The trunk fell heavily to earth with a mighty explosion of leaves, limbs and twigs. Large branches snapped like twigs in the collision with the ground. Branches the size of legs and as long as her car bounced away from the tree with the force of the fall. Millions of leaves flew upward, caught on a gust and slammed against her sunroom glass. One of the maple's large branches, larger than most of the others, bent with the strain then snapped under its own weight. The limb sprang into the air like an arrow shot from a bow. The splintered limb rotated in a great arch as Evelyn watched, unable to move. She saw it fall to the ground, summersault and then crash through her floor-to-ceiling glass wall.

Evelyn screamed, her legs still frozen in terror, her eyes wide, yet she was still holding tight to that Bloody Mary. She narrowly missed being impaled by the jagged end of a branch. Broken shards of glass sprayed her body. Following the sound of shattering glass came the howl of a hot wind, followed by stinging drops of rain and bits of debris blowing through the gaping window. Just as suddenly, a second tree toppled. This one landed on

161

top of the first. This finally jolted Evelyn into action. She tossed the cocktail glass, scooped up her running shoes in one hand and grabbed the green, floral cushion off the swing with the other. She sprinted into the interior of her house, dashing for her only place of safety — an interior bathroom.

Her spotless bathroom contained one white commode, a white, ceramic pedestal sink, a matching white washer and drier, and the only antique she owned, a huge claw-footed, white, porcelain cast iron bathtub. She raced down the short hallway, running straight for the tub. She leapt over the tall sides as if she were once again a teen running hurdles. She dropped her running shoes by the drain, crouched down with her head on top of them and pulled the cushion over her body. In terror, she pinched her eyes shut as tight as she could. The last thing she uttered was one long and terrifying scream, as the same wind that uprooted those trees began to uproot her house.

Evelyn's roof was the first thing to fly away. The wind peeled off the rooftop like one might rip a sheet of paper from a pad. It ripped off several others throughout The Plains. Exterior walls fell next, spinning or rolling away. Pictures and awards on Evelyn's walls flew in every direction. Closets of clothing exploded, sending contents everywhere. Wooden dressers collapsed as easily as cardboard boxes. Once filled with carefully folded socks or running outfits arranged by color, the contents disintegrated like tissue paper flushed down a toilet. Her pantry, stocked with neatly arranged boxes, jars, cans and all things edible, collapsed into heaps of soggy garbage that was kicked in further disarray by the relentless wind. Everything, even things bolted to the earth, vanished in that dark and sudden storm. Thunder boomed like artillery shells, shaking the ground. Lightning struck the earth in flashes brighter than a welder's torch. Everything that resisted this wind was beaten down to the very pavement by torrents of water.

Vern Hart listened to his radio warning of approaching severe weather. He was standing in the small office of his auction house. He pulled out his phone and immediately called Belle. "They say it's going to be bad, Belle, I think you should go to the basement, just to be safe."

"Oh, baby doll," Belle began, "you just worry 'bout me too much."

Belle had just stepped out of the shower and had wrapped herself in a robe. She applied eyeliner and shadow in front of her vanity mirror as they talked. Her phone was on speaker beside her bottles of perfume. Satisfied with her handiwork, she wrapped a towel around her wet hair and slipped her feet into slippers

"No, I'm serious, honey. They say this is a big storm on its way. I need to know you'll be safe."

"Well, OK, but what about you?" she chided. "Are you going to be safe?"

Vern pushed back his trademark ball cap and leaned against the big steel safe, in a pose suggesting a certain degree of casualness. But inside he was overly concerned. "Listen, Belle, I'll be fine. I'll lock up and come right home. But you go to the basement *now,* and you stay there!"

This was a first, Vern commanding Belle to do anything. He might have bribed her. He might have begged her. But Vern never ordered her. Vern was too fearful that dictatorial behavior would send his pretty wife packing. Vern often imagined that Belle would someday leave him. That was the last thing he wanted. Losing her was his constant and only fear. Maybe she wouldn't abandon him for someone else, but she might just up and leave because he didn't deserve her. On this occasion, the approaching storm called for him to act differently. This time, he was more afraid she would lose her life than he was afraid of losing her love.

Belle, for her part, had never known Vern to raise his voice, ever. This new sternness startled her. She picked up on fear in that voice. *He's serious. Is this storm really to be so bad?*

"Baby doll, I hear ya. I'm heading for the basement as we speak. Come home right now. I'll have a Mystic Mama waiting. You hurry. OK?"

"Gotcha, toots. I'll see you in fifteen minutes." Then he added, "I love you," and disconnected.

Belle obeyed her husband. She walked straight for their kitchen, where she pulled two bottles of Mystic Mama from the fridge. She walked down the hallway toward a door that opened to the stairs descending into the lower level of their home. She opened the door, and careful not to stumble in her slippers, stepped down the carpeted stairs into their big, comfortable recreation room.

She knew the storm had arrived when the lights in the windowless room flickered momentarily then went out. Belle found herself in sudden and total darkness. She groped around in search of an end table. Finding the corner with her knee, she fumbled in the darkness with her hands for a drawer. Once located, she pulled the drawer open and rummaged around until she touched the flashlight she had been searching for. The light was one that could be worn as a headband, leaving the wearer hands-free.

With her head wrapped in a terry cloth turban, the straps were useless. Holding the little light in one hand like a traditional flashlight, she fanned the beam around until she located the short refrigerator under the bar. Belle put both bottles inside to keep them cold. There was no electricity to do so. She shrugged. What else could she do? She went back to the couch and lay down, snapping off the light and removing the heavy turban from around her wet hair. In the darkness, she closed her eyes and listened to the muffled sound of wind and rain above.

From the outside, their house looked like a single-story ranch built on a slab. But the Harts had a half basement, their rec room, under the main floor. Extra insulation made the lower room extremely quiet. The shelter served her well this day. But even though soundproof, Belle could feel constant thunder outside. She was blind laying in the darkness, so she could not see the lightning that accompanied the thunder. Fifteen minutes passed slowly in darkness. Vern still did not come down to join her. She started to worry. He should have arrived already.

The ceiling above rumbled and shook violently. She jumped. The racket made her increasingly edgy. Belle's face took on an eerie pallor as she looked into the glow of her cell phone. She planned to call him. The phone proved useless. No bars. No signal. A very loud clap of thunder shook the foundation and rattled anything loose. Belle switched the light back on to have a look around.

Things seemed OK. Sofa and overstuffed chairs in place. Large screen TV still firmly attached to the wall. Lamps sitting on end tables. The fierce noise above, however, continued, louder.

This must be like war, she thought. *People hiding down in shelters, listening to bombs fall.*

She could distinctly hear shrieking wind. Would this storm never let up? For the first time in their marriage, Belle felt a dreadful sense of foreboding for her husband.

Where is he?

She started to pace. She bumped her thigh into the corner of an end table. She curled up back on the couch once again, rubbing the painful spot that no doubt would soon turn into an ugly, purple bruise. But she could not remain still for long. Her mind worked overtime. *Maybe he's in the garage already. Yes, that's it. He's already home, his black Escalade parked right beside mine.*

She reassured herself that Vern was probably sitting in that car, listening for the latest weather report on the storm before coming down. She would find out, in spite of his orders to stay in the basement. She had to be with him.

Belle climbed the plush, carpeted steps, dark in places where the little light in her hand did not reach, lighting only the direction her hand turned it, and then only a few steps ahead. She pushed against the door at the top of the stairwell. The door was jammed closed. She pushed again. The solid door still would not budge. Shoving with her shoulder, she pushed again. The extra effort worked. The door gave way with a groan of protest. Something seemed to be blocking it.

A blast of hot, humid air blew her backward. The wind swirled around her, throwing back her damp hair and blowing open her bathrobe. The air smelled of rain and sweet, moist earth. The scent rubbed against her skin like the gossamer veil of a ghost. It swept past her bare ankles then descended the steps into the darkness below. This was the scent of the natural world, out of place, foreign, inside her home.

Belle was positive she had closed all the doors. Her house windows were never open. There was no need. Harts had whole house air-conditioning. She should not be catching the scent of anything from the outside at all. She rationalized that maybe she simply had not latched one of the doors as well as she thought. And this wind being so strong...

The interior rooms were dark, as if dusk had arrived early. She flipped a light switch before catching herself in the error. *Of course, no electricity. How stupid!*

The sound of falling water and howling wind grew louder still. Belle turned, and with effort, shoved the door to the basement closed. She still could not understand why it worked so hard when, just minutes earlier, it swung on hinges with ease. She moved toward her kitchen. The garage was just on the other side. That's where she would find Vern, sitting in his car. Belle turned the corner in the hall, stepped into the kitchen and that's when she saw it. Her car.

Nothing stood between her and her car. The wall that once separated kitchen from garage lay in shattered pieces all over the kitchen floor, with an enormous chunk leaning outward onto her front yard. A huge gap in the roofline allowed torrents of rainwater to cascade down onto the car and puddle up on her tile floor. Vern's black Escalade was nowhere to be seen. Her own white Escalade, its horn barely groaning in agony, was where she had parked it, inside what had once been their two-car garage. The big vehicle was half as tall as it had once been. Most of the garage roof had crushed the top of the escalade down onto the seats.

Just then another blast of wind collapsed the garage completely. The leaning wall of her kitchen groaned and slid to earth with a deafening crash. Rain, which had been falling away from Belle, suddenly blew all over her. Her robe flew open again, revealing her naked body. Stinging, cold raindrops drenched her in a sudden shower of water and dirty, flying debris. She shrieked, trying to shield herself without success, one arm across her face, another across her torso in a vain attempt at modesty. She spun around and dashed for cover, back to the darkness, back to the unknown.

16

The Tea Basket Quilters waited nearly an hour for the storm to ease up. Only then were they able to depart. The storm moved eastward to continue its path of destruction elsewhere. They, and everyone else who had sheltered inside the darkened restaurant, filed out of the unscathed building and dashed across the parking lot to their automobiles, dodging remnant raindrops still falling lightly in the storm's wake.

Rosie planned to drive back to The Plains with the still-shaken Carolyn by her side. Their homes were only two doors apart. The museum director said he needed to go back to the Historical Society to make sure everything there was undamaged. With the power out, that meant certain problems with their security system. He was positive he'd get called anyway — phone or no phone — by the city police department, if that alarm system had been triggered by the storm or by someone trying to take advantage of the situation.

Although he would have preferred to see Phoebe safely home, Evergreen, too, was a little jittery about his own belongings at the hotel. Still, he offered. Phoebe declined. She insisted that independent Nora ride home with her in the Bug.

Nora poo-pooed that with a wave of her hand. "I have my own car, thank you," and she explained that she only lived a short distance anyway, which was true.

Phoebe therefore made a solo dash for her yellow Beetle. She'd soon find out if any roads leading to her place in the country were blocked by fallen trees.

"Phoebe, dear," Nora called after her. "If you can't get home, you come back and stay with me tonight."

"Thanks, Nora. I'll get home. If not by one road, then by another. But I'll keep your offer in mind... just in case."

Phoebe returned to the older woman, gave her a hug and bid farewell to everyone again.

Arriving at her car, she noticed it looked clean for once. The wind and water had washed away the dust. *Well, that's one blessing*, she thought to herself. Once behind the wheel, Phoebe watched from her side mirror as Bill Evergreen unlocked his Mercedes and climbed in. Her radio came on, still tuned in to a satellite station playing only fifties music. As she punched the button to start the engine, Johnny Mathis, one of her all-time favorites, was singing:

'Though we may never meet again,
'It's not for me to say.'

Phoebe caught herself humming along. "Oh, good god!" She rolled her eyes in disdain and quickly turned the radio off. She pulled away, leaving Evergreen to find his own way to the hotel and the road back to Cleveland.

When all seemed quiet above, Belle re-emerged from her bunker. She looked like a drunk who had taken a shower wearing a robe. Strands of wet curls were plastered around her face and still dripped water from ringlets. Her blue eyes were gray with worry. The look of shock covered her face.

Rain water had found ways to flow into the darkened rec room where she had retreated and where she had dutifully remained until all the sounds of fury above had subsided. She shivered, more in fear than cold. In spite of the storm, the air was still hot, and now it was even more humid than before. She stumbled, closing the door behind her out of habit. There was little point. Half of her house had collapsed away, leaving a huge gap where no garage or wall remained. The huge opening exposed the kitchen and the rest of the house to the elements. Belle's car and her kitchen were partially obscured under a roof which tilted at an impossible angle, teetering unnaturally low. Part of the roof had come to rest on her once-pristine tiled kitchen floor. Splintered wood and pieces of asphalt shingles sprawled out into her yard. In her hand she clutched a useless cell phone.

Several minutes passed before Belle came to the full realization of where she was. She stumbled away from the house. One foot was bare, the other clad in a lone pink slipper. She turned back to stare in disbelief at her once-beautiful home. What she saw was a scene of devastation like none she had ever witnessed. Only then did she clearly understand the danger Vern had warned her about. Only then did she realize that she and Vern were homeless.

Vern.

Belle called out his name, like calling home a child. With no reply, she again yelled, louder. Again, she screamed, louder still, this time fear resonating in her voice. Then she began to scream out for him constantly, hysterically. She yelled his name over and over until finally, a neighbor, who had himself just emerged from his own less-damaged home, saw her standing half dressed in front of what little remained of her house. To him, Belle's house looked for all the world like a bomb had exploded on it. He jogged across the street to her side, as other neighbors, hearing her screams, were themselves beginning to emerge into their own yards.

Law enforcement was soon out in force across the county. Emergency services teams were deployed to the hardest hit areas which, except for one commercial building within the town of Athens, meant most were dispatched to The Plains. The elevation of the village proved to be a liability. Perched higher than Athens and unprotected by surrounding hills, The Plains was wide open to receive the full brunt from the passing storm. Trees toppled over along every street. They uprooted soil around their base or snapped in two, leaving jagged stumps wherever they fell over. Entire homes were destroyed or severely damaged in most parts of the town, while a few were mysteriously spared any damage at all.

The town's four-man street department, along with a small contingent from the county highway department, were soon deployed to tackle the mess scattered across every street. They began the backbreaking and time consuming task of clearing away trees. A single dump truck and one pair of workers arrived from ODOT, the Ohio Department of Transportation, to help clear the state route running down the middle of town. The mayor requested more, but one truck was all ODOT could spare. Many state highways across Athens and surrounding counties needed assistance, too.

Homeowners volunteered to pick up the slack. They emerged from their shelters to assess their own damage and pitch in on the cleanup effort. The town was soon abuzz with a raucous chorus of chain saws on every block. Power crews attended to fallen electric lines, blown transformers and snapped poles. Sheriff's department cruisers barred key intersections. They turned away nosy non-resident peepers trying to get a look at the damage for themselves. Hapless residents were likewise prevented from getting home. No one was permitted to enter until the roadways were cleared. There really was no open roadway in or out of The Plains.

A kid on a bicycle pedaled furiously to the firehouse. He was thrilled to be on an important mission assigned to him by his dad. The task made him feel grown-up and proud. He peddled as fast as his scrawny legs could pump his mountain bike. He jumped the bike off curbs, swung around fallen trees and plowed right through numerous puddles, toward his objective. He had been dispatched to report a hysterical lady who had emerged from the wreckage of her home and needed medical attention. She was over on his street, at an affluent subdivision, on the edge of town. He had to ride at least a mile to reach the station. He arrived, his shirt damp from sweat and puddle water, breathless with excitement to deliver his urgent report to the nearest blue-clad fireman.

"My dad said... you have to come right now..." the boy gasped between breaths. "There's a lady... she's not well... and they have her wrapped up... but she don't look too good... so I came to get you... to get her to the hospital... maybe... and my dad said... she don't have a house any more... and you gotta come take her."

The fireman on duty knelt by the boy and asked where he lived. Once he had an address, he patted the kid's hair and thanked him. He ushered the boy and his mountain bike away from the open station doors and spoke to his supervisor who then put the boy's urgent request into loud motion. A squad dispatched from the firehouse at once. The kid was left standing by to watch the bright-red emergency vehicle pull away. He covered his ears as the siren wailed.

The squad eventually arrived at its destination, but the journey ate up the better part of an hour. They radioed for help not half a mile from the station. Fallen trees made the street impassible. Civilian volunteers, armed with chain saws, swarmed in to come to their aid. Men shoved, pulled or hacked trees to open a slit on the street, barely wide enough to permit the vehicle through. The kid on his bike caught up. He stopped to watch the action. After several more stops to cut away fallen trees, they finally arrived, the boy and his bike waiting for them.

They saw the woman across the street from what had once been her house. She sat in a lawn chair supplied by the neighbor who first saw her. She was wrapped in a blanket and seemed to have recovered somewhat from her hysteria, but she looked to be in shock. She was a mature woman with a certain natural beauty about her, but she was wet from her ordeal. The kid on the bike rolled up beside his father. The little boy beamed with a look of pride and accomplishment on his pink, sweaty face.

The EMT who attended to her first, noticed she wore a blank expression. Eyeliner and mascara, which must have made her blue eyes radiant, streaked down her cheeks, giving her the appearance of a tattered zombie in a cheap horror film.

"Ma'am?" the responder said, as he approached and knelt in front of her. "Ma'am, are you injured?"

He asked her other questions too. All fell on deaf ears. Her eyes did not focus on him but stared blankly past him, toward the rubble from which she had emerged. The EMT did his best to check her body over for obvious signs of wounds. He then asked her, "Is there anyone we can contact to say we're taking you to the hospital?"

At last she looked up, staring directly into his eyes. She saw he was a uniformed man in blue. He was kneeling before her. Tears began to fill her eyes. They fell down her cheeks, streaming eyeliner even farther. In sobbing broken words, all of her fears surfaced. "I don't know... where he is. He didn't come home. I couldn't reach him... my phone is dead. I'm so afraid he's..." Her statement went unfinished. Belle was unable to speak the words she feared most.

The friendly neighbor pulled another EMT aside, out of hearing range of the woman on the lawn chair. "Her name is Belle Hart. That's what's left of her house," he said, indicating the half house with the collapsed roof. "She told me her husband didn't come home. His name is Vern Hart. He owns the big auction house on the edge of town. She thinks the storm caught him somewhere between there and here, because he apparently never made it home."

"Do you know what he drives?" the EMT asked the neighbor.

"Yeah, nice new caddy. Big, black Escalade. License number is H-I-S. Hers is still up there in the garage," he said, indicating the collapsed roof.

"Is anyone else around here hurt?"

"Don't think so. We're fine." They glanced around at the small crowd that had gathered on the lawn. No one requested aid. "Their house seems to be the only one damaged on this block. Like the storm pummeled it, but jumped over all the rest of us."

"If Vern Hart shows up, can you tell him we're taking her to the hospital for evaluation?"

"Right. Yeah, sure."

With that, the two EMT's helped Belle out of the neighbor's blanket and off the lawn chair, then up into the squad. One of the EMT's rode with her in the back, while his partner shut the doors behind them then crawled into the cab. He drove off, flicking on the siren once again as the squad drove back, weaving through a mess of fallen trees.

"But you don't understand — *we live here!*" the woman in the blue Ford Edge, with the real estate sign on the side, argued. "Both of us!"

"Nobody's going past me, lady," the deputy said. "The road isn't cleared. You couldn't get more than one block even if you tried. You're just going to have to wait. They'll radio when the road's clear. Then I'll let you pass."

"Oh, dear," her companion in the passenger seat commented. "What will we do?"

"I recommend you pull over there," the deputy said, pointing to the darkened gas station nearby. "Get off the road so the service trucks can get by." He could see that the passenger in the car seemed distraught. "I'll keep you informed. There's just nothing you can do, and you can't get past all the downed trees and power lines, anyway."

Rosie sighed, patting Carolyn's hand. "We'll do as he says. We'll just have to wait, dear."

She thanked the deputy then made an illegal U-turn in front of him and drove the blue Edge into the gas station lot where he indicated they should wait. Rosie made another smart U-turn maneuver to position the vehicle so they could watch the cop and eventually make an easy exit once he signaled they could.

He didn't seem to mind that she made the U-turn in the middle of the road. There wasn't anything in the other lane, anyhow. Rosie put down all the windows, shut off the engine and tuned in to the local radio station. She wanted to hear any news about the storm or about damage. She was informed immediately.

'The Athens county sheriff has issued a Level 3 emergency. No one, except emergency personnel, should be out on the roads. Anyone caught driving is subject to arrest.

We have been informed that The Plains community has been severely affected. Route 682, The Plains Road and Lemaster Road are closed. No one is permitted to enter or leave until roads are cleared and it is once again safe to drive on them.

Anyone needing assistance should call 911.

The fire department reports that several homes in The Plains have been completely destroyed, and many others damaged. We have word that some people have been transported to the hospital. At this time, we do not have the names of the victims, or their condition.

We will bring you updates as soon as they become available.'

"Oh, dear," said Carolyn. "I hope our homes are OK."

"'Oh, dear' is right," agreed Rosie.

Damage-assessment teams are not usually deployed so soon after a disaster, but this time, local emergency response personnel decided to get them out as quickly as possible, before darkness fell. Officials in disaster services had recently practiced various response scenarios. They felt prepared to assemble needed personnel, both paid and volunteer. Everyone was ready to deploy and perform their appropriate role as soon as they were called into service. Shortwave radio, ham operators, were the first to jump into action. They initiated procedures already in place, reaching agencies and personnel who no longer had telephone service.

A command center and staging area quickly formed southeast of The Plains in the parking lot of the local newspaper. Within two hours, a skeleton crew of assessment volunteers were promptly deployed in pairs as they arrived. Wearing special vests to identify them as officials, they were permitted, on foot, to pass cruisers blocking intersections to everyone else.

Even they were not allowed to drive in. Darkness would fall soon. They were dispatched to work until then.

The first pair of workers was assigned to the one neighborhood reported to have been hardest hit. This team included a retired vet, whose offices had once been located in The Plains. He was familiar with nearly everyone in town and knew them by their pets' names, like parents know others by their children's names. His partner was Sheila Harper, a clerk from the county engineer's office. Sheila lived in Athens, where almost every house had been spared serious damage. She knew few, if anyone, who lived in The Plains. Normally, she would have arrived home by that hour, but everyone, without exception on the engineer's payroll, had been deployed. With phones down and the Level 3 emergency announced over the radio, every disaster-assessment volunteer knew they had to report. Harper's office job was nonessential, so she had been assigned to train in disaster assessment. This was her first assignment. She was delighted to work with the man who had been her own dog's vet, up until his retirement.

As the two of them climbed over or went around fallen trees on their way to their assigned neighborhood, they chatted.

"God, Doc, have you ever seen such devastation?"

"Not here. Looks like a war zone."

"I should say! Where do we start our assessments?"

The vet flipped pages over on his clipboard as he walked. He checked a map he had been given, indicating the street they were assigned. "Right over there. I'll take this side of the first street and walk to the end. How about you grade the other side, and we meet up at the far end. Then we'll work our way east, take that little side street over to the next."

"Sounds good. Your walkie-talkie on channel two?" she asked, checking her own.

"Yes. Call if you need me. Channel one is reserved for emergency personnel."

They split up after climbing over another fallen tree blocking the entrance to their first street. He went left, and she went to the right side. They began jotting down house numbers and giving each a score based on their observations from the street. These were preliminary figures that officials would use to determine if they should declare a disaster emergency and seek state or federal funds to help in the recovery. They would turn in their score sheets to a supervisor back at the command station when they were finished. If there was still daylight, they would be assigned other streets to assess. Eventually, the entire town would have each home scored and the data collated. Someone at the command center would estimate the recovery cost associated with their findings.

The former vet had a longer stride than the shorter office worker, so he covered his half of the street sooner than she did hers. As promised, he waited for her to catch up.

"Other than trees and a few shingles, this part looks OK," she told him.

"I'll take the west side. You go east. We'll met up again at the end."

"Gotcha. See you soon."

The pair once again parted. Clipboards in hand, they continued to note house numbers, giving each a score from zero to ten, ten being a total loss and the zero indicating no visible damage. The former vet moved off quickly, and the office worker lagged behind once again. Her side of the street seemed to have been hit harder than his. Yards on her side rose slightly upward. Limbs from fallen maple and pines often obscured her view of what lay beyond. She struggled over fallen trees periodically to get closer to inspect some of the buildings, sometimes having to hunt for a house number.

At one place, she fought her way through a tangle of uprooted maples and came face-to-face with the first house to score a ten on her clipboard. The house had been a new one, by the looks of the others nearby. They, too, received somewhat higher scores on her sheet. But this particular one, however, was certainly a total loss. A white, antique bathtub was the only thing left standing in place. The house, if it had been one, had once rested on a concrete slab. The tub was now surrounded by empty cement block footers, where walls might once have stood just hours earlier. She had to guess what its number might have been, based on its neighbors. She stared at the scene with awe for several seconds. Her eye then detected movement. Something shifted inside the lonely bathtub.

Sheila's heart started pounding in her chest. As she struggled to quicken her pace up the litter-strewn lawn and around tree branches, she tried to avoid stepping on nails or shards of glass. Still climbing upward, she flipped on her walkie-talkie. "Doc? Doc! I... I found somebody. Can you come? I think somebody's hurt."

Phoebe's favorite way home was blocked by a hundred-year-old oak, sprawled across one of the county roads. She executed a three-point turn and backtracked to the nearest intersection, a narrow township road she had only driven down once since living in the country. She thought she remembered that the lane cut through a small wood lot, and the rest passed through pasture land. A few miles later, she came upon the hollow where the road traversed through the woods. A small tree leaned precariously over the lane. Phoebe estimated the trunk was high enough for her to squeeze the Beetle underneath. She advanced the little car, slowly edging under the small tree until hearing the sound of branches scraping the convertible top. She stopped, then backed up until she was clear of the tree. Not to be foiled, she punched a button above the window and put down the convertible top.

Once the dash light signaled the top was locked, she drove slowly forward. This time, the leaning tree only flipped water on her as she drove the windshield under its branches. She squealed as cold water droplets sprayed her face and ripped down her back, but she continued to edge the car slowly forward.

"Ha! Damn tree, thought you had me, didn't you?" she scolded.

Beyond the fallen tree, the road ahead looked clear. She pushed the button once again, which brought the top back up and locked in place, enclosing her once again inside.

At the next intersection, she turned right onto a county roadway. Here the road climbed out of the valley, until she traveled again along the ridgetop. The way seemed clear for at least a quarter mile ahead. Around a bend she came across another uprooted tree, a huge old sycamore laying across and totally blocking the road. Several locals with chain saws were busy hacking off branches. The crew looked like they might clear the road soon, so Phoebe stopped the Beetle a safe distance away and shut off the engine. She climbed out and joined a group of women standing in a yard nearby watching the workers.

"Your men?" Phoebe asked the group of four women.

They smiled at her. One spoke. "Wouldn't expect the county to come out this far. Probably everyone's working in The Plains. Radio said the town got hit real bad."

This was news to Phoebe. She had unwisely selected the public radio station to listen to after opting not to listen to Johnny Mathis. She should have known better, silently scolding herself. The university station covered such a vast area of the region that they hardly ever bothered to cover minute details of single villages.

"What did you hear?" she asked.

"We're on a Level 3. You better be careful you don't get arrested driving," one woman said, pointing at her yellow car.

Phoebe snorted. "If the engineer won't come out this far, I'm guessing the sheriff won't either."

They all laughed. People who lived beyond the city limits of Athens, the county seat, rarely, if ever, saw a cruiser, unless the deputy inside was delivering a subpoena or making a visit to a well-known criminal. The same went for the county highway department. If they weren't treating the roadways with tar and pebbles once every decade, or they weren't plowing after a snowstorm, they were not likely to be out doing preventive maintenance. Most folks living in the townships of Athens County, rarely saw road crews, sometimes not for months. Locals had learned to rely on themselves, a remnant, though necessary, behavior of the Appalachian way.

"You live out this way?" another woman asked, as Phoebe stood with the small party, watching the men cut up the fallen tree.

"'Bout four miles that way, over on the next ridge."

"Well, you might as well have a glass of iced tea while you wait. You take sweet or unsweet?" the woman asked.

"Sweet would be nice. Not much, though. I just had dinner in town."

"How was it in Athens?" another women standing nearby asked.

"Dark. Power went out with the storm."

"Same here. We heard on the radio that the weatherman said winds were clocked at one hundred and thirty miles an hour in some places. He said that's equal to a Category 4 hurricane on the ocean. Have you ever heard of such a thing? We lost our electric around six. But except for that and this tree, we all fared well. No damage to our homes at all, thanks to the hills we've got around here. The weatherman said houses got destroyed over in The Plains. Guess they got hit pretty bad."

The woman who had asked Phoebe if she wanted tea soon returned from her house, carrying a large glass with a long-handled spoon. She served her tea over ice. Little did she, or anyone else, realize this was to be the last ice some of them would have for a week. She rejoined the group standing together in what obviously was her front yard, thereby making her hostess of this little impromptu disaster party.

"Here ya go. Cold and sweet. I'm Helen Freeman," the woman said, handing Phoebe the glass. "Ted and my sons, RJ and John, along with these ladies' husbands, are down there on that tree," she said, indicating the crew reducing the tree to a log.

Multiple chain saws cut viciously into limbs. The men were stripping the fallen tree of its branches. The youngest boys, ten or eleven years old by the look of their small size, were tasked with the chore of dragging the limbs off the roadway and into the ditch.

"They'll have that tree cleared off soon. So drink up!"

For some who lived in the countryside, natural disasters provided opportunities to renew old acquaintances or strike up new ones. Groups of men donned brown coveralls, fired-up tractors, snowblowers or chain saws, and neighbors helped neighbors. Winter storms that dropped twelve inches of snow created rare but near-festive opportunities, as did this particular storm. Everyone emerged, eager to help. Cookies came out of freezers, and pitchers of cold water or iced tea filled glasses. Conversation helped to pass the time for the idle among them. Old friends huddled over hot cups while they warmed up after plowing out each other's drives in the winter. Tractors come out to pull cars out of ditches or, in this case, to shove tree trunks off roadways. Sometimes women pitched in. But for this evening's disaster, the women of this group elected to sweat off the event just standing by and supervising. The never-ending heat and humidity made work uncomfortable, even after this storm.

"So maybe the worst didn't come out this way," Phoebe observed, as she sipped on the cold beverage. The ice felt good, trickling down her throat. She enjoyed the sweetness.

"Would seem so. I s'pose you'll find your place will be OK. Anybody home?"

"No. I live alone," Phoebe said.

"Well, you have to stop back again sometime, after this is all over," her hostess, Helen Freeman, said.

Phoebe smiled. She was often overly cautious around strangers. This Helen Freeman seemed like a nice person though, and friendly, like her companions. But Phoebe so rarely drove this way, she knew she would probably not pass by again anytime soon. She thanked the woman for the invitation just the same. "Do you work anywhere?" Phoebe asked, just to keep conversation going.

"Here on the farm, that's all," she explained. "We raise market lambs and chickens. We sell direct to a restaurant in Columbus."

"Wow," Phoebe said. "That's a long way away. Eighty miles or so?"

"Closer to ninety from the farm. But they pay top dollar, and they're happy to get pasture-fed organic meat. Even our chickens are pastured."

Phoebe listened politely as Helen explained, more than Phoebe cared to know, about the process of raising stock that could be classified as 'organic' or strictly 'pasture-fed.' She heard where the animals went to be processed, too. Phoebe didn't like thinking too much about the word, 'processed' and what that really meant for the lamb or rooster.

"So you see, we can ask and get top dollar for our meat. We make enough each year to keep ourselves clothed and fed. What about you?"

"Oh, I'm retired."

"But you look so young!"

"I started work right out of college. Hit my thirty years of service a decade ago and quit."

"What do you do with your time?"

"I have a little vegetable garden I tend, and several flower beds that keep me busy and I piece quilts for fun."

"Oh, I love quilts!" Helen said. "Do you hand quilt them?"

"No. I prefer machine quilting. Do you quilt?"

"Why, yes I do. I just joined a new guild, too. We're called the Shining Stars. Do you know it?"

Phoebe knew of Evelyn's guild and nodded her head.

"We've been selling raffle tickets for this beautiful quilt by Avery Underwood. Do you know her?"

Again Phoebe nodded.

"You should come to one of our meetings, but I don't know when the next one will be," Helen said, with great enthusiasm. "I'll bet you'd love it!"

"I'm not so sure your president would love seeing me there. She quit the Tea Basket Quilters not long ago, in quite a snit. I'm one of their members."

"Oh. I wasn't aware of another guild, or that she quit it. She didn't say," the woman commented. "What happened?"

Phoebe tried to explain. "Evelyn believed we should not hold an auction, but rather raise money the way we had always done so, with a raffle. She quit guild because we voted for the auction. So you're selling the raffle tickets she wanted us to sell. I am pleased to hear Avery provided the quilt. I'm sure it's beautiful. Avery does nice work."

"So you plan to hold an auction?" the woman asked.

"Already did. Auction was this afternoon, long before the storm arrived."

"Out of curiosity, if you don't mind sharing, did you do well?"

"Astoundingly well," Phoebe said, without betraying the total.

"Well, congratulations then. I hope we do OK with our little raffle. Evelyn seems to think we'll win a longarm quilting machine."

Phoebe smiled. "I don't think that will happen."

By then the men with chain saws had finished removing all the tree's limbs. They retreated to a spot out of the way of the tractor with a fork attachment on the front. The man behind the wheel eased the fork under one end of the tree and began to push it forward. One end of the tree moved off the road. The other end pivoted backward. He backed up, repositioned the tractor more to the center of the log and then gently shoved it forward again. This time the long trunk rolled completely off the roadway. With the roadway cleared, the men approached the tree with their saws and began sectioning off chunks.

Phoebe returned the tea glass to her hostess, with thanks and a goodbye. She retreated to her car, turned over the engine and felt a blast of refreshing, cool air through the vents. She still had four more miles to drive before reaching her cabin. She hoped she would come upon no more downed trees along the way. However, meeting more neighbors would be nice. Maybe informative, too.

The retired vet reached Harper's side quickly, running with those long legs of his. Together they picked their way carefully through what remained of the house. Sheila kept her distance once they reached the bathtub. The vet pulled back a green, floral cushion which had been on top of a person laying in the tub. He saw a wild mass of red curls, and the frame of a tiny, barefoot woman clad in a blue jogging suit. The bathtub drain was apparently plugged, because she was laying in six inches of dirty water. If not for the running shoes tucked under her chin, the woman might have drowned in the tub.

He touched her shoulder gently and spoke. "Can you hear me?" he began. "Are you able to move? Are you hurt?" As he waited for a response, he noticed no sign of blood on her or in the water. He turned to Sheila. "Switch to channel one and report finding a survivor. Female. I'd say around fifty, sixty years old."

Evelyn stirred slightly. Every muscle in her body ached. She was disoriented. Why was someone talking to her? Why was she wearing her clothes in the tub? Why was she even in the tub at all? She managed only an inarticulate groan.

"Easy," said the vet, as if calming a nervous horse. "We'll soon have you out. What's your name?"

"Ev... eh... lyn," she managed to mumble.

"Well, Evelyn, let's see if we can get this water drained away."

The vet fumbled around her head and under the running shoes as carefully as he could, until his fingers located the drain hole. He discovered that her red hair and the shoes had formed a tight plug, preventing water from draining out. He carefully removed the shoes from under the tangle of hair. He then pulled a mass of orange curls out of the drain and gently brushed wet locks away from the woman's face. She looked extremely pale and thin. The water drained away immediately.

"I think you should lay still until paramedics arrive, just to be on the safe side, in case you're injured," he told her.

Evelyn didn't care. She felt water drain away from her body. She also felt an uncommon gratefulness that there was someone looking out for her. Then she passed out.

The next morning continued hot and muggy. The temperature climbed to one hundred degrees, making recovery difficult for those on the job.

"Where's the owner?" asked the man beside the cop.

The disaster-assessment volunteer and a sheriff's deputy were searching the rubble of what had once been Hart Auction House. The structure, which had once stood as a vast, cavernous pole building over a cement slab, was now a massive pile of splintered poles, mangled roofing and soggy insulation, tossed forward over a crumpled black Escalade. The deputy knew Vern Hart. He knew the Escalade was his without having to call in the license number. That the car was still on the premises meant that Vern was also. The deputy surveyed the scene of devastation. He thought he'd find Vern, but he was uneasy about the condition he'd find him in. He ordered the volunteer to go around to the other side of the rubble.

"Be careful. Don't crawl up over anything. Just use your eyes and ears. Listen. Call out if you hear anything!"

The volunteer circled the enormous pile toward the right. The deputy circled left. He got as close to the Escalade as he could without adding his own weight to the metal siding laying haphazardly over it. He could see where the windshield should have been. The glass was broken out. Particles littered the crushed hood and dash, and sparkled on metal roofing nearby. He didn't have a clear line of sight inside the vehicle.

"Hello!" he called out toward the Escalade, his voice big and booming, just like Vern's. He listened intently. No response came back. He detected no movement inside.

The disaster-assessment volunteer was duplicating the deputy's approach. He called out Vern's name periodically, then stopped to listen for a response. He, too, neither heard nor saw anything in reply.

The two met at the back of the exposed slab. Poles snapped in two and walls ripped from the foundation were all pummeled to the ground. The direction of the wind collapsed the entire building forward on top of the Escalade, tossing lighter pieces out into the gravel parking lot beyond. The deputy was certain no one inside could have survived. He shook his head in resignation. The two men walked side by side back to the waiting cruiser.

"This is a ten, a total loss," said the volunteer, making notes on his clipboard. "Man, I sure wouldn't want to be inside when that storm hit."

"No kiddin'," commented the cop. He opened his cruiser door, reached for the mic and reported his location. "Send in the K9 unit. We have a possible fatality."

The volunteer touched the bill of his ball cap, indicating he planned to move off. Damage assessment was one thing, but he felt squeamish about finding bodies in rubble. He wanted to leave to continue his task elsewhere.

As he walked off, eager to avoid what might come next, the deputy decided to walk the perimeter one more time.

He continued to call out Vern's name as he walked around, waiting for the county's search and rescue and K9 unit to arrive. He was certain their canine officer would successfully sniff out the body. The handler would release the dog to traverse the rubble where a heavy man shouldn't go. If anyone was underneath the pile, the added weight of a dog wouldn't cause further injury to a live victim. Big if. But if a body was located, the rubble could be put aside and the person retrieved.

Officer Dale and his canine partner, Ulla, arrived on the scene by the time the deputy completed a second circuit of the fallen auction house. Roads and streets were slowly getting cleared. Vern's place was on the edge of town. It had taken all night, clearing downed power lines and trees, to reach his part of town.

"God, what a mess!" declared Dale, stepping out of the vehicle. He opened the rear door of the cruiser to let the dog out. She was a big breed, a Malinois, used by the county for a number of scenarios. Today's challenge was either a search and rescue or a cadaver search.

"Bring her over here. Vern Hart's the owner. This is his car. Let Ulla get the scent from it."

Officer Dale, with Ulla on a leash, approached the semi-crushed Escalade. Dale commanded her to search, releasing her from the leash. Full of energy and eager to please her handler, Ulla immediately began to sniff the outside of the car. Dale gingerly stepped under collapsed roofing to the Escalade's door. With some difficulty, he pried open the passenger's door as far as the rubble on top allowed. Ulla squeezed past him, into the vehicle interior. She wiggled over the seat to the back then came back to the front. The dog gave no indication that any person was inside.

Officer Dale called the dog out and rewarded his canine partner with her favorite toy — a ball. The two moved away from the car, then the cop took her ball and signaled for Ulla to search. Without hesitation, the dog bounded off, her tail flying back and forth with glee. She leaped over splintered two-by-sixes and twisted rooftop metal, with her nose close to the surface. She crisscrossed warped and bent roofing and splintered lumber numerous times. Sometimes she would vanish behind a portion of the structure that protruded upward. She'd soon come back into sight again, her tail still flying and her nose at work. The dog's excitement was an obvious indicator that Vern's scent was all over his former auction house. That made the dog's search more challenging.

Several minutes passed while she searched. Then the dog stopped. She sat down on her haunches, facing Officer Dale. She was signaling to him. She had located her quarry. Vern.

"Shit," said the deputy to his fellow officer. "I'll call it in."

Officer Dale called Ulla to his side, clipping the leash back on her collar. He gave the dog her favorite ball once again and praised Ulla for doing her job well. The other deputy dispatched the dog's findings.

The distant sound of a siren slowly approached. EMT's were on their way. When the vehicle arrived and the men exited, Officer Dale unleashed Ulla, commanding her, once again, to search. She galloped across the fallen building and immediately sat down in the same spot on the pile of rubble where she had previously indicated she had located Vern Hart.

Dale called the dog back, again rewarded her with the ball and led her back to the cruiser.

The two EMT's who had just arrived began to crawl gingerly over the top of the flattened auction house to reach the location indicated by the Malinois. One laid down on the roofing, trying to peer through a crack into the darkened space below. The two men spent several minutes in conversation, assessing how best to get to the body through the tangled heap of metal and wood.

"Gonna need a 'hoe for this," said one. "Big rafters down there, each one laying on top of the next."

"Did you hear something?" asked the other, still lying prone. He wasn't sure if his ears had picked up the sound of debris shifting below, or if he had heard something else.

"What?"

"Shhh. Listen!"

184

17

$\mathcal{N}$ora arrived home the previous evening, relieved to find no apparent damage to the outside of her house. At first glance, only the yard seemed affected. Leaves ripped from trees littered her manicured lawn everywhere. To be safe, she decided she would call on her handyman soon to ask him to do a thorough walkabout, including up on her roof. Assuming she had no electricity, Nora did not bother trying to open her garage door with the remote. Instead, she used a key to let herself in through an outside door. Once inside, she absentmindedly flipped the wall switch to turn on her kitchen light. She was, indeed, among those in Athens without power.

Her car would have to stay parked outside until her handyman arrived. He would have to release the track motor and lift the heavy door manually. The thing was too heavy for Nora to budge. She picked up the telephone receiver and listened for a dial tone. Of course, landlines were also out. Nora shrugged off the inconvenience. Her handyman knew she lived alone. He would no doubt check on her tomorrow. He was a good helper and a nearby neighbor who may, she assumed, have storm damage of his own to attend to.

Nora went to a hall closet and pulled out a box of battery-operated candles, as well as some wax candles in a pleasing array of scents. She busied herself leaving a fragrant trail of them around her house, in preparation for the long, dark evening ahead. In her bedroom closet, she retrieved a battery-powered radio. She returned to her living room where she put the little radio on a stand nearest a window by a chair. She then retrieved fresh batteries from the kitchen and busied herself replacing old ones. She closed up the battery compartment to the radio and tuned in to a local station.

'...Several homes were completely destroyed, with most of the reported damage occurring in The Plains. The county remains under a Level 3. Stay tuned for further developments, as they become known. We return now to our regular program.'

"Oh, dear, did you hear that?" Nora asked the radio.

A 'newfangled' song, as she called them, began to annoy her. She lowered the volume, growing suddenly concerned for her guild friends who lived in The Plains. She knew that Rosie and Carolyn lived practically next door to each other. Belle Hart, and even Evelyn North, also had homes in The Plains. With no way to contact any of them, Nora had to calm her impatient need-to-know and console herself with the knowledge that at least Rosie and Carolyn themselves were safe. She knew them to be wise women, and therefore, if their homes had sustained damage, they would undoubtedly have the insurance coverage and the wherewithal to set things to rights. Then she wondered, had they even yet arrived home?

She pulled a quilt out of a basket beside the chair and ran her hand along the edge, looking for the last place she had stitched the binding to the back. She found where she had pulled up the thread to await her return. She plucked a needle out of a pin cushion beside the radio on the stand. She squinted in the fading light, looking for the eye of the needle, then she threaded the strand through it. With a sigh, Nora turned the binding over to the back and continued the task in the fading light of the evening. While she plied her needle to fabric, she let her mind wander, thinking about her friends.

As Nora settled in her comfortable chair, Carolyn and Rosie passed the time fidgeting in Rosie's Ford parked at the gas station, watching nothing but that deputy sheriff's cruiser blocking them from their destination.

"Holy moly," Rosie muttered, growing more impatient with each passing hour. "Do you think that guy will *ever* let us go home?"

"He probably forgot all about us, Rosie. Maybe we should go ask him again if we can go home *now*."

"Good idea. After sitting here two hours, I have to pee!" Rosie said, as she fired up the Ford, put it in gear and aimed for the cruiser.

When she pulled alongside the deputy's car, Rosie rolled down the window. She told the uniformed sheriff their exact addresses and asked, once again, if they could pass.

"We've been away from our homes all day, officer. I'm sure our husbands must be worried sick about us. And I'm telling you now, that if I don't get to a bathroom real soon, I'm going to be in serious, serious trouble."

The deputy gave a half smile and said, "Wait here." He turned his back to the women, reached into his car through an open widow and picked up the radio mic to speak.

Rosie could not hear his words, but he soon returned.

"You have to follow my instructions to the letter. Do you understand? All roads aren't yet cleared. Some are still quite impassable."

Rosie nodded with eagerness.

The deputy pointed down the main street, his beefy hand indicating precisely where she had to turn off. He was directing her down streets she would never have taken, but she understood he was relaying the only way cleared so far.

"You won't be able to drive all the way up your own street. Don't leave this car in the roadway. Pull completely off the road so trucks can pass. You'll have to walk a block, maybe two, to get to your houses."

"Thank you. We'll do exactly as you instruct, to the letter. Thank you again." Rosie looked to her companion with a smile, put the Ford in gear and drove away from the cruiser, down an isolated main street, making her way, finally, toward home.

"Oh, dear, I hope everything's OK at home," muttered Carolyn. "I pray Ben is OK. And say, what was all that about *our* husbands, anyway?"

Rosie, who was single, only smiled at her longtime friend.

They were, in fact, able to get the Ford to within five hundred feet of their homes. Several old silver maples, toppled by the fierce winds, lay blocking the roadway to vehicular traffic. But the fallen trees allowed passage of two elderly women on foot, who were both clutching handbags and walking briskly toward their respective bathrooms. Other than the mess of uprooted and downed trees, everything else looked as well as could be expected on their cul-de-sac. A few shingles littered the street here and there, but all the houses they passed looked to be OK from their observation point, hustling down the middle of the lane. Both women were relieved to see that their neighbors had dodged the severe damage reported on the radio.

Ben Ashcroft greeted his wife with a welcome and reassuring hug at the front door where he had been standing vigil. A quick embrace and a peck on the cheek, Carolyn assured him she was unharmed but in dire need of their bathroom. She immediately dashed past him on her urgent mission.

Rosie, who lived only a few doors from her friend, arrived to her seemingly unscathed house without electricity. After her own potty stop, Rosie made a cursory round of each room to assure herself that all the windows had survived and no water damage appeared anywhere. Satisfied, she immediately went back out the front door, heading straight over to Carolyn and Ben's house to check on their situation.

Phoebe finally arrived home to a pair of anxious, prancing pugs as she opened the front door. She was quite relieved to find no damage whatsoever to her log cabin. The pugs were obviously upset with her for having been absent during the storm. They told her so in no uncertain pug voices. Their 'woo, woo, woos' always meant that Phoebe had been naughty. Their master had broken a pug rule, a serious transgression. Phoebe hugged each pug in turn then walked with them outside toward her garden. She wanted to inspect conditions in the vegetable patch. Both pugs followed and relieved themselves after circling repeatedly in an effort to find the absolute best spot to pee. Duties completed, they began their serious inspection of the wet grounds and garden.

Phoebe pushed through the garden gate to find that her vegetable garden had fared badly. The wind did blow this far south of town. Her beautiful rows of corn stalks listed ninety degrees toward the east, flattened by the strong winds. Bush beans were pressed to the ground, with leaves and beans covered in brown clay. The heavy rain had rushed over everything the wind had flattened. Cucumber leaves were stripped from their vines and plastered against the inside of her seven-foot, welded wire perimeter fence. The naked vines still clung tenaciously to a wooden trellis that supported them. Developing cucumbers dangled like enormous earrings from their skinny, green, leafless vines.

The perennials had fared better. Though the asparagus fronds were also askew, they were long past production, so they were of little concern to Phoebe. The fruit trees were relatively young and had withstood the winds, having lost only a few leaves. Her young blueberry bushes seemed well enough. But standing there, observing her garden, Phoebe could see that she would have to wait several days before she could clean up the mess and restore order to her beloved garden. The clay would require days to thoroughly dry up. She was sad to see evidence that much of the rain water had merely run across the garden on its way down the south-sloping bed. This had not been the gentle, soaking rain she had longed for. Even her garden hose, which lay down the middle of the garden, was half-buried, hidden under eroded soil that had washed over the top of it.

The pugs had wandered off to inspect a nearby toad under the asparagus fronds. Phoebe sighed then called Stitch and Medallion to her side. She pushed through her garden gate, pugs at her heels, and returned to the cabin. Night would come soon. She needed to find her flashlight and kerosene lamps before darkness. To her dismay, the evening was still hot and disgustingly humid.

Avery never saw a movie. After the harrowing experience of enduring the storm from inside her truck, she drove away from Larry's as soon the storm eased. Few vehicles were out on the streets or the bypass. That was fortunate. Traffic lights were nonfunctional everywhere. Shops at the mall, the big grocery store, and all the fast-food joints along State Street, were dark and appeared empty. Some of the establishments had front doors ajar with an employee or two standing guard, probably, she assumed, to turn away customers. The movie theater was also dark. No business had electricity.

It was a wonder to Avery why commercial places didn't keep some form of old-technology backup systems to handle simple cash transactions in cases of power outages. Then Avery thought that maybe most people don't use cash any more. She herself had started relying more and more on a debit card, leaving funds in the bank. Was money just data on some bank computer? Every transaction these days required the use of electricity.

She recalled, as a kid, hearing about cash registers that did not use electricity to function, at all. They relied on an operator pressing certain tabs to ring up sales, with the resulting sound of a little bell to announce the cash drawer flying open. But of course, that contraption required tellers who could not only operate the register, but more importantly, to calculate in their heads the correct amount of change to return to a customer.

Those were the days, she scoffed to herself.

She recalled a big bulldozer operator who always fiddled with his change every time he paid for lunch. He hated carrying coins in his jeans. He was forever converting smaller denominations into quarters. Every time he'd pay for lunch, he'd hand over a fistful of coins with bills, which always exceeded the actual cost of his lunch, but would return one quarter to him in change. The poor pimple-faced boy behind the counter could almost never calculate the difference. God forbid if pennies and nickels were involved in the transaction. That usually resulted in a blank stare of dumbfoundedness or beads of sweat appearing on the young, hairless upper lip of the cashier. Avery chuckled with the memory, one of the few funny ones she remembered of her days on the road with the guys.

With a sigh of regret, Avery made a U-turn at the empty movie parking lot and drove back toward her home. Her apartment was on the first floor of a two-story, four-unit building. Aside from being small, constructed more with college students in mind than families, the small complex was well made, located in a relatively quiet neighborhood and set close to the street. Two upstairs apartments had private steps leading to their entrance doors, set directly above the back doors of each downstairs apartment. The effect gave each lower apartment an overhang, protecting its rear entry. Avery's lower apartment was faced with brick, well insulated and clean. Each apartment was well maintained, unlike some of the other student rentals around Athens. The complex was elevated above floodplain on a raised lot which was composed of a paved parking lot to the rear and a tiny, grassy strip of lawn to the front. The owners kept the grass mowed in the summer and the parking lot plowed in the winter.

Upon arriving at her apartment, Avery discovered a window pane in the kitchenette broken out by flying limbs. Tiny shards of splintered glass fanned across her linoleum floor. Avery sighed with weariness, but in fact, she was grateful one broken window was the only damage she had to face. She quickly retrieved a broom and dustpan from the hall closet and set about sweeping up the shattered glass. She emptied the glass into her trash can, creating the sound of a second crash. She scanned around, satisfied that she had most, if not all, of it located and binned. Her next problem was a wet floor. A puddle had collected, in the absence of glass in the window. In her efforts to clean up glass, she'd spread the water all over. Most of her floor was now wet. Avery sighed again. She exchanged the broom and dustpan for a sponge mop and bottle of floor polish.

Avery debated whether to leave the gaping hole where the pane had been, or to place something over the opening, before she tackled the floor. Having some airflow across the floor seemed like an attractive idea. She decided otherwise. Waiting an hour for the wax to dry, with an open window, probably wasn't the smartest thing to do. Avery didn't know if more rain and wind were predicted. She set aside her mop temporarily and retrieved a chunk of cardboard destined for recycling. She fashioned a temporary replacement for the missing pane, using scissors and duct tape from a cabinet drawer.

Satisfied her repair would hold, Avery finally tackled the chore of her wet floor. She waxed her way out of the kitchen then set the mop aside. Finally, she made the rounds of her small apartment, checking for any further damage. Everything elsewhere seemed to have survived intact. She decided to open her front door to admit air since there was no functioning air conditioner, and she'd worked up a sweat mopping the floor. The storm had done nothing to reduce the humidity. Tomorrow she thought she might check on her guild, make sure that members of *both* her guilds were OK.

18

The clerk and retired vet wrapped up their first day's disaster assessment, after the squad hauled away the tiny woman rescued from the solitary bathtub. Their discovery put their recordkeeping task in a whole new light. The excitement gave them a new sense of worth. As they walked together toward the command station, they engaged in animated conversation about their unexpected discovery. Both agreed to return the next day, if needed, to assess additional streets. Perhaps they would find and save yet another soul, though chances of that were slim, and in reality, neither really wanted to find anyone else. After all, they were not first responders.

The vet departed as soon as he turned in his reports, but Sheila Harper decided she'd wander back toward the lone bathtub. She could not get the image out of her mind, so stark white and out of place, perched over the dirty rubble that had once been that woman's home. Sheila simply had to return. She planned to snap a photo before total darkness fell.

In the excitement of the moment, discovering the woman in the tub and calling for help, she had not once thought to make a digital recording of the scene. She now planned to post a picture of the lone tub on her Facebook page. She'd tell her friends about finding the woman crumpled inside, laying half-drowned in water and covered over by a big cushion. She'd tell about the squad arriving, its sirens ablaze, then hauling the woman off to the hospital. Maybe the weird image of the claw-footed tub would get lots of shares — hundreds, thousands, maybe go viral. Wouldn't that be cool? The thought excited her. Nothing she had posted had ever gone viral.

She walked back toward the street where they'd found the woman. Another short distance up the lane and she arrived at the lot. There stood the lone, white porcelain tub atop a heap of crumpled lumber and busted drywall. Sheila pulled a cell phone out of her hip pocket, framed the scene on her little screen, then touched the phone and took the photo. The light of day was fading fast. The shot turned out to be of very poor quality. She deleted it. She needed to get in closer, or the next one would be washed out, as well. She needed the flash close enough to clearly light up the weird spectacle. Carefully stepping around the remnants and scraps of the woman's former home, she found a spot that seemed perfect.

She was up close now, standing within a few feet of the tub. Her feet were anchored on a slab covered in tile. She thought she might have been standing in the woman's former kitchen. She noticed small holes in the tile, a short distance away. Copper pipes protruded through them, twisted and snapped off near the top. She imagined a sink probably rested above them, but that was now gone. One entire wall lay nearby teetering on its side, a built-in oven still attached, but its door gaping open at an odd angle. Bringing the phone up in front of her face, she framed the image and once again touched the camera.

Her second shot was a keeper. Satisfied, she typed a brief comment then posted the image to her Facebook page. She pocketed the phone, took one final look at the tub and then let her gaze take in the rest of the devastation that lay all about in the fading light. Nothing appeared salvageable. Every item exhibited signs of having been recklessly tossed about then drenched in dirty water: a toaster oven all banged up and missing its door; dishwasher pods spilled from a plastic tub and dissolving on the dirty lawn; kitchen utensils strewn all over. Still, she didn't want to make things any worse by stomping anything deep into the mud. So she carefully turned to retreat back through the littered yard.

Her heel snagged something, which sent her off balance. She stumbled off the tile, falling down toward wet grass. With a spin and quick footwork, she faced the direction of her fall. She was able, just barely, to spare the indignity of landing in mud. Instead, one foot slid forward, landing her on her other knee. The sliding foot stretched to its absolute limit out in front of her. She glanced quickly around to verify no one saw her ungraceful maneuver and was relieved that she had fallen down in privacy.

As she attempted to right herself, two items ahead of her forward foot caught her eye. One was a purse which she assumed must have belonged to the woman in the bathtub. The other item was a large, clear plastic bag, containing what appeared to be a blanket. Toppled kitchen chairs had concealed them from street view. She could make out a bit of writing on a corner of the bag. Was it a note? Once upright, Sheila stepped forward to examine the object more closely. She turned on the light from her phone for assistance. The purse on top was still fastened shut, its contents intact. She thought she would deliver the purse to the authorities at once. The woman probably needed ID at the hospital and perhaps other documents within. The note inside the bag turned out to be a label attached to a quilt. The label read:

A Mystery Quilt
Pieced by Avery Underwood
Quilted by…

There was more, but she stopped short at the name. Avery Underwood seemed familiar. After a few moments, she recalled a face to go with the name. The face belonged to a tall woman with short, cropped hair, wearing large, studious glasses. Sheila remembered her from the office. Underwood had dropped off a resume, hoping for work. Everyone had been impressed and much in awe of her credentials. The county engineer told Sheila he was planning to call her in for an interview soon.

This blanket, or rather this quilt, is hers? Why is it here in The Plains?

Sheila remembered Underwood having listed her home address as a street and apartment number in Athens. She decided, at that moment, that she'd take the quilt, too. Next time she got back to the office, she'd look up Underwood's phone number and give her a call. Perhaps she was mistaken. Maybe she'd look up Underwood's address first, just to be sure she was correct in her memory, that Underwood did, in fact, live in Athens. Maybe Underwood had moved. No, that couldn't be. The skinny little woman from the bathtub was definitely not the tall and boyish-looking Avery Underwood she remembered.

Sheila Harper needed to get to her car. Darkness had fully descended. She worried that she might be mistaken for a looter — even though she was in fact a looter — by walking off with someone's purse and quilt, neither of which belonged to her. Thank goodness she still wore the vest identifying her as a county official. She'd drop the quilt off in her car, then the purse with the authorities inside the command station. Tomorrow, before coming back, she'd go to the engineer's office early and pull Underwood's file.

Cuts and bruises walked in and out of the hospital's ER, following the derecho. The evening presented a steady flow of patients for the hospital staff to treat. Nothing had been too serious — no major traumas, and fortunately, no deaths. Only a few arrived by squad, and fewer still had to be admitted. When the EMTs, bringing Belle, radioed ahead that they had another woman, probably in shock, the staff was more than ready to receive and treat her.

The nurse on duty met the EMTs rolling the woman in on their gurney and immediately began taking notes on a clipboard as they reported the woman's vital signs. She smiled down at the bedraggled face, put a warm, gloved hand on Belle's arm and assured her everything was going to be OK. She then indicated to the EMTs which bay to park Belle into for the doctor on duty to perform his examination. They obeyed, quickly rolled the gurney into bay #3 and together transferred the wet woman off the gurney and onto the waiting examination bed.

The EMT in blue, who had first attended to Bell, gave her hand a squeeze and promised they would find her husband and the two would soon be reunited. He and his partner then departed. The ER nurse pulled curtains around, enclosing Belle inside a temporary room. She began to hook an assortment of small devices onto Belle's body. She put adhesive pads onto Belle's chest and belly. She clipped a thimble-type monitor to a finger and a blood pressure cuff to her arm. All these were connected to wires leading to monitors that soon began to chirp, beep and hum. The blood pressure sleeve suddenly swelled tight around Belle's upper arm, held her for a moment and then soon released her from its grip. The nurse had just finished with the monitoring devices when a doctor entered through a gap in the curtain wall.

"Hello," he said. He introduced himself. "I'm Doctor Bu." He hovered over Belle, taking hold of her wrist and feeling her pulse. "Can you tell me your name?"

Belle looked at him, dazed, her heart rate elevated with fear and uncertainty. The doctor appeared foreign, Middle Eastern maybe, or Asian. Belle wasn't sure. She didn't care. Though the man spoke with a slight accent, she understood the question. She did not, however, reply.

The doctor calmly repeated the question again and looked into her eyes, as he tickled the bottom of her foot.

Belle's knee jerked the foot away.

The doctor continued to smile.

"Belle," she muttered.

"And your last name, Belle?" he asked.

"Hart... I'm Belle... Hart."

"Where do you live, Belle? What's your address?" Doctor Bu asked, as he tickled her other foot and watched that foot jerk away from his fingertips.

Belle remembered, slowly. She saw a place in her mind's eye — bronze house numbers positioned beside a bright-blue front door on a gray house. She remembered that she had helped to create its beauty, with color and furnishings that she had personally chosen. She had tried to fill that house with all the love she had for a man... her husband. Then the scene she remembered, clouded. The idyllic vision faded. Her beautiful illusion was slowly replaced by a devastating image of a new reality. Only half a house formed in her mind this time. She saw a crushed white Escalade under shredded ruins of what had once been an immaculate garage. That was slowly replaced by the scene of litter from trashed building material, strewn across a manicured lawn. Tears began to well up in her eyes.

"It's gone. It's ruined." Belle began to weep.

"Yes. Yes. I understand, Belle," Doctor Bu said patiently, as he cupped her chin and shined a penlight across each eye. "You've been through a lot, I know. They told me. But I need you to tell me your address, if you can remember it. Your house can be repaired in time. It's you we need to attend to right now. Tell me your street address. Please?"

Through a moment more of tumbled thoughts, Belle repeated a number, with difficulty. Doctor Bu glanced over at a monitor. Her heart rate was beginning to slow. The nurse by his side scribbled notes on a clipboard, as she recorded information about the ER's newest patient. Bell tried to focus on the two forms standing beside her bed, attending to her. She took in the curtain walls drawn closed, and she smelled the antiseptically clean space. She blinked up at harsh lights above her body. Slowly the images brought Belle back to the present, in both place and time. Then her thoughts abruptly returned once again to Vern.

Belle sat up, reached out and clutched Dr Bu's arm in a tight grip. Her heart rate jumped. "Where is he? Didn't you tell him I'm here? Why isn't he here?" She had grown frantic again.

"Who is *'he'*?" Doctor Bu asked calmly, prying Belle's grip from his white lab coat, taking both her hands in his own.

"Vern! My Vern! Where is Vern?" came Belle's desperate plea.

Doctor Bu continued to question the woman, in a calm voice. "Was Vern with you when the storm damaged your house?"

"No! He phoned. He told me to go to the basement. I did. He never came home! I don't know where he is! Please, find him! I need him!" Belle's heart jumped again. She grew increasingly agitated.

Doctor Bu nodded calmly, squeezing her hands still held in his own, then eased her back down onto the bed. "We'll look for Vern for you, Belle. You must try to relax. Let us worry about finding him." The doctor turned to the nurse, ordered a mild sedative then turned back quickly to Belle. "Let the nurse get you out of your wet clothes and dried off. Shall we? You need to warm up. Your hands are like ice. Are you cold? She'll get you warm blankets and some medication to help you relax. I'll inquire if anyone has seen your Vern. I'll come back in a few minutes to do a thorough exam. OK?"

Belle understood. She was in no position and without energy to object. She had just barely enough of her wits to realize that this man might find Vern for her. With hope, she watched the doctor vanish beyond the curtains.

The nurse set down her clipboard on a nearby table then turned all her attention to Belle. "Let's get you out of these wet clothes like Dr Bu ordered."

Doctor Bu walked quickly into the hallway where the EMTs were completing the tasks associated with securing equipment to their now-empty gurney. They were just about to leave for the squad.

Bu called out, stopping their departure. "The patient said Vern is missing, that he wasn't at the address where you found her. Would you relay that information? I am assuming 'Vern' is the same Vern Hart of the auction house in The Plains. Probably her husband."

"Already done, Doc," one of them said. "She still frantic to find him?"

"Oh, yes. I don't think she'll calm down completely until she does."

Again, a weak and barely audible groan emanated from below the rubble. Both men heard it this time. The EMTs looked to one another with the realization that Vern Hart was below them, alive.

"Get that equipment here *fast!*" shouted out one to Officer Dale. We've got an *injured* victim below!"

The deputy immediately called for assistance, on the cruiser radio. He repeated their request for a backhoe, not to retrieve a body but to pry a building off a live victim. "ASAP," he told the dispatcher. He repeated the location a third time then waited until he heard the acknowledgement from the voice on the other end. He put Ulla into the back seat of the cruiser then joined the EMTs. All three big men began to claw and pull away splintered wood, sheet rock and roofing. They clawed away any material they could in an attempt to uncover the victim.

The skinniest EMT reached through an opening located under an exposed truss. His fingertips waved impotently in the darkness below. Then he tried to wedge both head and shoulders into the small opening, but that maneuver proved futile. He was too broad shouldered. Nothing gave way. He threw up his hands in frustration and returned to the task of prying away more rubble with his bare hands. After several sweaty, useless minutes of labor, he was convinced they would reach the man below only with heavy equipment. The roof was still nailed to cascading trusses, preventing one human from hoisting up anything substantial. Each truss compressed, one on top of the other, had collapsed like fallen dominoes. There looked to be no way for mere human strength to reach the man trapped somewhere below. Heavy equipment was going to be the only solution to rescue this guy.

Minutes passed as the EMTs and the deputy continued to pry off what they could, making little headway. They had only managed to remove enough roof metal and wood to widen the small gap into a somewhat bigger small hole. Still none of the men could squeeze through.

Finally, a tractor-trailer bearing the logo of a local equipment rental company, came to a noisy stop down on the street. The owner was behind the wheel. He pulled the rig close to the lot. With a great blast of air, releasing brake pressure, he threw the truck into park, set the brakes then jumped down from the cab.

Two other men climbed out on the other side of the cab. As an efficient team, they hastily unhooked an orange track hoe on the flatbed, letting chains fall noisily to the pavement or onto the steel bed. One of the men climbed up and got behind the controls of the big machine. He fired up the engine which belched a plume of diesel exhaust into the air. With a skilled driver at the wheel and the owner and his companion to help guide, the heavy track hoe inched off the bed, down heavy steel ramps and onto the roadway. The tracks of the machine ground regular scars deep into the warm asphalt, as it turned and maneuvered toward the collapsed building.

The equipment owner raced ahead and was on top of the rubble, bending down beside the cop and EMTs, before the lumbering machine reached the former auction house. He, too, was assessing the pile through the small hole which gave him an incomplete glimpse of what lay beneath.

"I need to get a look under here," he said, with frustration in his voice. "I can't see a damn thing. We could kill your guy if we don't know what we're dealing with below. Anybody have a flashlight? A camera? A phone? Anyone have one of those selfie sticks?"

"Got something better!" the deputy replied.

The officer left the small group of men and sprinted quickly to his squad car where the engine continued to idle, providing cool air for Ulla's comfort. He opened the back door and the Malinois hopped out with a ball in her mouth, tail wagging. She was ready to play her favorite game of search!

From the trunk of the cruiser, the officer removed a leather harness that the dog sometimes wore and a small video camera from a storage compartment.

The equipment company owner soon reached his side and realized what the officer meant to do. "How do you attach the camera?" he asked.

"Never have. Still working on that problem. You got any ideas?" the officer asked.

"Duct tape! Got a roll in the cab. Be right back," he said, then bolted for the semi cab in the street.

By then another sheriff's car had arrived, as well as two more vehicles bearing reporters from local papers. The street was beginning to resemble a parking lot. The sheriff recognized the reporters at once and ordered them to keep out of the way.

"Sure thing," one newspaper reporter said. "Who's the victim? Can you give us any details?"

"Not now. Later," the sheriff barked. "You'll get your story after we have the guy. Now shut up. Stay back. Let these men do their job!"

With duct tape in hand, Officer Dale attached the little VCR to the breast plate of Ulla's harness. The camera was occasionally used to record incidents for the sheriff's office, which could be used later in court proceedings. Today the deputy was going to send Ulla down a hole to make a recording they hoped to use immediately.

With the dog's complete cooperation, the officer attached the harness around her then led his K9 partner to the top of the rubble, where the small opening had been widened just enough so the dog would be able to crawl through. He switched the VCR to 'on'. He checked the device to be sure the light on the camera was also on, then he pointed a hand down into the dark hole.

"Search, Ulla. Search."

As soon as Ulla squeezed through the opening and disappeared into the darkness, the deputy urged those standing nearby to get quiet.

The deputy bent over the opening to listen. He poked his head into the gap as far as possible, listening to the dog's movements. He could see the glow of the camera light on her harness, bobbing, descending away from him. He could hear Ulla panting, heard her footfalls as she scrambled over rubble unseen by him. He caught the sound of metal clunk up against something — the camera on her breast collar perhaps. Then he was briefly blinded by the bright light of the camera, swinging across his own eyes. Ulla had, no doubt, turned. She was probably sitting to signal finding her quarry.

"Good girl," he said. Then, "Ulla, come!"

Ulla obeyed. The dog promptly poked her nose and head through the opening. The deputy helped her squeeze completely out. He gave her the ball reward that she eagerly accepted. He then pried the camera off her harness. As he fiddled with buttons, the men crowded around, each trying to place himself where he could better see the images on the little video screen.

At first, a jittery belt, holster, gun and uniformed belly came into view. The deputy had turned on the camera as he knelt in front of the dog. There was a blur of scenery as he released the dog, ordering her to search. She was spinning round to depart in the direction he'd ordered. The hole came into view, bouncing up and down with each step of the dog's eager prancing. The tiny screen continued to show the image of the hole growing larger, eventually filling the entire screen. For a moment, all went black. Ulla had entered into the darkness of the cavern of rubble below them.

Slowly, the camera on her chest adjusted automatically to the lack of ambient light. A jerky image came into view, lit by the video camera's light. Nothing but blur passed by with each step the dog took. Two-by-sixes that were part of a truss came onto the screen. This vanished. Dust and dirt clouded the screen shot as the dog crawled further down into chaos. At one blockade of lumber and metal, the dog appeared to have veered left. Her paws alternately came into view as she crawled, belly down, along a slanted wooden plank.

Soon thereafter, the image of a man's torso appeared on screen. They saw a plaid shirt dusted with debris. The men above broke their silence with quiet exclamations of success. The man in plaid lay face down, his arms splayed outward. The lower portion of his body was hidden, obscured from view by a large object at his side. The object appeared solid, wood or perhaps metal. The man's image vanished in another blur, as Ulla spun around and sat on her haunches beside him. She had successfully found her quarry once again.

The men above could see he was lying under what had been the roof of the auction house, with little more than twenty-four inches of clearance above him. The space offered barely enough room for the Malinois to crawl under.

Each man who had watched the scenes pass in quick, blurry succession, were trying to solve problems in their heads. The contractor's eyes were fixed on lumber positions. He was trying to estimate to what depth the dog had descended, what objects might shift if pried upon, and which direction she had traveled beneath him.

The deputy was concerned with anything that might injure Ulla. There might be upended or exposed nails to pierce a paw or rip open Ulla's flesh. Were there jagged spears of glass or wood that might put out an eye or rip through fur and flesh?

The EMTs concern was not for the dog. They wanted to see the victim. In what position was he be pinned? What was his condition? Was he bleeding? Were any injuries visible?

Only Ulla wanted to have fun and play ball.

The deputy switched off the camera then looked up at the three men who hovered above his shoulders.

An EMT spoke first. "Looks like he's flat on the concrete floor. He might have head or back injuries."

The contractor commented next. "Anybody have any idea what that is beside him? If solid, it might prevent further collapse when we try to pry this up from over there." He pointed to the near side of the collapsed building. "We might be able to lift all of these trusses at once and hold them up, while you guys go in and drag him out."

"No dragging," said the other EMT. "If he's got back or neck injuries, dragging might paralyze him. We need to carry him out on a backboard."

"Agreed," said the other EMT.

"Well, we could try lifting the collapsed rafters higher, but not all of them at once. We'll have to peel back one truss at a time until we lighten the load," said the contractor.

"Then get started," ordered the deputy. He snapped his leash onto Ulla, who was still holding the ball in her mouth and stood ready to heel. Everyone followed Ulla, and all climbed down off the rubble.

The deputy returned Ulla to the back of the cruiser and shut her in. He then gave a brief report to the Sherriff standing nearby. The contractor returned to his crew. He yelled up to the man behind the controls of the big track hoe, pointing toward the edge of the roof where he was to begin the task of removing debris. The EMTs returned to their squad, extracted a gurney and retreated to a location a safe distance away to wait for their opportunity to retrieve the victim.

The reporters witnessed this sudden flurry of activity. They had been standing idle on the street, beside their cars. The action brought them to attention. They both ignored the sheriff's earlier order, and bolted, sprinting toward the waiting EMTs, for a statement.

19

Avery drove out early the next morning before breakfast. Sleeping had been impossible in the ninety-degree heat of the night. Power at her apartment was still off. She heard on the truck's radio that the Level 3 emergency had been lifted everywhere in the county except in the town of The Plains. She decided her first stop would be at the Tea Basket hall, which was near her apartment. If Nora had not opened up this early, she'd drive over to Nora's house to see how the older woman had fared.

She parked the big truck near the hall. To her surprise, the front door was unlocked. The door gave way to the scent of fresh-brewed coffee. Lights glowed from the ceiling. Cool air from a functioning air conditioner enveloped her body and felt absolutely refreshing and welcome. Without electricity, Avery had suffered all night long, even with her apartment door wide open. She hoped she didn't smell of sweat. There was no water pressure for a shower.

Nora turned around to see who was entering the hall. From her location in the kitchenette in the back of the room, she recognized Avery's tall frame. Nora was attired in a crisp, wrinkle-free, pink linen top and matching trousers. The storm had obviously not damaged her extensive closet.

"Hello there!" the older woman called out, with a big smile on her pink lips and a wave of the hand. She adjusted her large, red glasses and asked, "Need a cup o' joe?"

"Hi back at ya," Avery said. "I see we have electric here. You OK? How's your place?"

Nora poured out a cup of coffee then returned the carafe to the counter. "Oh, yes. We got electric early this morning. It's on at my place, too. I thought I'd just come over here in case others needed a cool oasis. Air conditioner works just fine. How about you?"

"Still in the dark on my side of town and still too hot for comfort. I had a busted kitchen window pane, but that's all the damage my place sustained. How about here? Have you been upstairs to have a look see?"

"Oh, yes. I've been here for some time. I'm a morning person, you know. Everything seems all right. But I was wondering about the girls, you know, our members, if they're OK."

Nora had gone to the guild hall more as a way of alleviating worry, rather than because she was an early riser. With no way to contact her members, she needed to do something constructive, hoping her brood of quilt sisters would perhaps come home to the hall to find her, their mother hen.

"Yeah, me too," Avery said, as she took a careful sip from the dainty cup Nora handed her. The little cup of coffee was hot — too hot to drink — but a welcome gesture. She set it down to cool. "I have the roster here," she said, placing a clipboard on the table beside the coffee. "I thought I'd try to visit as many as I can reach today, to see if they're OK. Maybe I should tell them you're here with hot coffee and cold, welcoming air-conditioning."

"Oh, that would be so thoughtful of you," Nora said, as she sat down across the table from Avery. "But you can't do all that alone." Nora's mind was instantly busy thinking of possibilities to help.

"What do you suggest?" Avery asked. "It's only you and me."

Nora adjusted her red spectacles. "I suggest you start your visits here in town. If your stop reveals our member is OK, ask her to contact one of the other members on your list, who lives near. Every stop then doubles your efforts!"

"Sounds good," Avery agreed, taking another tentative sip from the steaming cup.

"And do tell everyone you see to report here if they can; after they make their contact, of course. We can all assist anybody who needs shelter or help. Then, before you leave the city, come back and report your findings. Tell me who's OK, and who's in need. Sound like a plan?"

"I can do that. Oh, and one other thing, Nora. I have the membership list with me of the Shining Stars, too. I'm going to include them in my rounds. Would you mind if I also have them report here if need be?"

"Oh, my, yes, do!" Nora said. "By all means! We must stick together… like all the pieces of a quilt! You can't check on anybody in The Plains, yet.

Evelyn lives in The Plains, you know. I wonder how she fared. I understand no one's allowed to drive there."

"That's what I heard on the radio, too. Sounds bad. Do you suppose Carolyn and Rosie are OK?" Avery asked.

"Oh, yes, I know they're well. We were all together at dinner after the auction. That's when the storm hit. I just hope they were able to *get* home."

Avery highlighted names with addresses in town, which indicated most on each page. She drained the little cup of coffee as she scanned her lists one last time. She stood. Nora took the empty cup from her hand and walked with her to the door.

"You tell anyone who needs *anything* to come here, even your new guild members. We'll have a home for everybody who needs a place to stay, no matter what guild they belong to."

Avery smiled, gave Nora a hug then left immediately for her truck and drove off toward the nearest address on her roster.

By eleven o'clock, the number of women in the hall had grown exponentially. Obvious to Nora, Avery was making good progress on her rounds. The Tea Basket hall was bustling with women from both guilds. Telephones were still not functioning. Most whose homes were in Athens continued to go without electricity. The unbearable heat was miserable. Someone had started a list on a flip chart. One woman wrote the names of everyone who was OK, down one column. Besides that, along a second column, she listed the names of everyone whose home had sustained damage, adding a note of what that person needed. Some requested a generator. Some asked for gas for a generator. Several requested ice. The column of those who were OK was by far the longer of the two. As each name was added, Nora sighed contentedly with relief.

Missing were names and conditions of those who lived in The Plains. But Nora had taken it upon herself to scribble both Rosie and Carolyn's names at the top of the OK list. She had no clue what condition their homes were in. No one would know until Avery could get into, and back out of, the town.

Avery returned shortly after noon. The fast-food joints on State Street had apparently had their electric service restored and were back in business. Someone had subs delivered to the hall. Several older women, whom Avery recognized as Shining Star quilters, were seated among those she knew to be Tea Basket quilters. Members of the new guild were serving up the recent delivery of subs. Everyone seemed to be talking at once, jockeying around the pile of wrapped sandwiches piled high on the table, preparing to share the meal. When Avery entered, they looked up. Suddenly all got quiet.

Avery was overcome with an unusual feeling of embarrassment by such immediate attention.

Nora broke the silence. "Come have a sandwich, girl! Tell us what we don't know. Some Shining Stars are treating everyone to lunch! Our family is growing, as you can see! We've been making new friends all morning, and we need to hear what you've found out and where you're off to next." Nora was in her element, the mother hen with her chicks, clucking and encouraging each one with seemingly inexhaustible delight.

Someone shoved a paper plate into Avery's hands as she approached the table. The cardboard dish was piled high with potato chips and what appeared to be half a cold ham and cheese sub with shredded lettuce and a tomato slice. She was ushered then deeper into the crowd, where she soon relaxed enough to accept all their attention.

"Thanks, Nora. Hi, everyone," Avery said with a smile.

Someone rose and offered Avery the empty chair. She sat down and eagerly bit into the sub. She hadn't realized how hungry she was, until that moment. Other than the cup of coffee Nora gave her hours earlier, she had gone without food since Larry's hot dog the day before. Nora soon appeared through the crowd, bringing her a cup of hot coffee in a different little cup than the one earlier that morning. Avery glanced over to the columns of names as she chewed. She realized that the names far exceeded the number of women she had personally contacted. She was grateful to know that Nora's suggestion of 'spreading the word' was working to good advantage. She also noted the short list of names who had suffered damage or expressed a need for something. After swallowing a half-chewed chunk of her sub, she was able to speak. The women gathered around, eager to hear her report.

"I've been to, or arranged to check on, all the members' homes here in town, or very near all of them — I think. I'm going to head out into the countryside next. Still no cell phone reception."

Someone interjected with, "No landlines either!"

206

Avery produced her rosters, which someone accepted. "Here's my list of those who are OK. No one I met with, needed much. So I guess I just keep on doing what we started this morning. I'll visit as many places as I can and tell everyone that the hall is open if they need it."

One of the Shining Star quilters spoke up. "Why don't you let us help you contact the country folks, Ave?"

Avery's heart made a little leap. Someone had given her a pet name. She was feeling like she belonged to them, that they could take liberties that only friends might take with each other. It hadn't occurred to Avery to ask for help. She had always been very independent.

The volunteer continued, as Avery finished off the last of her sub. Another sandwich suddenly appeared on her paper plate. "We can divide the county up by townships or quadrants. Are there enough of us here who can pair up and drive out to help?"

Avery was impressed by members of the new guild eager to aid in her quest. Many of the Tea Basket quilters were elderly, and most of them lived within the city limits. But there were still many in outlying areas that Avery wanted to check on. Having help to do so would certainly speed up the process and reduce the miles she would have to drive that day.

"Fantastic!" she said. "How do you want to do this?"

One woman produced a county map, from who knows where, and another woman called out for volunteers willing to drive. The drivers were asked to find a partner to go with them as navigators, then they gathered around the table where Avery sat munching chips. Everyone else was urged to shoo. In less than twenty minutes, women from both guilds had claimed a section of the county to canvass. They tore names and addresses from Avery's rosters of anyone in their assigned portion of the county. Avery was left with her own little stack of torn strips of paper containing the names she would visit. Nora began to reassemble the ragged strips onto a blank sheet of paper by the use of copious amounts of scotch tape.

"You would have thought somebody would have found scissors. But no. No quilt maker in her right mind would use good fabric shears to cut up paper! There! Looks like a bad job of piecing, doesn't it? It's my rag quilt of names, just for you!" Nora said, as she held up the finished sheet for Avery to see.

After everyone took a turn with the scotch tape dispenser, seven teams had their own sheet of names to contact.

Leftover subs vanished from the table as pairs of women, forming the seven teams, all departed the hall on their assigned missions, fortified with the remnants of the day's lunch.

"If the phones worked," Nora commented, "this would be a lot easier. We need a phone tree. I'm going to mention that to Carolyn, so she can put that topic on the next agenda."

Avery still sat at the table and watched the teams depart. She was surprised at how well the women from the two groups were willing to work together. She was also very relieved to find her self-imposed task greatly reduced as a result of that cooperation. She scanned the scraps of her shortened list that Nora had taped together. Her eyes fell upon the name of Lois Caldwell, both Shining Star secretary and Tea Basket member. Avery arched an eyebrow and adjusted her own glasses with interest. She decided to stop at Lois' place first. She knew only a little about the woman whom she heard was a farmer. Lois was the one who always wore an oversized floral dress to meetings. She had never had a meaningful conversation with Lois, even as Shining Star officers. This was an opportunity to see for herself what Lois' farm looked like and get to know her better. The urgency of her task had been immensely relaxed by the many volunteers. She could now afford to take more time at each stop. She would definitely not rush her time with Lois. She hoped she'd find that both the farm and Lois had survived the storm well and that they could chat.

20

The GPS in her Ford had never led Avery astray. Every county road she traveled down that afternoon was littered with wet leaves and small twigs. One road was completely blocked by a big, silver maple uprooted and sprawled across both lanes. The necessary detour was not due to the GPS' error.

Avery wondered if the obstruction had been reported. She decided to leave that task to locals. As soon as she turned the truck around, the device in the dashboard recalculated. Her alternative, backtracking half a mile to an intersection with a township road, proved free of any more fallen trees to block her progress. Several turns later eventually brought her to her first destination.

The pitiful condition of county roads compared to the excellent status of the township lanes failed to surprise Avery. The County engineer, Dolittle, avoided using any expenditures for preventive road maintenance measures. Therefore, she fully expected to find the same deteriorating conditions elsewhere, after what she had found driving to Ximi Ling's. She bounced over washboard on the hills. She dropped her wheels into multiple potholes in the valleys, camouflaged beneath puddles of water left behind by the storm. Along the straightaways she saw frequent signs of old erosion, flowing in ditches filled with brown, muddy water. The neglect offered Avery ample opportunities for swearing. The big truck soon looked like it'd been on a mud run.

During the ten-mile drive to find Lois Caldwell's place, an idea began to form in Avery's mind about a possible future. The idea she had been thinking about related to her career in civil engineering and about wanting a job. That idea was developing slowly into a plan, one which included the women of both guilds, whom she was getting to know, and the community she was getting back in touch with after so many years away. This notion of hers was ambitious, foreign to her solitary nature and very, very far out of her comfort zone. Her idea actually frightened her. But it offered one possibility where she might be able to work for the engineer's office in a capacity other than laborer. Maybe.

Before she could fully realize all the ramifications of her plan, Avery's GPS announced, "You have arrived at your destination."

The Caldwell home where Lois lived, worked and sometimes, as she often reminded people, pieced a quilt 'when time permitted', came into view. A large mailbox bearing store-bought numbers on the side, matching Lois' address and letters, spelled out 'CALDWELL', confirming her GPS announcement.

A simple, faded, wooden sign reading, 'EGGS $2/DOZ', hung askew on the side of an ancient, wooden outbuilding. The shed leaned slightly toward the roadway. The wide, wooden planks appeared to have been painted, perhaps a century earlier. It was covered by a rusted roof of standing rib metal. The shed sheltered a small but newer model farm tractor of bright orange, in the aisle, sitting as if within a covered bridge. One side of the shed was closed in with equally ancient slats of wood spaced several inches apart, unpainted and weathered. Avery assumed the shed was a corn crib; indeed, it was stuffed to the rafters with dried, yellow corn still clinging to cobs. A small trapdoor, set high on the wall in the aisle, hung ajar above the tractor, with corn cobs exposed, perched perilously, ready to fall onto the tractor and dirt floor below.

A clapboard farmhouse, freshly painted white, looked conspicuously well-kept, a few yards away. Fronds from a pair of lush ferns swayed gently in the breeze hanging under gingerbread surrounding the porch. Geraniums of red and pink, in large terracotta pots, lined each step leading up to the porch to a closed front door. The screen door, the wood painted blue, wore a 'Welcome' sign, like the pendant on a necklace. One lone rocking chair suggested this was the residence of a single person. A bright multi-colored quilt, folded neatly was draped over the back of the rocker offering a charming touch of comfort for the one who lived within.

That someone was just then lumbering toward Avery's truck from a barn beyond the shed. This person wore not the usual gingham or printed voluminous dress of Lois Caldwell, but was clad in a short-sleeved, blue T-shirt under faded bib overalls. The denim knees were stained with mud and grass. The figure inside them wore a tattered, straw, cowboy hat and a holster strapped around an ample girth.

Avery could have sworn that a gun was parked in the holster. She had never seen Lois looking like this, ever. She forgot to speak. Instead, her jaw fell open in stunned silence.

Lois hailed the tall gent getting out of the big Ford in front of her house. She raised an arm up to block more sun from her eyes. The gent was a tall, bespectacled woman.

"Oh, it's you!" Lois bellowed, once she was near enough to make a positive ID. "You lost?"

"No… not lost… Lois, I've never seen you… like… this," Avery stammered, as she continued to stare, open-mouthed, at the secretary of the Shining Star guild.

"Well, heaven's sake, you don't think I'd cut trees and fix fence in my Sunday best, do ya?"

"Ah, no… It's just that I've never seen you wear anything *but* a dress. I didn't recognize you… in coveralls."

"Well, I suppose you do now; recognize me, that is. So why *are* you here?"

Avery smiled. "I came to see you, to see if you were OK after the big storm."

"Really?" Lois was pleased. This was a kind gesture on Avery's part. Such kindness should not be forgotten. "Why don't you come in? It's still hot as blazes out here. I've finished my fence repairs for the day and I can offer you a cold glass of water, if you'd like to join me."

Avery accepted and followed the woman up the front porch steps, past the colorful geraniums. Avery noticed drip pans under each pot, still holding water from the storm. Lois pried off her mud-encrusted boots outside the screen door then led Avery inside. The bulb in a lamp on a small side table gave a warm glow to the furnishings, indicating to Avery that Lois at least had electricity. The farmhouse was small but well appointed. The wooden floors gleamed with fresh wax. Lace curtains let afternoon light brighten up a rose-colored carpet on the living room floor. Lois motioned Avery into a modern kitchen, with a matching stainless steel stove, refrigerator and dishwasher arranged in an L of light-cherry cabinets. They were not new appliances, but they were polished and well cared for.

Lois opened the refrigerator. The interior was well stocked, to Avery's brief glimpse inside. Lois withdrew a pitcher of cold water, retrieved two tumblers from behind one of the cabinet doors then turned to face Avery. Lois' face was flushed with either heat or embarrassment. Avery wasn't sure which.

"Water is OK, isn't it?" Lois asked.

"Of course. Thank you. I love your house. It's charming," Avery said.

"Thanks. Me and my late husband bought the farm right after we got married. Been here almost…" She paused to do the math in her head. "Been here forty-two years."

Both women quickly drained their glasses. Lois poured herself a second.

"'Nother?" Lois asked, indicating a refill.

"I'm good. Thanks. Like I said, I came out to see if you needed anything after that storm. I see now you're fine. You have electric and…"

Lois interrupted with a shake of her head, while swallowing her second glass of cold water.

"Nope. No electric. But I have a standby generator. That's why I have juice. Had it installed after my husband passed. He always fiddle-farted around with a portable generator. Electric goes out all the time out here, with trees falling across power lines. But he was a big, strong man, so he could handle that portable. Me? Well, I have too little time, now that he's gone, to be haulin' that ol' thing out in twelve inches of snow, or in pourin' rain during a storm like yesterday, a hookin' it up, firin' it up and running to town for gas all the time. So I used some of the insurance money he left and got one of those standbys installed professionally. Don't have to raise a finger any time the power goes out. 'Lectric goes out a lot this way. Generator just fires itself up, shuts off the power company lines, then pops my circuits back on one at a time, and I'm in business! Don't matter if it's minus twenty degrees or a roasting ninety-five degrees like today. Best investment I ever made since he passed."

Avery listened with interest. This was news about a woman Avery was discovering to be most interesting. Lois was not one to talk during meetings, so Avery knew only what other people said about her. They said she was shy. Obviously, that was wrong. But they also said she was dependable. They thought she lacked much creativity in her quilt making. They said she didn't have a sense of humor, either. But nobody could remember Lois ever criticizing anybody's sewing, their quilting or their situation.

Avery took this opportunity to press for a bit more. "I saw corn in the crib, and a tractor. Do you still farm without your husband?" Avery asked.

"Oh, sure. I bought the corn, though. Farm's too hilly to grow rows and rows of corn. I put up hay for my cows, though. Keep hens for eggs. Sell 'em at the Farmers Market in town. And I raise vegetables for the market. Doesn't leave much free time to piece quilts, though. But I do what I'm able, when I have time," she added.

Lois downed a third glass of water. "Sure you won't have another?" she asked. "I've been cuttin' up a fallen tree and restringin' the 'lectric rope where the tree fell over the fence line. Been out since the rain let up. I'm dry as the desert sand."

Once again, Avery politely declined her offer. Lois shrugged and returned the pitcher to the refrigerator.

"Can't say I'm in need of anything, unless one of you wants to come out here and shoot copperheads for me if I come upon 'em." She patted the gun in the holster strapped to her ample hip.

Avery laughed at the thought of elderly Tea Basket quilters picking up any gun and knowing how to use it. "I suspect you'd be out of luck. Listen, I should move along. I have others to check on, so I better get going, if you're sure you're OK."

"Oh, sure. Are you finding ladies with needs?"

"Sadly, yes. Most, so far, still don't have electricity. Several, who don't have generators like you, have gone to the Tea Basket hall. I think probably a dozen might stay overnight, because it's too hot back home. Power's back on at the hall, so it has air-conditioning. But not all of Athens is back up. Some of the women at the hall have health issues and so need a cool place to spend the day and night."

"Well, maybe I should go lend a hand," Lois offered. "I have a couple of cots I could take, and an air mattress. I could take fresh eggs for breakfast, bacon from my freezer, and more. I could cook breakfast for them tomorrow morning."

Avery watched Lois, her hand held up to her chin, forming a plan to be useful.

"I'm sure the ladies would appreciate anything that would make their stay more comfortable," Avery said, impressed with Lois' generosity. "I'll be off then, to my next stop. Might see you again this evening at the hall."

Lois smiled and nodded. Avery returned to her truck. If Lois was going to work at the hall, she saw no need to send Lois out to check on anyone. The next closest stop would be Ximi's. Avery waved goodbye from the cab and reset the GPS to a new destination, hoping the device would pick township roads to get her back to the highway, then on to Ximi's.

Lois waved back. She unbuckled the gun belt and let the holstered gun dangle from her hand. She watched the dirty truck pull away, then she retreated inside to clean up for a trip into Athens. But first she had to jot down a list of supplies needed for the Tea Basket hall, before she showered and changed.

21

The local newspaper did not print or deliver the day after the great storm. Emergency services equipment, vehicles and personnel still occupied the newspaper's parking lot. If not for their presence, the lot would have been empty. No electricity had yet been restored to the building, nor to any part of The Plains, the devastation having been so widespread. Most of the county, in fact, was still in the dark on this first day after the derecho. Power was slowly coming back on in pockets. Utility crews would work around the clock for days yet to come. Their goal was to restore power to the county seat, Athens, first. Then they would serve other less-populated areas, as they could. The power grid in The Plains had received so much damage that officials estimated it would take crews several days, if not weeks, to compete all the necessary repairs to restore service. For now, getting roads cleared so that crews could reach all the homes and businesses, was the top priority.

Radio reports were the only way to learn how widespread the storm had been. Not just Athens, but many hundreds of thousands across several states had been affected. Athens residents would not read about the man located under the rubble of his business nor the efforts underway to rescue him.

Once the track hoe arrived on scene, the number of spectators increased around what had once been Hart's Auction House. It had been reduced to a great heap of metal roofing and splintered lumber. Rubbernecking neighbors heard the racket of machinery and saw emergency vehicles traveling to the scene. This unusual activity soon drew a small crowd of idle kids and adults, standing in the street to watch the action unfold, pointing to something or someone that would periodically attract their attention.

Emergency scanners picked up the initial plea for heavy equipment. The flash that a survivor had been located under a heap of rubble brought out more press. They parked their vehicles haphazardly along the roadway leading to Hart's Auction House on the outskirts of town. Three more press vehicles joined the first two cars. The university's student newspaper sent out a team in one car. A TV crew from the capitol arrived in a colorful van, hoping to film the rescue. A regional radio station sent its reporter to the scene in a van marked with its call letters and numbers along both sides. Adding to that congestion was the empty flatbed, its engine still idling.

Several sheriff's cruisers and one ambulance with its emergency lights flashing wormed its way up the drive to what remained of the auction house. By now the local sheriff realized that he had a crowd-control issue. He barked commands, ordering a couple of uniforms to clear the street and open it up to emergency vehicles only.

Ulla was napping in the back seat of the cruiser, her chin resting on the ball. She was the only living creature nearby unconcerned with the activity taking place on the knoll. Everyone else's attention was fixed on the big track hoe, its operator, and the huge pile of rubble blocking its path.

The machine belched diesel as it lumbered toward the collapsed building, puffing and chugging, its tracks rattling noisily on the asphalt drive. The boss directed its approach, from ground level. He indicated with hand signals, drawing the machine to a spot not far from the gap from which Ulla had not long ago emerged.

"Get some of this debris pulled away," he yelled up to the driver.

Carefully, the operator inched the bucket out, over then down onto the nearest rubble. He made the movement look as easy as if he were sticking a spoon into a bowl of cereal. In this case, the spoon weighed over two thousand pounds, and the cereal was definitely shredded. He repeated the maneuver several times over, each time pulling back chunks of wood and siding from around the collapsed trusses. The boss, by now, had climbed perilously to the top of the heap near Ulla's hole. From that position, he hoped to see and feel if anything had shifted. Soon enough there came a point where something did shift.

A screech of metal, sliding across pavement like fingernails on a blackboard, pierced the air as the track hoe pulled more debris back from under the pile. One of the trusses buckled and snapped with an explosive crack. The idle crowd that had been watching with interest let out a unified gasp. The boss up on the heap lost his balance and stumbled to his knees.

He quickly righted himself and waved off the track hoe operator, with a shout. "Yo! Hold it! Stop! Stop! Time to start raising it!"

The track hoe operator stopped, lifted the arm of the track hoe's bucket then inched the big orange machine in close. With years of practice and skill, he slid the fingers of the bucket down and under a corner of roofing. In small increments, he edged the machine closer still until the arm was bent at a severe angle, all the while careful not to move the heap of debris. He stopped, securing the machine by dropping a blade on the front all the way down to the ground. He then nodded that he was ready to lift the roof.

His boss gave him a thumbs up.

The driver waited until he was confident the man was down and a safe distance from the collapsed roof. Then with steady gentle pressure on a control stick, he inched the corner of the roof upward.

Slowly and deliberately, he began to raise the bottom truss. As that truss ascended, it caught and pushed the next truss upward. Those in turn pushed up a third. The operator and his machine were creating access under the collapsed mess for the EMTs standing beside the squad. Metal roofing screamed in protest. Nails popped and rattled down metal. The skillful operator continued to lift the collapsed roof, another inch, then another. When he had a space off the ground nearly four feet high, he stopped and signaled his boss. This was as far as he could raise the structure, fearing the trusses would buckle and fold in onto the victim somewhere underneath.

It was now time for rescuers to risk their lives underneath. As two men in blue rushed past the track hoe, the boss whistled loudly, stopping them. He bent down, picked up a pair of hard hats and tossed one to each man.

"Be safe, fellas. Don't risk getting your own heads crushed. If we tell you, you get out, fast, no matter what. Work fast. It's not safe, and I don't know how long we can keep this heap from crashing down."

Each EMT donned a hard hat. The pair then crouched down and disappeared under the collapsed roof into a dusty darkness.

They flipped on flashlights and examined the danger hovering overhead. One of them scanned forward into the darkness, looking for something big which would be located near Ulla's quarry. Thirty feet ahead, he could just make out something. He thought it looked like a large safe. A truss had folded over top of it, forming a wooden tent. There beside the safe, under the tent of splintered lumber, lay the dust-covered shape of a motionless body, a dirty red ball cap laying upturned on the concrete floor nearby.

The EMT touched his partner's shoulder and pointed. They were going to have to crawl to reach their victim. Both of them would not fit into the tiny space afforded by the folded truss and tangle of splintered wood. They could see that whatever the solid item was beside the man, that the way the truss fell across it, the victim appeared to be in a far safer position than they were. One of the EMTs held back while his partner duck-walked as far as he could. Finally, he was forced to drop onto his belly and crawl the last few yards in order to reach Vern's side.

The EMT who stayed behind retreated out from under the rubble. He sprinted to the nearby waiting ambulance and retrieved the gurney standing by. Once back at the entrance to the gap, he lowered the gurney as far as it would collapse. Strapped onto the bed lay a backboard. He pushed the gurney ahead, and following, once again disappeared into darkness. By the time this EMT had pushed the gurney as far into the hole as he could comfortably waddle, his partner had reached Vern's side and was attempting to assess the man's condition.

Vern Hart lay face down, his head bleeding from a deep gash to his skull. The EMT reached around Vern's neck, located his carotid artery and soon felt a pulse. The EMTs exchanged words in the darkness. The backboard delivered by his partner soon slid within reach of the prone rescuer. With much difficulty, working in the cramped, hot space, the EMT struggled to wedge the backboard under Vern's head and neck and then under his body. Slowly he slid the board farther and farther under the man's broad shoulders, deep chest, stomach and finally past the man's waist. By the time he stopped for a rest, the EMT's uniform was drenched in sweat and grime. He wiggled backward and away from Vern until reaching his partner's side.

"I need air, partner. Take over. I'll get a rope for that backboard. We'll have to pull him out. No way one of us can pull the guy along. There's not enough room for leverage."

His partner acknowledged with a nod. The dirt-covered, sweat-drenched EMT departed the darkness for air and a rope, while the other crawled deeper into the confining space at Vern's side.

"Hey Vern!" he said. "Vern, ol' buddy, can you hear me? We're going to get you out of here real soon. Can you hear me, Vern?"

The motionless form groaned.

"That's right! You're lying on a backboard. We're going to pull you out real slow. Can you tell me if you hurt anywhere, Vern?"

Vern mumbled something.

"Can you feel your arms?"

No answer.

"Can you move a foot?"

No answer.

"If you feel pain, I need to know, OK, buddy?"

Vern groaned and mumbled incoherently again.

Something bumped the EMT's back. It was the end of a rope that his partner, who had returned, had tossed forward. With practiced movements, the EMT laying prone near Vern fastened a knot to the backboard. He gave a tug to confirm the rope was secure then called back to his partner, unseen behind him at his feet.

"Inch him out."

The EMT who had delivered the rope said, "You'll have to shinny backward ahead of the board. Yell if we need to slow down or stop. We have deputies at the other end. They know what to do. You ready?"

"Ready."

A whistle from the rear EMT signaled two deputies to begin pulling on the rope, dragging the backboard their way at a rate no faster than a turtle might crawl. Keeping ahead of Vern, one EMT wiggled backward on his belly, keeping one hand on Vern. Minutes passed as the three figures inched back toward the opening offered by the track hoe. Slowly, Vern was pulled on his sled, in the dark, toward a throng of waiting emergency personnel and spectators outside.

Thirty feet later, Vern arrived at the waiting gurney parked just inside the rubble being held aloft by the track hoe. The EMTs yelled for the deputies to stop. On their knees now, either side of the backboard, they hoisted Vern up and onto the wheeled gurney. Still in cramped, dark confines and beneath dangerously splintered rafters, they detached the rope from the backboard. One of them then tied the rope to the gurney. A check of the knot once more confirmed the rope was secure, and the EMT called out to the deputies to resume pulling.

Minutes later the gurney exited the opening, and Vern Hart was out from under the cavern of rubble. Next crawled the EMTs, looking as soiled as their patient. But their work was hardly finished. They now needed to get Vern into the squad and to the hospital.

Though Belle had suffered no physical injuries sheltered in her basement, she had been held overnight for observation. Her anxiety over her missing husband and the knowledge she was alone and now homeless, gave the admitting staff sufficient reason to admit her. She had been cleaned up, sedated and then wheeled into a room to spend the night. A second hospital patient occupied the other bed in her room. The privacy curtain pulled between them prevented either from seeing the other. Belle Hart rested uneasily that night, in spite of sedation. She lay awake for hours on the bed nearest the open door. She watched in a daze as nurses and staff passed by, their white shoes quietly kissing the floor with each step. Her unseen roommate beyond the curtain snored loudly in the bed nearest the window. The intermittent snoring annoyed Belle greatly. Coupled with worry for Vern, she slept very little.

Sometimes the other patient awoke with a start, heart pounding wildly in her chest. She'd forcefully calm herself with deep breaths then stare out her dark window in silent numbness, until falling once again back into a restless sleep.

A hospital aide walked quietly into the room on morning rounds. She smiled at Belle, asked her to fill out a checklist for what she wanted for breakfast, then went around the curtain to the other bed.

"Good morning, Evelyn. How are you feeling today?"

Evelyn stared blankly at the woman in pink scrubs. She *felt* like crap. The sleeping pill they gave her the night before left a nasty taste in her mouth. She ached everywhere. She hated being treated like a helpless child. She hated the woman in pink. She hated pink.

"Here's a breakfast menu, dear. Check off what you want to eat. I'll be back in a minute to collect it. You have no restrictions, hon, so order whatever you like."

With that said and the menu delivered, pink scrubs disappeared back beyond the curtain, past Belle's bed and out the door.

Belle couldn't help but hear the short one-sided conversation from her location only a few feet away. She wondered...

"Evelyn? Evelyn North? Is that you, baby doll?"

Evelyn's heart jumped. It couldn't be..."Hart?"

Belle slipped bare feet onto the cold hospital floor and pulled back the privacy curtain to see for herself. There on the other bed lay the skinny, haggard form of Evelyn North, her mass of disheveled, orange hair looking worse than ever. Belle stood over her roommate, looking down at her for several seconds. She thought Evelyn looked quite pitiful. She wore a faded hospital gown matching Belle's own, but about ten sizes too large for the woman's small frame. Her complexion was paler than Belle could ever remember. She bore dark circles under both eyes. Her glasses were missing.

"You look like shit, baby doll. Why are *you* in here?"

Evelyn wanted desperately to do only one thing — her usual thing — to run away. But today she couldn't. She froze, lay perfectly still and felt trapped like vermin in a leghold. She squinted, trying to focus, unsuccessfully, on Belle's face. She least expected to find herself sharing a room with Belle Hart. *Of all the people in the entire universe, why did the other patient in this room have to be Belle Hart?*

"Are you sick?" Belle asked.

When no response came back, immediately Belle's attention waivered. Her thoughts were never far from her worst nightmare, and they drifted away from any curiosity about Evelyn North, for whom she cared little. She glanced out the window at the gray parking lot below. Her eyes took in the green hills which lay beyond the brown water of the Hocking River. Belle's thoughts were suddenly remembering the storm, about seeing her house, or what was left of it, and about Vern. Tears welled up in her eyes. An ambulance with lights flashing was arriving at the hospital as she looked on.

Evelyn heard Belle sniffle. She was strangely, deeply touched that Belle seemed to care. She could not have imagined Belle would give a damn what her condition was, especially after the crap she had pulled on her, the Tea Basket Quilters and Vern.

"I lost my house," Evelyn barely whispered.

Belle heard her voice. She looked down at Evelyn, as the woman's words slowly sank in. For a long time Belle just stood staring, teary-eyed, barefoot, forcing her thoughts back to the present.

"What? What's that you say?"

Evelyn tried to speak up. She felt like she had slept all night with cotton stuffed down her throat. Her voice was raspy and weak.

"My house… was destroyed. Everything I have… had… is gone."

Karma, baby doll. Karma. Couldn't have happened to a more deserving piece of shit than you. Try to take everything away from somebody. Then somebody or something's gonna do the same to you.

"How about you?" Evelyn asked, not certain what Belle's reply would be.

Belle took a deep breath, letting the air out slowly, getting her anger under control. "Same here, only I still have part of a house left." A nagging block of ice suddenly formed in the pit of her stomach. Tears rolled down her cheeks again, seemingly without cause. But she did have a reason. "Vern's missing," she whispered.

Evelyn took the words in.

Missing. Missing? "What do you mean?"

"Vern never came home. I don't know where he is." With this confession, tears fell freely from Belle's blue eyes. She began to sob uncontrollably.

Evelyn groaned as she forced stiff, skinny legs over the side of her hospital bed. She lowered her bony feet down onto the floor. She limped over to Belle. Then Evelyn did something she had not done in… well… ever. She put her arm around another person in pain.

"I'm so sorry. I'm so sorry your Vern is missing. I really am. It's dreadful to be alone and scared. You must ache for him. I wish that I had not treated you, both of you, the way I did. Now he's gone. Will you *ever* forgive me? I know I'm not liked, that all I deserve is your contempt, but really I… I…"

Belle had no words of comfort to return to her blackmailer. She was not ready to forgive. She could only weep for Vern. But as was Belle's custom, she automatically put her arms around Evelyn's bony shoulders, to reciprocate the hug. Hugging was something Belle always did and probably always would do, no matter who.

"I'll think about it," she said between sobs of anguish.

A nurse in the ER was the one to connect the dots. She recalled a woman in shock the evening before, whose name was Belle Hart. This new admission, a man with a serious head wound and body injuries, getting wheeled into the OR, was also named Hart. She quickly checked the computer screen, searching for the woman's name. Next, she called the nurse's station on Bell's floor, exchanged a few words with someone on the other end and then hung up with a smile of satisfaction.

The nurse on Belle's floor walked immediately into Belle's room. She located her, out of bed, crying in the arms of her roommate. The nurse went to her, turning her away from Evelyn and taking hold of her by the shoulders.

"Belle? Belle! Your husband is downstairs. He's here at the hospital. He's alive. He's being taken to surgery right now."

Belle was stunned silent. She could hardly breathe. She felt weak and yet she felt immense relief and joy. Tears continued to tumble down her cheeks, but they had turned into tears of joy.

The nurse ushered Belle back into her assigned hospital bed and put her under the sheets.

"You stay right here. There's nothing you can do. We can't have you hanging out in a waiting area in that hospital gown. I'll make arrangements from the OR to call as soon as they have news… any news. I'll tell them what room you're in. OK?"

"Surgery? What's wrong? What's happening to him?" Fear abruptly returned again when she finally recognized what the nurse had said. Belle realized something was terribly wrong if Vern was going into surgery.

"I don't have any more information than what I just repeated. I'll find out who the admitting physician and the surgeon are. I'll have one of the doctors come talk to you as soon as possible. You just stay put in bed, so we can find you. I don't know how long it's going to take before someone can tell you anything."

Evelyn emerged from behind the privacy curtain. She walked over to Belle's bedside. "We know each other," she explained to the nurse. "I'll stay with her. I'll keep her company."

Belle looked to Evelyn in surprise at this rare demonstration of kindness.

22

$\mathcal{L}$ois Caldwell made good on her promise of help to Avery. She secured holster and side arm, cleaned up and changed clothes into more respectable go-to-town garb — an enormous, floral, cotton, tent dress. Thirty minutes later she arrived at the Tea Basket hall in her truck. She backed the pickup over the curb, leaving the front half jutting out into the street. The back half of her truck blocked the sidewalk. She then proceeded to drop the tailgate and unload the back. She pulled the cots out of the truck bed first. Then she heaved a rectangular plastic box off. The heavy case landed with a thud on the sidewalk. The case had built-in wheels, making it possible to drag, rather than carry it to the door of the hall. Inside the heavy case was a queen-size air mattress.

She returned to the cab of her truck to retrieve more items: coolers laden with fresh eggs, meat, jars of strawberry and peach jams she had put up herself, and several bags of frozen hash browns acquired on sale at the store on a previous shopping trip. Lois loved hash brown potatoes, especially if all the prep work was already done. Lois loved potatoes. Period. Spuds were her favorite food in all their forms: hash browns, mashed, O'Brian's, baked, scalloped, and any way anyone might prepare them.

Nora Radnor stood gawking from the door of the Tea Basket hall, which she held open, watching Lois repeatedly come and go. Ladies inside the hall came to the door as soon as they realized what she was doing. One would take an item from Lois as she arrived at the door. Another would take that woman's place, waiting to accept the next item.

"What are you up to, dear?" asked Nora. "Are you moving in?"

"Looks like it, don't it?"

"What is all this?"

"Avery told me some ladies planned to stay the night, seein' how they didn't have 'lectric. Got beds an' breakfast for 'em. I'll be back in the mornin' to cook."

Nora raised an eyebrow and adjusted her red glasses in amazement. The news quickly filtered around to others inside. With many hands to lighten the work, cots and air mattresses disappeared up to the second floor. Another cluster of women were chatting appreciatively in the kitchenette as they transferred cartons of eggs from one cooler and bacon and sausage from another into the refrigerator. Bags of frozen hash browns flew into the freezer.

"Are you staying overnight with us, dear?" Nora asked.

"Nope. Gotta care for my animals. I'll come back 'round six tomorrow morning an' fix breakfast for ya. Just leave a note by the stove how many I'm to cook for. And be sure I can get in!"

"That's very nice of you," Nora told Lois. "You will stay in the morning though, and break bread with us, won't you?"

"Oh, dang. I forgot bread! Sure. I'll be here."

"Not to worry, dear. Electric's back on down on State Street. We'll buy bread and anything else we need. Thank you. You're so thoughtful and generous. You're amazing!"

"K," Lois replied, with a smile. She retreated from the doorway, with empty coolers, and lumbered back to her truck to load them in. She climbed in after storing everything then drove the truck off the sidewalk, heading back home for another change of clothes in order to complete evening farm chores.

Discussion broke out inside the hall as to what else was needed for a lovely breakfast. A few of the Shining Star members retrieved purses. Soon, singles, fives and tens started piling up on a table.

"Your guild members are all so helpful," noted one guest, as she dropped a few bills onto the growing pile of cash. "I wish our new guild was so altruistic. All we're doing is collecting money to try to win Molly Menear's longarm quilting machine. The money we get from our raffle quilt is going to her race team."

"We know," admitted Nora. "We knew you were selling raffle tickets. We held an auction for the same reason yesterday afternoon, before the storm hit. Evelyn North belongs…" Nora caught herself. "Evelyn… *used* to belong… to the Tea Basket Quilters before she started your guild."

At the mention of the redhead's name, some of the Shining Star members within earshot took pause. They commented to each other, imagining whether Evelyn had survived the storm intact or what damage, if any, might have occurred to her house in The Plains.

"Does anybody's cell phone work yet?" someone asked aloud.

A shuffle could be heard as several women dug into totes or pockets to retrieve useless cell phones. The answer was a collective groan of denial.

"I wish there was a way to reach everyone," Nora said. "Avery is trying so hard, but it will take her quite some time. I have no idea if anybody can yet drive into The Plains."

"The radio said just a few minutes ago that the Level 3 emergency has been lifted," someone said.

"Oh, good." Nora replied. "Maybe we can find somebody to drive over."

"I'll drive," a Shining Star quilter volunteered.

"Marvelous," Nora said. "We need addresses of all members who live there. Maybe a Tea Basket can go with you to navigate."

While efforts ensued to locate what remained of Avery's torn roster, Ximi Ling walked through the front door. Avery had found her at home, safe and her place undamaged. Alerted to possible needs at the hall, she drove to Athens to join her guild friends.

"Wow, hi!" she said, seeing the meeting room so full of women, some of whom she recognized from the Shining Star Guild, many of them busy with a paperwork project at a table.

"Just in time, young lady," Nora said. "Can you go with this gal to The Plains? She's going to see if all our combined members who live there are well, or if they need anything."

"Oh, sure. Be glad to," Ximi said.

As soon as a short list of names had once again been ripped from remnants of the shredded roster and reassembled onto another sheet of paper with tape, Ximi took the tattered list in hand. She and her driver then departed for The Plains.

Another mixed group of Shining Star and Tea Basket Quilters debated the benefits of oranges over bananas, as they attempted to put together a grocery list of additional breakfast items needed to accompany the bounty brought in by Lois. They were finally in agreement. They would buy both bananas and oranges to make a fruit salad. They would buy enough food for tomorrow's breakfast, and perhaps lunch and other breakfasts to come. After all, they were flush with green. A foursome scooped up the cash that had been piled up on the table. They soon followed Ximi and her driver out the front door.

The reconnaissance team of Ximi Ling and her Shining Star driver returned to the Tea Basket hall shortly before nightfall. They had good news and bad news to report.

"Oh, you should see what we saw," Ximi began. "Some houses were terribly damaged. Evelyn's house is *totally obliterated!* Nothing but an old bathtub stands on her lot! Belle Hart's place is a mess — looks like a bomb went off in her garage! We could see her car there. It was squashed under the roof. We went to the house, or what's left of it, to look for her, but we couldn't find her. The whole side wall of her kitchen was ripped off."

"The Plains is a mess, though you can drive down most of the streets now. Sheriff's cars are stationed at both ends of 682, to slow rubberneckers down. People everywhere were cutting up downed trees. Junk is piling up in front of places. Lots of people are out trying to fix rooftops and porches. Looks like disaster services took over the newspaper's parking lot."

"Did you meet up with Carolyn?" Nora asked.

"Oh, yeah. She's fine. So's her place. And we talked to Rosie. She's OK, too. They'll come by tomorrow. We told them what was going on here, that you had everything under control, so they said they might just as well stay home tonight.

Nora chuckled at the thought of 'being in control' of anything, especially of her guild. She was dismayed to hear about Belle's house, somewhat less so to hear of Evelyn's place. But still, she wondered what might have become of the redheaded she-devil.

"Will you be staying the night, dear?" Nora asked Ximi.

"No. I'm fine at my place. When I left, I still didn't have electricity. But I've got my chaise lounge set up on the back deck. I guess I'm sleeping out tonight. It's so stinkin' hot indoors by the end of the day, that I can't sleep upstairs. I have my bed on the second floor. I doubt trying to sleep on the sofa will be possible. It's just too hot. Too humid. I don't think it's any cooler than one hundred degrees inside. If I camp out after the sun goes down, at least I'll be trying to fall asleep in somewhat cooler air."

"Oh, dear," said Nora, who was unfamiliar with 'sleeping out' and was distressed at the notion of trying to find any comfort at all on lawn furniture. "Well, dear, if you change your mind, you come here, no matter what the hour. And do come in the morning. Lois promised to return at six to cook breakfast for everyone. Will you join us?"

"Thanks. No. I'll be OK. Just tell Lois I said hi."

With a hug for Nora, the young woman departed.

Nora returned to her enjoyment of being a hostess. Throughout the day, she had given tours for small groups of Shining Star members unfamiliar with the luxuries of the Tea Basket hall. Her guests oohed and awed as she led them from room to room on the second floor, explaining what each was used for.

"This is where we'll install the Gammill," Nora explained to one pair of Shining Star quilters, as she showed off the big room. Catching her thoughtless optimism in the presence of the competition, she hastily lessened the blow as best she could. "That is, if our guild collects and donates the most money for the cause."

By sunset, the room with the design wall had been converted into a temporary dormitory. Lois's cots and air mattress were arranged in a single row against one wall for sleeping. Women who had unluckily drawn short straws would find themselves sleeping on the floor on the far side. Some of them had returned from their homes carrying quilts and pillows for extra padding. They arranged these less-desirable beds with the hope that no one got stepped on in the night should anyone have a late night call of nature.

The second day following the storm, arrived as hot and miserable as ever. That morning, however, the scent of frying bacon and fresh-brewed coffee roused several who had slept the night upstairs in the Tea Basket hall. Lois had returned. The coffee pots awaited each woman descending the stairway. A queue of pajama-clad women, with disheveled bed hair, formed at the door to the only bathroom.

Someone commented, "It's just like retreat!" which returned chuckles from several standing in the line.

Lois discovered loaves of bread on the counter, bought from the store the day before. She browned slices for toast and already had some piled high on a platter on the table, alongside her jars of strawberry and peach jam. Several egg/cheese/bread/sausage casseroles baked in the oven. The sound of frying eggs, with the scent of bacon, filled the air as Lois, attired anew in another large, floral dress, bustled about the stove.

"Grab your favorite brew," Lois commanded, as she flipped eggs over in a large frypan. "Bread's on the table. Casserole will be out in five. Eggs comin' up. I got six over easy right now. Taters O'Brian are ready, too. Bring a plate and come an' get it," she announced.

Each woman took a plate from a stack Lois had arranged on the counter. They spooned potatoes from platters Lois had cooked. They filed past her still flipping over eggs. They seated themselves around tables pulled from storage and set up in the hall the day before. Soon, Lois joined the diners, her forehead damp from her labors, a white apron still tied around her ample waist.

Ladies feasted on eggs, breakfast casserole, fried potatoes, bacon, an orange-banana-grape fruit bowl and coffee. What had at first been a bountiful collection of food was too quickly diminishing into nothing but crumbs and leftover conversation. Lois was the first to polish off her O'Brien potatoes. She stood to get seconds, just as Rosie and Carolyn walked through the front door. Several women seated around the tables waved or mumbled brief greetings to the officers of the guild. Nobody stopped talking or eating.

Lois was dismayed when she arrived at the empty platter and recognized the need for more potatoes. She scraped off the serving dish onto her own plate and gobbled down the last spoonful. Now was a good time to cook up more, she decided. The task would only take a few minutes.

"Come have a seat," she instructed Carolyn and Rosie, pointing toward her vacated chair. "I'll fix more 'taters. You want eggs?"

"Yes, please," said Carolyn. "Sunny side up, if you will. Two."

"I'm good," said Rosie, who had already eaten. "We've got news of Belle and Evelyn."

The announcement drew everyone's attention. Even Lois paused at the stove. Conversation quieted as the women seated around the table paused to hear.

"Belle is OK. She's only shaken up. Her husband, Vern, however, was seriously injured. He was trapped inside his auction house when the storm hit. The whole thing collapsed onto him. He was rescued. Belle is at the hospital with him. Evelyn is also OK but sore from her ordeal. I would think she'll have nightmares about it forever. She survived the storm from inside her old bathtub. The entire house was destroyed around her."

A murmur of concern filled the air.

"Rosie and I think we should help Evelyn. Everything she owned was scattered far and wide. We thought we could locate anything salvageable from the ruins of her home, while she's in the hospital. I thought some of us could go gather up whatever we can find. We can store her things out back in the hall garage until she figures out what to do with it."

With little else to do until power was restored at their homes, several women agreed to help. A plan quickly developed to return to their homes, gather up empty boxes, then meet at Evelyn's address by nine.

Avery arrived at the hall just as they were in discussion about the salvage operation about to take place. Rosie brought Avery up to speed with their plan. Immediately Avery agreed to drive her truck to Evelyn's. She volunteered to haul the boxes back to the Tea Basket hall and be the one to put everything into the shed. If needed, she'd return to the site repeatedly.

By midafternoon, the temperature in Athens County exceeded one hundred degrees. The volunteers had to quit. The intense heat and humidity drove everyone indoors, even those trying to restore order to their damaged homes in The Plains. Folks all over the county retreated to air-conditioning if they were lucky enough to have it. Those still without power had to find less comfort in lawn chairs under the shade of a tree or a building, or go to one of several cooling shelters established by the local Red Cross.

Many of the quilters retreated wearily to the hall, with its air-conditioning running full tilt. Nora was ready when the troops from Evelyn's place clamored through the door. She had directed a group of older quilters to prepare pitchers of ice cold tea, lemonade and water for the returning workers. The heat had worn them down. There was little conversation among them, quite unlike the morning. Most of the women were not accustomed to so much stooping, bending, toting and walking, their age and arthritis having forced them to forego much previous activity in that respect. Several of them wanted nothing more than to cool down and take a long nap. Others simply wanted to wash the sweat off and cool down.

The company of volunteers had retrieved some of Evelyn's garments, most soiled but cleanable. Avery transferred all the clothing into four large trash bags. Wet running attire, T-shirts, socks and foundation garments amounted to most of what the ladies had collected from Evelyn's yard. Nora instructed Avery to put the bags into her car. Nora planned to go home later to do laundry for Evelyn.

They also salvaged undamaged cans of food that had survived the hit, and quite a number of running trophies. Avery unloaded these boxes and stacked them up in the guild's garage.

"Gosh, it's bad," one of the Shining Star members commented, as she sat gulping down a tumbler of ice water. Both her glass of water and the woman were sweating. "Evelyn has next to nothing left. Really! Maybe we should do something else for her."

"Like what?" asked another.

"Well, I don't know. *Something*."

"Well, maybe we can donate part of the money from our raffle sales to Evelyn," suggested Avery.

Even though she was not one of their members, Rosie quickly spoke up. "No way!" she objected. "First of all, Evelyn would probably take exception to losing her chance at that longarm. She'd throw a royal, hissy fit as a result. Secondly, she would undoubtedly be sorely offended if *anybody* offered her *any* form of charity. She's stubborn like that. I suggest you talk over any idea you may have, with her first, before you make a grave mistake. You really don't want to get that woman's hackles up."

Avery pictured Evelyn as the Tasmanian devil cartoon character, coming at her with hair pins flying off in every direction, orange-colored hair exploding outward, long claws extended, all spittle and snarls. She shuddered visibly. "You're probably right."

23

*T*he duty nurse picked up the phone. The call was from a volunteer manning a small desk in the OR waiting room. She listened to the message then hung up and went immediately to Belle Hart's room. Vern was just out of surgery and moved into recovery.

"The surgeon will come here to talk to you shortly. He'll answer all your questions and tell you how your husband is doing."

Belle took the news with mixed emotions. She felt both joy and fear at the same time. She swung bare legs over the side of the hospital bed and put a hand over her mouth, trying to stifle a sob.

Evelyn heard the comments, then footfalls as the nurse left. She came around the curtains to Belle's side of the room. Evelyn still wore the loose hospital gown that made the redhead look even tinier than she was. She sat down on the edge of the bed beside Belle. She laid her hand tentatively on Belle's shoulder in what she imagined might serve as a sign of comfort.

"He's out of surgery. So that's good. Whatever they did is done. Don't waste time worrying when you don't know what to worry about."

Belle looked over at Evelyn, puzzled. This was strange behavior for Evelyn. "Why are you being nice to me?"

Evelyn let go of her companion's shoulder and lowered her hands into her lap. She clasped both hands together and dropped her head. *Why am I being nice?* "I don't know. Maybe... maybe it's because I don't see you as a threat... any more."

"A threat? Me? A threat?"

"I mean... well, before... you and Vern stood in the way... in my way. I wanted to beat the Tea Baskets to that Gammill. I didn't care how. I just had to stop you from getting it. I had to eliminate everything in the way of that. Tea Baskets having an auctioneer was my number one priority to eliminate. Now with Vern... not gone, but banged up... I figure, what's the point? He's out. Right? Crap, what's the point of *anything* I've tried to do?

Might as well have been me under a surgeon's knife. I've lost everything. I don't have strength to fight for anything any more."

Belle sat in silence, an expression of doubt fixed on her furrowed brow, listening to this woman's confession.

Evelyn continued, "You see, I never could please anybody. I stopped trying a long time ago. Just spent my whole life running away. Foot races at first, to get away from anyone who said I was a failure. Who was I kidding? Huh? I guess just myself. I ran from supervisors. They all considered me a pain. Even you all, Tea Basket Quilters, you all thought I was useless. When I was president, I saw the looks on everybody's faces, the contempt. I heard the grumbles behind my back. Then Molly offered up that Gammill. As expected, nobody in guild would listen to my idea to win it. So I ran off again, formed my own guild. I did what I had to do to get what I wanted, the way I wanted. But then this storm... this storm's destroyed everything. My house is gone. My car is gone. My stuff, too. Everything. So nothing matters any more. Nothing. I have nothing. I am nothing. Just like everybody thinks."

Belle was clearly seeing an Evelyn she had never quite understood or cared to understand. She saw a tortured little person this day. For the first time in her recollection, Evelyn North was cowering. Gone was her demanding, snarky voice. Gone were all signs of tyranny and superiority. This was the same person who had always put everyone else down in an effort to elevate her own sense of self. Still, Belle could not bring herself to sympathize with any pain Evelyn was feeling.

"You treat people like dirt, Evelyn. That's why nobody's ever happy with you. The way people respond to you has nothing to do with thoughts about your abilities. It has everything to do with your damn attitude. You're a bitch toward everybody. No wonder nobody wants to work with you, or follow you, or be a friend. The world don't revolve around you, Evelyn. Believe it or not. You make your world the way you treat it. You want people to be nice to you? Then you gotta be nice to them, doll. Shucks, you go 'round blackmailing folks 'cause they did something stupid when they was a kid. You're going to find you made an enemy, not no friend."

Evelyn continued to hang her head, hands still folded in her lap. "I guess you're right."

"Dang right, I'm right."

"I'm sorry. I don't know how to be nice... or how to make friends, I guess."

"Well, first you gotta start seein' people as friends, not enemies. Break that nasty habit of threatening others. You might see there are folks out there who could like you. You might actually make a real friend, somebody who will always be there, willing to help you."

Evelyn remained quiet as Belle scolded her. Perhaps there was some truth in what Belle said. But it was also true that Evelyn had never cared to learn how to be nice or how to be a friend.

A physician wearing a white lab coat walked into their room.

Evelyn looked up, realizing he was there to talk to Belle. So she mumbled, "Later," and retreated to her own side of the privacy curtain, where she crawled into her bed and curled up under the sheet.

"Mrs Hart?"

"Oh, Doctor, how is Vern? Can I see him? Is he going to be OK?"

The doctor smiled reassuringly, extended his hand to Belle and shook hers gently. "Slow down, slow down. Vern will be fine, with time. I assure you. He suffered lacerations on his head, and a concussion. We've stitched up his wound, but he'll have a nasty scar, I'm afraid. His hair should cover that up in time. We gave him a haircut he probably won't be fond of when he looks in a mirror. His collarbone was broken, as well as an arm. The radius was fractured in three places. We've set the arm and have immobilized his upper arm and shoulder. The shoulder will have to remain so while his collarbone heals. You'll find that we tied him up, so he won't be able to do much of anything for himself for several weeks. But as near as we've determined, he suffered no internal injuries. He's going to be bruised and sore for several days. But considering everything he went through, he was very lucky."

"Where is he? Can I see him?"

"He's in recovery. After he comes out of sedation and his vitals are normal, we'll move him into a room. You can see him then. Now, how about you?"

"Me? What do you mean? I'm OK, just shaken."

"Well, you may want to wear something a little less *institutional* when you go to see Vern. I just spoke to your attending. He told me the squad brought you in yesterday. He only kept you for observation. He's releasing you today."

"Oh! Oh, my. Yes. I never thought about how I must look. Frightful, am I? This thing is kinda drafty, but I have no clothes with me." Belle fanned the skirt of her hospital gown, like a little girl showing off an apron.

"Have the nurse contact someone to bring you street clothes. By the time you're dressed and ready to present yourself, Vern will probably be in a room."

"Oh, thank you, Doctor. You've made me feel better, knowing Vern's not on death's doorstep."

The surgeon released Belle's hand, with a final goodbye squeeze, gave her shoulder a reassuring pat then left the room. She sat back, her heart feeling lighter, her future much brighter. On the other side of the privacy curtain lay a small red-headed woman curled up in a fetal position, who was very much alone and feeling unloved.

An aide soon popped into their room to take down a name and phone number to contact. As if Belle could remember any phone numbers. With the advent of cell phones, her habit of memorizing phone numbers had gone the way of the dime store's nickel-plated cash register. Belle wasn't sure she was correct with any of the numbers she recited to the hospital aide. She told the aide she hoped they were.

The aide, who knew that phone company crews had restored service to some areas, returned to the nurse's station and pulled out a phone book kept under the counter, to double-check the accuracy of Belle's list of numbers. She could verify two of the four. The first number she tried was not in service yet. The last number rang in, but she got only a recording. She left a voice mail.

Lois Caldwell returned home, shucked off her floral dress for barn clothes, then rushed outside to do chores. She fed her chickens, collected a bucket of eggs and tossed bales of hay to her cattle. After she returned to the house, she discovered a message waiting on her answering machine. She punched the button on the device and listened.

'This is Sandy Drew at O'Bleness. Belle Hart gave me your number. She and her husband are here at the hospital. The doctor has released Mrs Hart.

However, she wants to stay by her husband's side. She needs a set of clothes to wear. She thought you might be able to help in that regard. Let me know if that's possible, as soon as you get this message.'

Sandy had left a callback number that Lois returned at once. She knew where Vern and Belle Hart lived, of course, but explained she didn't have a key to the house. Then she remembered what she'd heard about the Hart home. Maybe a key wouldn't actually be necessary. She agreed to get clothes for Belle and deliver them to the hospital as soon as possible.

Lois had to change clothes again; out of bibs and back into her common sense going-to-town attire. She sighed heavily at the thought. With much grunting, fumbling and wobbling about, she peeled off her sweaty coveralls and tried to slip under a cool dress. The back of the dress rolled up like a window blind, behind her neck. It hung up on her damp shoulders. After several attempts of ineffective squirming and grasping, she was finally able to snag the edge of the hem and pry the fabric down and over her hips. Once again she crawled into the cab of her truck and drove back toward town. Bypassing Athens, she drove up the highway to The Plains. She'd have to rummage through Belle's damaged house to find a frock for her guild sister to wear.

Lois drove as close to the wreckage of the Hart home as she dared. No one had yet made any attempt to clean up the site. She wanted to avoid getting a nail in a tire from all the debris scattered across the drive. That's all she'd need in this heat. *Fixin' a flat in a dress!* Junk lay everywhere across the lawn, the driveway and out into the street, stuff which only yesterday had been part of Belle and Vern Hart's home.

Lois parked her truck in the street and turned off the engine. She walked around the garage, looking at the roof and the wall laying on top of Belle's flattened Cadillac. She shuffled unsteadily up a lopsided ramp of fallen garage doors, toward the remains of the home. Treading as carefully as she could, she clumsily made her way up through the gap where a wall had once stood. This brought her to solid footing on a tiled floor of what had once been the Hart kitchen. Conditions inside the house were surprisingly better than she had expected to see. Once under the main roof she recognized a neat home, with furnishings still oddly in place, untouched by the wind. Being inside the house, however, felt creepy. Lois did not like snooping around someone else's home. She had to force herself to concentrate on her quest for Belle's clothes. *Where is Belle's closet?*

Lois assumed she had arrived at the master bedroom, with its king-sized bed, plush carpeting and fine wooden furnishings. Here she began her search in earnest, by opening and peering behind several closed doors, one after the other. Master bath behind door number one. Obviously Vern's closet behind door number two. And a third door opened to another small room whose purpose Lois could see, at once, was Belle's sewing room. Maybe at one time the room had been a spare bedroom, or maybe a nursery. The space appeared then to be a studio for Belle's creative side. She had arranged an efficient triangle of sewing machine, workstations for cutting, and a large cabinet, covered with a reflective cloth, for pressing all of her seams. This was not what Lois was seeking, so she closed the door and moved on. Opening a fourth door, she finally discovered Belle's closet. The size alone made Lois gasp in awe.

This was like no closet she was familiar with. This was a whole room, filled floor to ceiling with women's clothing. An overabundance of garments were hung neatly on hangers, against two opposing walls. Between them, at the far end, was a wall covered floor to ceiling with a mirror. In the dim light, and for a brief moment, her own image gave her a start. As her attention was drawn again to the clothing, Lois realized she had never seen so many pretty things in one place in all her life, except maybe in a department store. Lois' collection of dresses, shirts and dungarees fit into a space no deeper than twenty-four inches and no wider than thirty-six inches. Hers was an old farmhouse closet. Everything she owned hung on one single rod. Belle's closet had tiers of rods that ran the length of those two walls, which she estimated to be at least ten feet wide.

There were rods fastened high to hold slacks, long skirts and gowns in every hue and fabric. Some of the gowns even glittered. Lois stepped closer and let her fingers caress the softness of a pale-blue chiffon number, which she pulled out to admire. She visualized Belle wearing the formal gown, looking like a queen. Then she thought about Vern. *Bet this number puts a real sparkle in his eyes,* she thought. Carefully she allowed the dress to fall back into place. She examined more rods, some low and others high. Here she discovered jackets, shirts, vests and other tops. Everything appeared to be sorted by season. Wools and heavier fabrics in one section for winter wear, light cottons in another for summer. She noticed recessed lights above, and without thinking, flicked a light switch to get a better look.

Of course, power's out. Dummy.

Lois tried to recall an outfit that Belle had earlier worn to a guild meeting. She combed through the collection to locate what she thought she remembered. She sorted through dozens of clothes, taking her time, before picking out what came close to the picture in her memory. She turned around to discover that the fourth wall held floor-to-ceiling shelves filled with neatly arranged footwear. Trying not to count them, she selected one pair of sandals from a shelf bearing dozens of them. She saw high heels, wedges, loafers, winter boots and fashion boots; so many, in fact, that she shook her head at this display of excess. Lois, herself, owned one pair of barn boots, one pair of work boots and two pair of sensible town shoes. Her own humble shoes resided woefully on the floor of her tiny closet, except for the barn boots, which she always parked outside her door.

It took additional time for Lois to locate Belle's foundations. There, again, Lois' eyes popped. From a tall, narrow dresser she opened drawer after drawer, where she was astonished by yet another abundant collection. This treasure trove was composed entirely of 'unmentionables', as she called them. She held up a red teddy for close inspection. She was both aghast and in awe at the delicate contraption. *How can a woman pee wearing one of these!* She was positive she would never have to face that problem, and as a result, would never know the answer. *Yes, positive I'll never know how.* Lois carefully folded and returned the teddy, grabbing instead a pair of tan — *probably called ecru* — lace panties, and of course, a matching lacey, tan bra — two other items Lois figured she'd never own. *Lace panties with a matching bra? Good lord!*

Half an hour later Lois lumbered into Belle's hospital room, bearing a brown paper sack with the change of clothes she had collected. She blinked in surprise to discover Evelyn North laying in the other bed. The privacy curtain had been pushed back so that both patients could converse eye-to-eye.

"Um, here's your clothes, Belle," Lois said, handing the bag over to Belle while still staring at Evelyn.

"Oh, thank you, baby doll," Belle replied, taking the sack out of Lois' hand and giving the big woman a hug around the neck. She realized Lois was still eyeballing Evelyn.

"Evelyn's my roommate. They're going to let her go home, too," Belle announced, as she let go of Lois and darted into the bathroom to change. Belle closed the bathroom door behind her, leaving tiny Evelyn looking up at the much larger Lois.

"Only I have no home to go to," Evelyn sadly whispered.

Lois took this news in stride. She was aware that Evelyn's house had been destroyed. "The girls have been to your place and gathered up some of your stuff," she said matter-of-factly.

Evelyn sat up, slack-jawed, silent and stone-cold still.

"Nora's washing up what clothes they found. Avery put your other stuff in the Tea Basket's garage. Some of the ladies have stayed overnight at the hall. You could, too. But maybe you'd like to come home with me instead, seein' as how you don't much like Tea Basket gals any more, I guess. You could stay at my place as long as you need to, if you want. I've got a spare bedroom you can use. I figure you can stay while you figure out what to do 'bout your place."

Evelyn didn't know what to say. Women were coming to her aid without her asking? Lois was offering her a refuge? These were some of the very people she'd displayed a contemptuous attitude toward, bad-mouthed, bribed and coerced. She remembered Belle's lecture.

"Why?" *Why would anybody want to help me?*

"Why what? Why can you stay with me? Or why don't you like Tea Basket Quilters?"

"No. Why would you, or anybody, help me? I'm the last person on earth anybody should want to help."

"You're right there, toots. You're a hard one to like. But when tragedy strikes, people open their hearts and homes, and they come to the aid of folks in need. People don't do nice things for others for a reason. They help 'cause it's simply the right thing to do. That's all. It's what friends do."

Belle emerged from the bathroom in her own clothes. She wore a fancy robin's-egg-blue T-shirt, with matching embroidery around the neck, a pair of tan, linen slacks and the brown sandals Lois had brought in the bag. She'd smoothed back her hair to look presentable. Lois had found and tossed a brush into the bag, as an afterthought. Belle's blue eyes sparkled with hopefulness.

"Good job, Lois!" she said, giving the woman another hug. Doing a small spin, she asked, "How did you know this is one of my favorite outfits? Thank you so much. Now, if you'll excuse me, baby doll, I've got to go find Vern."

Lois watched Belle leave the room, then she turned back to Evelyn. "So, can you leave now, or do you want to stay? I've got little time to stand around here doin' nothing. I have things needin' my attention back on the farm. Already been away far too often today. You going to stay here, or do I drop you off at the Tea Basket hall, or are you gonna come home with me?"

Given the alternatives, Evelyn knew now was the time to make a decision. Lois made clear, with arms crossed over her ample chest, that she expected an answer.

"They put my clothes in this locker. I'll get changed and go home with you, to your farm."

"Awesome. Get a move on then. Don't have all day, ya know."

"Oh, my god!" Evelyn said, opening the locker door designated for her bed.

"What?" Lois asked.

Evelyn stooped over and picked up a purse from the floor of the locker. "This is mine!"

"Yeah? Well, shouldn't *your* purse be with *your* stuff?"

"No! The last time I saw this purse was at my kitchen table!"

"Oh."

"I have no idea how my purse got here."

"Well, somebody put it there. Can you wonder 'bout this mystery later? I'm getting' hungry. We need to go."

Evelyn gathered up the running gear she had worn the day she sprinted down her hallway and jumped into her claw-footed tub. She also picked up the damp running shoes that she had used to cushion her head at the bottom of the tub. She went into the bathroom to change and soon emerged looking rumpled but fully attired. Her head of orange curls refused to be controlled. They suggested she'd been blown around by a tornado or, in this case, one of the nation's worst windstorms to ever cross the Mid-Atlantic States.

"Ready?" Lois asked.

"I guess."

24

$\mathcal{P}$hoebe slept poorly the night after the big storm. Like everyone else, she suffered miserably in the heat without power. There was no air-conditioning to remove the humidity inside her cabin. She could not run a fan to circulate air. The night was so oppressive, and all she wanted was to stop sweating. It was like picking beans in the noonday sun. As always, she hated to sweat.

Because of their short muzzles, Phoebe's precious pugs could not tolerate the heat, either. They panted constantly and moved frequently in search of cooler spots on the hardwood floor. They would spread out, bellies flat, legs stretching ahead and behind in a sploot. Stitch, Medallion and Phoebe spent the night in constant motion, dogs panting, owner fanning herself.

Part of Phoebe's unrest also came from nagging thoughts. Interesting thoughts, maybe. Impossible thoughts, probably. Useless, sleep-depriving thoughts, definitely. They swirled about her mind without end, scenarios that came and went, only to return over and over again, each time in a slightly altered form. Like a song in a loop, they drummed on in her brain, beating out an irritating rhythm that added to her restlessness. Unable to sleep, she was defenseless against their onslaught. They ran amok in her imagination, with William Evergreen playing a major role in every one. Phoebe could not get him out of her head.

By three a.m., according to the wind-up clock on her nightstand, she gave up and got out of bed. With pugs at her heels and wearing only a light strapped to her forehead, she went from room to room, opening windows wider, both upstairs and down. Some had never been opened since the cabin had been built. Thoughts of William Evergreen tagged along like one of her pugs. There was no respite.

After all the windows were wide open, she could almost feel the slightest of night breezes begin to flow into her stuffy house. She imagined her cabin a living thing, now able to breathe. Maybe if she gave herself permission, she might feel different, too. Tiny no-see-ums passed through the screens on the damp, night air. They pinged her forehead and cheeks. She snorted and shuddered as she blew them out of her nostrils, thrashing at the air to fan them away. The bugs were like her inescapable thoughts. Hastily, she thought to snap off the light strapped to her forehead, which attracted them. Now useless, she yanked the strap off then felt her way into a darkened kitchen.

Once at the sink, Phoebe drew a glass of water from the tap, using her thumb to estimate how much the water had filled the glass. She guessed, from the long length of time it took to fill the tumbler, that power was also off at the rural water district pumps. That meant a boil order would be issued. She took a sip, but the tepid water offered no satisfying relief. Next, she pulled open the door to a dark and equally warm refrigerator to search the interior, boredom leading her on an unnecessary quest for food. Feeling around, she located a water jug she kept on the top shelf and guessed, by its heft, to be full. Satisfied to know she had safe water for a while, she felt around for any form of edible snack. Disappointed, and also grateful that nothing appealed, she shut the door. She and her pugs wandered out onto the cabin's back porch.

A wooden porch swing hung on chains from the rafters. She chose to recline for a while. However, after several painful minutes with her back pressed against the slats, she rose. She returned to the dark interior of the cabin, knocking about blindly, then returned with two thin dog beds which she unceremoniously tossed under the swing, then once again retreated back inside. While she was gone, each pug selected a bed of its choice. Both circled around its chosen cushion several times before settling down.

Phoebe emerged wearing shorts and a T-shirt and carrying one of her quilts. By the light of half a moon, she folded the quilt neatly over the hard wood planks of her swing. With a small throw pillow for her head, she resumed a prone position, swaying gently back and forth above her two companions. Even though somewhat more comfortable, she still did not sleep soundly the rest of that night. An occasional mosquito buzzed her hearing, threatening to bite. Dew wrapped itself around her body, leaving a sticky film on her legs, arms and neck. Between these annoyances and the call of morning birds, she awoke before dawn. She sat upright, feeling tired and stiff. The rising sun was beginning to creep toward the forest treetops. Already, this new day promised to be intensely hot. With that irritating thought, she retreated into the cabin with her pugs in tow.

Phoebe needed to make breakfast. Kibble under a can of wet dog food for the pugs, as usual. They were soon happily snorting, loudly gobbling up everything she'd put into their bowls. She made a peanut butter sandwich for herself. Her hunger was satisfied but not her sense of pleasure. As she chewed on the sandwich, Phoebe realized she could have used a lighter to circumvent the need for electricity to spark a flame on her pilotless gas stovetop. That thought, which had been slow to occur in her sleep-deprived mind, meant she could at least have made coffee, tea or a bowl of oats. She sighed. She would remember tomorrow. All was not lost for the day or days ahead.

She rummaged in her pantry and found cans of soup, an unopened box of pasta noodles and a small jar of spaghetti sauce. No, she would not starve without the electric company's service. But what to do to pass idle time? Phoebe was always busy doing something. In addition to sweating, she also disliked being idle. Nothing was on her to-do list in the aftermath of this storm. Nothing came to mind to hold her interest, either. She sighed wearily once again in mild frustration at having grown so bored so quickly.

There would be no weeding in the wet soil or blazing sun this day, not without a hot shower afterward. Without water pressure, there would be no shower. There would be no laundry to do, nor vacuuming, nor any sewing at her machine. She finally decided, if her hands stayed dry, she might hand applique or maybe embroider. But she cautioned herself. If the heat made her hands sweaty, she'd have to forego even those activities. She was well aware that oil and sweat from hands could permanently stain fine linen. What then to do?

She went to her stack of plastic boxes containing projects as yet unfinished and some not yet begun. She passed over several linen samplers in various stages of progress. She rejected them, feeling it was best to play it safe. Linen was expensive, and the projects inside the storage boxes were very detailed. Finally, she found something to divert her hands, and maybe, thoughts of William Evergreen. She pulled out an autumn-themed, wool candle mat from the stack of UFO bins. If she stayed out of the sun, stitched on the west porch in the morning, moved to the east porch in the afternoon, perhaps she could avoid some of the day's heat.

On the porch once again, a slight but effective breeze embraced her, as heavy, humid air flowed past her cabin down into the wooded valley behind her house. She made relatively good progress on the little piece of wool, in spite of frequent breaks to dab her forehead with a limp paper towel. Several shades of brown turkeys with orange tail feathers danced around an eight-inch circle of black wool. The finished mat would look nice, she thought, placed on her coffee table this fall, with a stout orange candle centered on top of it.

Phoebe used a simple whip stitch around each tiny shape, which formed turkey bodies, tail feathers, heads and wattles. There were many little pieces to attach, so the task kept her mind busy for several hours, for which she was grateful. She wrapped black cotton floss three times around her needle then reinserted the needle near where it emerged, creating little French knots for each bird's eyes. She then adorned the project with other more intricate stitches, adding the final elements the pattern required. Careful embroidery created yellow legs and beaks for each fat and whimsical bird.

She was just about to create the final turkey beak with three strands of yellow embroidery floss, when her cell phone rang inside the cabin. She jumped at the unexpected sound.

It turned out to be a familiar male voice on the other end, a pleasant and welcome voice that made her heart skip. "Oh, hello, Bill. I'm surprised my phone works *(and it's you)*. What's up?"

"I just wanted to see how you fared last night. I heard on the news that several states east got hit pretty hard. Thousands lack power and phone service. That was a powerful storm we had. But here in Athens, power is coming back on slowly. Cell towers seem to be working now, so I thought I'd check on you."

"Here in Athens? You didn't go back to Cleveland?"

"Couldn't leave, puddin," he said.

Puddin? Oh, lord... a term of endearment.

"Local sheriff put the place on lockdown with his Level 3 driving restrictions. Oh, and an announcer on my car radio said route 50 to Marietta was closed due to downed trees. Couldn't get to 7, so I didn't bother starting for Cleveland. Extended my stay at the hotel of darkness. I've wanted to call you several times, but I didn't have service until now. So, how are you?"

"Bill, you know I'm fine. We were together. My place is fine, too."

"Do you have power?"

"No."

"So what are you doing with yourself?"

"Sewing."

"How can you sew without power?"

"By hand."

"Oh, I see."

There was a long pause between them.

"Maybe you'd like to do something else with your free time."

"Can't think of anything."

"Oh, sure you can. How about taking a trip? I do have to head back to Cleveland. I would really appreciate your company on the long drive."

What should I say?

Just then, Stitch and Medallion started chasing each other's curly tails around Phoebe's legs. They snuffled, snorted and sputtered, as pugs are known to do.

"I have two dogs to care for, Bill."

"I have no problem with dogs. Pugs, I think? You told me at dinner. I like pugs. My back yard is fenced, you know. Do they travel well? Do you have leashes for them?"

Phoebe had leashes. She had a harness for each pug, too. They were licensed, had all their shots, and they loved to go for car rides. Mostly because they could sleep. It was Phoebe who, at that moment, needed a jerk on her own leash. She needed a better excuse than pugs in order to weasel out of this invitation… with a man… with Bill Evergreen.

"I don't know, Bill…"

"Listen, puddin, I really enjoyed talking with you yesterday. It's been a long time since we did that."

"Yes, it has been."

"I was hoping to spend more time with you, now that I've found you again. You wouldn't have to stay at my place. I'll put you up at a hotel as my guest, if you'd feel more comfortable. But I'd like to catch up. I... you... we're both... at an age where... well..."

"Well, what?"

"Well... life grows short for us. Don't waste this opportunity. I know we'll be good friends. We are friends, I think. Aren't we? At least, I hope we are."

Phoebe remembered pretending to be Bill's friend. Hiding a deep affection for him was one of the hardest things she'd ever done in her young life. She had to stifle her desire to pursue the young Bill Evergreen. He was betrothed back then. Phoebe's sense of right and wrong, and her moral compass, kept her at more than arm's length. But now, maybe she had a chance. He had mentioned he was a widower now. But would the memories of his late wife get between them? Phoebe, of course, had no way of knowing. But she hoped it might not.

"Let's spend some time together. Just you and me. Enjoy each other's company for a little while. What else have you got to do?"

"Well..."

"Listen, I'll show you around Cleveland. Besides, the lake breeze might beat this stifling humidity down here in the hills."

Part of Phoebe was thrilled — that part of her that was once again a young girl on the precipice of love. Simultaneously another part was petrified — that part which had become her instinct for a pain-free life. The idea of escaping the heat and boredom, of spending time with someone she really did like, and with her precious pugs in tow, sounded perfectly delicious. But the thought of her being in the company of a man she had once loved so desperately, meant she might open up old wounds and perhaps end up with new ones. And then, there would be plenty of explaining to do to her Tea Basket friends.

Her quilting friends, like Nora, had been confidants who, over decades of shared classes, retreats, luncheons and meetings, had been led to believe that Phoebe liked... no... that Phoebe Prescott... loved... the single life and living alone. She'd have to admit she'd manufactured that long-held image when, in fact, that was not completely true. Phoebe had lived a lie. Phoebe Prescott thought maybe she had fallen, again, for this man from Cleveland. Years ago she had fallen for Bill Prescott, back when he belonged to another. The day Bill Evergreen proposed marriage to her roommate,

Phoebe suffered the worst heartache she had ever known. Would complications follow with this reunion?

Complications were the things she truly disliked, not people. Phoebe had simply lived a life trying to avoid complications. She had wasted forty years avoiding love, in order to avoid the pain of complications.

Belle got directions to Vern's room, at the nurse's station. She left at once, walking briskly down the hallway, wearing the crisp outfit Lois had brought her. She scanned the room numbers as she passed, eventually coming upon the number she was looking for. The room was located in the surgery wing on the same floor but some distance from her own room. The hallway looked exactly like the one in which she had been housed overnight, but this wing seemed quieter. Yet the staff there appeared to be busier, as nurses in colored scrubs came and went frequently from room to room. Belle walked around a medicine cart parked outside Vern's room, then she stepped quietly through the doorway. She had found her Vern at last. Her heart began to pound inside her chest, and tears welled up in her eyes even before she saw him lying in the bed.

Her man's arm was enclosed in a cast and strapped to his chest with a cotton restraint sling, just as the doctor told her it would be. His ever-present glasses were missing. His eyes were closed. Dark, yellow skin, a sign of developing bruises, formed under each. A coppery-yellow film graced his forehead — beta dyne maybe. The stain continued upward into his hairline and surrounded a row of stitches starting at his temple and ending, the length of a pen, along his scalp. That side of his head was shaved bare. The zippery stitches belonged on Frankenstein, not on her Vern.

Belle went to his bedside and gently touched his free outstretched hand. A needle taped to the back of his wrist was attached to an IV tube hooked to a bag hanging from a hook above his head. His heart rate was still being monitored, as a machine beeped rhythmically and displayed each beat of his heart with a jumping line on a screen. His heart seemed strong, the lines looked regular. A tear rolled off her cheek and dropped onto the sheet covering his body.

Vern had always been robust, lively and very much engaged with the world around him. She had never known him sick, ill or injured. Seeing him lying so quiet, knowing he had been hurt, filled her with a sense of panic which threatened to overtake her. This vision of him prone, silent and unmoving frightened her. Belle emitted a sob and wiped away another tear with the back of her hand.

Vern stirred with the sound of her sob and her touch. He opened his eyes. A few heartbeats passed on the monitor before he recognized her. When he focused on her, he smiled weakly and moved his hand to take her fingers in his.

"Oh, baby doll," Belle uttered.

"How do I look?" he whispered weakly.

That he still possessed his sense of humor brought a smile to her face. "Nobody'll know you when you leave here. You got a real punk do. Gonna have a nasty scar, too."

His smile widened then faded away with a sigh. His words were slow to form. "Lost everything, Belle. All gone." He was aware of what had happened. "I'm sorry I've let you down."

"Oh, baby doll, don't you worry 'bout a thing. We'll be OK. You're alive. We're both alive. We have each other. That's all that matters."

Vern uttered a sobbing sound himself, which frightened Belle even more than his appearance. "Don't leave me," he begged.

"Leave you? Why on earth would I leave you, baby doll? I love you, even with that awful haircut. I'm never going to leave you, Vernie. Never."

"But I don't have a thing, any more. What can I offer?"

"I don't care about stuff, baby doll. If I didn't have you, *then* I wouldn't have anything. Baby doll, you're all I need. You're all I've ever needed."

Vern and Belle were both crying. Their joined hands had grown damp with the anxiety of losing each other. Vern's cheeks were rosy, and tears rolled down to his ears as his head lay motionless on the bed.

"I can't give you anything any more. I'm ruined."

Belle wiped away her own tears then his, and she smiled down at her husband as she squeezed his fingers. "Wasn't I poor when you met me? I been there before, baby doll. Bein' poor don't matter. We can climb out of this setback together. I still have a license to cut hair. I can work, so we won't starve while you're laid up. I don't care where we live, either. Don't matter to me what we drive, or even if we own a car." Then, as an afterthought, she said, "Don't matter what happened to you yesterday, or what I did a long time ago. As long as I have you, I have everything I could ever want."

Vern listened. Her words allowed him to relax. He believed her. Perhaps he could stop worrying. He began to let loose of his fear of abandonment. If Belle was saying what she honestly meant and what she truly felt, as she seemed to be saying, then she was right. In time, and with each other, they would build a new life with whatever scraps they could piece together, just like one of her beautiful quilts. Everything, he assured himself, would be put to rights with time.

By then the IV drip, which included timed pain medication, began to take ahold. Vern felt tired and closed his eyes, letting go of his wife's hand. He drifted off into a dreamless sleep, a sleep now absent of a recurring nightmare in which he always woke up to find himself alone.

Belle walked to the only chair in the room and sat down to wait with him. She'd be there by his side forever. No doubt in her mind. Someday soon Vern would leave the hospital, and she would be there to help him. And as ugly as that haircut was, he was hers, forever. She'd find her clippers in that wreck of a house and give him a buzz cut. While she sat to wait with him, Belle began to make a mental list of things she could do. In a day or two, she'd call the insurance company. When he was ready to go home, she'd rent a car. And while their house was being repaired, they would go live on Vern's *Mistress*, the little sternwheel river boat moored downriver in Gallipolis. If it was still there.

For Avery, the day following the big storm proved to be a busy one. She had been able to reach most of both guilds' members to check on them. Thanks to Nora's suggestion, volunteers recruited along the way, sped up the process. Avery was happy and excited to be so involved: delighted to see women from both guilds working together, assisting anyone who needed help. The efforts to salvage items from Evelyn's place was the most interesting part of the whole affair. Many of the Shining Stars were not aware of Evelyn's volatile nature. But even those from the Tea Basket guild that did know her, never hesitated to lend a hand, policing her yard and gathering up pieces of the woman's life that had literally been scattered to the wind.

Avery drove to the hospital that evening. Once there, she learned that both Evelyn and Belle had been discharged. Avery did not know that Belle remained, sitting by her husband's bedside. Avery was also unaware that Lois had acquired a new housemate. She reluctantly left the hospital, turned on the coolness of her Ford's AC and drove to the stifling heat of her apartment, content with the knowledge that she had made a difference to some that day.

She flipped the switch inside her apartment door and was happily surprised when the lights came on. She went about closing windows left open during the night hoping for any flow of air at all, then turned on the air-conditioning. She opened her small and ancient refrigerator freezer to assess what should be hauled out to the trash. The rental did not provide the latest frost-free kind, but rather an ancient appliance with a tiny freezer compartment. All the ice which would have been condensed around the metal housing had melted off. Avery assumed nothing was safe, so she began the task of pulling out packages of soggy meat and tossing them into her nearby waste bin. Unfrozen bags of vegetables flew across the room next, landing into the trash can. The electricity must have just come back on, she thought, because nothing had, as yet, refrozen.

Returning from the dumpster with an empty bin, she noticed the light blinking on her home answering machine. Her landline was back up.

"Ms Underwood, this is Sheila Harper, with the county engineer. We wondered if you could come in for an interview. In light of the current situation around the county, the engineer asked if you would call us back at your earliest convenience."

Sheila left a callback number which matched the one Avery already had programmed into her cell phone. Her phone now indicated adequate bars to return the call. Before she could punch up the county engineer's number, a second message came over on the answering machine speaker.

"Ah, Ms Underwood, it's Sheila Underwood again. I was doing disaster assessment over in The Plains yesterday, right after the storm, and I came across a quilt with your name on it. Would you give me a call about it? You can reach me here at work."

25

*N*ora, Carolyn and Rosie sat around a table on the first floor of the Tea Basket hall. They were talking over coffee and cookies when Avery walked through the door, carrying a large plastic bag. Nora waved and motioned for her to join them.

"What are you up to, girl?" Nora asked.

"You won't believe it when I tell you."

The friends all looked to each other, intrigued.

"Try us," Rosie said.

Avery unzipped the bag. Carolyn stood to help the tall woman once she saw the queen-size quilt fall out. Carolyn held one corner, and Avery backed off, holding the other, allowing the quilt to unfold. The two women raised the quilt as high as their arms allowed, for Nora and Rosie to view. Carolyn did her best to peer round to the front side while still holding her end high.

"This is my quilt. Well, no. Correction. This *was* my quilt. I donated it to the Shining Stars. It's our raffle quilt."

"Beautiful!" said Nora.

"Oh, my, yes, very nice," agreed Rosie, still craning her neck to view the quilt.

"Evelyn took this quilt home with her on the day of the storm. When the derecho destroyed her house, this quilt and everything inside went flying. A damage assessment worker found both Evelyn's purse and this quilt when she went back to get a photo of Evelyn's bathtub. You remember, the one we heard that she jumped into, the only thing that didn't blow away. Anyway, this worker reunited Evelyn with her purse through the Sheriff's office, but she held this quilt back because of my label. She thought this quilt was mine."

Avery passed Carolyn her end of the quilt to exchange ends, in order to reverse its orientation for the little audience of admirers. Nora and Rosie then saw the machine-embroidered label on the back. Carolyn craned her neck around again so she could once again see.

Avery continued. "This woman recognized my name from my resume at the Engineer's office. She recalled that I didn't live in The Plains. So when she found the bag with the quilt bearing my name, she kept it. She wanted to find out if I still owned it, and she had to be sure where I still lived — Athens, or in The Plains. She wanted to return the quilt personally, plus she had to contact me for the office. I met up with her today when I went for an interview."

"You have got to be kidding!" said Nora. "Your name on the label got the quilt back to you?" She turned to her guild sisters, with a finger held aloft for emphasis. "See? What have I always warned you girls about? We must always put a label on the back of every one of our quilts. Here's a perfect example of one reason why."

"Uh, huh."

"I can't believe it!" said Rosie. "And look how it survived the storm; as clean as a brand-new fat quarter!"

"We used this sturdy plastic bag for transporting it to raffle sites. That's what protected it."

"Well, I'll be," said Carolyn. "What a miracle."

"You are so lucky, girl. But do tell, what's this about an interview?" asked Nora.

"Yes, well, that's another reason I'm here. Um, they liked my resume, and I guess I interviewed well. They hired me on the spot. The engineer's office is under a lot of pressure to clear off and repair storm-damaged roads as soon as possible. They wanted me to start immediately. I'm not going to be around, due to the job. I'm not sure what to do about the Shining Star Guild. We don't have a regular time or place to meet, and I haven't been able to find Evelyn. I'm thinking I'll have to drop out of both, since I accepted this job and won't have free time."

"Nonsense, child," Nora said. "You just keep your membership with the Tea Basket Quilters. If you can't make our meetings, that's fine. We'll keep you in the loop and on the roster. I can't help you with your other guild. Did I hear you were one of Evelyn's officers?"

Avery nodded. "VP."

"I know where you can find Evelyn," said Rosie. "She's staying with Lois. She moved into a spare room at her farmhouse."

"You tell Evelyn, that if she wants to use our meeting room for her guild, she can do so. You girls agree?" Carolyn said, looking to the others for approval, which they all gave readily with nods. "Most of her members have been here after the storm, so they know where it's located. And you can leave your quilt right here, too. Make it easy for whoever takes over your raffle duties."

Rosie spoke up. "I hear you've got a schedule of places to sell tickets every weekend. Even if you can't do that work, I'm sure someone from Shining Star can take over."

"I'll open the hall for them, if they wish to leave your quilt here between sales," Nora said.

Avery and Carolyn refolded Avery's quilt and returned it to the plastic bag. Avery zipped the bag shut and set the heavy bundle on the table. "I'm so happy I found all of you. Nothing ever seems to upset you. You always welcome everyone with open arms, and you're always there when anybody needs something. Thank you all."

Nora came around the table and gave the tall woman a hug. "Now, how about some coffee? I suspect you'll be driving out to Lois Caldwell's place to see Evelyn. You don't need to rush off, though. She isn't going anywhere. We can chat awhile longer. We still have a few cookies left."

"Thanks again. And yes, I need to talk to Evelyn and Lois."

Nora, ever the hostess, retrieved a big mug of hot coffee for Avery. "This should keep you here a while. Now, tell us all about this new job of yours."

Avery took a careful sip, savoring the flavor and her association with Nora, Carolyn and Rosie. "I'm the new Assistant County Engineer."

Carolyn Atwood leaned back in astonishment. She listened to Avery Underwood describe her prior experience and how they fit well with her new duties at the engineer's office. She, too, sipped her own coffee and observed Rosie, Nora and Avery. Her own thoughts drifted to the whole Tea Basket group. She thought about all of the quilters who had stepped up to make their auction a small success — no, a *huge* success. She glanced across the table, feeling a sense of deep appreciation for her friends. Her best friend, Rosie, was peppering Avery with questions.

Rosie wore a customary, blue, two-piece business suit, looking professional as usual. Rosie had always been Carolyn's foundation rock, always there to ease the woman's unfounded worries. She'd been a friend since college, and she would continue to be a friend forever.Rosie glanced over at Nora and saw the elderly woman was taking in every word Avery said. Nora was always attentive like that, and she too had always been there for Carolyn. Nora was the one who kept the guild hall running smoothly and made sure every person who entered was made to feel welcome. As a founder, there could have been no better individual.

Whatever mishap, problem or unforeseen danger that Carolyn could imagine, rarely did anything go wrong. Part of Caroyn realized that her worries were useless, but she could not help herself. Worry was in her nature. She sighed contentedly, taking another cookie, followed by a sip of coffee, thinking about the future of the guild. She was happy that her role to play next year would be less when her tenure as president came to a close. Perhaps she might enjoy guild a bit more when she had less responsibility for it. She realized, as she sat among this group of women, that they were the ones who made her look good as their president. Her time in office would be remembered fondly, and her reputation solid, a reputation she probably didn't deserve at all, certainly not without Rosie, Nora and all the others.

Avery drained her mug of coffee at the same time she concluded telling the others about her new job. She left the Shining Star raffle quilt on the table for their safekeeping. Nora agreed to be responsible for it. Avery bid them goodbye and left the hall, bound for Lois Caldwell's farm to see Evelyn.

The drive along the county roads was the usual frustrating experience for Avery, bouncing and swerving around potholes the whole distance. Now she'd be in a position to do something about the problem. By the time she arrived at the farm, her truck was covered with dust and mud. Avery stopped in front of the Caldwell farmhouse and climbed out. Red geraniums still lined the porch steps, and large, green ferns still hung under the gingerbread around the porch. There were now two white-painted rockers on the front porch, each draped with a colorful quilt over the back. As Avery walked toward the farmhouse, the blue screen door swung open wide and Lois emerged.

"Looks like your truck needs a bath," she said, indicating Avery's Ford, the engine ticking under the hood as the metal cooled.

"Always looks like that when I come out your way. I understand Evelyn is staying out here now."

"Yup. She's out back. I gave her my pistol and told her where all the snakes were. I showed her how the gun fired and how to reload. I figure taking out her anger on other vipers would do her a world o' good. We practiced about an hour ago. She's on her own now."

Just then the blast of a gunshot rang out from beyond the corn crib and barn.

"S'pect she's found 'em."

"I need to talk to both of you about guild."

"What's up?"

"I took a full-time job. Don't think I can serve as vice president any more."

Lois' eyes widened with surprise. "Well, I s'pose we better go find Evelyn and tell her. Don't think she'll be too happy to hear this. She isn't too happy about much of anything any more. We'll take my truck, unless you wanna drive yours. We'll be off-road about a quarter mile."

"I can drive. Tell me where to go."

The two women climbed into Avery's truck. Avery engaged the four-wheel drive and drove onto one of Lois' hayfields. Lois directed Avery to keep the big truck along the fence line, which Avery did. She could see previous tire impressions blazed by Lois' truck or tractor, which had flattened the tall grass, leaving a path. Soon they came upon Evelyn standing alone near a small stack of old, rotten fence posts, pistol in hand, taking aim at the posts. She was dressed in a lime-green running suit, her orange hair poorly stuffed under a straw gardening hat that obviously belonged to Lois. Evelyn heard the truck approaching and turned around, squinting, trying to identify the occupants.

"Maybe I should take the gun away from her before you say anything," Lois said.

They looked at one another and broke out in laughter.

Avery stepped down with ease and closed the door behind her. Lois found herself on the downside of a slope, which offered a challenge for her exit. She hung on to the grab bar and tried to slide down to the running board, simultaneously twisting her bulk around in order to land on the ground backward, clinging to the door to remain upright. Her exit was not graceful.

"Oh, it's you," Evelyn said, when she finally recognized the two women climbing out of the cab.

"Sorry to hear about your house," Avery said, approaching Evelyn.

"Yeah."

"You planning to rebuild? Maybe stay here with Lois while the work gets done?"

"Haven't decided."

Avery nodded as if she understood. By then Lois had caught up, and she stood between them.

"I came to let you know that I accepted a job. I start tomorrow."

"Oh. Oh? Tomorrow?"

"Yes. I'm going to work for the County Highway Department."

Evelyn thought this over. She knew instantly that the implications meant that Avery's free time would be limited. "Guess that means you won't be able to sell raffle tickets on week…" Evelyn stopped mid-word. The blood drained from her face, and her complexion grew suddenly more pale than usual. She took a step backward, her knees weakening.

"Oh! Oh, my god, the quilt!" she said, collapsing to the ground in a sitting position.

Lois and Avery stepped quickly to her side.

"You OK, Evelyn?" Lois asked.

Evelyn looked up at Lois and then at Avery. "I haven't seen the quilt since before the storm. I forgot all about it. I put it on a kitchen chair. Then the storm hit and I ran and then…"

Avery knelt down in front of Evelyn, placing her hands on the woman's shoulders. "It's OK, Evelyn. The quilt is safe. Someone found it and returned it. It's at the Tea Basket hall."

Evelyn blinked with astonishment. She let the word 'safe' sink in. She pushed up a pair of new drugstore reading glasses which had slipped down the bridge of her nose when she fell on her rear. "You have it?"

"Yes. It's fine. No damage. Perfect condition. Ready to sell more tickets."

Evelyn let out an audible sigh of relief.

Lois took the pistol still clutched in Evelyn's hand and immediately checked to be sure the safety was latched. She then helped Avery lift Evelyn up off the meadow grass.

"That's why I'm here, to tell you about the quilt," Avery said. "That, and I don't think I can live up to my commitment as your VP. I won't be able to spend the days and hours I intended selling tickets. I thought you should know, in case you want to appoint a replacement."

During her day following the derecho, spent in the company of Lois, Evelyn was trying to slow down, to observe things and people in the world around her, to take time to appreciate them. She had taken Belle's words to heart. Evelyn was now making concerted efforts to treat Lois, her hostess, like a friend. She had helped her with chores. She tried not to complain or to roll her eyes at any of Lois' habits or requests. Evelyn discovered, to her surprise, that sharing a simple conversation with Lois, from the comfort of a rocking chair on the front porch, was not only pleasant but something she actually looked forward to.

Evelyn looked up at Avery who had been instrumental in the success of her raffle — of the *Shining Star's* raffle. And here Avery stood, apologizing for not doing more. This must be, Evelyn thought, another way to treat friends. Make every attempt possible to avoid problems with each other.

"I think Lois and I can handle it, with help." She added, "It'll take everybody in guild to fill your shoes, though."

Avery smiled. That was the first compliment she'd ever heard Evelyn utter. "Thanks, that means a lot."

"How about we head back to the house?" Lois suggested. "It's about time to eat, and I have a hunger for fried potatoes."

26

The Tea Basket hall was abuzz with Shining Star members. Twenty women were present to attend their second meeting, and the first since the big storm. Many of them had visited the hall following the storm and were familiar with the layout of the building and the rooms upstairs. A few of them asked Nora if they could show around their fellow members who were unfamiliar, just for a look see. Nora was delighted to grant permission.

Evelyn was present, too. The redhead made an effort to talk to Nora apart from the hubbub of the small crowd. She pulled the older woman into a corner of the kitchenette, where they could speak in private.

"Lois told me what you did for me. I didn't get a chance to thank you for washing up my clothes," she said.

Nora smiled and pushed her big, red glasses up. "It was something we all did, Evelyn. I couldn't wash what I didn't have. The girls rounded up all the things they could find undamaged. Avery helped too. She hauled everything here and unloaded all the boxes into the garage out back. All I did was a few loads of laundry."

"No, you did more than that. I want to thank you."

"Really, it was nothing."

"Well, I want you to know I'm grateful, to you, to everybody."

"We all know you've lost everything, dear. We're happy we could help in a small way. Have you decided to rebuild?

"I'm, ah, I'm not sure if I will. I need time before I can decide. Lois told me about a group that takes people all over the world, on tours to different places, like a travel-abroad study group for seniors. I don't know. Maybe I'll take one of those tours, just to get away and forget about my problem for a while. Maybe, after that, I'll decide what to do about a place to live. Lois said I can stay with her as long as I want."

Nora smiled. "Lois is a good person. You won't find a better friend."

"Yeah. She finds nice things to say about everybody and everything. She even says nice things about cow manure... and me."

Nora laughed. "Your meeting is about to start. Now scoot, before your new vice-president takes over."

Evelyn glanced across the room toward the dais where Lois stood waiting. "Yeah, I better get going. She'll make me sell raffle tickets if I don't do my own job."

Tiny, redheaded Evelyn, attired this day in a purple running ensemble and matching running shoes, walked briskly across the room to take her place as presiding officer beside the much larger form of her new vice president, Lois.

Nora had the opinion that Lois could do a fine job as a guild president. *Maybe I'll ask Lois if she would be interested in running for the Tea Basket presidency. Carolyn's term is soon up, and the guild will need a new presiding officer.*

She heard Evelyn call the meeting to order. The first thing on her agenda that day was telling Shining Star members about Avery's job. She asked for a volunteer to serve as their secretary, noting that Lois had agreed to fill in as vice president. Several hands shot into the air.

It occurred to Nora, as she watched the Shining Star meeting get underway, that her own Tea Basket Quilters could use a few new members. It was gratifying to see so many hands. Nora was always on the lookout for new members willing to step up and take charge. She might try raiding the Shining Stars after their meeting was over. She took her cup of coffee and left them to their business, climbing the steps toward her favorite room to work on a bit of sewing. Along the way, she paused as she passed the big room favored by her friend, Phoebe, for its design wall. She wondered briefly where Phoebe had vanished to, but the question was soon replaced by another thought. *Yes, this will be the perfect home for that Gammill, when we win it.* With that conviction, Nora continued toward the room reserved for applique, and her favorite chair and a project that awaited.

Since Belle will be living downriver with Vern on their little sternwheeler, and Avery will be preoccupied with a new job, the Tea Basket Quilters could definitely use a few replacements. Maybe, if Evelyn takes that journey, I might encourage a few of her Shining Star ladies to consider joining our Tea Basket Quilters.

She arrived at the comfortable chair, her latest block untouched, waiting for her to complete a bit of reverse applique. She placed her coffee on the side table and picked up the block to find where she left off. As Nora considered her idea, she realized she was planning to do exactly what she had originally accused Evelyn of plotting. She herself was now planning to raid the membership of another guild. She giggled to herself. But unlike her imaginings of Evelyn decimating Tea Basket membership, Nora felt sure that this time there would be a sharing of both members and accommodations. Both guilds might grow bigger and stronger, as a result.

Now wouldn't that be something?

Epilogue

Late October finally replaced the heat of that long, muggy summer, with crisp, frosty mornings. The hillsides shimmered in greens, a few golds and the occasional orange splash of maple leaves. The chain saws had months earlier finished cleanup work on fallen trees. The wood had been offered up as free firewood. In The Plains, the house once belonging to Evelyn North had been bulldozed, the lot reduced to a flat meadow. Grass, a foot tall, waved in a slight breeze where her bathtub once stood. The unmowed lawn gave the vacant lot a very unkempt look, which riled some of the nearby fussy neighbors.

Evelyn didn't care. She rarely drove by. She spent her days on the Caldwell farm. She had decided to take a tour to South America this winter, with other seniors. She told her friend, Lois, that she'd make up her mind about what to do with the lot after she returned. Maybe she would rebuild. Maybe she wouldn't.

Lois understood the difficult decision Evelyn faced. She was aware that Evelyn was far from destitute. More than needing a house, however, Lois knew that what Evelyn needed was time to heal old emotional wounds and soothe some deep scars left behind as a result of a difficult childhood. Perhaps not building would be a good thing. Total destruction might signal a total break from her past. Whatever her little friend decided, Lois was confidant Evelyn could find eventual peace, if that's what she wanted. Perhaps she could find a bit of tranquility while travelling abroad. Perhaps Evelyn would even return to Athens with a renewed spirit, and hopefully a subdued temper.

Crews had also hauled off to the landfill the piles of lumber that had once been the Hart Auction House. A new structure was quickly taking shape on the original concrete slab, yet another reminder of the severity of that summer's windstorm. The Hart home, a few miles away, was also undergoing major repairs. The Harts, like Evelyn, decided to take this opportunity of homelessness to travel. Vern's broken bones were on the mend. His wife, Belle, fussed over him around the clock, as they made their way slowly down the Ohio River on his sternwheeler, *Mistress*.

Nora received a postcard from Belle stating that they had arrived at the Mississippi and had decided to turn the boat south and make their way on down to New Orleans. Maybe they'd berth long enough this year to enjoy Mardi Gras.

Phoebe Prescott was dividing her time between her cabin in the country and William Evergreen's house in Cleveland. She had purchased and installed special doggie safety seats for the small back seat of her VW Bug, for the comfort and safety of her two pugs, Stitch and Medallion. Nora, Carolyn and Rosie couldn't quite believe that she was dating, when they heard the news. But the news had come directly from Phoebe, so it had to be true. Still, the fact was hard for the friends to picture. Phoebe, after all, had always declared herself to be a confirmed bachelorette.

Phoebe had finally confided in them, one Sunday in Nora's back yard over brunch, that she had held a secret crush on Bill ages back when she was a coed at the university. But because he was her roommate's beau, she was unwilling to act on her feelings. Instead, she denied herself the opportunity and resigned herself to keeping her feelings bottled up. But then, when she met him before the auction and learned he was a widower, she decided to take a chance on love at long last.

Nora, Rosie and Carolyn all congratulated her and wished her the best.

Phoebe announced that one of her sisters, Robin, would be staying in the cabin off and on during her absence, just to make sure the place was cared for.

Nora immediately jumped at this opportunity to invite Robin to join the Tea Basket guild.

"She does piece quilts, doesn't she?" Nora wanted to know.

Phoebe agreed to pass along the invitation but said her sibling hadn't caught the quilting bug yet. They weren't to expect much out of her.

Nora suspected that Phoebe was perhaps not forthcoming about Robin's skills with needle and thread or with a machine and fabric. Nora guessed, therefore, that Robin was an excellent quilt maker.

These friends and all the other Tea Basket Quilters gathered together this chilly autumn morning, at the hall, for a brief meeting and highly anticipated ceremony. The meeting space was filled with women milling about, all talking at the same time, trying not to seem too anxious to invade the area where Molly Menear, their guest of honor, was setting up an elaborate display on top of several eight-foot tables along the front wall. Phoebe assisted her as she unpacked her wares. Not one to miss an opportunity to promote her business, Molly had arrived with six huge bins of fabric, patterns, samples of finished projects and all kinds of sewing necessities she was positive the Tea Basket Quilters would enjoy seeing — and purchasing — after the ceremony.

Today, the Tea Basket Quilters were to honor Molly's Thimble and Chatelaine Quilt Shop for awarding the Gammill longarm quilting machine to their guild. No other group had come remotely close to donating as much money as they had. Their little quilt auction had been such a success that the local paper published a two-page spread in one of the Sunday editions. The article included a full page of photographs taken by Ximi Ling on the day of the auction. She featured several of the little quilts. The editor insisted she include one photo of their auctioneer, William Evergreen, and another of their officers, Rosie Dyer and Carolyn Ashcroft. Ximi received credit as the photojournalist, which pleased her to no end.

Those same officers were now about to ask Molly to cut the ribbon which blocked passage this morning to their second floor. Perched in the center of the room with the design wall, now stood Orpha Kidwell's Gammill. Orpha had been Molly's sister who had passed away due to complications from breast cancer. It had been Orpha who was the Thimble and Chatelaine's long arm quilter. Carolyn was to give a short speech, thanking Molly for the donation. Molly was to give her own speech next, explain her decision to give her sister's machine away and express her faith and gratitude that it would be well cared for. She was then to cut the ribbon barring the stairway, officially handing over ownership of the Gammill to the Tea Basket Quilters. Following that, the members would be allowed to ascend the steps to see their machine and get a little hands-on time guiding the controls.

Many new guild members helped fill the hall to overflowing. Some of them were also members, and even officers, of the Shining Star guild. Nora had prepared two forty-cup urns of coffee, plus a large bowl of punch. She looked at the gathering and then to the dwindling stack of mugs. She was worrying they might run out of cups before they ran out of drinks, when members were to return back downstairs for cake, cookies and more coffee following the ceremony, and of course, to engage in a bit of shopping at Molly's display.

Lois Caldwell, in one of her print dresses, stood in the kitchenette sipping punch beside Nora who was adorned in a crisp, white, linen pantsuit. Together they observed ladies taking their seats. Nora decided to divert her worry from coffee cups to something more meaningful.

"You know, Lois," Nora said, "You could become an officer of this guild, too."

Lois was taken aback and paused in her attempt to down a mouthful of punch. She was quite happy to have advanced rapidly from secretary to vice-president and then to president of the Shining Star guild. She had never once considered the idea of holding another office in her other guild.

She finally swallowed. "Nah, not me, Nora," she said. "I've got more than enough on my plate with the Shining Stars and the farm. But thanks. I'm of a mind that *you* should serve the Tea Baskets as president. And don't tell me 'no'."

Nora was about to object, but Lois stared her down. Nora could not find words.

Lois continued, "Been talkin' to folks. There's a move afoot to submit your name as a candidate on the slate of new officers for next year. Don't mean to scare ya, but ain't no other names bein' bantered about yet."

"But dear, I don't know *anything* about being a president," Nora began, "And I'm so old."

"Like you think *I* knew how to be president? If I can do it, *anybody* can. I learned that if you can stand up in front of gals and speak your mind, then you can preside. Don't matter how old you are, neither. Nora. You're respected, very much so, by everyone. That there's all the credentials you need."

At that moment, the sound of a gavel hitting the table drew their attention. Carolyn Ashcroft stood on the dais, waiting for everyone to find a chair and settle down. Molly Menear had joined her and was taking her seat of honor next to Rosie. Nora and Lois walked obediently to where they had left their purses to reserve their seats in the front row next to Phoebe.

Carolyn beamed. She smoothed the front of her blouse and placed the gavel on the table in front of her. This had indeed been a wonderful year for the Tea Basket Quilters. She looked over the packed room, with pleasure. Upstairs, thanks to their efforts and Molly's generosity, the Tea Basket Quilt Guild had a Gammill, and in just two more months, someone else would stand in front of the group as their presiding officer.

"Ladies," she announced loudly, "I call this meeting of the Tea Basket Quilters, to order."